The
Celtic
Kingfisher

&

The Key to the Secrets of the Ancients

by

Rory Macquisten

TWO BOOKS ALTERNATING WITHIN ONE

Published by:
M.10 Services, P.O.Box 7, Exmouth, Devon EX8 5YT

British Library Cataloguing in Publication Data
A catalogue record for this book is available
from the British Library

ISBN 0 9539841 0 9

DEDICATION

This book is dedicated to my wonderful wife
Jacqui and my two sons Euan and Connell.

The front cover design was created by Alasdair Urquhart a Scottish Contemporary Impressionist
artist. He has exhibited paintings in the top galleries all around the U.K. and has on several occasions been sponsored by fine art publishers. He has won the Elizabeth Greenshield scholarship
twice and spent a year as the residential artist at the Grizedale Society in Cumbria. Alasdair inputs
a spiritual and emotional dimension into his work in a way that provides a vitality to his paintings
that reaches out at you. This makes him one of the most exciting painters in Britain today.

CONTENTS

LIST OF ILLUSTRATIONS

ACKNOWLEDGEMENTS

There are a number of people I have to thank for assisting me in one way or another in writing this book. If I was to name everyone that influenced me, I would have to go back to very early on in my past and even then I would probably miss a few people. However there are some that readily come to mind and I would like to give them some credit.

Firstly I would like to thank Dave A. who, but for the fact that a cow kicked him in the head, would not have found time to read through my first draft. Whether or not the damage impaired his sense of judgement is open to debate and his full recovery was hopefully not delayed in digesting the contents of the book. I would also like to thank Alex A. an old friend from University. Having lost contact with him for many years, he reappeared by fortunate coincidence and gave me much needed encouragement at a moment in my life when I needed it most. Thanks should also go to Roger P. for his assessment and timely advice and to Ian W. who added insightful comments about how to improve a couple of the chapters. I would like to thank the many people that have read the manuscript and pointed out the corrections needed to make it more readable.

Much of this book was written as a result of exploring what lay behind coincidences. There are many people who helped by introducing me to their friends and colleagues and who lent me or suggested that I read certain books or articles in magazines. I would like to thank all of them, and in particular Anton R. who is still guiding me in the world of N.L.P.T.M. His input into my work has allowed it to come across in a far more effective manner. Thanks must also go to Alasdair U. who, having read my manuscript, very kindly agreed to give of his time to produce a marvellous front cover design.

I would like to also thank my sensei at the Banyu Hatten School of Aikido in Exeter, Devon, Geoff F. and his wife Jacqui. Having also read and assessed my work, he continues to teach me to new levels of pain in the dojo. Whether this is his way of repaying me for the pleasure or part of the life-long learning process also remains to be seen.

I would also like to thank my wife Jacqui and my two sons Euan and Connell who allowed me the time to write. I know that the venture took longer than initially expected and much of the time should have been spent with them. I apologise to them for that and promise to be more careful in future.

I would also say that I have proposed several new and controversial theories in this book. Those people that I have mentioned within the texts do not necessarily share these points of view.

FOREWORD

This novel book offers the reader a glimpse of science inside and outside the framework of thinking by extending the possible or even the probable, to meet up with the ancient methodologies that date back well over ten thousand years.

It may be that such a synergy will one day become the foundation for a better understanding of ourselves and the world in which we live. With guidance, of the nature found in this book, it may well be that this can begin to lead us to the utopia of choice and freedom that currently seems to constantly elude us in this present age.

My work with N.L.P.™ is my attempt at speeding up our evolution towards this and I welcome Rory's work as I do all works that pursue this worthy goal.

I recommend that you read this book with the open mind that it demands and then go on to look for, and explore, the path that is right for you.

Enjoy your journey.

Dr Richard Bandler

INTRODUCTION

You are invited to go on a journey of discovery to find a connection between modern science and ancient earth and human energies. Within the pages of this book, you will be given the necessary information that will eventually enable you to discover for yourself a startling link that has fantastic implications for mankind's future development. Recent revelations in a wide variety of seemingly different fields have now allowed this link to come to light. It is only when you have begun to understand a whole range of information that this all starts to become clear. However, in order for you to reach this understanding, it is necessary that you read things that you might not normally choose or wish to read. Subjects that, in your past, may have left you uninterested or even bored will, in this book, be read in a new way. By the way it has been written, what at first may not seem clear to your conscious mind, will reach through and be understood by your subconscious mind. This will occur more and more as you progress through the whole book and at the end you will feel that a form of 'coming to know' has happened and everything has finally become clear. How this all works you will also come to understand as you read through the book. So please persevere through those chapters that you are less familiar with and you will be rewarded. This form of 'coming to know' process plays a crucial role in the overall awareness of the link, which is why the book is written in a particular style and manner.

It is for this reason that it contains both a story and a scientific journey. Both are interrelated and each is written to assist in the understanding and enjoyment of the other. Balance in all things in life is a key to retaining ones health and staying refreshed. The brain has one side that is logical in nature, whilst the other is creative, and as a whole we have a basic need for an equal use of each. This book, by the way it is written, will hopefully bring you that balance as you come to understand it.

For these same reasons it is also written with the chapters alternating from novel to non fiction. Rather than being frustrated by this style of presentation, I would ask that you accept that it is done in this way for your overall benefit. You will go on to find that it can add to the suspense and enjoyment of the book as a whole.

This method of presentation also adds an interesting dimension to the novel in that it increases ones beliefs and pushes back the boundaries of your own imagination. The non-fiction content of the book covers a variety of areas and starts with what we have learnt from studies of identical twins. This helps to establish the idea that we have different paths in life that are open to us and that we can, at any time, choose which way we want to go by how we wish to think. The concept of a time cone is then introduced purely in order for you to have a framework with which you can build your understanding as you continue through the book. Your own path in life could be inserted upon this time cone model and you could imagine where your past and future paths might lie upon it. This has greater relevance as you learn more toward the end of the book. The subject of success is then covered and this assists us to see what is actually happening when we wish to obtain a particular outcome from out of all those that are possible in the future. This has relevance when we read what physicists have to say about our world and the way we observe things in it. This act of observation, in its various forms, involves a form of 'collapsing' all the possible paths that are open to us into the one we encounter in our present. It is this 'collapse' that is explained in more detail from a scientific viewpoint and which is integral to our connection.

Chapter six covers some of the strange information that has resulted from the work of these scientists and it is worth mentioning at this stage that some of their latest theories are beginning to support many of the core concepts that encompass eastern philosophy as we know it today. This chapter is also the first in the book that might give you a clue as to where the connection exists. The work that these physicists then carried out brought them to looking at how the mind might be working and this leads us to the same area in chapter eight. With some fascinating research now being done on consciousness and how it arises, the book covers some of the more tangible subjects like the workings of the brain and goes on to cover the programming of the mind and its related phenomena. A final look at some of the more microscopic workings of the brain, and where this 'collapse' might occur, leads us to the forefront of modern day research and provides a definite link with the mind and quantum physics.

Chapter twelve starts afresh and tackles the connection from the other end by looking at human and earth energies and progresses back towards quantum physics and the mind. This culminates in several new theories on the ancient world being presented as well as providing some startling evidence as to how pyramids might have once been used and how they might be used in the future. The book concludes by outlining the connection in more detail and discussing its consequences on both an individual and group basis. There are a few parts to the book that give the reader practical information that they can try in their own homes. All I would say about these sections is that you should keep an open mind, give it a go and notice what happens. Don't take the written word as definite proof that it works, take your own judgment too.

Having given you a brief outline of the book, all that remains for me to do is to wish you much enjoyment in your reading. For obvious reasons though, I would ask that, when you have finished the book, you consider other peoples fun by telling them of the book and not about the link. I would also suggest that for maximum benefit, the reader should resist the urge to go straight to the end of the book.

WARNING

Some of the sentence structures in this book may appear to be grammatically incorrect. They have been written in this way for a purpose. N.L.P.[T.M.] and Grammar do not always share the same structure.

The Celtic Kingfisher

CHAPTER ONE

AN OMEN

I'd finished. After seven long and hard years of having to memorise every single spoken word, relief and elation now raced all the way through my body. Its tingling warmth spread inside me and gave me a lightheaded feeling that I'd never known before. It all seemed like the perfect beginning to my new direction in life.

The sun had long since started its descent through the skies as I begun to head back down the mountain. The thick clouds were still below me, hanging over the glen like a soft fleece. After carefully retracing my steps down the first icy part of the rock-strewn path, I stopped to look back over my shoulder at the old man. He was sitting on his wooden seat, leaning against the wall of his hut looking calm and contented. Having done his part, he was now relaxing in the warm sunlight, gazing up at the brightly lit, snow covered peaks. I paused for a moment waiting until he saw me. When he did I smiled, waved and continued on, following the well-worn route that wound its way down toward the cool, dense zone of cloud. As the mists wrapped around me, the cold and damp seeped swiftly through my skins giving me a chilling reminder of the perils that these parts could deliver the weary traveller. I hurried on thankful that I'd made this journey countless times in my mind as well as by foot.

As I reached the trees visibility began to return and with it the closeness that can only be felt inside a dark wood on an overcast day. I'd been through here many times but had never ventured far off the path. The lone cry of a wolf howling off to my right quickened my step and I found myself having to control my breathing to calm my all too imaginative thoughts. I reached the clearing where the track crossed a wee burn. Its icy waters pooled at the base of a small waterfall. I liked to stop here and eat some oatmeal cakes whilst relaxing against the trunk of a leaning pine. I could then reflect on all that I had learned that day and repeat it over again in my mind. More often than not though, my mind wandered and I would conjure up the wild fantasies of bygone years. I would make up battles between humans and the Sidhe, the little folk. Brownies and Thrummycaps, shape shifting Kittywitches, Trows and Peerie Trows and many other types of fairy would all fight together using their magical powers against the cold metal of swords and shields. I could make the trees move, the animals speak and lightening strike all with single thought. It was little wonder my sister called me a dreamer. Perhaps it was this that made my father finally despair in me ever becoming a true warrior like himself. After years of trying to train me in the 'Island' arts of unarmed and armed combat, he realised that although I had an aptitude, my heart and mind had always been elsewhere. He had finally relented and with my mothers support, I was allowed to go and learn from Dugald, the Island's Seannachie, a learned man gifted in the art of Storytelling.

It was not Dugald and the tales that I was learning from him that was on my mind now though. Nor was it the impending initiation into the school for Aes Dana on the mainland. What had caught my eye and had stopped me in my tracks was the sight of a beautiful male kingfisher. He was perched on a branch overhanging the pool and was staring, with keen intent, down into it. His head turned toward me as I crouched down to watch him and he let out a shrill whistle. A respectful awareness hung in the air and after a while he turned his head away. Moments later he swooped, flying low and straight over the water. I watched in awe at his accuracy and sense of purpose. A momentary twinge of envy stabbed me from within. His graceful flight continued, direct and undeviating straight toward the face of a huge, upright boulder at the edge of the pool the other side. Half a breath later there was a dull thud.

Thoughts failed me. Powerless to move, I watched as the dead body fell straight down into the water and then slowly floated towards me on the current. Its lifeless eyes looked up at me as it passed and without knowing why, I reached out with my hand and cradled the bird out. Images started to flash through my mind. What did this mean? Why hadn't the bird made any attempt to alter its course? Not even at the last instant! Had it just been a huge mistake, an oversight? A miscalculation? Maybe it had been distracted, obsessed by its prey. Surely not. This was definitely a powerful omen, the meaning of which I was at a loss right now to even guess at. Trembling a little, I made a hole in the ground near to the branch I had first seen the bird. As I laid him in it, I pulled out three short bright blue feathers and three orange ones and wrapped them carefully in a piece of soft tweed. My rituals complete, I walked on heavy of heart and foot, my mind though was racing. What did all this mean to me? Where was I now going to? What purpose was there to my life because of this? Everything had been so unclear in the past and I thought that I had just begun to gain some sense of direction. But now this! Such a clear sign filled me with a sense of fear and fore-boding.

The path ended as I came out of the woods and I could see Donan Broch in the distance. Its circular, dark grey, stonewall towered above the thatched roundhouses nearby. It looked a formidable sight with the setting sun outlining it against the backdrop of the Gruinard Sea. The faint outline of the four guardians, pinnacles on Cae Carn Beag, could be seen in the distance. I'd never been to the mainland before and my coming trip would bring me close to this mountain as the Aes Dana, the learned men and women who would give me my final test, were only to be found at Invercarrie, the nearby capital and home to the queen.

My mind wandered again to my oncoming task. It was the end of seven years training with Dugald and if I was to become a Fili, a Poet, I would need to pass trials of memory and imagination. I would have to repeat word for word all eighty stories and fifty poems. Only then would I become known as an Anruth, someone who could practice the art throughout the land. I loved my work, there was nothing more enjoyable than holding everyone's attention in the middle of a well-crafted tale. What had always concerned me though, was how I was going to survive afterwards. Fili were always welcomed wherever they went. They were fed well. But what of the future, it always seemed so uncertain.

As I passed the outfields that I had ploughed myself with Ard and Oxen, I wondered at what might have been if I had been happy to go along with my father's wishes. He had been a warrior who had fought well for the clan chief and had been given a large part of the Isle of Seigg to raise his own clan. A strong community had built up here around the broch with many ways of life. My elder brother, Cethan, had felt comfortable with the role of a hunter. He spent most of his time away in the woods on this and other islands. My sister Mairi had always helped my mother making clothes and preparing food. I, on the other hand, had never felt interested in farming the land. It was my father's wish and I'd tried to get into it for his sake. In the end, however, we had reached a concession. I agreed to put the time in for him, so long as I had been allowed to visit Dugald and to learn my chosen craft from him.

Dugald had turned up at one of those opportune moments in life that can only be looked back upon as some form of a coincidence. The tiny currach he had been sailing had been blown off course by a strong gale during the Time of Ice. He had seen the lights from our fires and made for shelter. As was customary we bade him and his skipper to enter into the warm broch and fed them well. When he had finished eating he repaid us with a story. It was a night I will never forget. As he sat by the fire turning the wheels of the bellows, he took us all away from our current lives and into a past land full of majics, fairies and gods. A land frequented by our forefathers, a land where people still had the power to cast illusions and spells, a land where warriors were both brave and foolish and maidens were as fair as snowdoves. I had been transfixed and ever since had wished to be able to repeat such an epic tale. It had taken days of persistence on my part in order to get my father to allow me to study with him. Dugald on the other hand didn't seem at all surprised. He had long since decided to stay with us on the island and been more than happy with the idea that I would bring him food in return for my tuition.

I'd now reached the infields where we also kept the hives. Bees had been a main part of my life since I had first tended them when I was six. They were one of the things I would really miss. The first sweet sip of your own mead was always an occasion to savour. I could easily accept my lot in life and settle down to farm here when I was around my bees. Something inside me though, had always nagged me into thinking that there was more for me to do. It felt like there was a mission to be completed, but of what I had no idea.

I looked up at the buildings now only about five hundred strides away. There was smoke rising from the broch. That seemed strange. It was far too early to start the fires. Perhaps my mother was brewing up one of her cures. Her father had been a man of learning, skilled in the art of herbalism, and she had acquired many of her ways from him. She had been named Etain after Etain Echrade, the fair maiden that Oengus, son of the Dagda of the Tuatha de Danaan, had longed to marry. Her powers of beguiling had been strong and she had bewitched him into wanting her by appearing to be the most beautiful woman he had ever seen. My mother, it was said, was also blessed with fair looks and luckily for me also had a large amount of influence over my father. It was finally with her help that my father changed his mind and allowed me to pursue my studies.

My thoughts though were interrupted. Something was not right, my step quickened and I broke into a run. Where was everybody? At this time of day people would be all over the place. I rushed up the stone steps to the front door of the broch. It was half open. Ducking down inside and hurrying quickly along the short entrance passage, I was faced with about twenty people all turning their heads towards me. On the ground in the centre next to the fire in the hearth lay my father with my mother kneeling beside him.

"What's going on?" I shout, louder than I had meant to, but my voice was filled with desperation.

"There's been a raid," replies Donn instantly, looking me straight in the eyes. "Your father, Donal mac Donal's close to dying."

Donn was a young lad going on ten years and he already considered himself to be a man but his distraught expression as he looked at me brought back the boy in him. The shock at his words also ran right through me. My father, my invincible father, now near to death! I moved quickly past the others that had gathered around and knelt down next to my mother. She looked at me and tears began to well up in her blue eyes.

"How is he?" I ask, trying to sound calm as I put my arm around her, but my voice is full of nerves.

"Donal's been badly injured Fionn, his leg is broke and he may have lost the use of his left arm. He's taken several deep cuts there and has lost enough blood to fill a loch. Your dad does nay bruise easily, yet he has some mighty wheals on his head. I'm not sure if he'll overcome all of these things." Her head shakes from side to side.

I leant over his body and was immediately struck by how small he now appeared. My mother had done a good job bandaging him up and staunching the flow of blood. The poultices she had applied had plenty of fresh herbs blended into the wounds. He lay still. The only sign of life was the slight rise of his chest as he breathed.

"How long has he been like this?" I ask, now turning to face her. Everyone in the room had moved in closer. I looked up and round at all the gathered faces.

"Since midday." Whispers my mother. The pressure is starting to tell on her and she wipes back a tear. I reach over and hold her tight and looked round for Mairi. There are several moans from behind me and it starts a few others crying.

"Mairi." I call. There is no answer, the crying becomes louder and soon everyone in the room joins in.

"Where's Mairi?" I call more loudly and this time anxiously.

"She's been taken." Says Donn nervously.

"What!" I say, my voice now rising with anger. I peer at all of the nearer faces again, my expression requesting some explanation.

"They came..." Donn continued, "three of them, all heavily armed with black targe and sword. All wore a strange plaid we'd none of us seen before. Yet Donal fought all three at once, even wounding one, but they were too much even for him." He joins in crying with the others.

"Calm down Donn." I say, with my heart thumping inside my chest. "Tell me what you saw, starting with my sister."

"They grabbed her on the way out, the big one put her on his shoulder and went off with the other two following. I followed as far as the rise. I had to hide so that they couldn't see me. They went down the coast to their currach and got on board. I couldn't do anything to stop them." He calls out with his arms and hands wide open in a gesture of despair.

"Then what?" I urge him on.

"They just set the sails and went." He replies and I can see he felt miserable remembering it all, especially his helplessness.

"You did good." I say reassuringly, but impatient to know more. "What happened to begin with then?"

"I was helping Donal feed and milk the cattle beneath us, Mairi was up above cleaning. Your mother had gone on one of her collecting walks along the beach. They must have come really quietly because the first we heard was Mairi screaming for help. Donal grabbed his sword and rushed straight up there. I followed him and when I got up the ladder there was a terrible fight going on. One of the men was attacking Mairi; the other two were slashing at Donal." He stops talking and hangs his head.

"What's up, Donn?" I ask in a quieter tone and placing my hand on his shoulder. I watch his face as tears begin to fill his eyes.

"I ... I ran off to get help. "Donn stammers out, "I should have stayed"

"Be off with your silly ideas Donn, you did the right thing for a man of your years." I say hurriedly, pulling him toward me and giving him a manly hug.

At the use of the word 'Man' he cheered a little. I still wanted to know every little detail so I probed him for more.

"I ran around outside shouting for people to help, but no one was around." He continues, "When I got back they were leaving with Mairi. I went straight inside and found Donal lying there. His last words to me were to follow them."

Turning to look at my father again, confusion sowed its tiny seed in my mind. Why? Had they really come for Mairi? How come they left my father alive? There were too many questions left and my mind raced furiously for answers. Everyone gathered in and around the dark chambers of the broch was silent and looking at me for some reaction. I gradually realised that they were expecting me to take charge. I got up, slowly summoning all the control within me.

"I'd like you all to leave now, you can help most by getting things back to normal as soon as possible. Everything will be all right." I say hoping to sound convincing but not very sure of myself. "Jamie, I'd like you to stay behind with Donn."

As the others left, I turned to them both. Jamie was seven years older than Donn and already one of the fastest runners amongst our extended family around the broch. He knew this well and was proud of the fact and showed it by choosing to wear little that might restrict his ability. His leathers barely covered his loins and his chest had begun to heave in anticipation of some action.

"I want you, Donn, to show Jamie here, where you saw these cowards leave. Jamie, I want a thorough search of the area, they must have left some clue as to whom they were. Take two others to help you. You've about an hour of light left if you hurry."

Even before I'd finished speaking Jamie had turned to run outside shouting at Donn for directions and yelling at him to keep up as best he could. I turned to Donal and knelt down again.

"How's he doing Ma?" I ask with a tone that insists upon the full truth.

"He's fighting demons, Fionn." She replies shaking her head from side to side, "He ne'er been afraid of a good fight but he's more years than he looks and this is the worst I've ever seen him."

As she stopped talking her long blond hair stopped swinging and it now hung down in front of her and onto his chest. Only the slight rise and fall of her shoulders as she breathed gave any sign she was awake for she had sunk into her deep meditative trance of healing. Her mood set me to thinking as well and memories began to stir in my mind of the days of my youth spent with my father. Looking back now, there never seemed to have been enough of them. A picture of him began to form in my mind. A healthy warrior clad in clan plaid, sword and skeann dhu in each hand with a beaming smile. He was towering over me at the end of the first lesson he had ever given me.

I reached out to feel his forehead but at the touch my arm jolted back as what felt like a spasm ran up my arm. His eyes opened and his head leant up toward me.

"Fionn." He says effort written all over his face. "You... must... get it... back." Having finished, he fell back into his deep slumber.

My mind raced, what did he mean? Surely he meant Mairi. I turned to my mother with a puzzled look on my face.

"What's he on about Ma?" I say with rising curiosity. "What's he talking of?"

"The Crown Helm." She replies calmly, half murmuring as if in some half sleep.

"What?" I'm not sure I hear fully as I'm certain I'd never heard the words before.

"The Crown Helm." She says louder. I turned and gave her a strange look intending for her to give me more of an explanation. As I did Donal's head rolled back to the side and he fell back into his dreams.

I look back again to my mother who sees I'm not going to give up without more of an answer.

"Go and look in your dad's chest by the bed. In there you'll see a smaller tin and silver casket. Tell me what you find." Her voice sounds almost forlorn and with signs of resignation.

I'd never been near the chest in my life and had never even been told of the contents, let alone seen them. To be told now to go and search it sent my mind reeling. For years, as a boy, I'd longed to do just this, but now feelings of curiosity were heavily mixed with those of awe and dread at perhaps at what I don't find.

I half walk, half run across the circular open room only to find the chest with its lid forced open. Looking inside there were pieces of gold, silver and iron, some strange ornaments but no tin and silver casket.

"It's not here." I call out. A moan came from Donal, as though somehow he had heard what I had said. "What was it, why is it so important?"

"Donal mac Donal, was holding one of the four parts of the Crown Helm. A helmet once made for the High King Diarmait mac Cerball, near four generations back now. Your father was entrusted to care for one of the pieces by Amairgin, king of the Milesians after fighting alongside him against the Fir Bolg. I've no idea how he came by it or indeed of its importance. Your dad would hear nay talk of the matter and indeed wished to keep such things secret, e'en from you, till the time was right."

"And what of Mairi? Why would they take her if they only came for the helm?" I shake my head in my failure to understand.

"I can nay say. What e're it is, it does nay bode well." Forewarns Ma in her broad mainland accent that she always resorted to when using one of her more common phrases. I left her to get on with her work and went outside.

I sat on the steps contemplating all the recent events. The sun had gone down and the light was fading when Jamie and Donn ran up. They halted at the bottom step and looked up, faces red and heavy of breath. I looked at them both expectantly and it was Jamie that spoke first.

"There's evidence of a camp last night. They seemed to have been well prepared, like broken men paid for their work. Arriving early will have given them time to scout out the land and make plans. They knew exactly what they had come for and where to find it and they timed their raid almost to perfection." He punches his right fist into the palm of his left hand as though to quench his rising anger by smiting an imaginary foe. "I don't think they meant to get into any fights. They either hadn't seen Donal, as he was down underneath with the cattle with young Donn here, or almost certainly they underestimated the old man." He pauses a moment to catch his breath. Then, as though remembering another fact, he continues. "Ha! At least one of them won't sleep well tonight. The cold edge of his sword drew blood, there were stains on some stones above the moon tide mark." Jamie stops and smiles at his last words. I can imagine him savouring the picture of the wounded man in pain.

"What makes you think they didn't want a fight?" I say breaking off from my own thoughts.

"There are footprints that showed that they were travelling light. They would not have wanted to be caught. The person that wanted this deed done, wished to go in and out quickly."

"Could you see anything to suggest which direction they might have been heading?"

"No, but Donn reckons they went North with the wind. If they'd planned well, they would have wanted to get away in the most favourable circumstances. That leaves two possible destinations Killiecraigie to the North and Invercarrie if they double back and head west. There was no way they'd risk the rocks at night at any of the other possible coves along the coast to the south."

"If the cargo they are now carrying is that important to them, you're right." I add. "Well done, now go off and fill yourselves with some hot broth. We'll talk more on the 'morrow."

I got up off of the steps and went back up into the broch and over to Donal, he was breathing more easily now but still asleep. My mother sat next to him holding his hand so I settled down the other side and pondered my next move. After what seemed a long time spent in silent deep thought and having had no revelation as to what I should do next, I lay down to go to sleep.

A loud groan next to me woke me in the middle of the night. I leant over and saw Donal stirring. "Donal!" I whisper close to his ear, "It's me Fionn. How are you feeling?"

"Son?" He mumbles half delirious with the lack of sleep and an unclear head, "Is that you?" He wakes a little more and reaches up with his good arm to rub his eyes.

"Aye it is."

"I feel like a hundred wounded wolves that have been stung by a thousand bees. By Cuchalainn's great rod of iron I'll string those cursed cowards across the highest thorn tree on Siegg!" He tries to thunder out, summoning all his strength for one of his customary oaths.

It was not full of his usual gusto but it was a good sign he was on the mend.

"Calm down now, there's plenty of time for that. You must rest more first." I say with a smile beginning to cross my lips.

"Fionn." He continues, with a more earnest tone. "Did they take Mairi as well?"

"Aye, I'm afraid they did."

"Damn! May the Sidhe from the Otherworld haunt them for ever." He explodes, which starts him off in a fit of coughing. I turn him slightly to his side to ease his convulsions and then have to hold him down to resist his efforts to get up.

"Stay down Donal, you're going nowhere in your condition." He lies back as my mother appears.

"How is he?" She says.

"Good enough to swear by the power of the fairies against all his enemies." I reply.

"That's good." She smiles and leans over Donal. "You go back to sleep now, we'll sort things in the morning."

"There's no time." Donal urges, "Fionn, you must prepare to leave. With Cethan away for many days you're the only one here who can do what needs to be done. You were to leave tomorrow anyway, so nothing will look strange. Take this ring and go first to Drummorchy and seek out my old friend Conal Brus. Show him it so he knows who you are and tell him what you know. He'll know what to do next. I know you've to go to Invercarrie to meet with the Ollamphs at the Aes Dana, that could be a fortunate coincidence... Fionn," he says with a grave tone that I'd not heard him use many times before, "you must rescue Mairi and, if possible, an item I believe they came here for."

"The Crown Helm." I say.

"Yes. How did you know about that?" He says abruptly, his face tightening.

"Ma told me. I asked her what they might have come for."

"Well it's time you knew anyway." He sighs with an air of relief. "I was asked to safeguard one piece of the helm by Amairgin, king of the Milesians. He had one of the other two pieces." He coughs, still having difficulty talking. "The other two's whereabouts were still unknown."

"What's so important about the helm? Why four pieces?" I ask, my mind still full of even more questions I wanted to ask him.

"It was made for King Diarmait to represent the four lands he brought under his control. While the pieces were joined together, it came to symbolise the strength of unity amongst the men in those lands. It locked them in peace in a similar way the that pieces were locked together." He pauses, seemingly to choose his next words carefully. "People came to believe that the wearer of the helm gained power from the helm itself. Recognising the dangers that potentially posed, the king, before he died, divided it for the future safety of his kingdom. It was possibly a grave mistake. Not long afterwards feuds turned into battles, battles turned into wars. The peaceful times were over and, ever since, men have had to watchful."

I knew the stories of the wars, many of them were lodged word for word in my memory. But I had never known or heard tell of any crown helm. My first thoughts were that my stories could become much more colourful and intriguing, if I added this one fact.

"How come so few people know about the helm, surely the tales told would have mentioned it?" I ask.

"Such was the power of a few people at that time. They decreed to all the 'gifted ones' that this should be omitted from all forms of communication on pain of death. This was an attempt to diminish the power that the helm was felt to hold. Secretly, I believe that all those in control sought out the pieces for themselves for their own selfish reasons. This drove the helm into the regions of myths and legends, poorly retold by common folk and soon forgotten."

"But who's looking for it now and why?" I ask, hopeful he might have some idea.

He shakes his head. "That's something you must find out. Find Mairi and you'll find who." He lies back down screwing his face up as the pain increases. "I must rest again." He leant back down. "Fionn, you're due to take the boat tomorrow, anyone else going with you would signify to someone that there was a change of plans. That might well lead them to take action that would endanger Mairi. I cannot stress the importance of keeping this whole thing secret." With that he shut his eyes. The whole conversation having sapped him of whatever energy he had left.

I rolled over onto my back and looked upwards. As I did so, I slipped my father's ring onto my middle finger. It was a loose fit and I ended up turning it repeatedly whilst I was alone in my thoughts. The sound of the wind outside whistled around our small settlement, a door slammed the other side of the yard. Other than that, nothing else stirred. By habit, I reviewed the day's events, including my father's final words. Something troubled me though and at the back of my mind somewhere there was something that didn't quite seem right. Using the memory techniques that Dugald had taught me, I tried to access all that was relevant. Dugald's image kept appearing in my mind. Something he had said. Then I had it. I had to see him again before I left. It meant leaving before first light in order to get back in time for the boat, but I had to go. It was something he had said when relating a story about the High King Diarmait. Had he known about the crown helm? I had to know and what's more, I felt I had to know as much as was possible if I was to have any success at all in rescuing Mairi.

I rose again after only a short rest. It had been a tiring night and I still felt weary from it. Putting on my leathers and fleece coat, I crept quietly out. Snow had fallen lightly in the night and there was a soft covering of white on the ground. One of the cows lowed as I headed off up toward the glen. The geese cackled but became quiet as I neared them. As I lengthened my pace, my legs began to ache. I managed to reach the woods of Glean Coul as the sun began to rise. A warm red glow spread from the East, right up through the pass that led to Lairg. The towering peak of A'Cailleach loomed ahead, its snow capped peak now brilliant in the morning sun.

The rising, twisting and turning path was damp and shaded. All my efforts failed to fully warm me. At last I reached the clearing with the waterfall and my thoughts switched to the events of the previous day. I reminded myself to ask for Dugald's thoughts on the Omen. What relevance did it now have in the light of the events at the broch? I felt for the six feathers still wrapped within my pocket and found a strange comfort in their presence.

On reaching level ground after the woods, I could now see Loch Cailleach. Next to it on the left was the small peat and stone hut that Dugald and I had built together. Dugald was sitting outside it and as I approached, he looked up.

"Fionn." An element of surprise shows in his voice, "I ne'er expected to see you again so soon. And what troubles are following you, for sure this can nay be yet another goodbye."

"Dugald, it is surely good to see you this fine morn. Forgive me for I've forgotten to bring our normal fare today."

"Will you nay fass you'self laddie, I've a pot of porridge and some of your fine honey. Sit you'self down and let's enjoy the moment." He gestures pointing to the food on the table in front of him.

I sat down and he brought me a bowl of the porridge to which I added, and stirred in, a large lump of honeycomb. We ate in silence as we always did. Eating this way I always found to be deeply relaxing and in these circumstances it helped me enormously. Having found I was hungrier than I thought, I finished quickly. I sat still and watched him enjoying his food right up to the last mouthful. When he'd finally finished, I spoke.

"Dugald, the broch was raided yesterday. Whoever it was took Mairi and an object that Donal had in his safekeeping." I pause and watch as his mouth slowly drops open, registering the shock.

"Is everyone well?" He enquires quickly, showing his obvious concern.

"Donal was seriously hurt trying to stop three of them. Everyone else is fine, except that they have Mairi. I just hope that she's been treated well." I continue as his gaze met mine. "The reason I've come back up here, " I change the subject, "is because of what Donal told me. I thought you might be able to help." I stop and look over at him for some indication and feedback.

"I'll try, what is it?" He says after a moment of silence.

"Do you remember the stories you told me about the High King Diarmait?"

"Of course!" He replies tersely, impatient with my common fault at often stating the obvious.

"Well, at the time you referred to it as incomplete, as though at some point there would be more to tell. Is there?"

His wrinkled face fixes me with a long hard stare as though he is trying to read my thoughts. I find my mind thinking about the crown helm. I had resisted mentioning it first, hoping to prise out information from Dugald beforehand. It was a mistake. I could feel myself regretting that I had chosen this course of action with someone who had become a good friend. Donal had, after all, only a short while ago sworn me to secrecy.

The silence continued and I sensed that it was still my turn to speak and to tell all. Guilt from both sides made me feel queasy. I had to open up.

"The object they stole from my father was a piece of the Crown Helm." I almost shout it out. Relief gushes through me, mixed with extreme guilt.

Dugald's look turns from a wry smile to one of amazement. The ruddy cheeks of his face begin to turn an ashen shade of gray.

"That is something I hadn'y wished to hear although I can nay really hold you to blame." His words were slow and without the usual rhythm and zeal so commonly found in an accomplished Seannachie.

"You were right to come to me lad. Indeed, you've developed a rare talent that remembers detail such as that. You're right the story was incomplete. It would appear however that you already have the missing information. Tell me what you know and I'll add what I can."

I related all that had happened since I last saw him, including the omen of the kingfisher. When I finished, he sat back on his seat, stretched out his legs and with his hands resting by his side and looked up into the skies. I watched him while he seemed to be carefully choosing his next words.

"Fionn." He starts, "As you get older, one of the strange things you discover in life is that it appears to be that events come round again, like a wheel. Then again, looking back at the coincidences that have happened to me throughout my life, it might also appear as a straight line. By that I mean that events appear at first seemingly obscure and diverse, but are, in fact, linked. That link eventually becomes as clear as a straight line leading in an obvious direction. Some men choose to ignore it; others embrace it. Neither is right or wrong. I chose to follow my instincts and that is why, probably, we are here talking this morning." He pauses and leans forward. "I never told you where I was heading that day when I arrived. Your interest at the time was deflected by my story to you all. In fact, I was fleeing from Drummorchy on route to the Eastern Isles. The reason had to do with the Crown Helm."

My attention to what he is saying is now intense with curiosity. "Go on." I say.

"Whilst studying at the Aes Dana in Invercarrie, a few of us accidentally discovered reference to some drawings of ancient icons in amongst a pile of slates. As we were all looking for additions to our arts, we set out to look for these things. We eventually found carvings on some broken wooden tablets. There was one there that was clearly depicting the crown helm. Others, ones with oghams on them, outlined the story about king Diarmait. I thought nothing more at the time, but a few days later one of us died in mysterious circumstances. His body was later found washed up with the tide. Shortly afterwards, another disappeared. That left three of us. One I had known for many years, an ovate who went by the name of Angus Og. He was a remarkable seer with a gift that surpassed all of his peers. We put two and two together and decided to depart quickly and separately. I went south to Drummorchy and took the boat. He went west. All the time I was travelling, I had the feeling of being watched and being followed. After the storm, that feeling had strangely gone. Why and how I don't know but it was the main reason I decided to stay; the others you know."

"You mentioned three of you, who was the other one?" I ask cautiously, mindful of the power of names.

"The third man, for reasons of his own, didn't seem to want us around and we suspected he was planning to get rid of us permanently. He was a powerful and influential man, one that leaves you with an uncomfortable disposition in his presence and long after you've been with him. He was an Ollamph gifted in many arts, a man who neither Angus nor I ever really trusted." He pauses as though remembering a past wrong.

"His name is Callum Beg." He says in a sombre tone. "It is he, Fionn, that could well be the man who is behind this evil deed."

"What makes you so sure?" I ask.

"I remember the look in his eye when we first found the evidence. He said something that, at the time, seemed quite strange. His exact words were 'At last I've found it'. On reflection, I believe he had known of the helm's existence but was looking for evidence that could support it. If he could prove its existence beyond doubt, then the story he would tell could change people's belief's to suit his own purposes. Add to that the actual complete helm and total power over those people would be his for the taking."

"You don't suppose he has all the pieces do you?" I say.

"Up until now I didn't even believe in its existence, I thought the bits we found were reference to myths. I hope that for all our sakes he has not found them all. The power he could then wield over people would be terrible and lead to the loss of freedom for all men throughout the land."

I look up and see that it is time to leave. I would have to run most of the way just to make the boat. I get up reluctantly.

"Dugald, I must go. What will you do?"

"What I have to. When they discover you, as they no doubt will in time, it will lead them to me. I must not put your clan in danger with my presence here any longer. I will leave a message with your mother as soon as I've made certain preparations."

He gets up and we begin to walk together back down the path. There is a silence between us as we both feel that this could be the last time we see each other. "Fionn." He says after a while, "There is a place on the mainland that Angus and I agreed we would meet, or leave message for each other. You have a passable understanding of the ogham words and could read any such message. I believe also that it's your destiny to meet with Angus. He will help you more than I ever could when it comes to interpreting your Omen. The answer to that is most definitely linked to all of this."

"How would I find Angus? Should I find this place first?" I ask, my mind fuelled with questions.

"When you get to Invercarrie, go to the Bridge Inn. Ask for the owner, a man by the name of Leag. Mention my name to him. If he has no ideas where Angus might be found, then I suggest you try to reach this secret place of ours in the Southern mountains."

"How do I find that?" I wondered out loud.

"There's a cave on the west face of Ben MacDui. It's at the top of the scree slope behind a large boulder that's the shape of a bear on its hind legs. The best way to get there is from the Well of Lecht just outside Drummorchy. Follow the path on through the Strathyre Forest till you emerge at the base of a large cliff. Go off the track westwards till you get to a burn. Follow it up till it's safe to cross. You'll know when, it'll be obvious." He smiles at me. "There's no easy way back after that. Keep the mountain on your right and you'll come round to the slope I mentioned earlier. If Angus is alive, he'll have left a sign as to how he can be found." He stops walking and talking at the same time, turns to me and hugs me in a warm manly embrace. "Take care lad." Without the words coming to me, I nod and smile then turn to go on my way.

The whole clan had assembled by the time I returned. The currach was stone-anchored just off the shore and was ready to go as soon as I had come. I went straight up into the broch to see how Donal was.

"Donal, how are you feeling this morning?" I say as I see him sitting up.

"Like a wounded Boar after Beltane that's been left to lick his wounds without dignity. Strengthless like Senba's son, by Demne if I catch up with those curs I'll fert them alive." He curses feigning more anger than his body can really cope with.

I smiled, now knowing he was better, but I still looked him over. For a man of his years, only his wild gray hair and his bushy beard made him look old. His skin had a ruddy brown colour and would have had more lines but for Etain's cooking. His cheeks were well rounded from being fed well and it was that, that took the years off of him and made him look younger.

"He will walk with a limp in future." Says Etain, "I am not sure about the arm, we'll have to wait and see."

"It'll be fine woman, you worry too much. Get me that package I asked you to make ready." He points over to the corner of one of the

29

Broch's chambers.

Etain left and in a short while brought back a bundle of tweed and handed it to me.

"Inside, son," says Donal, sitting up as much as he could, "are some vitals to help you. There's bars of iron, gold and silver, people talk with a clearer mind and will forget less in the sight of these. Go now, don't worry yourself about us, we'll be fine. Bring back Mairi and that which was stolen from the clan." He reaches across and with his two hands grabs me firmly around my right forearm.

With that, he leant back on his good elbow and eyed me firmly. I turned to put my arms around my mother, whose eyes had started clearly to water, and I said goodbye. After that I went straight outside, glad of the fresher air and a chance to breathe out my emotions. As I walked down to the beach, my friends and relatives all wished me good fortune, some handed me lucky herb charms; others gave me food.

Nearer the water's edge, I heard the skipper shout at me to hurry up. I waded out till I was waist deep and waited for the currach to draw nearer. The sails were already set and the circular anchor was slowly drawn up. As it rose, the boat swung closer and I jumped up, caught the side and hauled myself in. At once we were moving. It all happened so fast it felt like a dream. I stood looking back at the waving figures on the shore and it slowly dawned on me that I'd only ever been out fishing before and only then in a small coracle and always in sight of shore. I'd also never been to the mainland. Feelings of excitement and trepidation welled up within me, each struggling to become the more dominant feeling. It was a close tie between them.

The Inner Islands

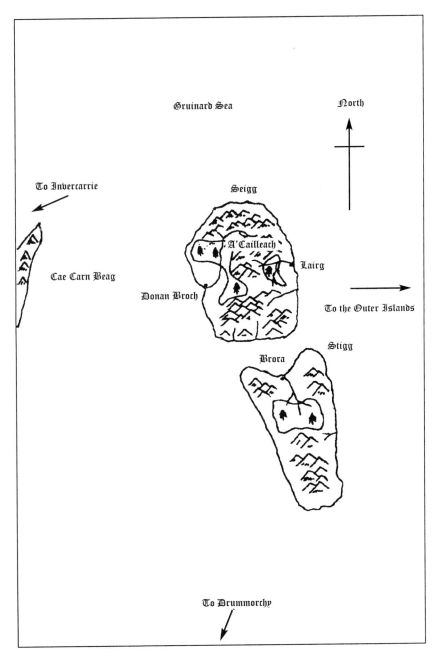

Gruinard Sea

North

To Invercarrie

Seigg

A'Cailleach

Lairg

Cae Carn Beag

Donan Broch

To the Outer Islands

Stigg

Brora

To Drummorchy

CHAPTER TWO

OF TWINS AND TIME CONES

Anyone who sees one of the great ancient monuments around the world for the first time is always struck by the same thought. They have all previously underestimated its actual size. Not until you are right there next to one can you appreciate not only the enormity of it, but all of the work that must have gone into erecting it. Standing next to them almost certainly fills everyone's mind with many questions. Who were these people who built this? What reason did they have to build it and why place it here? Perhaps more commonly asked. How did they manage to build it? Pyramids all around the world have fascinated modern man. Monuments built with huge slabs of stone, some up to 100 tons in weight, have left us transfixed with thoughts of ancient technologies now lost to man.

Studies of the ancient Egyptian and Mayan texts leave us none the wiser. However in between some of them, there are some vital clues. Piecing together these and adding to them knowledge that has come from research in more contemporary subjects has led to a conclusion that has dramatic implications for mankind. The priests in power at the time these constructions were built were known to hold the keys to all this ancient lore. They were its sacred guardians only passing down their information by word of mouth to carefully chosen individuals. It is no doubt at all that these people derived their strength of position in society because of the mental powers that this knowledge gave them. It was a knowledge that utilised and understood the concept of 'Energies' and their relationship with the mind. It is by looking into the power of the mind now that we can begin to see what it is that they seemed to be able to do.

However to find the answers to all the above questions we must ensure that everything we look into conforms to current day scientific theory and fact. Science must link up with the past and be able to explain some of the phenomena found there. Understanding that science is therefore necessary if we are to begin to understand how these ancient priests managed to perform the acts and deeds that are written about in the texts. Our journey begins by investigating how we as individuals link up with the overall answer as part of the solution needs to explain the connection we hold with the universe as a whole.

One of the biggest questions that a person can ever ask of themselves is "What is my role in life?" The dilemma in answering this, the same faced by Fionn, is considered by many people at some point in their life. To assist in providing an answer to this question and to also help in our quest to find a link between modern science and ancient energies, we must first look at the following two areas of study: – Past and future light cones and the studies of identical twins. This will allow us to produce a model with which we can use and follow throughout the book as we gather together all the relevant information.

Initially, we will look at the studies of identical twins in order to see the way we are affected by our genetic make up and by the experiences we encounter. We will then progress to see how all our possible directions in life can fit into the concept of a light cone.

2.1 Identical Twins

Francis Galton (1822-1911), a British psychologist at University College London first suggested that a study of twins might determine how much of a person's character was inherited and how much was affected by the environment that a person was brought up in. Monozygotic twins were chosen as they were considered to be identical genetically. This allows an observer of any experiment to assume that there is a form of control on one side and that any changes in character ought to be solely down to environmental differences. Dizygotic twins were considered too different genetically to be of the same amount of help.

The study of genetically similar people is perhaps validated by work that had been carried out on the common fruit fly Drosophilia. Research on this fly provides us some of this interesting information on genetics and the environment. If you take genetically similar flies and non genetically similar flies and subject both groups to rises in temperature then, as the flies grow, a change is found in the number of facets in the eyes of the flies. For those that are genetically similar the changes are the same. This is not so for the other group. It shows us that the role the environment plays on genetically similar bodies can result in similar changes on those bodies. It is thought that this could be the same for humans and that by analysing the character and behaviour of identical twins we might be able to determine how much of an influence the environment has on human development.

One of the most comprehensive analysis on twins was carried out by R.W. Wilson (1979) with the Louisville twins study. 374 pairs of twins were studied on children from the age of 3 months to 6 years. Monozygotic (M.Z.) twins that were reared together and those reared apart were also studied. Results showed that with age M.Z. twins grew more alike in I.Q. and Dizygotic (D.Z.) twins grew less alike in I.Q. It prompted a saying by Wilson that 'all that can be inherited is a potential.'

More recently, an American scientist Tom Bouchard (1990) conducted a summary of over 100 worldwide surveys on M.Z. twins and came up with an answer, now generally agreed by everyone today, that a person inherits 50% of their character and 50% is down to their environment.

From what we have understood up till now, we could assume that we are all genetically programmed from conception (with some of us being similar as in the case of twins), yet we are environmentally directed and affected from the moment we are born.

Looking further into studies between M.Z. twins that were reared apart and those reared together, further information is revealed to us. The differences between the two groups were analysed and the results were found to show that stress plays an important part in their upbringing and why they differ from each other.

Before continuing, we must consider what is meant by stress and how we choose to be affected by it. Stress is an internally created reaction to an external experience. Two people can experience the same events, one person can choose not to become stressed and yet the other can choose to become highly stressed. Imagine sitting in a traffic jam in your car with an urgent meeting getting closer to its start time. The person behind you in the traffic is also late for the same meeting. The circumstances are now out of your control, how you choose to react at this point (leaving aside the possibility of getting out of your car, leaving it where it is and running to the meeting) will have no effect on the outcome of arriving on time to the meeting. Many people however allow themselves to become stressed in this situation and act out many related mannerisms (like hitting the steering wheel). The person behind however could choose to handle the situation in a completely different way. They could accept that they were going to be late and that there was nothing that they could do from that point to alter the outcome. They might resolve to leave even more time for subsequent meetings and accept that they hadn't left enough this time. They might also consider it was their fault and not the fault of the traffic. This course of internal reaction to events is one that allows much lesser amounts of stress to build up. Both cases show a different internal reaction to the same event. One person chose to become stressed; the other did not.

If we were to bend a straight metal rod a small way it would return to its original shape. If you bent it too far, the metal would become stressed and return to another position, leaving the rod with a bend. The resultant change has resulted in metal damage called strain. The difference is in the amount of stress an object (or person) receives and the flexibility of the object (or person).

In many cases of identical twins, parents can easily be the initial cause of stress between siblings. This is often due to their desire to make them similar and equal or different and individual. Strain has been witnessed in many cases with these children because of a number of actions that the parents have taken. The end result produces a rivalry and, as life goes on, a form of competition can grow between the twins. In the severest of known cases a murder has occurred with one twin killing the other.

Another extreme form of stress was witnessed amongst twins found in the concentration camps in World War Two. The infamous Dr Mengele from Auschwitz conducted tests on over 3000 twins. He would test one of the pairs of twins to see how germs worked on their body and then compare its effects with the other twin. Poison gases and viruses were also used. Only 161 people survived these tests. Among them was a ten-year old girl called Eva Moses Kor who was similar to her twin sister Miriam. Eva chose to block out the tests in her mind and mentally fought against them. She endured a massive amount of stress in doing this and because of that went on to become a fundamentally different and also a much stronger person from the one she and her sister used to be.

When studying twins that live together in harmony and who also have a relatively stress free life, the occurrences of similarities between them become much greater, even to the extent that on many occasions even their occupations have been found to be the same. Some even declare that they are incapable of separate thought. In these cases where one twin has died, the remaining twin has described feelings of 'electrical jolts'. Some people have gone on to term this a sort of 'spirit separation'.

Although many twins say they were 'one person', it is recognised that their brains are unique to each of them. They may do the same type of work, but they think differently. In the few cases of identical twins being reared apart from birth, again in a relatively stress free way, similar roles and characteristics are also seen. One case in point involved two fire chiefs living in the middle of the U.S.A. As babies they were adopted and brought up separately, yet they met 30 years later by accident, and found that they only lived 65 miles apart and had many similarities, likes and dislikes. Even their mannerisms were the same, like the way they drank their beer.

Twin studies over the last three decades, in four countries, have yielded remarkably similar results. Robert Plomin and John C. DeFries carried out some of the latest research on twins. Robert Plomin is the research professor of Behavioural genetics at the Institute of Psychiatry in London. John C. DeFries is the Director of the Colorado Institute for Behavioural genetics. Their own Colorado project, launched in 1975, looked at adopted children with regards to intelligence and their genetic or experienced characteristics after periods of adoption. They were surprised at the strong genetic trend that carried on after adoption. In fact it increased in the years up to the mid teens age. Further studies revealed that these genetic or hereditary abilities continued well into adulthood and old age. Today it is now still felt that, in the general population, genetics accounts for between 50% and 60% of a person's character.

In May 1998 Robert Plomin and various collaborators reported in the journal Psychological Science that they had discovered the first gene associated with general cognitive ability. This is strong evidence for a genetic influence in a person's abilities.

When we look at all the evidence, it would appear that we are born with a genetically predetermined character and even, quite possibly, a genetic path or role in life. If we followed this path, it would be one where we would fit into an environment with which we were brought up in. We would conform unquestioningly to its dictates because it seemed to naturally suit us. If we suffered little or no stress, then we would be likely to play out the role that we were genetically meant to. What it was and how we turned out as people, would be subject to one's initial genetic coding and subsequent external direction due to the environment that we passed through.

This could be similar to many other life forms on this planet, albeit that they would be living on a more primitive basis. Two examples that exhibit this similar path are that of worker ants and drone bees, but there are many others in the animal kingdom with greater or lesser complex genetic roles. Each appears to have a form of genetic program that they carry throughout their life. Earliest examples of this can be found in the fossil record. Trilobites, miniature crab-like creatures found around 250 million years ago, burrowed around in the mud in several different patterns depending on the activity they were pursuing. Their ordered patterns indicated that their programs were not random in nature but had a simple but predetermined route. It may not have been always fully carried out, but that would have been down to the changing environment.

However, as soon as we are born, we can begin to make choices. We can choose whether or not we want to be affected by our environment in a certain way. We soon learn, as do animals, what gives us pain and what gives us pleasure and we normally seek out the latter through choice. This ability to choose allows us to deviate from this so-called 'genetic path' if we decide and /or desire to.

Therefore, if we were to choose to select an alternative path to our genetic one, it would appear that in order to follow it we have to subject ourselves to some degree of stress. This would be due to having to carry out some sort of an internal change from our norm. Interestingly enough it has also been proved recently that you can trigger a genetic change in an organism by subjecting it to a form of stress. Our D.N.A. is made up when twenty-two amino acids are stringed together in a row and then all folded up in the right way. This action is done with the help of 'servant molecules'. The presence of a particular servant molecule, known as HSP90, makes the resulting shape of an organism orthodox as opposed to mutated. Even when there are mutations within the construct of the D.N.A, this molecule irons out these problems and the mutated forms don't get expressed in the finished organism. However when under stress, this servant molecule gets diverted to other functions and any mutations present in the organism are allowed to surface and an unorthodox shape results. One can think of several examples in our geological past when this must have happened during the course of nature's evolution. In our own case, it would appear to back up the fact that stress can result in allowing some change to surface from within us as we evolve as a person throughout our lives.

As to whether we should follow our genetic path or allow ourselves a degree of stress in order to follow another path is not the question at the moment. What is important is to say that there is no right or wrong path for someone. There are, in fact, many options and choices that can be made or taken. All of the paths are neither right nor wrong, yet some may be more apt or convenient as we shall see later on.

On the subject of stress, it is important to realise that if one wants to achieve certain things there is often a price to be paid. Some people choose not to pay this price; some pay too high a price. There is a subtle difference here in the words used. We will see later on in the following chapters how important words and their meanings are and the effect they have in the programming of a person's mind. Here, however, the difference is in the word stress and stressed. Stressed implies a threshold has been passed and that damage has been done (Like the bent metal rod) and physicists refer to this as strain (also mentioned above). Stressed also implies that this threshold has been reached and that if pressure is then released, a return to the new starting position is more than likely. A gentle, ongoing and continuing level of stress, and one that does not result in strain, will enable one to create change without personal damage. One related point that is worth mentioning here is that of blood pressure. We all have changing blood pressures throughout the day and these are regarded generally to be in close correlation as to how much stress we are under. High blood pressure can be a good thing under certain circumstances and it coincides with periods of high stress. Too high a pressure for too long is considered by the medical profession to be unhealthy and will result in putting a strain on our bodies and will eventually damage them. However it is undoubtedly very necessary to have short periods of high blood pressure if we are to succeed in certain activities. We will return to this important point in chapter ten when we look at how the brain might work.

Stress can therefore be seen to be either positive or negative, depending on whether or not we are in control of the situation we are in and how we wish to view it. We may well set off on a path of our own, but end up on one controlled by someone else and doing something that we do not really want to do. This can lead to enormous amounts of negative stress and can only be reduced by taking steps to become internally driven and acting on our own accord rather than someone else's.

At this point we could take a highly positive stance with regards to the future, in as much as it now appears that although we have a genetic role in life, it is also seemingly possible for us to achieve anything we would like to in this world by following a different path. How we can use this information brings us to the next area, that of past and future light cones. I like to also refer to them as time cones.

2.2 Past and Future Light Cones

Let us first imagine being in deep space with a space suit on and holding an extremely powerful lamp. Let us also consider that time has slowed down considerably and that the speed of light is now only about five miles an hour (and for the purposes of this example it is not relative to the observer). If we were to switch on the lamp we would see light go out in all directions. Someone five hundred metres away would see an expanding area of light with ourselves at its origin. Soon it could have passed the onlooker and continued its outward path. The same thing would happen at the normal speed of light but it would be impossible for us to see it happen. If we were to now consider this picture over a period of time, we could represent what was happening in the form of a light cone. Scientists have long since known that nothing in this large-scale physical universe travels faster than the speed of light. So when we look at a light cone it appears to have a circular edge at the top that starts from a single central point. That single point would be where and when we turned on our lamp. The circular area at the top would be the current extent of the light from that lamp at that future point in time. A similar analogy can be seen when a pebble is thrown into the middle of a still pond. The concentric ripples travel outwards from the middle over a short period of time. If this was represented on a time chart, you could see the first ripple reaching a circular limit at some future point in time, just like a cone of light.

Diagram 1 shows two cones, one inverted on top of the other. These are past and future light cones. The point at which the two cones meet

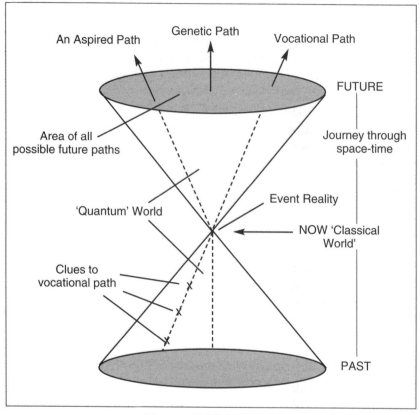

Diagram 1 Light Cones

in the middle is represented as now, in the present. This could be thought of as the place where we, in our space suits, turn on our lamps (or the point the pebble enters the water). The future light cone represents everything that can happen in the future from our present position. The one and only limit to this is the speed of light as nothing we can do physically from that starting point can be done faster than this speed. Consequently, we can consider that all of our possible future paths or courses of action in life, must lie within this cone. The flat surface at the top end of this cone represents all the future possible points in space-time that we could end up in. Any future path, or future position in life, that we can consider in our minds, from our current starting point at the tip of the cone, must fall within this conical area.

Physicists also talk of a past light cone. This confines all our possible past individual histories to lying somewhere inside of this past light cone. The set of events that fall inside the past light cone are all those from which you are able to reach the present position. This is a concept we will return to later in this chapter, but for now the past light cone area does contain some clues. These are indications that will help us find our possible future path and this is done by looking for any trends within past events and then projecting that trend into the future.

When looking at both past and future light cones we could theoretically track our known past journey through life to the present and then plan the path of our choice up into the future cone. Whatever vision or goal that we would wish to aspire to, would be found at some future top surface in the future cone. Obviously if we did nothing more about reaching this goal within the space-time limits we had specified, then it would soon fall outside the boundaries of our particular cone at that present time. Action and planning would be necessary if we were to succeed in reaching that particular desired outcome. We will look at powerful ways in which this is accomplished in chapter four.

We can now see how these light cones can be used to represent our journey through life. Our next step is to superimpose three, out of the many possible routes, onto these cones. This can be done for the past as well as for the future. The only condition again, is that they must all pass through the point at the present. The three routes we are initially concerned with are the genetic path, the aspired path and the acquired path. The genetic path is the one most natural to us initially, but from conception, we are subjected to experiences and are 'externally led' away from this path towards an acquired path. We are also 'internally directed' as we have goals and ambitions and it's because of these that we have an aspired path. As we progress through life, we can elect and take (albeit sometimes with difficulty) the routes and directions we wish.

The genetic path, for pictorial ease, can be drawn as a line in the centre. This will represent a journey through life where an individual is able to follow their genetic role in life. This is unlikely as these days there are more and more experiences around that can affect people, thus affecting their future direction. However the line can be imagined to exist as something that has been left over from our own evolution. Though the path might lie dormant within us, we have seen from the studies on twins that our genes still have a strong influence on us and can influence much that we do. This inherent genetic force will constantly be at work within us as we progress along any path we choose in life.

Throughout life, external forces and experiences can affect a person and they will often end up following one of the many possible acquired paths. It is likely that this is a path with an ever-changing direction as influences and experiences come from many directions. It is most usual for younger people to begin to follow these acquired paths as they begin to learn and experience their way through life. Their teachers, their peers and the environment they are brought up in, will influence them. However, whilst they are learning and being influenced they still possess a 'mind of their own'. This is stronger in some people than others and can give rise to problems when bringing up children in ways that conform to societies dictates. This leads us to the next path.

The aspired path, and there are many that can be chosen, will follow a route heading toward some alternative destination. This will be an 'internally directed' path as opposed to the genetic path that will be 'genetically led' and the acquired path that is 'externally led'. This internal direction, seen more commonly in those people of a stronger will, will lead to new paths in life being established. People selecting aspired paths are those that create and do new things in life and those that produce new outcomes by applying their own thoughts and visions and feelings to their work. We will look at the nature of internal and external directions and experiences in more detail in later chapters as it has a bearing on our own heading.

These paths can be regarded as that of the differing routes taken by some of the identical twins that have been observed. A path close to the genetic path could represent the one where the twins suffered little or no stress and were happy to go along with the dictates of their stable environment. This 'go with the flow' genetic route would be the opposite from the one where the twins incurred much stress. Depending on whether or not it was positive or negative stress, it would also lead to different end results. The negative stress, due to the lack of feeling of control over one's situation (i.e. being externally led down a path one didn't want to go), would lead a person in one direction. The positive stress (perhaps caused by being in control, internally directed and proceeding in harmony with one's wishes) would lead in another.

Diagram 2 shows three arrows of possible paths. To go to one side requires internal direction and leads to an aspired path, to go the other way implies being externally led and leads to an acquired path. To go

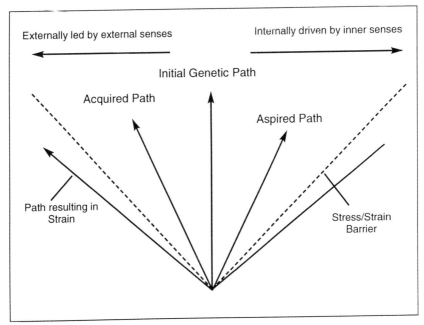

Diagram 2 Directing your future path

too far, too fast in each of these directions results in too much stress and the effects of strain will begin to show in an individual. The one side represents control over one's situation; the other being controlled. The degree with which we are happy with that situation will determine the amount of positive or negative stress we give ourselves. Again it is important to say there is no right or wrong path as we, as individuals, are all different and like and want different things in our lives. However at any one point in our lives we are proceeding in one of these three directions. As to how far in one direction will depend on how much we also let the other two come into play in our lives.

The outcomes of these paths could, quite possibly, lie far away from one's inherent genetic path. These could also include paths where goals or outcomes have not been reached within the space-time limits of a particular cone. They still could be attained, but that would need extra time and require following the necessary goal setting principles (covered in chapter four). To get back onto one's genetic path could also be possible but that then would require an internal direction and a form of control in order to accomplish that specific goal.

Probability will also have an effect on the outcome we desire. The further away the outcome is from one's starting point, the less probable it becomes. If it is to be achieved within a specific time frame, more internal direction is needed which in turn will require increased stress. This is only a danger if one goes beyond the stress/strain barrier. An example would be the desire to be Prime Minister in the next ten years when you are not even a candidate at the local elections. It's not an impossible task, but extremely unlikely and one that could probably make you stressed trying to achieve it. Not reaching that goal within the next ten years can be represented on the 'time' cone model as the outcome having fallen outside of the cone and missing the 'present' position at the tip of the cone. That is not to say it will never be possible, it's only now impossible within the time frame that you set your goal. To alter this and to put it back into your future time cone, would require putting a new time scale on your goal of perhaps twenty years. This more reasonable, and importantly believable, time frame makes the goal easier and will be possible with probably only a healthy amount of stress.

Now we have a framework with which we can understand people's roles and paths in life. We can begin to use it in order to understand our own pasts and where our futures might lie. This time cone framework will also provide us with a useful goal-setting model and become the basis for understanding in the connection between science and eastern philosophy.

The first place to look for future trends is the past. Trends found in our past will begin to give us some indication of our genetic route and our chosen aspired route. Whether we would seek to choose either of these two, or any other, is not in question here. All we are seeking to do is first to understand the principles. I am certainly not suggesting we all stop what we are doing in order to follow our aspired paths, although it would lead to some extremely interesting conclusions!

To look for our genetic blueprint, it would make sense to start with our parents and then their parents. Trainers have known for many years of the benefits of breeding horses. Farmers also go to great lengths to breed animals that best fit a particular purpose they have in mind. There is no reason that humans should be any different, whatever the thinking might be behind any process. Physical, inherited characteristics in children are obvious to parents and they are often heard to comment on which features come from which relative. Parents also witness emotional characteristics that are similar. There have been studies on adopted children that have often shown up complete character miss matches between adults and their adopted children. This has been proved time and time again, irrespective of the new environment with which the children have been brought up in.

In many cases children follow their parents into similar occupations. Many might say that this is because there is an easy route laid out for to them. But this is precisely why and how people carry out something that is close to their genetic role. Some of these children are happy to allow themselves to be led by their genetic make up and incur little or no stress at all when following this path. This is not always the case and sometimes children follow one parent's profession only to find that it was not for them. They become stressed as they try to follow what they think is right for them. But, these children must remember that they are the product of two sets of genes from both parents and they are more likely to have some combination of genes that might indicate that their path lies elsewhere. Looking at parents professions, activities, interests, and possibly combining two or more groups of these, could begin to show a 'questioning descendant' their own possible genetic path. How successful that person is at following that path is a completely different matter for two reasons. Firstly, because as soon as they used some 'inner direction', it would mean they would be beginning to deviate from that path and starting to follow an aspired route. Secondly, if they allowed themselves to be influenced by external events and experiences, they would drift away onto more of an acquired path.

The search for an aspired path, and in particular the one aspired path that could be termed vocational and closest to our vocation in life, requires us to take a much more 'in depth' look at our pasts. If we are to assume that our aspired future paths can be found as a result of using our own inner direction, taking decisions and actions by ourselves, then in our pasts we must look at the outcomes of events when we took similar actions. As our vocation in life is personal to ourselves, it is not likely to be one that has arisen as a direct result of the influence of someone or something else. Looking back at the most memorable times in our pasts, moments that filled us with a passion for some new subject can then become guidelines to our vocation in life. To find these clues though, we must be sure to only include those times that were specifically due to, or resulted from, decisions that we made ourselves and not other peoples. It is an analysis of these events, which could also be termed coincidences, which will eventually show a trend and help lead us to our vocational path in life.

2.3 Coincidences

The Swiss Psychologist Carl Jung studied and wrote about a subject he called 'Synchronicity'. This was the study of meaningful coincidences and their underlying reason. He believed them to have a naturally connecting principle but without an obvious link. He felt that this awareness of a coincidence was a form of attunement by ourselves to the mystery of an underlying principle of order in the universe. If this is the case, then these meaningful coincidences would appear to occur more frequently when we are aligned with our vocational path in life.

Our own attunement is therefore really only attained when we elect to be internally directed in pursuit of our aspired vocational path. This vocational path would then be just playing our own part in the underlying principle of order within the universe.

Coincidences can range from various occurrences like chance events to those things that surprise us and intrigue us. They could be those things that appear to be connected to some mystery that we are engrossed in or even strangers that we meet that might influence us by doing something or saying something. Anything that falls outside of logical expectation and along the lines of instinct, and resulting from our own actions, could be a clue from our past as to what our vocational route might be. An example could be as simple as taking the dog for a walk in the woods and meeting someone on the way. If you had been told to take the dog for a walk in those woods and followed the track you had been recommended to follow, then the meeting would have resulted as a direct experience of being externally led to that meeting. If however you had decided to do all those things on your own accord, then there might well be relevance attached to any meeting. This then needs to be explored further.

James Redfield in his best selling book 'The Celestine Prophecy' describes the feeling of being 'Energised' when such a coincidence occurs. This he refers to as a form of being internally excited in some way. The feelings that surround these moments helpfully make them more memorable, and this makes it easier for us to pick them out of our pasts. Redfield goes on to say that they also appear to occur most readily when we are in a highly expectant state. This expectancy is a powerful inner emotion that we will discuss more when looking at how to be successful. He goes on to say 'Coincidence is the mechanism of growth, the how of evolution'. By this I think he is referring to our own evolution throughout life and our quest, should we choose to take it, for our own aspired, vocational path.

Some people call this aspired 'vocational' path one that's closely tied to ones intuition and one that is quite literally a 'calling'. It is the process of making your way towards something and is therefore more of a direction and a destiny rather than a goal. The emphasis is on the journey and not the end of the journey. Those people who say that they were 'called' or were 'on a vocation' talk of feelings of no escape and of being on a sense of a mission. Marilyn Ferguson in her brilliant book 'The Aquarian Conspiracy' describes an almost universal feeling of change that is occurring within ourselves. Many people have begun to experience the transformation she talks about, both on an individual and collective basis. This could also be thought of as beginning to follow one's vocational path.

Buckminster Fuller, inventor of geodesic domes and many other scientific discoveries, called his own commitment to his work 'mystical' and 'The minute you begin to do what you want to do, it's really a different kind of life'. Many others report that they are co-operating with events rather than controlling them or suffering them. Many successful people will admit to similar feelings in their past as they made their progress toward their destiny.

All of this can serve to assist us in our understanding of our own direction in life and how we can reach our aspired paths and our chosen goals. It might also assist us in understanding what our aspired 'vocational' path might be. The first question to ask ourselves is "What events have occurred in my past, that were directly as a result of actions taken by myself, that either fascinated me, intrigued me, affected me, energised me, or left me feeling connected to some higher sense of direction?"

In some cases you may feel that there are very few, too few to find a trend, or even none at all. In this instance you must return to the first part of the question that refers to actions directly taken by yourself. It may well be that there are not sufficient numbers of these. The solution is to look for some adventure. This could be on a physical, emotional or mental level. This should and must lead to far more interaction with other people.

If you get out and about, read more, talk and listen to more people, then more coincidences will occur. It is also important to remember the two-way nature of communication. Information can always be exchanged between people, but for it to be beneficial for all parties you must seek to give as well as receive. In our example of walking the dog in the woods, it may be that the meeting was far more important for the other person and that something you say has real meaning for them and their life.

This makes meeting people and exchanging ideas and information a truly exciting experience. With a practice of past reflection you will find certain times are more evident and memorable and eventually you will even reach an awareness of them occurring in the present. It's on these occasions that flows of energy are most easily experienced and this is something we will be discussing more of in chapter twelve.

The culmination of just this sort of exercise resulted in the writing of this book. Looking back in my past left me perplexed initially due to my variety of activities, achievements, interests and events. Nevertheless I sought to find a common thread to it all. This I believe I have now achieved and the discoveries I have come across have lead, in part, to the writing of this book.

2.4 Summary

In summary, we have learnt from the studies of identical twins that our characters are partly affected by our genes and partly by our experiences. How we allow these experiences to affect us and how we manage our levels of stress will determine our path through life. To a degree we have a genetic role in life although we can elect to follow alternative paths. If we choose to be more 'internally driven' rather than 'externally led', then we can select an aspired path and attain the goals we set for ourselves. If we analyse our own pasts along with our coincidences and any synchronicity, it can give us a clue as to our calling in life and our 'vocational' path.

All of this information can be represented on a past and future light cone diagram. The light or time cones are based on the representation of a mass that is in existence at the present time (where the tips of the cones meet at the middle). This mass occupies a point in space-time that is now. It has many future options open to it, as long as they fall within the boundaries of the speed of light for its current position. If we theoretically substitute the mass for ourselves, we can now consider it as our model and that we are at the start of a variety of options of paths in life.

In later chapters we will return to the picture of light cones in order to fully appreciate their connection between our goals, science, space-time and ki energy. It is important to do this to be able to understand how new realities occur and how we as individuals are party to the process. The reality of some of the phenomena that are associated with the ancient priests can then be more fully understood and appreciated.

In chapter four we will begin to look at the goal setting techniques that have been learnt from some of the most successful people from all walks of life. Their simple rules and techniques will shed further light on how to reach our chosen aspired paths and even our aspired vocational path. A look at the nature of success is crucial as it is the precurser to the creation of a new reality. If you want something like a vision to become real, then understanding the common principles of success are paramount. Applying these principles to our own quest then begins to provide us with some initial clues as to what the key to the secrets of the ancients actually is.

CHAPTER THREE

ON TO THE MAINLAND

I moved clumsily forwards, clambering over the bundles of cloth that lay on the bottom of the craft. As it pitched to one side, I grasped at the nearest object. It happened to be a leg. Looking up to apologise, a large wave broke over the bows and the full force of the spray caught me straight in the face.

"Sit down at the bows!" The deep, rasping voice of the owner carries over all the sound. He is obviously used to these circumstances. Dutifully and thankfully I obey, as best I can.

"We'll be out of the break in a minute." He calls again. "When I call out next, mind your head. We'll be going about."

I turn to look at the man next to me, with a look on my face that's got the question 'what does he mean?' written all over it. He returns my glance with an expression of disgust and rising anger. I remember his leg.

"My apologies." I say, "It's my first time." I feel even more of a fool for having said that, and the look he gives, convinces me that he fully agrees with me.

"Ready about!" Comes the cry. I notice that my wary neighbour leans forward and I remember the warning just in time. A thick wooden boom swings around over our heads and the currach now appears to be sailing along just out from the breaking waves and following the line of the shore. I breathe a sigh of relief and try to settle myself.

Having passed the shore break, the boat now moved in a gentle rolling action and I felt I had more time to get used to my new surroundings. I was sitting on a plank of oak that stretched the width of the craft, some three paces from side to side. Timbers of all sorts formed a cross lattice from the bows to the stern. Thin layers of oiled soaked skins were stretched to their limits across the underside of these struts. There was not much to stop a well-aimed or misplaced foot from seriously damaging the boats seaworthiness. I remembered the skipper's first words to me, the same thought had probably crossed his mind more than once with novice passengers like me. There was a large central mast well supported at its base by the thick beam of the keel. The boom that had nearly taken my head off was now leaning off to the leeward side pulling the thick cloth sail into a curved shape. The timbers creaked even in this light breeze and I wondered how the whole rig could possibly survive anything stronger.

At about twelve paces long, it was one of the larger vessels to be found trading amongst the islands. Ruadh, the owner and skipper, had several regular routes around the islands. This was his two day round trip, stopping occasionally at Donan broch, then round the corner to Brora on the isle of Stig. Then there was a short open sea journey to Drummorchy.

After a night there, he would return to Invercarrie. All this of course was weather permitting. If the winds were unfavourable, it could take several days. However, as the Time of Winds was approaching, and our pace already seemed reasonable, I didn't think dead lines were going to be a problem.

I was due to stay with him all the way to Invercarrie as had previously been arranged over two moons ago, but in the light of recent events I had decided to stay in Drummorchy, meet with Conal Brus, and then make the remaining part of my journey on foot.

Alone in my thoughts, I cast a wary eye around at my new companions. Ruadh was one of the hairiest people I'd ever seen. Small in stature, he still managed to look an imposing figure. Standing at the stern, his arms and body were draped over the tiller in a comfortable accustomed manner. He gazed steadfastly ahead. We'd spoken only a few times before, on a few of the previous occasions he had stopped at the broch. I knew him to be a genuine man who was happiest when at sea. He prided himself in knowing all the tides and currents around the islands. The hidden rocks and sand bars were all places he had once used to fish. Now though, through reasons only known to him, he had turned to ferrying people and their goods around. His presence was reassuring and I felt I was in good hands. Aside from Ruadh, there was the man I had landed on earlier. The earlier exchange of glances left me with no uncertain feeling that the man had no intentions of talking to me. I had also felt a distinctly unpleasant air of disquiet whilst sitting next to him and had therefore slowly edged my way along to the furthest end of the bench seat. With the few looks he'd made in my direction, I'd also begun to sense an evil presence. The hairs on the nape of my neck had never lied to me. This feeling was enhanced by a strange, faintly familiar smell that I'd also eventually tracked down to be emanating from this stranger, though I hadn't managed to identify it. I could feel that my curiosity was becoming noticed, so I consciously looked over to see if I could see what Ruadh was looking at. After a few minutes and having drawn a complete blank, I resolved to find an answer to my last question and made my way aft.

"Ruadh." I began cautiously.

"Yes Fionn. How can I help?" He replies, seemingly grateful for some conversation.

"I was just wondering what it was you were actually looking at?" I wave vaguely over the side.

"For. Looking for." He states with his lips beginning to smile at one end.

"Looking for?" I enquire again, now slightly perplexed.

"Ah Fionn." He pauses, and puts his thumb and forefinger on either side of his chin and begins to slowly stroke his beard. "The sea and the sky are fair and fresh today, howe're I need to become one with them in order to spy any tell tale signs of anything out of the ordinary. If there is, it might spell danger. Storms come quickly, reefs can rise up nearer the surface and the shifting currents can quickly ta'e a boat onto rocks." He turns and looks at me. "Do you ken lad?"

"Aye, I think so." But not really sounding that sure. He senses my lack of understanding and continues.

"Do you see that patch of slightly lighter coloured water a way ahead of us?" He points.

"Aye." I reply after a few moments.

"It's a de'ils current, the waters there flow different. It's nay a problem for us, but they sometimes spread as the tide changes. If that happens we must alter course to avoid the rocks on the point. The current would want to take us that way. We need to round close to the point to enter the sound of Stig in the right position to get safely to Brora. If we mess it up, its far harder to avoid the ledges and their rips on our approach."

"Ah." I say, just beginning to have an inkling that there was far more to this art of sailing that was first apparent.

My disquiet returns as we approach the point.

"If I can gi'e you one piece of advice Fionn." He pauses to check that he still holds my interest, which I acknowledge with a slight nod. "It's something that's seen me through many a spot of trouble." He leans nearer and I lean toward him too. "When e'er you find you'self unsure of your position an' ken not which way to turn, look for those things around you that are not normal. It's them that tells the story you need to know. To do this, I fix a beady eye around me and become aware of what I feel out of the corner of it. If there's anything there, then you'll know soon enough." He leans back and his half smile returns. "What you do then, I hav' nay a clue. But I know this, what you may have noticed and your next action is always connected in some way or another."

I am left to ponder his words as he looked back out toward the point. The sound of the waves breaking on the shore had begun to get louder and now started to mingle with the calls of the kittywakes and the gulls that were flying nearby. Their noises reminded me of the hours I'd spent as a boy playing along the top of these very cliffs. The whole length of this part of the island had no path down to the sea. Seeing it from this viewpoint was strangely refreshing.

We rounded the point uneventfully and the boat quickened as the currents swept us along. I watched everything in a fixed stare trying to notice any abnormal things out of the corner of my eye like Ruadh had said. Unfortunately everything seemed new to me and my attention was distracted on several occasions, to the extent that I wondered whether or not his words would be of any use to me at all. I deduced that I would probably have to first appreciate what was normal in the first place and in order to be able to do that, I would have to experience an awful lot more than an average young man from the islands. I supposed that it might well be that this was the beginning already.

The approach to Brora was rough and the curragh was being thrown from side to side as the waters ran over the shallow shelves of rock in the channel. The few huts that I could see were low to the ground and well dispersed, nothing like the imposing sight of the broch. It was as though the settlement was nestling behind whatever shelter there was, in an effort to keep out of sight from passing craft. I knew defense was always a priority and guessed that there must be something else more substantial elsewhere. Islanders were known to be canny and crafty, and these folk were probably no exception.

Ruadh swung the boat expertly in behind the short stone pier. On it stood around twenty large islanders with blue painted faces; dirks at the ready in one hand and targe in the other. It was often a custom to greet everyone in full battle dress, visitors were tolerated, but were meant to have no doubt that the clans here, would stop at nothing to defend what they had. My earlier thoughts seemed to be correct.

Several of the younger men eyed me up and down as though they were sizing me out for a fight. I had no desire to disembark so happily stayed put. A few packages were lifted out and several more brought in.

"Careful with that one." A voice calls out and a man appears from behind the others clutching a parcel of hide from under one arm and staff in the other. His face was unlike any that I had previously seen. He had a dark complexion and short black hair with a few grey curls. His attire showed him to be a man of wealth. A thick gold clasp held his leather wrap firmly about him. Two large bracelets and rings with several large jewels on matched them. I imagined that he was probably one of the more successful traders around these parts, however I was surprised that I had not heard or seen him before and why he had not visited our broch.

I watched with growing curiosity, as he turned to the clan chief before boarding our curragh. With what seemed an excess of zeal, they embraced and slapped their arms around each other. The visitor then slowly and carefully took a ring off of a finger, one with a large red stone, and offered it to the chief. He responded with a well-rehearsed decline, but it barely concealed his greed.

"You're too much Col Oig." Booms the chief, taking the ring. "Be off with you now before I change my mind. Fare well my fine friend."

"Thank you again most kindly for your hospitality which, by the way, far exceeds all that is offered here among the islands." Comes a rehearsed but humble reply along with a slight nod of his head. With that, the aged traveller turns and places his staff carefully onto an oak plank and steps on board.

"Cast off at the bow!" Cries Ruadh and immediately we are under way again.

The whole process took under a sun's width and I wondered why the haste had been important. Surely we were not that short of time and would reach Drummorchy before nightfall.

Ruadh hugged Colin Oig like an old friend and beckoned him to take a seat at the front, which he gratefully accepted. Passing me, he turned and offered me his hand in a gesture of friendship. I took it, unsure of my feelings toward this imposing man and mumbled a word of greeting, then looked away.

I immediately regretted my apparent coyness and lack of manners. As he took his seat, I looked over toward him again. How had this stranger managed to conjure up so many awkward feelings inside me. Those of ineptitude, shyness and fear had all welled up within me, yet mixed with them, there was a distinct impression that the man meant me no harm. In fact, it was almost the opposite. I resolved that it was probably a mixture of my new mode of travel and that I was not yet that used to meeting with new people. If that was the case, it was a pretty poor start for a young Seannachie.

With the current and wind against us the shortest route, back up the sound, was out of the question. The only option was to follow it down and sail around the far side of the Isle of Stig. We would then have a short spell of open sea before we would catch sight of the mainland.

The currach ran with the wind as we went down the straits and with the cliffs either side of us, it got us up to a breathtaking speed. I looked back and saw our long white wake in the water and noticed a broad grin across Ruadh's ruddy face.

"The God's shine on us today Fionn." He says almost shouting his enjoyment. It was obvious he loved the sea with a passion.

I smiled back at him and turned to look in front again. This time I saw Colin Oig and the cowled one, deep in conversation. Anyone could see that they had known each other for a long time and were in fact on friendly terms. My suspicions about the two of them began to rise, but again for what reason I had no real idea.

We rounded Stig and fell into its wind shadow. As the boat slowed, the quietness and peacefullness became apparent for the first time. I started to survey my new surroundings eager for new experiences and material with which I could embellish my stories. The dark grey skies had now allowed a small patch of blue to appear, the sun's rays shone through it lighting up a ring of sea some way off near the horizon. An eerie tranquillity had begun to surround us. 'Shelter before a storm' ran through my thoughts.

It wasn't long though before the peace was broken, we rounded the island and fell into fresh new winds and open sea.

"All to the windward side." Calls Ruadh. Again I obey, following the others, my life really did appear to be in his hands.

Looking forward, I could see no sight of land and Stig behind us was getting smaller. My thoughts turned to the great sea commander, Manannan. It was said that he drove chariots as easily over the waves as over a plain. He had a boat that sailed itself called the Wavesweeper and could either stir up the sea to help or hinder those who ventured on his waters. I knew of the stories and had learned many by heart, but only now did I wonder at their real truth. Just in case they were, I mumbled a lorica to myself and made a promise that if my voyage was uneventful, I would repay him with much praise when next I was called upon for a story.

Half way across, I began to experience strange feelings both on the outside and in the inside. The boat was at one instant on top of a wave and the next completely dwarfed by it. Fast then slow, up then down, there was no respite. My stomach wrenched at its sides for stability but found none. Even the sight of land did little to cheer me, nor did the constant requests to join in the conversations.

At last I could see the lights of Drummorchy. I had arrived. It was nearly dark and the evening fires had been lit. The winds had settled and, with a lot of mental concentration, so had my innards. Ruadh had expertly brought the boat around the to the lee of the stone and wooden pier and had tied it up.

"Fionn." Calls Ruadh, lending me a hand up. "Be sure to stop by the inn tonight." He finishes with one of his usual smiles. I half expect him to continue, but that would be akin to his purposely perplexing demeanour. So I just smile back at him.

"Sure, I'll look forward to it." I add, not knowing quite what I might be letting myself in for.

I clambered on to the jetty and nearly collapsed as my legs half buckled beneath me. A loud guffaw came from Ruadh as I reached out with my hand to stop myself falling. My other two travelling companions looked back and I could only imagine the smiles on their faces in the darkness. I walked guardedly over the wooden planks all the way to the shore and into the small crowd of locals that had gathered there.

My first thoughts were to get out of my wet clothes, but this settlement was completely new to me. I resolved instead to first find my father's friend Conal Brus. I walked up to the first stranger.

"Hey, do you ken a man called Conal Brus?" I ask the nearest local.

"Have you anything to sell?" Comes the reply from the oldish man.

"Nay I've not, I've nought to trade. I am just a traveller." I reply. His interest in me is instantly lost and he walks away muttering to himself and joins the crowd now establishing itself around Col Oig.

I turn to a young lad not far away who seems unable to get close enough to them. "Hey! Lad. Do you ken where I might find Conal. Conal Brus."

"Sure, just follow the track there till you see his sign. Are you selling?"

"No, but thanks. What sign might that be?" I reply. But he was off. I was obviously of no use to him either.

I had no real choice but to follow the track and see where it would lead. It was fairly dark now and the light escaping from the leathered flaps barely lit the way.

The muddy path wound its way past several roundhouses both large and small but all with steep conical thatched roofs that nearly reached the ground and similar to those we had on the islands. After only a few hundred steps away from the main group of them, I came upon a large stone. On it was a carved picture of a salmon, a totem to those that respected wisdom. Next to this was a muddy path with occasional large flat slabs leading to large round thatched hut with a tall entrance passage in front. The fires were on and I could hear laughter and merriment coming from within.

I bolstered up all my remaining energy and courage and walked up to the entrance and slapped the thick leather flaps three times. The sounds inside ceased and I could hear the footsteps of a large man approaching.

"Who calls at that this time of night? Friend?" Comes a low and powerful voice.

"My name is Fionn mac Donal, of the clan Donal, from the Isle of Siegg." I say mustering up as much dignity as I could, given my present condition.

The skin partition is pulled wide open and a giant of a man is silhouetted against the firelight. "Welcome Fionn mac Donal of the clan Donal, my house is your house, come in. Come in and let us see the son of an old friend." He rumbles with deep warmth to his voice.

I enter and step cautiously down through the narrow passage made by the woven hazel screens and into the circular room. The relief that I felt at being asked inside quickly fades and turns to mild panic as I see four more new faces staring at me. "D'nna be afraid, young Fionn, let me introduce you to my family. My wife Aine, my daughters Niamh and Brigid and wee Davy my young son." He turns to me and looks me over, "My indeed, you have the face of your old man. Tell me, how is he? Still cussing his way through life?"

"Aye, he is." I say remembering my fathers last few words. "Good evening to you." I look at each of them in turn. "Thank you kindly for receiving me at this late hour."

They each eyed me back with a friendly smile and, in the firelight, I noticed the facial similarity between them all. Each had the same shape of nose, straight and slightly pointed in an attractive way and all had dark brown slightly wavy hair and blue eyes.

"Not at all lad. Come sit down by the fire, tak' off those wet clothes and dry yourself." Says Conal with genuine kindness in his voice.

At that Aine and her daughters get up from their seats and offer me the best place. Although I am well aware of this practice, I am unused to it being directed at my benefit and the others immediately feel my angst.

"Come now, Fionn." Says Aine "Settle yourself, you must be hungry. Can we get you some broth? Girls, fetch some soup for the man. Davy, go cut some bread."

The place became a hive of activity as each sought to help me. With every moment my indebtedness and comfort increased. Conal was a huge man, easily two paces tall and with shoulders that could block out sunlight. He looked as though he could appear quite menacing, but his face had a gentle appearance. His pale blue eyes and slightly curling short light brown hair added to the effect. I was slowly gladdened that my father seemed to have such a good friend in Conal. His wife Aine by comparison was tiny and only just the size of her eldest daughter Niamh. Despite this odd difference between them, Aine still managed to exude a fair amount of power over her man and it became obvious it was she who was in control inside her roundhouse.

With the broth filling my stomach and the fire warming me from the outside, it was time to quench their burning curiosity. Good naturedly, they had held back from questions whilst I ate and I knew that now it was my turn to repay them as best I could.

"I take it you came in on the boat. Tell us..." Cries Niamh almost bursting it out.

"....Hush now child." Aine cuts her off. "Let the man speak in his own time."

"Indeed I did Niamh," I reply. At the sound of her name she smiles and dips her head to hide it. "I can nay say it was a good or a bad crossing, as it was my first. To be honest Conal," I continue, leaning back against one of the nine upright posts holding up the floor above, "this was not a planned trip to see yourselves. We had some trouble at our Broch."

I explained everything that had happened in the last couple of days, all about Donal and much of what he had done since he had last seen Conal, which was nearly as long as I was old, and about my training with Dugald to become a storyteller. When I finished, there was silence.

"Fionn," Conal begins in a slow and pensive manner, "You seem to have a talent for your chosen art. Come we must talk some more, but not here. Ladies. Will you excuse us? I'd plans tonight to call on Lachlan down at the inn. Fionn will you join me?"

"Of course," I say, noticing however that the others appeared to be upset at losing their guest so soon.

"We'll be back before you're off to your beds." Smiles Conal, as he too had sensed the same feeling.

As we stepped outside, the wind had quietened and a few of the stars were now visible. Despite the season, it felt less cold now I'd found friendly company. We set off at a leisurely pace and the big man immediately began to talk again, this time with a friendly arm over my shoulder.

"What plans have you made, Fionn?" He starts brusquely.

"Well, none really, it's all happened so fast that I thought that I should take things as they happen and deal with them then." I reply.

"From what you've told us, I'm afraid that things might not be that simple. If your suspicions about Callum Beg are correct, you've chosen a very difficult man to cross."

"What do you mean?" I say, interested in knowing more about the man.

"Enough of him later." He dismisses. "First it's time to tell you more about myself and perhaps a little of what I know of your father. Forgive me for not asking this earlier, but these are strange times and to have done so in front of my family, would have been inhospitable of me when faced with a stranger in need. Did your father say anything or do anything with regards to myself before you left? Do you perhaps have anything that might prove you are his son?" I look at him straight in the eyes, trying to fathom what it was he might be on about, when it dawns on me." Yes, "I blurt out, hurriedly searching my pocket. I pull out my father's ring and show it to him.

He takes it and looks closely at it, but not in an examining way, more of one who is deep in memory. "Aye! You are who you say you are alright, he would not have given you anything else, if it was me he wanted you to meet with." He lifts his head up and looks me in the eye and continues.

"I was with him the day we first saw this." He pauses then takes a deep breath, "It seems so very, very long ago. Your father and I decided to travel South looking for adventure. As young men do." He adds as an after thought, "We joined Amairgin and his armies in many fights, first against the Firbolg, then the Tuatha De Danaan. No man would believe the sights that we saw in battle. We stood side by side against all types of demon. This was the ring I was given by Amairgin himself, for saving him from a fall in the midst of one of the frays. Later your father saved my life and I gave it to him. I've been indebted to him to this day." He pauses again and on a fresher note says, "Now I shall help you as best I can, in the hope that it will in some way repay what he did. "

"You've done much already," I reply hastily.

"Nonsense," He rebukes me, "There is plenty to do still."

"The first thing though, is to have a drink and toast old friends."

We came to the door of the inn and from the outside it sounded as though there was a lot of fun going on. He opened it and walked in ahead of me. I followed him into the warmth and broke into a smile at the infectious atmosphere of music and laughter that was all around me. I stopped for a moment to enjoy the feeling and to cast an eye over my new environment. It was another large thatched roundhouse but this time with a central stone fireplace and beams of thick oak radiating out to the dry stonewalls. The central stonework obscured those people the other side of it, but I guessed there were around twenty folk gathered here. The room was full of benches and tables and there was a long bar against the wall to my right. Conal made his way over there and beckoned me to follow. I walked over receiving a few odd glances on the way from the revellers. Further round and into the room, I could see Col Oig holding court, he was directly opposite from the bar. Ruadh was with him and he was the first to see me. I smiled and looked back to Conal.

"Here Fionn, the ale's not that bad," He advises, handing me a wooden tankard filled to the brim with a frothy top, "But it's better with a dram of me own." He breaks out into a broad smile and gives me a small silver cup with a clear sweet smelling liquid. I look at him and he goes on to say, "I make it myself and Lachlan and I sell the stuff." I raise my eyes up again from the dubious fluid to see Lachlan nodding to me from behind the bar. "The brew we make, we trade all around the area, some would say it's the best uisgebeathe in the highlands, but I would nay go that far. We supply many of the inns in these parts and I've plans for much more."

I raised the cup to my lips and knocked it back down my throat. My throat feeling instantly on fire and with the liquid further burning its way down to my belly, I reached for the nearest thing I could find to quell the pain, the ale. Three large swigs later and having just avoided my eyes watering, I turned to Conal and managed a smile. This was not a time to try for words just yet.

"By the Dagda's good word, you're your father's son indeed." He grins and slaps me on the back. All I could do was to grin back.

I decided to take a little more time to recover by pretending to study the room in more detail. There were a couple of burly youths arm wrestling each other with others cheering them on. An old man played on a wooden whistle and was accompanied by a man with an old war drum. There was another group, who were clearly becoming the worse for wear from drink, that were telling each other jokes and playing the woods and then there was the group around the trader. I noticed that my initial travelling companion had also joined them. This time he was dressed similarly to the rest but was still sat in such a way that I still could not get a clear view of his face.

"You look deep in thought Fionn." Guesses Conal, "What's on your mind?"

"I was wondering about my next move." I answer, looking down and away from him.

"I might be able to help you there." He stops and waits.

"Go on." I say, turning back to look at him.

"Well, I've done a lot for my age and I know a little about getting what you want in life. Surprisingly is not all down to fate, you can make a lot of your own luck."

"How's that?" I ask, now slightly intrigued as to what Conal was about to say.

"Achieving something is all down to planning, setting realistic tasks and getting yourself in the right frame of mind. Put simply in your case.

What's the position right now? How much do you know? What do you want to achieve and when? What are the routes to take? And which is the best one now?" He stops to check if I'm following him. I nod back. "That's the framework." He goes on, "The next thing is, that knowing that nothing was ever achieved without hard work."

"I know that." I interrupt, remembering the seven years studying with Dugald.

"That's good lad, but the bigger the task you set yourself; the more persistent you must be when times get tough. You need to have complete belief in what you are doing and make it part of the world of your thoughts and visions. Then, and only then, will things start happening for you."

"So what do you think I should do first Conal?" I ask, still a little unclear.

"First you need to know what you're up against. How much do you know about Callum Beg?" He lowers his voice for the last words.

"Very little, I was just going to go to Invercarrie and see what I could do when I got there." I say. It sounded feeble after having heard his previous advice."

"Fionn, if the man you suspect is behind all of this, then you'll need to know a lot more about him, before you'll know what to do. I'll tell you what I know first, which is not much."

"As you probably know the king died a couple of years ago. His wife, Irnan, was left with a son too young to take the throne. Callum Beg stepped in to help. He had become the chief Ollamph at the Aes Dana, something I might add he could only have achieved if he had had the support of the majority of Fili and Anruth in Invercarrie. To many it seemed quite a natural thing that he should assist the throne in this way, to others it was disastrous. However, for all the strange goings on we hear from as far away as we are, it would appear that the majority of the people are happy with the way things have been going. Trade is good."

"So what's the problem?" I reply.

"There have been disappearances, people have just vanished and there are rumours that he has brought back the black arts of sacrifice for his devinations."

My mind honed into full concentration at his last words and brushed aside any affects that I might have had from my drink. The concern for my sister was now uppermost in my thoughts.

"If it's any help," Conal continues as though he had sensed my feelings, "it's nearly eight full moons till Samhain. If these rumours are true, then it will be on that one night of the year, when the sidhe open their doors to the Otherworld, that he'll do his dirty deeds. Although the beginning of winter is seen by us all as a major festival, we often forget the darker side. " He finishes his words with an eerie note to his voice.

"Enough." I call out, not liking the way even my own thoughts were going. "Nothing's going to happen to Mairi."

"Aye, you're right and it's best not to dwell upon it." He adds changing his tone along with bringing finality to the subject.

We sit silently for a moment deep in contemplation and I take some more sups of the ale that is becoming sweeter with each swallow.

"There is a man here you should meet with. He may well be able to give you some up to date inside information as to what is happening at Invercarrie. He has friends in high places and on all sides. He's also one of only a few people that I know that has an ability to make friends with all types. That makes him a powerful ally. Come let us talk with him." Having said that, he takes my arm and starts to lead me across the room.

Almost before we set off in the direction, I had guessed to whom Conal was referring. Col Oig was holding a merry audience and in the middle of gesticulating to all those at his table when we approached. "Well, if it not our intrepid first time traveller." He calls out heartily, raising his arm toward me. "How are you feeling now? You certainly look better now than you did earlier."

"Well. Thank you," I reply as courteously as possible.

"Conal. Is this young man with yourself?" He looks up at the two of us now standing next to his table.

"Aye Colin, he's the son of a old friend of mine. It's good to see you're keeping well too." He reaches across the table and greets him with a short firm arm embrace.

"Life's been good to me as you can see." Pulling away from Conal, he makes a quick display of his extensive decoration of rings, amulets and bracelets and continues, "How can I help you? Are you looking for trade, I could sell barrels of your brew down South if you'll say the word. "

"Thanks but no, Colin, well at least not yet. No I was hoping to introduce you to Fionn here, but it appears you've met already."

"It was hardly what you might call a meeting. He said not two words to me since Brora." He adds quickly.

"Fionn's been in training to become a Seannachie and he off to the Aes Dana.."

Before he has time to finish Col Oig bursts into loud laughter. "... I'm sorry, it was just the thought of a man of words who'd run out of them."

"I'll ask you just once to take those comments back." I say in a low menacing tone and placing my hand on the top of my dirk. Conal stops my hand and I instantly feel the power come from that big frame of his.

"Stay your arm Fionn! Colin!" He calls and adds a look that the two of them seem to know well.

"Come, Fionn have a drink with me," replies Colin, "I meant my words only in jest and I am sorry to have offended you, I've had more than my fill tonight." He appeases.

I take my hand off of the dirks hilt and slowly release a smile as I sense his conciliatory tone. We sit down and Colin sends for two more ales.

"Now my friend, how can I help you both?" Colin says with a slightly more serious tinge to his voice.

"I was interested in knowing more about the Aes Dana at Invercarrie and in particular the chief Ollamph." I ask first. The words seem to carry a sobering affect on all at the table. But it lasts only a moment as Colin interrupts the silence that was developing.

"T'is perhaps not the time for questions of such seriousness. Come my future Seannachie let us hear what you are made of. Tell us a story that we all might enjoy."

At that he stands up and calls for silence until he has the attention of everyone in the room. "Tonight" He starts, "We have a special surprise for you all. Young Fionn here is a hopeful Seannachie and he's promised to give us one of his stories. "

With that he sat down leaving me to deal with the resulting silence. I turned to Conal who shrugged his shoulders and I'm left to cater to their desires. As all the revellers gathered in front of me, along with their drinks and benches, my stomach begun to twist. A thousand thoughts ran through my mind as to what story I should tell, when I realised my recent pact with Manannan the Sea Commander.

After a few deep breaths I began. "This is the Story of Cormac's Cup." A loud cheer goes up around the room and I feel I'm onto a good start.

"King Cormac mac Art, a noble and illustrious Celtic king, grand-

son of Conn, giver of the greatest feast of all time at Tara, was resting alone on the lawns of Mur Tea. As he lay half asleep in the morning sun, a warrior appeared from out of the early mists. This grey haired and handsome man wore a purple, fringed cloak with ribbed shirt and a branch, made from silver with three gold apples hanging off of its many stems, rested against his shoulder.

The King did not at first recognise that this magnificent sight was none other than Manannan the Sea Commander, Son of Lir, and that the branch he carried could give amusement, delight and healing to all that heard it when it was shaken.

I paused and looked about me to see if I had their attention. I did, so I continued in a loud and accented manner.

"Where have you come from, Warrior! " Called the King

"From a land where there is nothing but truth." Replied Manannan with a clipped accent to his voice.

"That's not like it is here." Replied the King, "Can we not make an Alliance, Warrior?" He continued.

"I would be very happy to make one." Said the warrior.

"Seal it by giving me the branch that you hold." Said Cormac greedily.

"I will give it to you as long as you grant me three boons when I return."

"They shall be granted." The king replied gleefully.

With that the warrior turned and left and Cormac had no idea where or how.

On returning to the palace, King Cormac shook the branch in front of his household and they were cast into a deep sleep for a whole day. They all marvelled at its ability to heal and to send people into beautiful slumber.

At the end of a whole year the warrior returned to the king and asked for his first boon to be given.

"What shall it be?" Calls the King

"I will take your daughter Ailbe." Said the warrior. At this all the women cried out but Cormac shook the Branch in front of them and banished their grief.

At the end of the second year, the warrior appeared again.

"What do you ask for today?" Says the king

"I will take your son, Carpre." Replied the grey haired man.

Again weeping and sorrow filled the halls in all Tara. This, once again, was dispelled by a shake of the Branch.

Again the warrior returned for his last boon to be granted. "I will take your wife, the fair Ethne the longsided daughter of Dunlang" Said Manannan, son of Lir and off he went. This was too much for Cormac and he went after the warrior along with fifty of his strongest men. They followed the stranger and his wife Ethne, all the way to a large and high mound. On seeing that it was a mound of the sidhe, his men drew back. It was well known by them that this must be an entrance to the Otherworld. A place inhabited by brownies and corrigans and people of the sidhe. They knew well that this was a place only for heroes and those gifted in the Arts.

As King Cormac approached the top of the mound he began to hear sweet and silky music, an entrancing song from the Birds of Rhiannon, who were often found the other side of the gateway to the Otherworld. He felt compelled to proceed to the top despite the calls from his men.

At the top, he entered the domain of the Blessed Isles and Cormac saw for the first time the unrivalled beauty of the place. A troop of majestic grey horses, with dappled manes, and another of purple-brown raced across the plain before him. Three trees of purple crystal glass were full of flocks of birds all in harmonious song

In front of him in the midst of this great plain stood a fortress with a wall of bronze. In the fortress was a silver white house, half thatched with the wings of white birds. A host of the sidhe rode around with lapfuls of the wings of the white birds trying to complete the thatching, but gusts of wind carried much away each time, filling the air like blossom.

Not far away he saw a man kindling a fire. Each time he returned with oak wood for fuel the fire, it had nearly gone out. His never-ending and futile task went on and on.

Looking round he sees another fortress, vast and royal, with another wall of bronze. Inside this were four houses and a palace with beams of bronze and wattling of silver, all thatched with white wings.

Then in the courtyard he saw a shining fountain. This Cormac recognised as the Well of Wisdom in the land of Promise. The fountain fell into five streams and from it, people were drinking. Above it all grew nine hazel trees from Buan. The nuts from these trees fell into the water and were being bitten by the large salmon that swam in the fountain. The husks from these nuts then flowed down the streams. The sounds of these streams were so soothing it took away all pain.

Cormac continued on into the palace where he saw a couple inside waiting for him. One was the distinguished grey-haired warrior Manannan, commander of the seas, magician and healer; the other was a beautiful golden haired woman. She was clearly the loveliest maiden Cormac had ever seen. Beside her was a golden helmet, the shine on which was as great as the sun. Her name was Fand and she was the wife of Manannan. This was the same Fand that had fallen in love with our hero Cuchulainn. She, it was, that had lured him into the Otherworld in order to get him to fight the Formorii, the ugly mis-shapen monsters that lived beneath the lochs and seas in purgatory. But that is a story for another time. I add, as an aside.

Today she stood unattended, bathing her feet in water over heated stones. Cormac was invited to bathe, which he did gladly and after a while a man entered with a wood axe in one hand, a log in the other and a pig on the end of a lead.

"T'is time to make ready, " Said the warrior. The man took the pig and struck it and killed it. He then cleft the log and cast the pig into a cauldron. "It is time for you to turn it." Said the warrior.

"That would be useless, " Said the Kitchener, " for the pig will never be boiled until a truth is told for each quarter of it."

"Then," Said the warrior, "You shall speak a truth first."

"One day, when I was going round my land, I found another man's cows. I brought them with me to the cattle pound. The owner followed me and offered me a reward to set them free. I gave him his cows and he gave me a pig, an axe and a log The pig could be killed each night and the log could be cleaved by the axe and there would be enough wood for the fire to boil the pig. There would be enough food for the palace as well. And in the morning the pig would be alive again and the log whole."

"It is the truth indeed," The warrior, confirmed.

The pig was turned in the cauldron and a quarter of it was boiled. The warrior then said, "Ploughing time had come and I went outside to see that it had already been done, and harrowed and sown as well. When I came later to reap it, I found it stacked in the field. When I desired to draw. it in, it was also done and still to this day we draw grain from it, yet it remains full." The pig was turned again and now it had become half cooked.

Now came the turn of the beautiful Fand. "I have seven cows and seven sheep. The milk from the cows is enough for all the people in the land of promise. From the wool from all the sheep also comes all the clothing they require. "At this truth the third quarter was cooked.

"It is now your turn, Cormac." Invited the warrior. Cormac then related the story of how he came to be there and how he had come to pursue his wife, daughter and son. With this final truth, the pig became fully cooked.

They carved up the pig and shared out the portions, but Cormac said, "I never eat a meal without the company of my fifty men." The warrior then sang a spell over him and put him asleep. After this he awoke and saw his fifty warriors and his son and his daughter.

Cormac's spirit was lifted and ale and food was given round to them all and they became happy and joyous. Then Cormac spied a cup of gold being handed to the warrior. He marvelled at the number of forms upon it and the strangeness of its workmanship. Manannan, noticing Cormac's interest said, "There is something even more strange about this cup. Let three falsehoods be said under it and it will break into three, it is better to utter truth. " This the warrior then shows Cormac by telling three lies and the cup breaks into three. "Now Cormac, I will utter three truths to restore the cup. Until today, neither your wife nor your daughter has seen the face of a man since they were taken from you in Tara. And your son has not seen a woman's face." The cup then became whole.

"Take your family and this cup so that you may forever determine between truth and falsehood. You can also keep the branch for music and delight. And on the day of your death they will all be taken away from you. I am Manannan, Son of Lir, King of the Land of Promise. The reason I brought you here was for you to see the land and learn the lessons that are here."

"The Fountain which you saw, is the fountain of knowledge." The warrior continued, "No one will have knowledge unless they first drink from the fountain itself and out of the streams. The folk of the many arts are the ones that drink of them all."

The following morning Cormac awoke to find himself on the green of Tara, along with his wife and his son and his daughter and the branch and the Cup.

This forever more became Cormac's Cup and it helped justice prevail throughout the peaceful realm until his death. Then, as was foretold, they remained not. There are some to this very day that think that Manannan's treasures have returned from the Otherworld. There's one that would claim that the Golden Helmet is amongst us right now.

With that I sat back and took a long swig of ale to wet my mouth. There was silence all around. I looked around me and saw faces deep in dream. Colin Oig was the first to clap. His noise broke the spell and soon there were cheers from around the room. I felt great.

"Come Lad, we must go." Conal is standing next to me amidst the noise. He reaches out his hand. "It's late and there's still much to say and do before tomorrow." Not fully understanding his haste, but recognising an air about him, I got up and followed him to the door. The sounds of the cheering and clapping could still be heard from the outside. We set off, back up the path the way we came down, and breathed in the cold fresh night air.

"It's a good time to leave with them wanting more, and more they would have got, if I'd let you stay. Fionn. That was a well-told story, but I feel I ought to give you a wee bit of advice. You must learn not to be so direct in your approach. Whilst you were talking, Colin managed to speak to me in private. What he said worries me, as it concerns you." He pauses as though wondering where to begin.

"Colin Oig is an old trading friend." He goes on. "It is only because of that, that he told me. Your directness, when it came to asking about the chief Ollamph, caused more than a stir with a certain party at the table, which I am sure you both intended and noticed, however strange things are afoot in Invercarrie. Your impending arrival there may well be already known."

My jaw dropped. "How can that be?" I manage to stutter out amidst my complete surprise.

"That's not important, what is, is that you are being followed." He stops and looks into my face. He can see my amazement turning to anger.

"The other man in the boat." I state, pausing momentarily.

"Yes." He says. "His name is Fiacal, one of Domnhuill Dubh's men, and one of the most dangerous. Watch yourself with him and don't ever get into a knife fight with that one, his reputation precedes him, even this far South!"

"Who's this Domnhuill Dubh?" I ask noting the warning. "And what does he want with me?" I walk a little faster to catch up with him.

"It would seem that there is talk that he might well be working for Callum Beg, which could well explain who was behind the disappearances. He's not a man to cross paths with, Fionn. My advice to you is to stay well away from him as well, if at all possible." He looks round and straight at me as if to reinforce his words.

"If I'm to do what my heart is set upon, I see little chance of that, Conal Brus. Can you tell me more about the man?" I enquire.

"I've not met the man, but I've heard that he's got his name Dubh because of his passion for the colour black. It's all he wears. That, and his reputation for enjoying evilness, is all that I know. Anything else is only heresay and useless to you." He stops and I get the feeling he is wondering whether to mention more.

The silence lasted for several moments and it gave me time to think. With his last words my thoughts went back to what young Don had said to me only yesterday at the Broch. The men that had come were wearing black, which to me was more than coincidental. There was a definite connection here. I hadn't mentioned this to Conal and for some reason I thought it wasn't important.

"What about this Fiacal, did Colin ever tell you anything about him?" I ask after a while.

"Aye, he did. It's not much better. He's Domnhuill's ear to the ground, his right hand man if you like. He wears a cowl to hide a massive scar that he got from an early childhood knife fight. There's some would say none can match him with a short blade now. Colin said that he thought something was strange, as he'd never known him ever to leave Invercarrie and he was certainly not someone who liked to take passage on the sea. When Col had asked him, he had come up with a fairly lame reason of collecting something here in Drummorchy for Domnhuill."

"How does Colin know these people? Can he be trusted if he keeps such company?" I ask, curious to hear Conal's answer.

Conal chuckles to himself and goes on to say. "The man is surely an enigma alright. He seems to know everyone and have no enemies. It must be an art he has practiced all on his own, for his own ends. And for him, those ends are material possessions. Why, I've no real idea, but if he does anything that'll be the reason behind it." He smiles at the simplicity behind the seemingly complex man.

"Would he not then sell what he knows?" I say more than a little concerned.

"I've asked him a similar question before and he said it wouldn't be good for trade in the long term. I believe him, as I have never found anyone to have a bad word for him."

At that, we'd arrived at his place. Inside his family were all waiting for us and it was Aine that spoke first.

"Did you two enjoy yourselves?" She asks slightly checkily, knowing we had both kept them from going to bed and from the pleasure of interrogating their visitor.

"We did." Replies Conal in a voice full of pretence authority and one that was responding back to his wife's playfullness. "And, I might add, Fionn here treated us all to a brilliant, refreshingly new, version of Cormac's Cup." He smiles, knowing the reaction he was going to get from them.

"No, No." Came the cries of all of them "How could you let him do that without telling us and letting us also hear? Fionn promise us you'll give us a story too. " Calls Niamh, half jumping up and down on her stool.

"That I shall," I say, "But I am afraid that it will have to be another time. From what I have learned tonight my plans must change, I am going to have to leave before dawn and I've decided its best to go to Invercarrie by foot and to arrive in secret."

"Leaving so soon. Mother! Please make him stay longer." Cries Brigid.

"Brigid, show some manners." Aine rebukes her. "Fionn. Come and sit with us by the hearth. You will be back again, won't you?" She says looking up at me and making her question sound almost like an order.

"Definitely." I say, moving closer and sitting down amongst them. "I'm just not quite certain when at the moment. I would like to thank you again though for your kindness in case I miss you in the morning. "

"Niamh." Says Conal in a questioning way. "You were going to Comrie in a few days to visit your friend, weren't you?"

"Yes, father." She replies, with a voice that begins to rise with a little hope as though she senses his thoughts.

"Well, why don't you accompany Fionn here as far as Comrie. He doesn't know the ways and I am sure he would like the company." He suggests with complete seriousness.

I raise both my hands to start to protest on the grounds of the possible danger but am interrupted by an eager response. "Oh thank you father. That's a lovely idea."

I look at Conal in order for him to notice my surprise. "Don't worry Fionn, Niamh's made the journey herself many times. Besides, you can go on the horses, which she can bring back later, it will save you a lot of time." He waves aside any argument I might have by brushing his

71

hand to the side.

I am a little stunned by the speed of all this and my silence is quickly taken as consent by all.

"Great." Says Niamh, "Now I'll get a story all to myself." She teases to the others, who are beginning to look enviously at us. "You will tell me one, won't you Fionn?" She looks at me to back her up.

"Of course, it will be small payment for your company and good direction." I reply as courteously as I can, having been put in these circumstances from no real choice of my own.

"Well, that's all settled then." Says Conal, "Off to bed now. Come here wench!" He calls mischievously to Aine. "Fionn, the girls here will show you where you can rest."

At that, he disappeared with Aine up the ladder to the sleeping room above. Brigid and Niamh took me over to a straw palliasse that they had already prepared with rugs and placed in front of the fire. They left me and went on whispering and giggling to each other. With nothing else left to do, I settled in and as soon as I was flat on my back, I found I was a lot more tired than I thought.

I am woken by a nudge in what appears to be still the middle of the night. It's Niamh. "What is it?" I whisper clearing my eyes and seeing her face close up for the first time.

She smiles at me. "Time to get up." She says coquettishly, "I've readied the horses and prepared us some food. We must hurry, I left you as long as I could." I got to my knees stretched my arms and rolled my head around in an attempt to waken. I need not have bothered for as soon as I was outside the chill morning breeze ran straight through me. I awoke instantly, my senses whirling. Niamh took my hand and led me through the darkness round the back to the stables. It felt warm and comforting to be touching her and I admitted to myself that I was glad of the company.

"We'll go south and then double back on the outlying fields around Drummorchy," she says, "just in case." She adds with another smile.

I found myself smiling back at her. She was certainly an impelling young woman. We set off in single file with her in front leading the way along a narrow path. There were fields either side of the track filled with cattle and sheep. The only signs of our presence came from our horse's deep breaths and the occasional bleat from a sheep. The night air had left a heavy dew and my legs brushed against the sides of the larger bushes and soon they were uncomfortably damp.

The narrow path needed all my concentration, on account of the fact that I was not an accomplished rider, unlike my brother. Niamh, on the other hand, seemed to me to have been riding for many years. She and her mount looked to be a lovely, matching combination. Her light brown horse went well with the colour of her cloak. Her long, dark, slightly curly hair bounced around behind her in a perfect rhythm with the gait of her steed. I found myself wondering about her, wanting to know a little more.

Having completed a near half circle, we reached the western coast road to Invercarrie. It was a well-worn track that was thankfully hard and dry. It allowed us to travel side by side and so we indulged ourselves in conversation.

"Do you see the sunrise over there, Fionn?" She says excitedly pointing out across Gruinard bay. "Isn't it lovely first thing in the morning, don't you think?"

"Aye, indeed Niamh, it's a fair sight." I agree, stopping to look for a moment.

"There's many things I'd love to show you on the way, Fionn. I wish ...." She stops and looks away out to sea.

"Fionn." She starts off again, "Are you hungry? I've brought us some oatcakes with dried fruit, we can eat on the move if you like." Her enthusiasm again fuels me in a mildly intoxicating manner.

"That'd be grand Niamh." I reply, enjoying the reaction in her when I use her name. Every time I had so far, it had provoked her to turn her head away from me. Her coyness and youthful naivity felt flattering.

We continued, walking our horses, and fell into more silence whilst we ate. Having a full stomach left me, again, feeling more than grateful at having come across such genuine generosity from the whole of Conal Brus's clan.

"Niamh, I truly appreciate everything you have done for me and in some way, I shall try and repay you. Will you accept, for now, a wee tale about Cuchulainn and his love for Emer."

"Oh please, it's one of my favourites." She mentions, now rapt with attention.

I begin to tell her the story, adding extra bits to those parts that I could sense she loved more and quickly passing those that held less interest to her. At the end she was in tears. They were tears of joy, happiness and sadness all mixed up, and were often to be found amongst an audience at the end of a tale. It was a sign of a good Seannachie and today it filled my heart to see her like this. I leant across and put an arm about her shoulders.

"That was beautiful. " She says wiping her eyes, "How do you do it?"

There was no short answer to give, so I stayed silent. We travelled that way for a while. The sun had come up and was now behind clouds, but luckily the winds had stayed away. The latter was in some small part due to the forest that was now to the left of us. On the other side, was the rocky shoreline that was a stone's throw away. It was covered in kelp and the salty smell that came from it mixed with scent of our horses leaving us quite heady.

"Around the next corner is Drumnadrochy. There are only a few crofts there and they keep themselves to themselves so they'll not say anything to anyone about us if asked."

"Fine." I reply now wondering what might be going on back at the pier when they discovered I was not around to join them. I also wondered about my kin at the Broch and how they might be faring.

"What are you thinking?" Asks Niamh now smiling again.

"Oh, just about my kin o'er yonder." I point to a vague area out in the bay where I guessed Seigg might be.

"Tell me about them." She continues sounding genuinely interested. As we passed through Drumnadrochy, I described my family to her and what life was like on the island.

Afterwards she says. "It sounds lovely there, I'd love to see it one day."

"One day you will." I reply, my mind still elsewhere.

After that, we were alone with our thoughts for a while. I was recalling in my mind all the events that had happened in the previous day, looking for signs, hidden meanings and just ideas for the future. It was a common enough exercise and I normally did it at night. Had I not been so tired the night before, I wouldn't have been doing it now.

"Look, Fionn." Niamh calls, "There on the left."

I looked to my left and see a stone with a picture of an animal head sculpted on it. They were common along main routes such as this and symbolised a boundary limit of an area that someone considered theirs. In this case their sign was a stag. It was also a sign of fertility.

I look back at Niamh. "Not the stone Fionn." She reddens, "The gap between the trees. It leads to a clootie well. Come on, let's leave a rag there and make a wish. I've always wanted to, but I've been afraid to leave the track on my own. Please Fionn, please." She begs, leaning forward over the head of her horse and turning her head to try and look me straight in the face.

How could I say no. Her persuasiveness was now becoming obvious to me. She was a woman who used all her womanly ways to get what she wanted. I could picture Conal Brus often giving in, in the same way as I did now.

"Of course." I say, "How could I refuse a young woman such as you." I reply with a slight air of playfulness.

She stops at those words and looks at me briefly. A serious look to her face instantly fades to a broad grin as she sees me smiling impishly. "Come, we'll walk the horses." She says.

We dismounted and led the horses through a barely imperceptible, narrow gap in the trees. The path we were on was strewn with old pine needles, broken twigs and small branches. It was obviously not used that often.

"We're now in the Strathyre Forest. Have you heard of it?" Her words sent a shiver down my spine as I remember them from before.

It was only yesterday morning, now almost a lifetime away, that Dugald had mentioned it to me. I'd not recounted that particular conversation to Conal and his family and had all but forgotten it as I had stashed it deep away in my secret memory. All Seannachie sectioned off their minds. It was one way to cope with the huge amounts we had to learn. Recalling it all was based on step-by-step techniques with access codes to each level. In this case I'd almost forgotten, as I'd not had time to go through the memory retention techniques necessary shortly after initial learning. I reminded myself to do that later in the day.

I went through Dugald's words again. He mentioned the Well of Leght, just outside Drummorchy in the Strathyre Forest.

"Niamh, does this clootie well have a name by any chance?" I venture.

"It's sometimes known as the Well of Leght. Why do you ask?" She replies casually.

"Just something someone said recently," I say not wishing to comment any further right now.

'Coincidences should always be looked into.' I hear the voices of my Father and Dugald in my head. 'There is always a reason, it may not be obvious straightaway, but there is always a reason.' they always said as well.

We approached the clearing and in the middle was a small spring. Surrounding it were pines, firs and spruces, but the clearing itself was mostly mosses and clumps of long grass. It made it very damp underfoot. On the lower branches of the trees, on one side of the clearing, there were large numbers of torn rags, many faded in colour. A few feet away there were some large flat boulders where people could squat down and fill their flasks. The waters from the mountains had seeped through the rocks and surfaced here just under a natural bank of earth.

It was a strange sight. The inner calm and beauty of the place had been scarred by the haphazard array of bits of old cloth tied to branches all over the place. We made our way around to the far side and I tore off a small piece of cloth from my bundle and gave it to her.

"Thanks," She says and ties it up next to the others.

She then turned, bent down and cupped a hand of the clear water and brought it to her lips. She leant her head back and, with her eyes closed, half drinks and half spills it down her neck. She then screwed up her face, as though in deep thought, whilst making her wish. It was a pleasure to watch her ritual.

When she had finished, she turned and walked away from me, enjoying the peacefulness of the moment. I was in no mood for what I had to say next. I had enjoyed the morning and this was going to be upsetting to her and possibly many other people.

"Niamh," I begin with a serious tone to my voice that she instantly detects.

"What is it?" There was concern in her voice.

"I'm going to have to leave you to go on your own."

"What!" the shock registers in her voice, I could see she hadn't expected this. "What do you mean? Is it something I've done or said? What is it?"

"No, it's nothing you've said or done, in fact I've really enjoyed this morning with you." I answer truthfully.

"What is it then?" She goes on, now in a more controlled state, albeit still obviously upset.

"The well of Leght was somewhere I'd been told about and there are things I believe I now have to do." I pause for a moment to look into her face. Her expression was like a child that had been scolded without knowing why. "It means parting company for now. I have to follow a dangerous route which is better I do alone." She looked at me not fully understanding but realising that I was deadly serious in my intentions.

"I'll be back as soon as possible. Your father told me you've a fine and delicate voice for a song and you dance the best reel in the whole of the South. I've a mind to see that for myself and to join you at the next Ceilidh." I could see this cheered her up.

"Fionn. Away with your lies." She smiles. "I don't understand why you've to go off now, but I know that you must. All I can say is to take good care of yourself. I'll be upset though, if you forget about the offer of a dance when we meet next. I'm holding you to that at least for leaving me so."

I walked with her in silence back down to the main coastal track. In parting, I gave her a hug, cheek to cheek, in a fraternal way and watched her ride off with the horses. She broke into a gallop without looking back and the last I saw of her, was her long dark hair streaming back over the top of her cloak.

I turned and made my way back up to the well. On foot and alone, retreading the same steps, saddened me, but I could also begin to feel a tinge of excitement starting at the thought of following a new path having trusted only my intuition. By the time I had reached the clearing I had begun to cheer up. Yet again, there had been far too many strong emotions for one morning.

CHAPTER FOUR

SUCCESS AND GOALS

This chapter sets out to look at what can be learnt about success and how and what makes people successful. We can then add this information to the time cone model we started building in chapter two. This will give us the necessary knowledge base with which we can progress to understanding more about the link that this book is about. In this chapter we will see that it is possible for a person to influence their future reality and follow their aspired path towards the goal that they want, purely by the actions that they take. How we influence the creation of reality is of crucial importance if we are to understand how the 'Ancients' were able to create all their phenomena.

One thing that has been learnt from the many studies of successful men and women is that success is not hereditary. If one looked at a cross section of people who had achieved success in their chosen field, one would see that in an average number of cases there were unsuccessful parents and grandparents. Although there are exceptions where we do find successful children who have successful parents, it's by no means the rule. One explanation to this last occurrence is that there was a good model from which the child could learn. Many people might say at this point, 'It's not what you know, it's who you know that helps you succeed in this world'.

The implication behind this being that a few people are born into the world with all the contacts they need to become successful, merely because of who their parents know. This is undoubtedly true in many cases but does not support the argument that success is genetically determined. It is true that the chances of success can be increased by selective breeding, such as can be seen by breeding racehorses, but this action does not offer guarantees. In many cases the probability of being successful is higher, but this is only because of a higher starting point. It is the action taken after birth that is of important to us. It is the decisions we make throughout our life that will either lead us to being successful or unsuccessful. As there would appear to be nothing genetic about success itself (i.e. there is no success gene), we can go on to deduce that everything we can learn about how to be successful, will tell us more about achieving an aspired path (or reality of choice), as opposed to our genetic path, on our future time cone.

Much has been written about the subject of success and how to be successful. I have read books on the subject, read biographies on successful people, listened to tape programs and interviewed over two hundred successful and unsuccessful people. I have also analysed my own successes and failures using the information that I have learnt. I should state right now that I have discovered nothing new about the subject. Everything I am writing about is already known. However I have discovered that there are rules and guidelines that can come out of an exercise of examining how and why people are successful. These can come under two headings and it is these that we are going to look at, as they have a bearing on our journey.

This chapter should not be taken as a complete guide to success as there are many excellent books on the market that will go into this area in more detail. What I do hope to achieve is to give the reader an indication of how and why people are successful and that if one follows the rules and guidelines, then there is nothing that a person cannot achieve in this world. The living proof is out there. All truly successful people know and follow these principles. For those readers that already know about this subject, please bear with me and enjoy the new angle of looking at it.

4.1 Goals

The first thing to do is to find out what defines and what is meant by success. Many distinguished coaches and speakers have said that 'success is goals' and everything else is commentary. Brian Tracy, a well-known personal development coach first mentioned this in his now famous Phoenix seminars.

He often quotes the following study on success and goals. Research done on graduates from Yale university in 1953 showed that only 3% of the class of seniors had written, set goals for their future. All people in the initial study were contacted twenty years later in order to see how they had all fared. It was found that the 3% that had set goals were in total better off financially than all the other 97% put together.

This was a survey that only concentrated on wealth alone. Success and the importance of having goals can be applied to all walks of life, whether it is in athletic competition, in the field of science, in the arts or anything else one would wish to succeed in. It is the underlying principles from all these areas that is of interest to us.

4.2 Climbing a cliff

One of the best analogies, which I use regularly when teaching people about goals and goal setting in our M.10 seminars, is to consider the whole process of climbing a cliff.

The goal is to reach the top. The broad concept is to first discover where a person is at present (in location, ability etc.). The second is to find out where they want to go to (Where on the top? Which part is the top etc.?) The third is to find all the possible routes available that can get the person to where they want to go and fourthly to find out which is the best way for that person.

A person finds themselves, in the first place, at the foot of the cliff. It might well appear to them to be an imposing sight looking up at it. At first glance, it seems both dangerous and nigh on impossible. Many people at that point might give up and go away with many, not unreasonable, fears. Others might just sit at the bottom and do nothing but look up at the top and dream of what it might be like if they were up there. Some might even think that it was within reach if they took a running jump and tried to grab onto the top ledge!

A few might actually start anywhere on the bottom and climb without looking up or down. They would miss out on planning a route and also ensuring they knew enough techniques to get past any obstacles on the way. They might well get to the top, but often they might also come to an impassable overhang or a slab with no holds.

Just one or two people (True climbers) would sit down, write out a plan, prepare well in advance and get the equipment they needed for the climb. They would look at all the possible routes, check the books for past climbs and decide where to put the pitches (The stages that a climb is broken down into). They would then begin to climb with the advance knowledge of obstacles and contingency plans to get around ones they came across on the way. They would look up and down without fear and learn from what they saw. They would reach the top without breaking the rules of safety and then go on to plan their next goal.

This last scenario outlines the first of the two headings that I mentioned earlier. This principle is to increase ones chance of success by doing all that is physical and practical to reduce the probability of failure. We will look at this again in a little more detail later on in the chapter.

To return to our successful climber we can now look at the second heading. This is the main and most important area that will determine whether or not someone is going to succeed or fail (fall?).

At all times the climbers will be using their minds, but each in different ways. They will not only be using all their external senses and acting and reacting on the information they receive from those sources, but they will also be using their internal senses.

Many of them will not have sufficient drive, persistence and desire to overcome obstacles, nor the sufficient belief in order for them to succeed. Others will not be able to visualise the actions they need to take without seeing themselves falling back down to the ground. Some will not be able to suppress the negative thoughts that arise in their times of fear and will be left frozen to the spot. A few will become impatient due to the length of time that is needed to go through the step by step practice of a new hold until they can do it every time. They will give up and perhaps claim that an overhang made it impossible for them.

One or two will have all the right inner control over their thoughts, their visualisations and their feelings (these three being their main inner senses). These are the ones that will reach the top and gain their reward.

To become successful, a person must set goals. To achieve those goals a person must first reduce all probability of failure through physical and practical means and secondly gain control over their inner senses and then apply them in a manner that is consistent with achieving their goal.

4.3 Goals and Time Cones

The next thing we must do is to superimpose this information onto our picture of a future time cone. Any future goal that we would wish to choose will lie somewhere at the top surface of our cone within certain probability limits. The more impossible the goal that we select (within that amount of space-time); the more it would be found toward the edge of the cone.

Easier targets would be found nearer the centre with increasing chances of probability. For the more improbable goals that we select, within the time limits we set for ourselves, the harder it will be to channel them down toward our reality. Should we do nothing about those goals or not manage to bring them to our current position, we would find that they then fall outside our cone of potential futures. The only resolve left in this instance, is to set the goal again within a new future time frame. (See Diagram 3)

Diagram 3 Light Cone with Cones of Probability

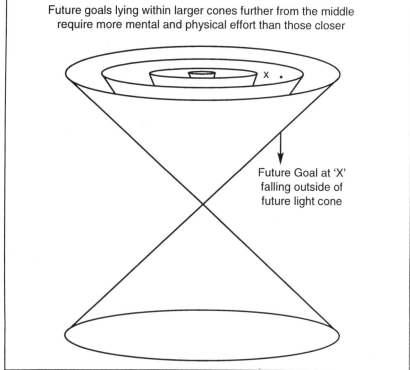

Future goals lying within larger cones further from the middle require more mental and physical effort than those closer

X

Future Goal at 'X' falling outside of future light cone

The time cone model we are using is based on the speed light can travel in a given time. As we operate at a vastly reduced speed, our own cone of possible future paths lies well within the light cone. This does not detract from using it as a model, but requires us to recognise that our model is a time cone within the light cone.

4.4 Eight steps to attaining goals in life

For those people who are interested in learning more about how some people are successful, the following steps have been chosen to give some idea as to how to find out how some people have achieved it. Please feel free to skip this section if you feel that this is going over familiar ground. The first stage in goal setting and goal attainment is to make all the necessary preparations to reduce the probability into a manageable proportion. The following questions will help identify those people who are more likely to be successful.

1. Firstly is the identification of their current position. Where are they now in life? This will involve an understanding about their past, their emotions, their likes and dislikes, their interests and their values. What are they good at and not so good at? What things are most important to them and why? What coincidences have occurred in their past and was there anything to be learnt from them?

2. Where do they want to be in 1, 5, 10, 15, 20 + years time? What are their personal targets, business targets, development targets? Why do they want these goals?

3. What are all the routes open to them, that they could take, in order to get to their goals? What extra knowledge will they require? How will they obtain it?

4. Who will they need to meet in order for them to reach their goals? What information do they need from these people? How will they help these people in order for them to want to help back?

5. What are the obstacles in their way? How will they overcome these challenges (Opportunities)?

6. Have they written down their plans? Have they prioritised which are more important than others and set deadlines for each one? Have they broken up their plans up into smaller, more tangible, daily, weekly and monthly targets?

7. Do they review their progress regularly, learn from it and update their plans?

8. Have they found out the price they need to pay? It may be in time, in money, in emotional terms, in physical terms or anything else. Have they then resolved to pay that price? If they cannot or will not, then do they need to review the goals that they really want and their priorities? Are they 'Paying the price' without incurring pain along the way? Many people make this mistake and lose the reasons they have for the goals whilst in pursuit of them. Do they enjoy the journey, not just the end of the journey? True climbers enjoy the climb as well as reaching the top.

Once a person has answered and accomplished all of the above, they will have reduced the probability of failure considerably. Their goals will now lie closer to the centre of their time cone but could still, given time, fall outside of it if they leave it at that and do nothing else.

4.5 Using ones inner senses

This takes us to the second stage and the one that concentrates on the continual use of our inner senses. It is perhaps the right time to analyse what is meant exactly by internal and external senses. Our five external senses are our sight, hearing, touch, smell and taste. These are internally matched with senses we can make up in our mind. If we close our eyes, we can still create, or remember, images with colour and movement. This is called visualisation. We can create, or remember, feelings and we can do the same for sounds and smells and tastes. When we talk, we hear the words we are speaking, we can recreate these sounds in our minds and we call them thoughts. Our internal feelings also cover a wide range of emotions that we call the kinaesthetic sense. These are the internal representations of our external touching and feeling. We will look more closely at these senses in chapter eight. To see exactly how important these inner senses are to us and our chances of success and also how much of a part control over the mind plays, we only have to recall the words of a world class athlete. Linford Christie, once the World Champion over the 100m, was asked what he felt gave him the edge over his fellow competitors. His reply was that at the end of the day, after all the training that they all go through, there was no real physical difference in what each person could achieve. On the day, however, it was the person with the best mental focus and control that would win the race.

The intensity with which we use our inner senses would therefore appear to be in direct relation with the outcome. The higher the intensity, control and focus; the more we are likely to have the outcome we want.

With all the effort the athletes put in before race day, in their training and practice races, it is strange that most personal bests and records are achieved on competition days. This is perhaps because it is on those days that they are best prepared mentally. We hear this same story across a huge number of sports. However, it is not just confined to sportspeople. Successful business people, scientists and artists will agree to the importance of using all ones inner senses and with maximum possible intensity.

Our inner senses can be looked at as either positive or negative. One can quite easily take this to mean that they are either directed toward and assisting the goals we want or that they are not.

One of the strange things that can be noticed about successful people is that they prefer to be around other successful people. If they meet a person for the first time they will carefully listen to the answer of their first question, 'How are things going for you?' or something similar. If the reply is not sufficiently on the positive side, they will quickly move on. Some will even do so in a rude way; others might do so in an unconscious way. The reason for their action, is that they are careful to guard against any negativity that might detract from the positivity they know that they need for their success. A person only needs to be around someone who is negative to begin to notice the effect it can have. I am not saying that people should start avoiding anyone who is negative, because it may be that it's part of ones path in life, at that time, to lift that person up from out of their negativity.

For those people that allow negative feelings, negative thoughts and negative visions to affect them, we must look for the reason why. In many cases it is down to the two greatest fears common to mankind.

4.6 The two greatest fears

These two fears are not present when a child enters this world. They are gradually instilled into children, to a greater or lesser degree, through their formative years. The first is the fear of rejection. This is built up with the early desire to be loved and liked by parents, family and friends. When there is rejection by one of them over something, a feeling of being unloved or unliked results. If love or friendship is offered conditionally to the child then they begin to feel controlled by that person and they then tend to strive to gain their love, friendship or attention. To be criticised by them, or ridiculed, leaves the child feeling rejected. In extreme cases it leads to a behavioural pattern that restricts the child on their later road toward success. Those children might not wish to even attempt to reach their goals lest their families or friends continue to criticise or ridicule them.

Salespeople have to regularly overcome their fear of rejection. Not everyone is going to want to buy from them all the time. Not taking this personally is the only way to get back out and try again. The customer is not necessarily saying 'no' to the person, only to the product or the service. They don't have to like this rejection, but they have to understand all the emotions they might feel when they do get turned down. This acceptance of rejection and learning to overcome this fear is most important if a person wants to travel the road toward success.

An example of this is found in the story about the rise to success of Mr. Soichiro Honda, the founder of the Honda Corporation. Whilst at school in 1938, he spent everything he had on developing a new type of piston ring for an engine. He first tried to sell it to Toyota but they refused it saying it didn't meet their standards. Only three rings out of fifty passed! His teachers and schoolmates laughed at his designs, yet he still continued to try to improve upon them. Two years later Toyota accepted his designs, but the war came and they rejected him again. Not wanting this to stop him, he decided to start up on his own. This too had its problems and rejections. The Japanese Government constantly refused his requests for concrete to build a factory. Instead of being down hearted he proceeded to invent a process for creating his own concrete and then went on to build the factory. It was bombed twice, but still he continued. He later sold the piston ideas to Toyota and went on to designing a bicycle that had a small engine. Most of his first customers considered that his initial model was too heavy and only a few were sold. Mr. Honda went through many more of these rejections. He was not deterred by this and went on to design the 'Super Cub' motorbike. This was much more popular and became highly successful. Today his corporation has a work force of over 100,000 people.

The second fear that limits people is the fear of failure. This has been cited as the number one reason why people under achieve in life. Early failures in life may well have been followed up by negative feedback from those people around them. Failing can then become associated with losing and is therefore thought of as something to be avoided. A person must become aware that failing is crucial if they are to become successful, as long as they are prepared to learn from the mistakes that they make. One only has to look at the long list of failures that all successful men and women have gone through in order to see this.

If Thomas Edison had given up after his first few attempts at creating the electric light bulb, we might not have them today. He spent hours and hours in his laboratory trying to find the right mix of metals that would allow electricity to pass through and give off a bright light. Each time however, the metal either broke or there was insufficient light given out. It was known as Edison's Folly and all the newspapers ridiculed him saying that everyone knew that the world would always be lit by gaslight. However when he was asked about his quest, he didn't see that he had failed. Even after 6,000 unsuccessful attempts, he still continued, saying to others 'I am not discouraged, because with every wrong attempt something is learned and I can then take another step forward'. After 11,000 combinations he eventually found a mixture of metals that worked.

It is easy to perhaps see that people need to conquer these two fears if they wish to progress toward their goals. However they must not be eliminated altogether. Fear is an emotion that must not be suppressed and ignored. It has evolved along with mankind and the animal world for good reason.

When I first started work as a structural geologist in the gold mines of South Africa, I was thrust immediately into one of the most dangerous working environments in the world. The number of fatalities throughout the course of mining was high and injuries even greater. It took 46 days for the mine I was working on to do one million fatality free shifts. Each person that went down and up counted as one free shift. In the three years I was there, the nearest our mine ever came was

13 days to go. For the superstitious amongst you, it was Friday the 13th that particular day and there were two fatalities. I'm mentioning this to you to explain a little about my state of mind in the early days of starting the job. At first your fears abound as you desperately try to get used to all the sounds and dangers underground. With every unrelated noise you jump, wondering what it was and whether it might affect you adversely.

After a few weeks of this, you learn to become accustomed to life underground with its various rules and hazards. However it's at that time that you can also find that you have suppressed your fear. You just can't physically and emotionally get on with your work and worry about your fears of dying or being injured. One common result is that you end up considering that danger is non-existent.

This of course is not the truth, for there is danger everywhere, no matter how hard the mines try to run as safely as possible. The results of suppressing my fears soon became noticeable. My surface life was becoming more and more irrational. I was living for the day in every wild sense that was possible.

After quite a long period of burning the candle at both ends, I was fortunate to come across a philosophy on life that allowed me to bring into question my actions and future path. Part of my work underground involved walking great distances to get to the working development ends. It was very often silent with only sudden interruptions of noise. This allowed me a lot of time to think. Out of all of this, I was able to develop a gradual respect for everything around me. I could become aware of the danger, analyse it in a logical manner and take calculated risks. It was this action that slowly diminished my fears and I eventually began to feel more in control.

Needless to say, life began to calm down for me back on the surface and I was able to proceed further in other directions.

Conquering fears by recognising them and then taking action is the only way to go forward in the quest for success. This action does not mean suppressing them and believing they don't exist.

Bjorn Borg had a reputation as being very cool on the tennis court, especially on vital points. Yet on being interviewed at the end of his competitive career, he confessed to having felt terrified and that it had taken all his courage to just keep the ball in play. His ability to recognise and conquer his fear and yet still appear calmly confident was undoubtedly a key ingredient in his successful career.

Something has to be found deep within a person, in order for them to overcome their fears. In successful people, they find out what it is and follow it up with action. By taking action it dispels their fear.

One could consider that there are no failures in life, only results. A person must therefore overcome their fears in order to achieve the results they want. Taking action to achieve these results must then involve reducing the practical and physical probability of failing and taking full control of ones inner senses.

4.7 Adding intensity to ones thoughts, feelings and visualisations

The next stage is to look more closely at the inner senses. From what we have learnt about successful people, we can now see that if we apply them all with sufficient intensity, we can have a greater affect over our choice of outcome. By reducing and coming to terms with our fears, we can make the outcome positive and in our favour. The opposite of this is also true. If we allowed our fears to rise within us, it would lead us to more negative thoughts, negative visions and negative feelings. If we concentrate on these with any intensity, we will arrive at the negative outcome that we are holding in our minds.

The first internal sense to study is the kinaesthetic sense. There are four main feelings within this sense and they play an integral part in our search for success. These are desire, belief, joy and expectation. There are others that are also important (some of which could be subtitled under these), but none more so than these four. A drowning man will have one desire on his mind, that of being able to breathe air again and to go on living. If that intensity of feeling for the desire to breathe can also found in a person's drive toward success, they would achieve all that they wanted. Desire and intensity go hand in hand. A person has to work out how badly they personally want something and then determine to keep that desire burning like an eternal flame.

Our internal world is made up of beliefs and values. What a person believes in and what they value must match with their aims in life. If they do, they will be able to build up a huge amount of self-esteem. They must then go on to make their goals believable. If they are too big, they need to be split up into smaller more believable goals. If this is not done, the mind won't take them seriously and will throw up doubts. A salesperson that has a range of products to sell will often find that they sell far more of one product that the others. It's not because it's the most popular product, because other salespeople in the region find it's just the same for them, but with a different product. In each case it is found that it is their belief for the product that allowed them to sell more of them than the others. Often when sales managers have a motivational talk on an old product (thereby rekindling the salesperson's belief) there is a surge in orders for that product.

Daley Thomson once said at an early age, "I always thought I was going to be the best at something one day." He even went around and told everyone, as his schoolmates will verify. His intense belief in himself, even though not focused at the time, became the foundation for his future success. Once he had discovered that the decathlon was the event for him, he only allowed himself to recall the positive experiences he had doing the event. Any failures were quickly learnt from and then discarded. This approach allowed him to keep his mind tremendously positive, an attitude that spilled over into all of his other senses.

Gerald Ratner, the chairman of the Ratner's jewellery group before it collapsed, was heard to say in a speech in London, that he considered that most of his products were 'junk'. The results were dramatic. Sales dropped instantly as belief went out the window. As old customers demanded their money back, new ones avoided the shops altogether. Belief is a powerful internal feeling and has tremendous influence. If held in sufficient intensity, it will bring your goals into your reality. Your external world will arise from a representation of your internal world.

Expectation is the third powerful inner feeling. Often associated with either being positive or negative, it's the actual feeling of expecting that is powerful. All successful people have developed an underlying confident expectation in everything that they do.

Steven Redgrave, the five gold medal winning Olympic oarsman, was once interviewed before the '96 Olympics. The interviewer persistently asked him what he and his partner Matthew Pinsent would do if they found themselves behind in the race at the half way stage at 1000 meters. Each time he asked Steven Redgrave replied that it wouldn't ever happen so how could he possibly answer. His expectation of winning was so high that the idea of being behind was not even a possibility. Eventually the interviewer turned to Matthew Pinsent and asked him what his partner would do if they were ever in that situation. He could only answer in a way that made it appear totally fictitious and said. "Steven would probably say 'Come on Matthew, they're rowing away with our medal!'"

With such incredible belief and expectation, coupled with intense desire, it was probably not surprising that they went on to win and retain their first place from the previous Olympics. Anyone who comes from a sales environment may well know the type of person that never knows where their next sale is coming from, yet still meets all their targets by the end of the month. It's only having interviewed a few of these rare individual's, that I discovered the one thing they have in common. They each have an incredible amount of positive expectation. They themselves will admit to not knowing where or when they will find the next bit of business, yet they are always confident and expect that it will come.

Joy is the other powerful inner feeling. With it a person can learn to love everything in life. Just recall all the really happy people you know or know of. They are all leading successful lives, in their terms and in one form or another, and it will have begun by being joyful and not the other way round. The lesson to be learned is to look and learn to live with joy. The alternative does not seem to me worth dwelling upon! Regular use of this emotion along with all the others is certain to accelerate a person on their road toward success.

It would appear then that we might actually be able to influence what happens to us, if we take the right steps and develop the power of our internal senses.

The second internal sense is visualisation. Every successful person makes pictures in their mind of what they are going to do in advance of actually doing it. The clearer and more intense they make this image, the closer it can become their reality. Downhill skiers can often be seen, at the top of the mountain before the start of their race, going through the course in their head. They crouch down as though racing and make the correct body movements of turning, jumping and leaning as they descend the course in their minds.

High jumpers are often seen doing the same thing before they jump. They play, over and over again in their minds, an image of themselves clearing the bar. When one athlete was questioned about why he took so long to do this, his reply was that he didn't want to proceed until he had cleared the bar in his mind. Because of what he was asking his body to do was verging on the impossible, his mind kept questioning his belief and kept knocking the bar down in his head. Only when he had sufficiently installed the new beliefs into his mind, did he see himself clear the bar. He then proceeded to run up and jump and achieve a new personal best.

Personal development coaches will all testify that visualisation is one of the most important tools required to achieve success. It's my belief that, as it's one of the three main inner senses, it has an equal part to play with the other two. Develop all three and major changes will come into a person's life. It is important that positive changes are made as negative influences will, in the same way, create negative outcomes!

The third internal sense is the auditory one. The internal sounds we hear in our minds can be made up anyway we like. Again the external and internal relationship between the senses still applies. In the case of internal sounds, the one we use the most is our thoughts (Although some people just hear music). The internal dialogue that a person has with their thoughts, plays a major part in how they achieve success. By internalising like this, a person is, in an important way, partly programming their mind toward a particular outcome.

Motivation is a side to communication that endeavours to get the listener to reach a higher level of achievement in whatever field it is being used. The commonest method employed to do this is through the use of words, said, sung or shouted. The listener hears the words in their mind as they are being uttered and in this way internalises them. In the short term, motivational talks produce fantastic results. In the medium to long term, without sustained motivation, the impact lessens.

All experts now believe that the only true motivation is self-motivation. Instead of another person's words that is heard in the mind, they are the individual's own words. This makes a tremendous difference, instead of being externally led, they become internally driven, under their own power, under their own choice.

Many successful people are often heard talking to themselves. It's not a sign of madness, it's their way of psyching themselves up for a coming event in their life. Many actors, entertainers and presenters use this method before going on stage. Sports people adopt the same approach before the start of their race, more so when the race is of a more dynamic and explosive nature and one that requires the body to respond quickly. They know that by doing this their mind can also be stimulated to produce useful chemicals like adrenaline.

What we actually say to ourselves will also have a massive impact on our outcomes. Again positive language will produce positive outcomes and negative language, negative outcomes. Just imagine telling a child that they are useless and that they will never amount to anything and saying this not just once but again and again. It is no wonder that in most cases where this sort of thing happens, the poor child has trouble at succeeding at anything. It takes a strong character to overcome this sort of motivation!

We shall see in chapter eight just how powerful this is when we look more closely at how language programs our minds. The hypnotist uses these concepts to great effect when they play around with our senses to create the results they want us to experience.

Each and every one of us is brought up hearing patterns in language. These can be any phrases that are repeated repetitively in the speech patterns of individuals. These patterns are most commonly heard on the chat radio stations. When listening to the patterns and not the words it becomes alarming at how often certain phrases are repeated. So much so that often the meanings behind them can be lost.

These patterns have been etched into those people's minds through overuse over many years. They become rather like a computer program, and when it comes for them to communicate, out the patterns come on a regular basis. The more astute, intelligent, knowledgeable and loquacious they are, the harder the patterns are to find. They are still there though and would, perhaps, represent a more complex program if we were to still use the computer analogy.

It would appear that people often repeat their favourite phrases and words, and that they do so because of the repeated internalising of them in their earlier life. All a person now has to do is to recognize that a reprogramming of their words and thoughts could lead them to become even more positive. This in turn will get closer to their desired outcome. In the case of our time cone model we could assume that this would be along our selected aspired path.

Winston Churchill, at the end of his career was talking to a group of schoolchildren and was asked in a question at the end whether he could give them one line of advice that would also describe how he had succeeded in life. His reply was this, 'Never give up, never, never, never give up.'

The power of this phrase, that one can imagine him saying to himself again and again through all the difficulties that he faced in his life, perhaps goes some way to explain his success and never ending determination to succeed. Perhaps more recent evidence of this can come from the game of football. The 1999 Manchester United football team went on to win the league, having been behind during many of their crucial end of season games. The intense determination and belief in their ability to come back and score enabled them to go on to complete the treble and collect all the major trophies in one season. Their 'never give up' attitude was what manager Alex Fergusson said was the main contributing factor in their amazing European champions league win over Bayern Munich. One-nil down at the end of ninety minutes, they went on to score two goals in injury time. With such inner control, drive and 'never give up' persistence, they attained the success they wanted.

To get what we want in life (achieve the reality we want), and as long as it is personal to ourselves, it appears that we must follow these two principles of success. It also appears to be necessary to ensure that we add maximum intensity to our inner senses. It's by our actions alone that we can make the difference to achieve what we want. We can actually influence the outcome! All successful people would attest to this fact. There is a well-known saying, 'If it's to be, it's up to me.' The brain is like a muscle in some ways. Memory techniques can be practiced and with a little effort amazing feats of memory can be exhibited. It's the effort that is the key. If a body builder stops exercising a particular muscle and then returns to exercise it several weeks later, they will find that they are unable to repeat what they used to be able to do. Only with further regular practice can they reach their old standard. This is the same with the mind. If we then apply this model to using our inner senses, we must begin to try a method of exercising them in order for it to produce the results we want. The more we exercise them; the more we get the results that we want.

I would like at this stage to suggest to you that you do not just take my word for it but to try out a small experiment. This is to try and influence the outcome of a free parking space. Picture someone pulling out in front of you. Expect and believe that the space will be there. Use the thought of 'Where is it?' Put this together with a sound logical approach, like waiting patiently at the entrance just long enough to carefully look around the nearer cars, (How many times has someone pulled out after you have passed?), and you will slowly find it begins to work. Keep it up and it will work more and more often. If you feel confident at doing that, try working on expecting a phone call. Maybe it will be someone who you have not spoken to in a while or a new business proposition. How many times have you thought about someone you have not seen in a while and thought that it would be nice to do so again, only to find that the person calls you a short while later? Try doing so with an air of expectation and take a note of any changes from normal that you come across.

A person can take this a step further and become an inverse paranoid (someone who is convinced that the world is out to do them good). The more a person can get to believe this, the more things will begin to happen in their life that will appear to be unbelievably good luck to anyone else witnessing it.

Now that we have added a little more information to our time cone picture, by seeing how to reach our aspired paths through goal setting and success principles, it is time to see how this connects with the physicist's view of light cones. In chapter six we shall look at quantum mechanics and relativity with a view to understanding some of the dilemmas that scientists face and how it all can affect us in such a positive way. We will also proceed toward looking at how these inner senses might be working within our brains and why it is that using them actually assists in bringing about the reality we desire. Understanding what is going on when we create our reality is the next step we must tread in our quest to discovering the link.

CHAPTER FIVE

TO SEE A SEER

I took a final look back at the clootie well, and the thought struck me that I ought to take some care to cover my tracks. If Fiacal had indeed been told to follow me, it wouldn't take him long to discover that I'd left Drummorchy by some other means. I retreated backwards towards the clearing wiping out the prints along the way. Afterwards, I went a few paces to the left and made my way through the undergrowth off to the left of the track, joining it again some way on. I made my next steps slowly and carefully, trying to leave as little evidence as possible of my passage.

It was an old disused track that seemed to turn and head north and continue on its way through the Strathyre forest. It was easy going and, at four paces, it was wider than I would have expected. I imagined that at one time it must have been in much greater use. However, I could only wonder as to where it was leading, as I knew I would be leaving it shortly.

The thickness of the trees and undergrowth either side of me provided me with plenty of protection from the weather. Now I was out of the wind, it had also become quiet but for the few sounds of nature. The occasional call of a capercaillie and the howl of a lone wolf reminded me of the company I now kept. I held my senses keen and quickened my pace. All in all I felt that I would be a lot happier out in the open.

As the track went on, there was still no sign of anyone having passed this way recently. I crossed several burns, some with stepping-stones and others requiring a careful jump. My mind went over my plans and preparations. I had rations for four days, but I wasn't really equipped for any hard weather up in the mountains. I would need to make Dugald's cave before the sun went down. The consequences of not making it were not worth thinking about. I wasn't sure what I would find there, I just felt that it was the right time to investigate further.

The track started to climb a little and it wasn't long afterwards that I came out of the forest and was greeted with the awe-inspiring sight of Ben McDui. Its slopes loomed up above me in a series of unscalable cliffs, scree slopes and grassy ledges. Other areas had large patches of snow and ice that seemed to cling impossibly to the steep sided rock.

The top of the mountain was out of sight, covered in the thick grey, snow-laden cloud that now stretched across the whole sky. The sun, now having risen up, had no chance of shining through. A grim thought struck me. The cave might well be above the cloud base and that meant there'd be no escape from getting wet right through my skins.

I left the track at the base of the cliff and made my way to the west, following the wall of dark rock. It appeared I was doubling back on the direction I had just come from. At times I had to squeeze my way between the trees and the cliff face as there was no path at all. This was definitely not a way anyone would have come through choice, but it was possibly the only known way to this particular cave from this direction. I pressed on, pausing only for the occasional swig of water from my leather sac.

At last the cliff on my right petered out into a steep but climbable slope. It made walking easier, but for the constant angle on the ankles.

Despite the conditions, I was not cold. My exertions had warmed me up and as I climbed further, I began to slowly take off some of my clothes to avoid perspiring. By the time I had reached the burn, I had stripped down to my waist.

The waters in it were flowing fast and rather strangely were heading in a direction away from the coast. There were large boulders strewn across and around it, each looked a treacherous step for someone trying to ford. I had no desire to get my legs and feet wet, especially if it was going to get colder higher up. Only the brave or foolish or probably both would cross barefoot, so I decided to follow the course up the mountain until I recognised the crossing point I'd been told about.

The few waterfalls I came to each required me to use my hands to reach the top safely. There was still no easy way over to the other side and the day was getting on.

The sound was the first I heard of it. A deep, thunderous and never-ending roar. As I reached yet another brow, I saw and heard the full force of a magnificent falls. It was hidden deep in a gouged out area of rock and had a narrow width at its top, over which its freezing waters sprayed out between two giant slabs of rock. The distance between the flat surfaces at the top was around three paces, with another three in height. I knew, just looking from the bottom, that this was the place Dugald had told me about. I understood then why he had smiled at the time.

Climbing up the side was easier than it looked. The main problem was that the holds were wet and slippery. The top was about the height of a good-sized pine tree. I stood back from the edge to regain my breath and take advantage of a wonderful view. It was my first real glimpse of the mainland. Off in the distance, even in the poorish visibility, I could see the fabled 'Inland sea'. This burn was probably one of the many that fed it. To the South there were low undulating hills, most covered with woods. Looking East, I could see the forest and behind it Drummorchy. To the West, the edge of the Southern mountains was all there was to be seen.

I had an almost impassable route up the mountain from here, or alternatively, I could jump across to the lower slab of rock the other side. I looked around for alternatives and noticed that someone had marked an arrow on the stone slab that I was standing on. On seeing that, I knew I had to cross. The jump itself was not the problem. It was just the knowledge that there was no easy way back, if there was one at all!

I took two steps back and went for it. Luckily I landed well, a twisted ankle now could well have meant certain death.

Proceeding on, I followed the mountain round and gradually made my way up higher and higher. The ground had become fully covered in snow and was still angled steeply. The cloud base was getting closer and I still hadn't reached the bottom of the scree slope. Time was not on my side either. I was now exhausted from the ascent and the temperature had begun to drop, if I didn't reach somewhere safe soon I would be in trouble. When I reached the level of the cloud, I stopped to put my clothes back on. Their warmth was reassuring. A few steps further and my feet broke through the snow on the loose rocks of the scree. There was now nothing else to do but to go higher. I had to find the cave. My very survival depended upon it.

For every two steps up, I slid back down one. My hands were cold and wet from the number of times I had to use them to break a fall.

Conditions were such that it was now a complete white out and I couldn't see more than a few paces in any direction. If it wasn't for the slope, I could not have even told which way was up and which was down.

At last I reached the top of the slope, there was nothing else but a sheer wall of cliff in front of me. I had no way of knowing how high it went. All I could do was to edge one way or another in the hope of finding the cave. That at least would give me some protection to get through the night.

I decided to head on to my left. Using my hands to guide me, I traversed along the top against the rock face. My progress was now slow and less demanding and, as I got my breath back, I began to feel the chill. Now was not the time to give in to fear, and I could feel that I had to fight it from building within me. Again I stopped to control my breathing, concentrating deeply on the simple, comforting rising of my chest as I slowly sucked in the fresh mountain air. With every exhalation, I felt slightly more renewed of energy and spirit. After a count of ten, I had restored my confidence fully so continued on.

After what seemed an eternity, yet was really only a further twenty paces my spirits were lifted, I'd reached a cave. Whether it was the one I was looking for, I didn't care for it was shelter.

Once inside, I immediately felt warmer. I was out of the mists and there was even sufficient light to see for a short way. I cast a keen eye on what lay about me, hoping to find something I could put to some use. Luck was with me. There were piles of wood against one wall, along with some large rounded stones. I set about making a fire.

Moments later, after a few misplaced sparks, my tinder had ignited. The shavings I'd sliced off the wood were fuelling the flames nicely. Before long, I'd added some of the logs and had a nice blaze going.

I took off some of my damper clothes, including my plaid wrap and positioned them carefully around the fire to dry them. Next, I made a torch out of a long thin branch and a piece of waxed rag that I'd found. If I was going to sleep in any peace tonight, I had to know that I wasn't going to be interrupted by a fellow cave dweller. Although I couldn't detect any smell, it wasn't sure yet that this place was not frequented by bears. I would need to check out the rear of the cave.

With my torch in my left hand and dirk in my right, I moved cautiously towards the blackness. Thoughts of Korrigans, small evil cave spirits, kept coming into my mind, springing out and attacking me from the sides and behind me. I knew they were part of folklore, but you have to ask yourself how these stories start, if there isn't some basis of truth.

The flickering light threw shadows all over the place. The ceiling was lowering and the walls narrowing and round a corner and behind a large boulder, I found a dead end. Relief was mixed with excitement as I saw on the ground a small cauldron and some straight sticks about a foot long in length. It was a definite sign that this was the cave I was meant to find.

Back at the fire, I set up a wooden rod that would hold the cauldron in the middle above the flames. I filled it with water from my sac and added some dried herbs for flavour. Whilst waiting for it to boil, I set about looking at the sticks. They had been so purposely laid down in a neat pile that they had to have more meaning. Sure enough, along the side, there were a few, barely noticeable, oghams. Anyone not looking carefully or unaware of the meanings might well have mistaken them for firewood.

I ate pieces of dried, smoked haddock and flat oatmeal bannocks. They never tasted so good. The hot drink was most refreshing that I'd ever had. The chamomile and spearmint had cleared my mind in an intoxicating manner and it was the first time I think I'd ever felt really alive. I was in total control. I'd risked a lot and I'd won through over adversity. I was on my own and instead of feeling unsure of things, I felt that I was on my way. My destiny awaited me, whatever it was.

My mind wandered back to the message that Angus had so cleverly left for Dugald. The trick in understanding the Ogham letters was not just in identifying the marks, it was reading between the lines. Visibly all that could be seen was a vertical line down the stick with various horizontal and diagonal lines either crossing it or one side or the other. Together they built up a picture in the mind composed of smaller images.

Once I'd put the sticks in order, fortunately the same order as they were cut, I could set about unravelling the puzzle. The wood was Yew, common enough but there were no yew trees close by. Was this a clue in itself?

The words I dissembled on the first branch were, dream, black, wren, sits in hazel tree, C.B., shield head, 2. People and names were often written code to retain secrecy, but I guessed that black wren referred to Black Donald or Domnhuil Dubn. Hazel was sometimes a nickname for the name Callum, so I inferred that the message was that Domnhuill was working for Callum Beg. The shield head was obviously meaning the crown helm and it appeared that they held two pieces. The fact that Angus was a seer meant that this whole message was revealed to him in a dream. As it was written on yew, a tree that only chieftains were really allowed to use, and it was specifically left for Dugald, I suspected that the gist of the message was a warning to watch out for those wearing black who were looking for him.

I was slightly disappointed with what I had ascertained from the message, but I took hope in the fact that Callum Beg might still only have three parts to the helm. The two mentioned here and the one recently stolen from my father. That might mean my sister was safe for a while longer, but then I had no idea when this message was written. He might have got all the parts now. I decided not to think of that possibility for the moment.

The other oghams were a little more perplexing. All I could make out was grey heron, village, legs, full moon, hunting, brown hare. No matter how hard I tried I could not make head or tail of it. I was getting tired so I decided to get some sleep. Often when one went to sleep with a problem, the mind would continue to work on it and the answer would be revealed in one form or another in the morning. It was with that thought that I put my head down and wrapped myself up in the now warm tweed. The fire continued to crackle and glow. I watched the changing colours deep within it and drifted contentedly off to sleep.

I awoke late in the morning, my fire had gone out and it was cold. Despite that, I felt terrific. Stretching as I walked to the mouth of the cave, I was greeted with one of the most beautiful sights I'd ever seen. The sun was already half way up and there were only a few wispy clouds high above the mountain tops. For as far as the eye could see there were mountains, some were snow capped; others just steep pinnacles of rock. In between these was a maze of dark, bowl shaped valleys dappled with shadow and sun. Below me there was a large round corrie loch, its rippled waters glinting in the light from above. I took a deep breath sucking in the beauty and hung my head back and closed my eyes feeling the warmth seep back into my face.

"I do the same thing every morning." A calm voice to my left says.

I spin around, cricking my neck in the process, to face this new intrusion into my world. A small, wizened old man sat cross-legged, leaning back against the rock wall. He continued to gaze out in front of him, as if in deep contemplation. I noticed a sturdy staff, within hands reach, the far side of him, and tried to work out if this figure represented any threat to me. I concluded not and relaxed my guard a little. He seemed to notice as he snorted what appeared to be a wry chuckle.

"Forgive me for asking, old man, but who exactly are you and what brings you up here so early in the morning?" I say.

"Funny thing," he pauses, "I was wondering exactly the same thing about you, only you are in my cave!" He replies.

"Your cave?" I reply, my lips beginning to curl up with a smile.

"Yes. My cave." He snaps back. "Not that I mind you using my things and as long as you replace what you used it's nay a problem to me."

"Then, I must thank you old man, for your hospitality allowed me a passable nights rest, which could have been a lot worse." I reply courteously, turning to fully face him.

"Come." He says rising to his feet in a nimble way that doesn't even see his hands touch the ground. "Call me Gus. Let's put some oats on the boil and break our fast. You can tell me all about how you came to be up in the mountains." He moves past me and into the cave.

"Would you be Gus as in Angus Og?" I say, my excitement rising at maybe having found the man so soon. I follow in behind him.

"Aye I might be, depends a bit on who wants to know." He turns round sharply, raises an eyebrow and looks me straight in the face.

"I am Fionn mac Donal of the clan Donal, from the Isle of Siegg. If you are Angus Og, then it's you I've come to meet with, at the recommendation of a Seannachie who goes only by the name of Dugald."

"Dougie, you were sent by Dougie you say," He says in a quicker tone, unable to suppress his own rising excitement. "How is the man? What is he up to these days? Forgive me, I am Angus." He remembers and embraces me warmly.

"He's well and sends his wishes. For the last seven years, he's been kind enough to teach me some of his art. I am on my way to the Aes Dana for their approval." I reply, trying to answer all his questions.

"So you want to become a seannachie do you. Well it's a fine ambition for a man to have, it's an art that will give both you and a lot of others great joy. Mind though, it's a double-edged sword at times. There will be many a time of solitude, for if you are going to be any good you'll need to travel to gain experiences." He says now starting to prepare the fire.

"Tell me." He continues, gently fanning the smouldering tinder, "Why did Dugald mention me and tell you about our secret cave?"

A small flame appears and Angus carefully arranges some kindling around it. It ignites immediately.

"It's a long story," I start, watching him and his technique.

"Good, I like them better. Go ahead while I do this, I'm listening." He busies himself beside the fire.

I start by telling him of Dugald's arrival at the broch. Then about my training and finally I mention the events of the last two days. By the time I had finished we had started to eat our porridge. It was unlike what I was used to, but not everyone was fortunate to keep bees like we did at home. Instead of honey, Angus had used a selection of dried berries that he kept in one of his many leather pouches he seemed to have concealed amongst his clothes.

Acquiring new tastes was something I had not expected or even thought of when I had set off. Life seemed to be full of changes for me at the moment. This particular one however was welcome and I finished it feeling both replenished and even more full of anticipation for the days ahead.

Angus continued to eat in silence. When he finished he put down his wooden bowl and turned to me.

"Well Fionn, for a young storyteller you've certainly started off with a clap of thunder. It also explains to me now why I came to be here today." He remarks, licking his lips.

"How do you mean?" I ask, slightly perplexed.

"Dugald and I, as you know, agreed to leave messages here for one another. I've only come back here a few times these last years as there were never any signs from him. Just recently, I had a series of dreams about a cave bear. As you know, we seers regard dreams with high levels of importance and always look for their meanings. In this case it meant to me that it was important to revisit the cave at some stage. Yesterday, I disturbed some bats in woods not far away, whilst I was searching for herbs. A common enough sight you might think but together, along with this urge to come up here again, made me think it was time." He pauses and seeing he has my attention he continues.

"I have a small croft down by the De'ils cauldron, the corrie loch you can see. I use it when I come up here and I stayed there last night. It's time I told you more about what happened after Dugald and I split up. You'll understand then why I keep myself moving on. I did indeed go West after we split, as Dugald mentioned." Angus continues after another short break, "On my first night out on the road to Port Athel, they caught up with me. Luckily for me my sixth sense was well tuned toward impending danger and I woke up before they found me. I just had enough time to sneak off into the bushes when two spears hit the sleeping bundle I'd left moments earlier. They were incompetents. They never even checked to see the body, they just rode off back up the road to Invercarrie." He stops, as if remembering the incident and I wait patiently ready to listen again.

"I headed on toward the Glencarrie loch and Achnacarrie where I had some friends. I didn't stay for their safety but they kindly gave me leave to visit cousins of theirs at Duntelve Broch on the North shores of the Inland Sea. There was an old trading route, used before the clan wars, that led South through the Strath Conan Forest and they guided me all the way to the Strath Eil pass. As you may know, the Southerners are a strange lot, least ways since losing the last of the great battles. However kin is kin and by way of repaying a past debt, the clan allowed me to stay at the Inchree crannogs." He chuckles to himself for a moment, as if remembering something funny.

"That's a strange place if ever there was. The're huge areas to settle and they choose to build an island on wooden stilts out in the sea. Their very nature is defensive and they keep themselves to themselves. They liked the idea of an ovate staying with them. The fact that I could sense danger was probably why they welcomed me." He pauses.

"Was that the village on legs," I almost shout, piecing together the puzzle of the previous nights oghams.

"Why yes." He looks at me with surprise clearly showing on his well-lined face. "So Dugald taught you the secret of the ogham script did he?"

"Only a little," I reply, "I couldn't get the meaning of the second message. What or Who was Grey Heron?"

"Grey Heron is a nickname for the clan chief at the Crannogs. If Dugald had found him, he could then have found me." He explains.

"I'm known as Gus down there, but I only visit once a month now as I travel a circle throughout the Southern mountains. It's my way of helping people as best I can and keeping in touch with what's happening. They soon discovered I wasn't dead and came looking for me. After a while they stopped which means I can move around more easily now."

"Who exactly are they?" I inquire.

"Domhuill Dubn and his men." He states in an accusing manner. "Under the authority of the Chief Ollamph of course." He adds. "Over the years, I thought I'd come to know him quite well. Now I realise he had learned ways of disguising his thoughts. People can come away from meeting him thinking he was friendly, only to suspect that later he was behind some evil deed done to them. No one has ever proved it yet, he's too careful. Nor have they proved a connection between him and Black Donald. The other message I left Dugald was about a dream I had. After that it was clear to me that they were together behind some of the worst atrocities not seen since the dark ages."

"What about the Crown Helm and why do you think he wants that so badly?" I ask.

"It's a power symbol. If he can reunite the pieces, it will give him popular support to take the throne.

"People either love or hate the man. At the moment he has the support of the Queen and is acting as a clan chief until her son comes of age. He's already very powerful and hugely influential over people's lives. However, I can see the dark side of him. He started as an Ovate like myself. I suspected even back then that he was dabbling in the old sacrificial rites. Death by air, by water, by fire and by earth." He accentuates these with hand movements. "The throws of death would focus his mind and reveal the future. For the prophecies to be even more accurate, the rites would be carried out at Samhain. The start of the new year, the beginning of seed fall, is felt amongst people like him to be the most auspicious time for sacrifice." He pauses again for his words to have full meaning.

They did. My mind immediately thought of my sister Mairi. Sacrificing local people was possibly getting difficult for Callum Beg, he had probably run out of criminals and now turned to raids on far off places, like the broch. She was in more trouble than I had previously thought. Still if it was Samhain, I still had some time.

"What more can you tell me?" I ask in earnest.

"For now, not much more. But tell me again exactly what happened when you saw the Kingfisher." He asks.

I repeat everything up to the point of the bird drifting down the stream in front of me.

"Never before have I heard of such a strange occurrence." He utters shaking his head. "It's truly one of the most awe striking omens I've ever heard tell." He gets up and begins to wander around in a circle with one hand on his chin. As he gets near to the mouth of the cave he stops and gazes out. Then after a while he twists at the waist and calls to me.

"I think I can be of some help to you on this, but I haven't the complete answer yet." He twists back again to look out at the view.

I get up and move over to stand next to him. We stay there in silence, watching and listening. The sun was near its zenith now. A lone eagle soared on the air currents above us. The only sounds we could hear came from the light gusts of wind that swirled about us.

"Fionn." He starts. "Before I can give you an answer, I must first explain a little about the art of divination. Come let us walk down together."

We set off down the slope, heading in the direction of the loch Angus called the De'ils Cauldron. It meant traversing some of the time to find safer ways, but apart from a few slips on the loose rocks and the patches of ice, we reached a level where there were soggy tufts of moss and peat and damp clumps of course grass. We could talk more freely now, without having to concentrate so much on the descent, and continued onwards side by side.

"Fionn." Angus starts again. "Did Dugald mention to you about the gifts of the Cauldrons?"

"Only a little bit." I venture.

"No matter." He continues. "To be able to receive the inspiration one needs to foretell the future, and indeed for the other arts, one must first align all three of the body's cauldrons. Only then will you be able to speak in truth about what will appear to you."

"I'm not sure I understand what you mean." I answer a little perplexed.

"I will explain more a little later, bear with me for now. Next a seer needs to open themselves up to the three illuminations. After that they may receive an augury. This sense of the future is, however, not necessarily what will happen."

"Now I really don't understand. If it's a true augury why does it then not occur?" I enquire.

"There are many futures Fionn, each with a greater or lesser chance of happening. The future at this point in time is fixed, but if certain actions are taken in the present, then that future can be changed." He pauses for his words to sink in. "The reason I am telling you this," He continues, "is because I don't want to unduly concern you with regard to your omen. Death as it was shown to you, does not always mean death to the beholder, sometimes can imply a change is coming."

His sudden serious tone had concerned me, was my omen really a portent of my own death. He sensed my fear.

"In this case, I feel there is no need for concern, so calm your fears lad. What is important here is that your spirit guide has identified himself to you." He stops to look me fully square on.

I stop a pace further on and turn back round towards him. He was now higher than me and I looked up and noticed how kind his eyes looked.

"There are things I can help you with here, but there are also answers I don't have. Your omen is meant as a warning, for reasons that perhaps now are clearer. It almost definitely refers to a major change in your life that, I think, has become obvious to you in these last days. What I don't understand is why your guide is a kingfisher and the relevance behind that. I have never heard of anyone before having that same guide. The second thing is that omens normally leave some extra indication as to what might be coming, and I cannot see it in this case. I believe, therefore, that I have only one course of action left."

"What's that?" I say.

"I must perform part of an act of Illumination, an Imbas Forosna."

"What?" I say my mind filling with questions again at a fast and furious rate.

"In good time," He turns and strides out downhill again.

I follow him, sensing that he had perhaps really stopped talking for my benefit. With my mind full of unanswered questions, I was left to focus on what was said. My thoughts went back to the kingfisher.

We reached the loch and now strolled easily along its banks. The water was a deep brown colour, stained by the peat that was all around. There was no other drink in the world that tasted as sweet and as tangy as that from a peat loch. I stopped and emptied my sac to take the opportunity of refilling it with this wonderful liquid.

Around the other side, we followed the burn that drained the loch down toward a small copse of trees. It was strange to see them up here at this height, but it was a sheltered spot. Just inside the wood was Angus's small round croft. It had been made with local stones, mud had been used to fill the cracks and there was turf for roofing. Shoulder high, it made for cramp living but at this altitude it was meant primarily for warmth. We crawled inside.

A small hole in the roof let just enough light in to see. A collection of furs lay wrapped in a bundle on a dried earth floor. Three large, flat, blackened stones had been set in the earth in the middle. Suspended on a tripod above them was a hook.

"We're out of wood lad, fetch us some will you, while I make some preparations." He orders lightly.

I reversed out on my knees as it was the easiest way. Outside I took my time in looking around. It was not a large wood, a well-thrown stone would have cleared its widest point, but it followed the path of the water for a good ten times its width. My eyes naturally fell to searching the ground for deadwood. Animal droppings were everywhere, this was obviously a haven for them.

I collected up sufficient wood for a day and a night and returned. Inside Angus had laid out his collection of plants and herbs and fungi and was sorting through them picking out those that he seemed to want. He worked in silence, so I set about lighting a fire. It was only mid afternoon and too early to eat but some hot scented water would go down well.

"Fionn, How are you at trapping?" He asks suddenly, breaking my chain of thoughts.

"I've done a bit. My brother was always more successful though, so I've not had much practice of late." I reply.

"Well this might be a little different. We need a Snow Hare for tonight's meal." He says.

"I have some dried meat we can share." I offer.

"Thank you, but unfortunately it won't help for what I have in mind. The Snow Hare is my spirit guide and to receive his help we must ask him to make us his ultimate sacrifice."

There were no words to say. Eating the flesh of animals, although often necessary was never done lightly. The act of killing and eating was regarded by many as a form of communication between all the parties involved. Each received benefit from each other. To receive more than just physical nourishment meant entering into a pact with the animal. The nature of your terms dependant on the benefit you required.

Outside Angus beckoned me to be quiet and I followed behind him and knelt down when he did. The damp ground slowly soaked into my leathers as we fell into a peaceful state of being at one with our surroundings.

After a while, I watched as a large, buck Snow Hare poked his head out of a nearby hole. If it had been my brother next to me, a slingshot would have stoned it by now. At five paces he never missed. Angus kept as still as a flag on a windless day. Slowly the hare fully appeared and hopped forward a couple of times. I watched as both the hare and Angus appeared to acknowledge each other. It reminded me of the time I first noticed my Kingfisher. The Snow Hare made a slow glance back with a turn of its head toward its burrow, then turned and hopped towards Angus.

When it was only half a pace away, he slipped out his Skean Dhu and reached forward with his free left hand. What happened next seemed to defy time. A gentle stroke and a flash of his right hand and it was over.

I'd seen many animals slaughtered before, but the peacefulness of this occasion stunned me. In moments it had been skinned, gutted and rinsed in the burn. The freezing cold waters returned a semblance of decency to the carcass and I felt the beginnings of a few hunger pangs.

I followed Angus back inside, keeping an initiates silence. He would talk in good time and I was certainly in the mood for listening. I watched as he carefully placed the hare on a long metal skewer and then laid it across two of the tripod legs that had notches in just for that purpose. He then pulled a small silver cauldon from out of the folds of his garments and started to fill it with his chosen ingredients. From the look of some of the more unidentifiable ones, I hoped the concoction was for him and not some sauce for the hare for both of us. With the little silver coire and its potion, now hanging from the hook, warming over the fire, he turned to me.

"Imagine your body has three cauldrons, one here," He points to his belly, "one here," He points to his heart, "and one here." He says pointing to his head.

"They are all either the right way up, on their side or upside down." He continues, "At anyone time they can be turned by various means. The lowest one, the Coire Goiriath or cauldron of warming, starts face up when you are born and is the foundation for all your vital physical health and energy. It becomes inverted if you become sick."

"The middle one is the Coire Ernmae or cauldron of Vocation. This is inverted in people who have no apparent gifts or skills yet. It lies on its side in those people who are aware of their gifts but isn't face up until that person becomes fully enlightened. The cauldrons position can only be overturned through your emotions. With joy, and pleasure, and being of a bright nature, you can turn this cauldron upright. With sorrow, and pain, and being of gloomy nature, you will invert this cauldron."

"The same is true of the third cauldron, the Coire Sois or cauldron of knowledge. This starts off in life in an inverted manner. Those people who are closely in touch with their spirit and who embrace their good emotions will turn their cauldron face up. Only then will they receive the knowledge that they require."

"All three of these cauldrons need to be aligned face up in order for a person to receive inspiration. In most people only the first is face up and the others face down. This closes off the many experiences possible in life. Any one cup that is inverted will adversely affect the other two."

"In divining the future we must become open to inspiration, we can then use the three illuminations."

"What are they?" I eagerly interrupt. He looks up at me in the now darker hut and I can both see and sense that he notes my true interest. I want to look away from under his intense gaze, but feel it is important not to. He looks back at the burning logs.

"The Imbas Forosna, the inspiration of the masters, is the first. We must first chew the meat from the hare, then later on fall into a deep sleep. In our vision dreams we will see the true augury and the wisdom of the spirit guide."

"After we've eaten comes the Teinm Laeghda, the illumination through the words of the chant of a poem."

"And lastly the Dichetal di Chennaib, a ritual invocation through touching objects relevant to the person whose future we are looking for. In your case have you anything that you think might help."

"Yes" I say excitedly. I took out my leather pouch and unwrapped the tweed bundle. I held out the three blue and the three orange feathers in my hand for him to see.

"This is more than I could possibly have hoped for." He exclaims throwing his arms open wide in a true gesture of amazement and thanks to the spirits. He then turns and says as an afterthought, "What made you take these? Why did you also forget to tell me? No matter, this will help and greatly enhance the chances of success." He exclaims, ignoring his own question.

He took the feathers from my hand and carefully placed them with a bunch of other strange looking objects.

"How's the food doing?" He changes the subject.

"Well." I reply, turning the skewer again so that it was not over-cooked on one side.

Angus reached up and lifted off his silver coire with a stout stick and sniffed its fumes. He then reached over and grabbed a handful of herbs and added them to the boiling mixture. His earlier use of the word 'we' worried me as I saw the concoction. Deep down I didn't want to go near it, let alone drink it. Having replaced it back on the hook, he threw the rest of the herbs into the flames. Smoke soon billowed out and filled the croft.

It was a pleasant enough aroma, yet it irritated my throat. One thankful effect however, which was instantly beneficial, was the effect it had on the midgies. Attracted by the light of the fire, they had constantly pestered me. The smoke seemed to disperse them well.

The meat was cooked to a golden brown colour with the legs darkening toward the blackish, charcoaled feet. Fingering it quickly, as it was hot, I divided it into two by breaking the spine. I gave Angus the choice and then sat back with my sac of loch water visibly by my side.

It was not the tenderest morsel I had ever eaten, but it was one of the most appreciated meals I had ever experienced. Angus sat cross-legged and, in between mouthfuls, was chanting some sort of a song that was unknown to me.

I ate in silence, sucking each of my fingers slowly and deliberately at the end. I watched as Angus now lifted off the silver coire and proceeded to strain its contents through a cloth into a larger iron cauldron. His chanting continued, he was well into his Teinm Laechda. My anxiousness grew as the moment approached when he lifted the bigger cauldron to his lips. I remembered the weird and poisonous ingredients.

He drank slowly and then placed the cauldron down on the side of him furthest from me. My heart jumped, was I relieved of this ordeal?

I could only wait and see. Curiosity was overwhelming me and I strained to make out any of the words he was chanting. All at once he stopped. There was a momentary silence and then the last sound came, it was the word 'Lugh'.

At that Angus carefully picked up the cloth and the feathers. He placed them in the palms of his hands and lay down flat on his back. Next he placed his hands, with the cloth and feathers, on his eyes palms down.

All that could now be heard was the crackling of the fire and the slow deep breathing coming from Angus. I could hardly move. I had been so engrossed in the ritual that my body had stiffened. Long moments later, I stretched out my legs and began to get up and back out of the small hut.

It was dark outside, the sun having gone down early in the mountains. Looking up, the sky was filled with stars. I walked out of the wood and back toward the loch. The reflection of a new moon greeted me as I reached the waters edge. It was a beautiful night and a wonderful time for my daily reflections. My earlier fears seemed to have left me and I decided that it was down to the fact that I was acting on my instincts and taking control of my own directions. Coincidences abounded which was a good sign I was doing something right. I doubted my father would have agreed. I am sure he would have done things differently. He would have said that I had become distracted. It was not the case though. I was still full of concern for my sister. I just had to keep an open mind and trust my senses. I knew I had to make a plan, but first I needed more information and this I was getting faster than I'd ever imagined. Angus had taught me how to become open to inspiration. If I could achieve that, I would receive all the information I would need. I needed to keep all my inner cauldrons in alignment face up. To do that, I needed to maintain a joyous heart, even in adversity. I needed to avoid becoming gloomy and despondent when times went wrong. All so simple to know, yet I knew would be hard to follow. I resolved to make that my first plan.

I went back down into the croft and settled down for the night. Angus was fast asleep, his body twitching as he acted out his dreams.

The next morning I awoke to find the croft empty, all Angus's gear had gone. I got up quickly and hurried out. It was another fine morning. Looking round, I saw the crouching figure of Angus over where we had first seen the Snow Hare. As I walked over, he heard me and spun around and stood to face me. Again I wondered at how an oldish man managed to move so nimbly. His face was stained with tears, but he was smiling.

"How are you this fine morning young Fionn?" He asks crisply.

"Very well thank you. Did you sleep well Angus?" I ask back.

"Under the circumstances, yes I think it was a good sleep of Incubation." He replies.

"Are you alright?" I say

"I was just burying an old friend. We used to spend a lot of time

112

together here. I used to bring him vegetables and roots."

My stomach began to feel queasy. We had just eaten his pet. I wanted to ask him so many questions but couldn't because I felt it had all been done on my account and I felt guilty asking for anything more.

"Come Fionn, we must leave, there is much to do and much to say and we have a long road to travel." He put an arm over my shoulder and we begin to walk back up toward the loch. "Did I say road, well I didn't mean it." He laughs. "There'll be no roads the way we're going."

It was the first time I heard the old man fully laugh. It had a dry chuckle to it and one that would easily bring a smile to others.

We set off North following a damp watercourse that fed the loch. It was mainly wet moss and peat and progress was slow and arduous. Our first aim was to reach the brow of a col between two peaks. Once over that, Angus told me, we would descend to a small loch and the falls of Bruar. We trudged onwards and upwards in silence, saving our breath.

By mid morning we had reached the col, it was marginally drier underfoot and we could begin to talk with more comfort.

"What do you know of the Samildanach, lad?" He starts.

"Only that he is spoken of in the legends and that he is supposed to be blessed with being skilful in all the arts."

"Aye that maybe so, anything else?" He probes.

"He is also known to be a magician and can bestow skills on any he chooses. Why do you ask?"

"Who told you about him?" He ignores my question purposely.

I stopped to think about it and tried to remember if I had heard anything about him before the arrival of Dugald at the Broch. I came to the conclusion that I hadn't.

"Only what Dugald told me." I reply

"That's interesting. Did he teach you any stories about him or how he came to be placed in the legends?" He continues.

"No." I say sounding perplexed at his line of questioning. "He just mentioned him by way of information that I could use at some future time. Come to think of it, it seems strange now you've asked about it."

"I met him once." He pauses and I stop, not quite sure I heard him correctly.

"What?" I say, confused by this admission.

"I said I met him once, briefly when I was a young lad." He repeats in a matter of fact manner.

"But how was that possible, you said he was legend?"

"I only said 'maybe' Fionn." He answers, "I had just decided to become an Ovate and was wandering in the Northern Highlands, searching as one does for some source of inspiration, when I decided to climb to the top of one of the 'Ben's' nearby. It was an easy climb and a good day for it. At the top, I sat down and began to contemplate what was to be in my life. The Samildanach appeared from behind me, having walked up the other side of the Ben."

"We chatted about many things and he told me much about things to come. He was a true Seer amongst all his other abilities. What he wasn't though, was a dead legend. His reputation has nowadays clearly preceded him and people now come to think of him as one. The reality though, is that he is flesh and blood. The reason for telling you this, is that his name came to me last night and again he appeared in my dreams. I saw the two of you talking at a Dolmen somewhere in the Northern Highlands. I didn't think that he would still be alive, as I would have thought that age would have caught up with him by now." He stops to ponder.

"My interpretation of last night is that I think that you are destined to meet with Lugh, the Samildanach. For what purposes I am not sure, but it has to do with Callum Beg. He also appeared in my dream and was in some conflict with Lugh."

"How would I find this man, Lugh?" I ask, tentatively.

"That is a question for which I have no answer. The only clue is to find the Dolmen. You must ask the folk in the North if they know of any standing stones, then trust your intuition. If you do that, I believe you will find your destiny."

"What does this all mean, Angus? I thought that I was destined to go to Invercarrie." I ask.

"Indeed you are, we are heading that way right now, albeit not by one of the easiest routes. You must attend your meeting with the Aes Dana and become an Anruth. You will meet Callum Beg in person and hopefully learn much about him."

"What about my sister and the Crown Helm?"

"The dream told me nothing about your sister and nothing about the Crown helm. That alone doesn't mean anything, we seers don't receive all the answers, if we receive any at all." He adds, smiling cynically.

We walked on and down towards Loch Bruar. The weather was holding up well for us. The sun was not always behind clouds and there was little wind. We would have preferred a warm wind, at least that would have kept the flies low and away from our faces. At times they were becoming unbearable. When we arrived at the Loch, I decided that I needed to freshen up. I stripped off and stepped carefully into the cold waters. With my feet slipping on the slimy stones, I had to occasionally reach down with a hand to stop a fall. Once deeper, I sank to my shoulders, held my breath and put my head under. It was instant relief. My head cleared and the buzzing sound had ceased. Only those who had walked in the mountains could really appreciate this brief respite from all the aerial pests.

Dried and dressed and ready to face the next onslaught, we pressed on Northwards. This time we headed up the Glen Beag towards the impressive sight of Ben Beag. It was one of the mountains that could be seen from Seigg because of its size. Its snow-capped peak had probably never even been climbed. The last part was sheer rock face on all sides. Although we were heading that way, we were going to cut to the right and over the col to Drumbeg. We could join the High road before passing through the Strathyre forest again, then go over the Drummorchy pass to Invercarrie.

That would take another days full walk, so we had to stay the night at the foot of the Ben. Angus knew the area well and from time to time would venture off up the slopes to the side and come back with some wild flower or herb.

"There's a place not far from here we can rest for the night. I wouldn't want to chance it on a cold night though." He calls out in front of me as though he was thinking out loud.

Some time later we came across nothing more than a collection of rocks. They were stacked up on three sides in some semblance of a wall. I resigned myself to an uncomfortable sleep.

Nevertheless, after we had lit a fire with the few branches we had collected along the way, we huddled together in good cheer. Angus told me about the reception I would receive at the Aes Dana and gave me good advice as to how to impress the elders there. I, in return, told him more about my time with Dugald and life on the islands.

The next day, I awoke first. The temperature had dropped and there had been a light smattering of snow in the early hours. Our wraps were covered with it. My bones ached as I stretched out and in doing so I woke Angus.

"I'm getting too old for this." He coughs, "Would you help me up Lad?" He calls holding out his arm. I take it and pull his light frame to his feet.

"Come old man." I smile, "You've a long way ahead of you yet." I say with double meaning. He smiles back at me and arranges his plaid wraps by slapping them down with his hands. It sends a spray of powdery snow up and over me. "You're right of course, you're the Seer around here." He jests, letting out a short chuckle. "We've no wood left for a fire, I suggest we press on and eat some fare on the way, what do you think?" He asks while picking up his pack.

"Sounds alright," I reply, my belly rumbling. He looks at me quizzically. I have to stop to think why he had done that as it was a look given in earnest. Then I remember the coire ernmae and coire sois.

"Actually I feel great. It sounds like a good idea Angus." I reply again. He smiles back the way a teacher might when a pupil had learnt an important lesson.

The snow had left the ground harder the higher up we walked. We moved faster but had to take more caution due to the unyielding bumps. Twisting an ankle out here would have been perilous for both of us.

The weather threatened to worsen at any time, dark clouds loomed from the west. The rest of the sky was covered in a thick white cloud that was slowly descending. To be safe we had to reach the col before being cut off. We pressed on hard our lungs bursting from exertion in the cold air.

Just before midday we reached the saddle between the mountains at the same time as the descending cloud base. A few drinks and a short rest, fuelled us sufficiently to begin our descent on the other side.

Just when I thought that things were getting to be easier, we encountered the first of the scree slopes and ledges. Each ledge was between five and ten feet tall with the slopes in between much wider but not too steep.

"There's two ways to tackle this." Says Angus, "The slow, hard and dangerous way or the fast, slightly easier but more dangerous way. Which do you prefer?" He offers.

"Do we have a choice if we are to reach Invercarrie tonight?" I reply, not liking either route anyway but having an awful feeling that it was going to be the more dangerous one that he had in mind.

"Not really. Come follow me, the safest way to start scree running here is this way. It's a bit hairy to start with, but fun from then on. Here you'll need these. Copy what I do." He hands me two strips of cloth and begins to tie his around his ankles as tightly as possible.

"What are these for?"

"To give your ankles some more support. I didn't use to use them, but I've got older and once twisted my ankle, now its improved things considerably."

I had no option but to copy him. When I was done, he led me carefully forward to the top of the first ledge. There was at least a ten foot drop onto loose rocks. He lowered himself to sit with his legs hanging over the edge, then lowered himself further until his elbows were higher than his head. With a wild shout he dropped off. I watched as he landed and slid for two to three paces on the loose scree. Two more strides, slipping with each one and he disappeared over another ledge. All the while letting out hoops of joy.

One of us was plainly mad. Him for enjoying it or me for attempting to follow, I wasn't sure. I jumped off. Off balance on landing, I slid on my bottom until I was bounced up by a larger rock. The sensation sent ripples up my spine. Two steps later and I was over the first ledge. This time I landed five feet down on my feet. A long slope stretched down in front of me. There was no sign of Angus. I was now travelling as fast as I could run on the flat, unsure if I could even stop myself if I tried. It began to become a little exhilarating and my anguished face started to allow its lips to turn their edges up into a smile. Soon it was full on fun and I too let out a hoop of joy. Then the next ledge appeared. My senses were jolted back to reality as I had no idea how big a drop there was the other side.

I flew for a moment, the Strathyre forest came into sight as did the familiar Gruinard sea. This time I landed straight on my bottom. Angus should have warned me about this I thought. I would have saved some extra cloth for padding there. Again I was moving, there was no stopping me. On and on it went until at last, nearly dead from the exhaustion of having to keep my legs going to stop me falling over, I saw Angus. He was standing and looking up at me. My concentration lapsed and I messed up the last ledge jump. It was a small one, but all the same I tumbled forward two or three times and landed in a heap beside him. He was roaring with laughter as I looked up at him.

"I'm sorry about that," He says reaching down to help me up. " I've never seen anyone else come down there before, it's quite a sight."

"By Demne's sword of fire, how did you ever discover that way to come down the side of the mountain?" I burst out as I catch my breath.

"By accident really. Now I do it whenever I can. I find it more stimulating than almost anything I've ever come across. Tell me how do you feel right now?"

He had a point, I really felt great to be alive and now I was, the whole experience had left me feeling wild with the joys of life. I could do or achieve anything. I felt invincible.

"I feel terrific." I cry out, "But if you pull another trick on me like that," I say pointing and looking back from where I had just come down, " I'll ... " I was lost for words and my smile turned to disbelief as I realised just what I had come down. I turned back to Angus.

"I wouldn't even attempt to climb that." I say, still pointing. He still smiles at me and we burst out laughing together again.

"Nor would I!" He laughs out even louder.

It seemed like a good place to stop for a meal so we gathered up wood from the forest next to the road and made a broth from our pooled provisions.

Having filled ourselves well and destroyed all signs of our presence, we set off North along the road to the Drummorchy pass. As we approached, our light conversation turned to a more serious note.

"Fionn," Angus starts, "I want to teach you a protective lorica. Lugh gave it to me on the mountain top and I have a feeling it is time I told someone else. As you know it's not just saying the words, it's feeling them and seeing them as well that counts. I believe that if Callum Beg has become as powerful as the stories I hear about him, then you will need to recite this to yourself in his presence. It will stop him from hearing your thoughts and from influencing you to do things against your will. Practice it and you will succeed all the more. If either you or he are talking then it will not work."

"Thanks Angus, I really appreciate that. How does it go?"

"I rise today, through the strength from the stars. Light from the sun, radiance of the moon. Splendour of fire, speed of lightning, swiftness of the wind. Depth of sea, stability of earth and the firmness of rock."

"That's beautiful." I say.

"Now repeat it." He says. It was no problem for me and I do it first time.

"Now do so with greater meaning and passion. The same intensity of feeling you had when you came down the mountain and this time say it to yourself not out aloud."

This I did and afterwards I saw Angus's face drawn back in awe.

"I've never managed to ever invoke this lorica with the same strength that I have just witnessed in you. Fionn, you had better use it carefully as it will signal your presence to those that are attuned to these things. That might be dangerous."

"Thanks Angus, for everything you've done to help me. Dugald has a good friend in you."

We reached the Pass as the sun began to go down behind the mountains. I was greeted with my first sight of Invercarrie. I'd heard much about the city but nothing had prepared me for the size of the place.

The Eastern Coastline

CHAPTER SIX

ALL IS NOT WHAT IT SEEMS IN PHYSICS

As just one of the many interconnected branches of science today, physics manages to present a fairly well defined image and understanding of how most things work. However, underneath this orderly view of the world things begin to get much more interesting. In order to understand the current theories of this subject we must behave like a detective who is faced with what seems like the perfect murder. At first there appears to be an absence of clues, but with a careful analysis of all things, down to the minutest scale, evidence begins to show. It is only by carefully unravelling a few of these vital parts, that we can begin to see clearly through to its murky, uncertain and complex foundations. It is for this reason and also for ease of understanding that I have summarised this chapter's main points at the end. For those of you that will be reading about the subject of quantum mechanics and relativity for the first time, it is recommended that you adopt the following approach towards helping you gain this increased understanding. By glancing over the summary on page 141 and then returning to read the chapter from the beginning, you will find that you will come to know the subject far better. If you are unfamiliar with the subject it is also suggested that a slower reading speed will assist in bringing about a greater awareness.

6.1 The Big Question

For the last century one of the biggest, and still unresolved, questions in the world of physics has been the ability to combine and explain what we see on a large scale and what we observe on a small scale. On the large scale, we have the universe and the everyday massive objects encountered within it. This 'classical' world operates on the clearly defined principles of Newton's laws on gravity and Einstein's relativity theories. Everything in this 'world' exists in an ordered basis. The planets orbit the Sun according to regular and predictable paths and other celestial objects move relative to one another in ways that can also be calculated.

On the small scale, at a subatomic level, things are quite the opposite. One of the first people to study objects on this scale was Max Plank (1858-1947). His work at the Kaiser Wilhelm Institute of Berlin led him to become the first scientist to create the quantum principle. This principle was the first attempt to describe the activity of objects at this scale. He later, along with Niels Bohr a Danish physicist, established quantum theory. This different theory was presented because, at the microscale of the 'quantum' world, objects did not move in a relative way but in a random manner. The mathematics that worked for the 'classical' world did not work for the 'quantum' world!

This left a huge dilemma for the physicists. How could two such different ' worlds' coexist together? Especially as they do!

The search for the answer has led to many new discoveries and even more anomalies. I would like to cover some of these anomalies in this chapter and for ease and understanding they have been summarised again at the end. The knowledge and familiarity of these strange facts, will lead the reader to a quicker recognition of the connection that I referred to at the beginning of this book.

6.2 Four Forces

To begin with we must look at the four forces that are found in the world. A force is defined as some thing with a mass that is accelerating. On a subatomic level the mass is considered to be a particle. It is the exchange of these particles, between objects of mass, which gives rise to a force. It helps to try to imagine that a particle looks like a sphere but without a definite surface.

Gravity
The first of these forces is gravity. It is the weakest force but acts over large distances. Any objects that have a mass have a gravitational field

of some degree and with large masses like the sun and the earth all the forces that are given out add up to produce a significant effect. We know that this force exists because we can see the effects for ourselves. Tides move in relation to the sun and the moon's position and there is the obvious fact that objects tend to fall when they are dropped. Whatever the mass of an object there will always be a gravitational field. The amount of the force depends on the density of the object. The larger or more dense the mass; the more the force. The popular example most of us know of is the 'Black Hole'. These highly dense features in our universe have extreme amounts of gravitational force, so much so that light itself cannot escape.

The particle that is generally associated with the gravitational force has been called the graviton. It is worth mentioning at this stage that this is an extremely elusive particle and has not yet been measured or even proved to exist beyond doubt.

If the particle can be proved to exist then the theory of quantum gravity can become a reality. Proof of quantum gravity has become the holy grail for many physicists. If proof of this were attained, it would be strong evidence for a link between the large 'classical' world and the small 'quantum' world.

However due to its theoretically infinitely small size, it is extremely difficult to measure. When we use a microscope to view tiny features on a glass plate, we are actually bouncing photons (particles of light) off of the object up through the microscope into our eyes. We can distinguish what we are looking at by the way these photons are distorted into a specific picture. However these photons are massive in size when compared to gravitons and it would be like using bowling balls to observe miniature ping-pong balls (The scale used in this analogy is also hopelessly incorrect, if it were, the bowling ball would be millions of times bigger). As there would be a negligible (or at least unmeasurable) deflection of the bowling ball in any collision between the two, it would be impossible to tell what had been hit from our observations. This makes it very hard to find a method of observing and identifying the graviton!

However, it is now generally agreed amongst physicists that quantum gravity must exist at the very smallest of sizes called 'Planks scale – 10_{-35} cms'. At this scale the graviton particle would be the smallest thing in the universe. (A few now believe that they might be found at 10_{-19}cms).

If we are to assume that gravitons do exist and then go on to take the sun and the earth as our examples, we can go on to state that the gravitational force between them is caused by the exchange of 'virtual' gravitons. This would mean that there is a two way, 'attractive' exchange of particles between the two large masses. They are called 'virtual' because they cannot yet be detected by particle detectors. The forces between all these individual particles would add up to give us the effects we see on the planet. It is called an 'attractive' force because although graviton particles are given out, from starting at the centre of a mass (like the earth), the result is an attraction to it. This two-way naturedness to gravity has been given added strength due to the latest theories that antigravity must also exist in the universe. It would appear from the latest research on supernovae (large exploding stars) that the universe is continually expanding and this is partly due to the repulsion effect of antigravity. The nature of particles and their antiparticles is explained later on in this chapter.

Electromagnetism

The second force is the electromagnetic force. This is the force that occurs between electrically charged particles like electrons. Electrons are the tiny particles with a negative charge found orbiting around atoms. As with magnets, the electromagnetic force between two positive or two negative charges is repulsive and between a positive and negative it is attractive. Originally it was thought that electricity and magnetism were two separate forces but in 1873 a Scottish mathematical physicist called James Maxwell produced a set of equations that proved they were one and the same. This was the start of electromagnetism and new laws of physics based on fields, like magnetic fields, and not based on matter itself.

A photon of light is the massless particle that carries the electromagnetic force. Photons are given out when an electron moves from one orbit to another nearer the nucleus of the atom (depending on the type of atom there are several orbits with electrons in, all found at different distances from each other). When this happens energy is released and the photon is emitted. We can easily observe these because they are the particles associated with light which makes this particular force very measurable using today's scientific equipment.

Weak Force

The third force is called the weak force and is found inside the nucleus of the atom. This force is responsible for radioactivity. There are three particles known as bosons and they carry the weak nuclear force. For the purposes of discovering our connection, no more is needed to be known about them for the moment.

Strong Force

The fourth force is the strong nuclear force. The nucleus of an atom is made up of neutrons and protons, these in turn are made up of quarks. The strong force is thought to hold the quarks together. The particles that carry this force are called gluons. There are many strange names for these particles and fortunately, for the purposes of reading this book, you do not need to worry about knowing all of them.

It is important to realise, that on this subatomic scale, forces don't act in ways we might imagine they do in the large-scale 'classical' world. When we push an object like a car, we are exerting a force upon it by transmitting power from our muscles through our arms and hands and onto the car. The contact between us and the car is a very necessary part of the procedure. This does not have to be the case down at the microscopic quantum scale. At this scale a force only appears as an interaction that occurs between particles. As two particles come close to each other, they interact and there is a form of exchange between them. It is this exchange that gives rise to the force. With millions of particles spread over large areas, forces can be carried over large distances. One only need see a powerful magnet at work to realise that the electromagnetic force can be effective over substantial distances. Metal can be made to counter the effects of gravity and rise up to magnets above them. The forces that operate when this occurs act in a similar manner to the way all the forces operate between particles. There is no need to have an actual contact between two pieces of matter, or the particles themselves, for a force to be able to be transmitted. Water moves under similar circumstances when the mass of the moon exerts its gravitational force. The graviton particles between the moon and the water interact and exchange the necessary force and we end up seeing its effects.

6.3 The Strangeness of Spin

All known particles fall into two groups. Those that make up the matter in the universe, which have a spin 1/2 (half) and those that give rise to forces between matter, which have a spin 0, spin 1 or spin 2. These 'spins' are described like this.

Spin 1 is when a particle looks the same only when it has been fully rotated around 360 degrees. No other amount of rotation will cause it to look similar to how it did before it was spun. An example would be like the earth spinning on its axis. It needs to complete a full circle, 360 degrees, before it arrives at the same position.

A spin 2 particle only needs 180 degrees of turn before it mirrors what it was like before it was spun. An example of this is a playing card like the king of diamonds. If it is spun half way around, it is indistinguishable from it starting position. A graviton is considered to be a spin 2 particle. This also mathematically displays something called chirality, a basic handedness. It can be either show a left handed or right handed spin. This chirality is something that can be seen in many things in nature. One example of this can be found in sea shells. They have a tendency to spiral in one direction or another when they are formed as the organism in them secretes the calcium carbonate.

A spin 0 particle looks the same from all directions no matter how much it is turned.

The particles that behave in an odd manner are the ones with spin $1/2$ (half). It is not until these particles have been fully spun around two times do they return to resemble their former selves. This would be like taking a playing card and turning it over two times only to find that you hadn't ended up with the original face up. Only by turning it over another two times would you return it to its original state! And these are the ones that make up matter! This led Wolfgang Pauli, an Austrian physicist, in 1925 to come up with his famous 'exclusion principle' which describes why matter doesn't collapse in on itself. He proposed that each particle (i.e. an electron) had its own orbit and level of energy. He went on to say that these matter particles all obey a law that states that two similar particles cannot occupy the same space and the same velocity at the same time. If one place is occupied at a low energy level by a particle then the next place a particle can go is to the next higher energy level.

6.4 Matter and Antimatter?

The phenomenon that matter doesn't collapse in on itself due to the forces from the other particles led to another discovery. It was Paul Dirac in 1928, Professor of Maths at Cambridge, who first mathematically explained the spin $1/2$ (half) of the electron. He predicted that it had a partner, an antiparticle, that he called the positron. The first positron was discovered a few years later in 1932 and we now know that all particles have an antiparticle. How these antiparticles fit in to the overall picture no one is sure yet! These anti-matter particles with mass and spin are identical to ordinary matter except they have an opposite charge. For example electrons are negative, positrons are positive.

6.5 Uncertainty!

Just as you might think we know something about particles, there is more uncertainty. Werner Heisenberg (1901-1976) in 1927 made a major discovery that there was no way that the position and the momentum of a subatomic particle could ever both be known. The more you knew about the position, the less you knew about the momentum. This led to his uncertainty principle which states that the uncertainty in a simultaneous measurement of momentum and position will always be greater than a certain quantity called Plank's constant (an extremely small number that Plank discovered could never be zero when he was trying to measure packets, or quanta, of energy). Particles therefore have no determinancy (meaning determining where they are and what they are doing), they are said to only have a quantum state. This means that they are thought of as having a combination of velocity and position. Quantum mechanics can therefore never predict an outcome or a definite result for a given observation, it can only predict a number of different possible outcomes and give us the probability of each. This introduces the random element, mentioned earlier and one that some physicists, notably Einstein, were not at all comfortable with.

6.6 Waves and Particles

This leads us to the next strange observation of particles. Isaac Newton and Christian Huygens (1629-1695) argued about whether light consisted of particles or waves. Newton thought of light as photon particles and Huygens thought of light behaving like waves. We all know that radio waves can carry different frequencies. When we tune into the different radio stations that are broadcast, we are changing the receptiveness of our radios to the different frequencies of the radio waves. Concentric waves, like ripples in a pond, can be imagined to emanate from the transmitters and wherever our radio receivers are, we detect these waves via our aerials and get the messages. These ripples or waves can be transmitted at different speeds or frequencies, but only those that are found within the band for radio waves are of any use to those people using radios. We know radio waves are frequencies of light that come from the invisible part of the spectrum and that there are higher and lower frequencies that can also be observed. As it is all part of the light spectra, we also have to come to terms with the fact that we know we can also detect particles of light. These we call photons. This is why Newton and Huygens found that they disagreed with each other.

Thomas Young in 1801 was the first to carry out a now famous experiment called the two-slit experiment (Diagram 4). The slightly concerning conclusion to this experiment, and one now accepted by the whole scientific establishment, is that there is a wave/particle duality. This means that particles, like photons of light, can behave like particles and they can also behave like waves. If you set out to measure waves, you find it behaving like a wave. If you set out to measure particles, you find particles.

The experiment works like this. You position a light in front of a card with two vertical slits (4.c). Behind the card you place a backing screen (particle/wave detection screen). The dark shadows and light patches that are naturally seen on the screen behind the two slits are called an interference pattern of light and dark patches. This is what we observe with two slits. There is no interference pattern with only one slit, just one light patch with dark shadow all around (4.a). If, instead of a light source, we place an emitter of particles, like an electron gun, in front of the one slit, we still just find a similar pattern of particles that can be detected (4.b). We can now progress to using a particle detector in front of two slits and proceed to send the electrons off one at a time toward them. If this is done several times and measured on the backing screen we have the strange result of still finding the same resultant interference pattern as from the light source (4.d). It would appear that each single particle somehow passes through both slits at once! If we then cover one of the slits from behind (4.e), the pattern disappears. How the particle/wave knows that the other slit has been covered or uncovered, and then goes on to either produce the interference pattern or not, is the question that causes concern. The only conclusion that sci-

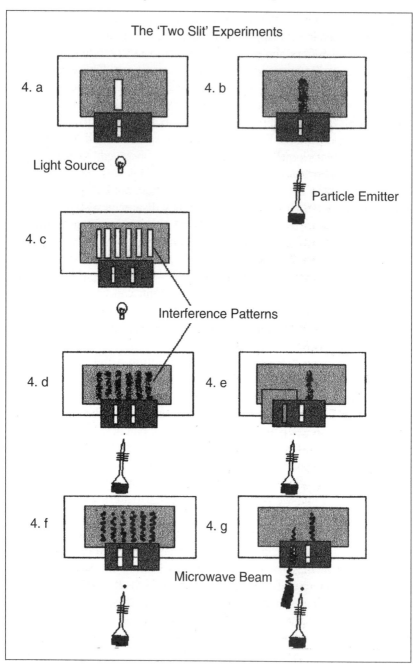

The 'Two Slit' Experiments

4. a

4. b

Light Source

Particle Emitter

4. c

Interference Patterns

4. d

4. e

4. f

4. g

Microwave Beam

Diagram 4

entists have come to, is that each electron/particle must be passing through both slits at once! The particle would appear to behave like a wave when it wants to and is only measured as a particle when a particle detector is used as the backing screen!

It was Louis de Broglie (1892-1987), a student at the Sorbonne in Paris that showed that this Wave/Particle duality was the same for all particles and could be extended to the whole physical world.

It was later deduced that it was the method of observation that played an important part in deciding what was being observed. A particle would be observed if using particle detectors and a wave would be observed if using wave detectors. It could be said that the method by which we choose to observe things in the world will have a high degree of effect over the outcome.

This two slit experiment was done again recently in September 1998 by Gerhard Rempe and his colleagues at the University of Konstanz in Germany. Rempe wanted to test the uncertainty theory by seeing if he could measure the particle without disturbing it. By bouncing weak microwaves off of the atoms going through the slits, they hoped to learn which path the atom followed through the slits (4.f & 4.g). The atoms used were large, cold rubidium atoms as these have many orbits or layers of energy states. The microwaves used were of sufficient energy themselves to only affect the outer layers of these atoms, whilst the internal states would still be able to keep a record of which path the atom had gone along. In other words they wouldn't have totally interfered with the atom by their observations. This should have meant that there still would be an interference pattern, but that was not the case and not what they found. This meant that the wave/particle duality theory was still upheld as the pattern disappeared, but it can't have been the act of observation that stopped the interference pattern as the microwaves were insufficient to do this on their own.

Yu Shi, a Cambridge physicist, studied the implications behind this experiment and deduced that what this meant was that the uncertainty principle wasn't wrong, but that it now can't explain the results of not finding the pattern. He further deduced that is was not the act of observation that causes uncertainty to be lost but, more importantly, the act of finding the path information. If you find the path of an atom, with or without disturbing its position, you will cause the loss of the interference pattern. Shi states that this loss of interference is always due to something called quantum entanglement.

If two particles meet or interact, then the two can become linked or entangled. They now cease to be independent of each other and can now only be described in relation to one another. This astonishing feature is explained more fully later in this chapter at 6.10 when we go on to look at non-locality.

By purely finding the path of an atom and not completing a full observation, an interaction has occurred between particles and the system is no longer the same. Entanglement has occurred.

6.7 Not a Universe a Multiverse?

Richard Feynman, a famous American scientist and genius of immense proportion, introduced a new way of looking at this wave/particle duality problem. He called it the sum over histories. He argued, along with concrete mathematical theory, that the particle didn't just travel on one path from the source to the backing screen but that it travelled by every possible path at the same time. Each of these paths would also have varying degrees of probability. It is important to add here that each of these paths have their own time and space (space-time) for reasons we will come to later on.

It has been further suggested that the universe didn't just have a single history but rather every possible history, each with its own probability! (Recall the past time cone) This would also be true for futures as well and is the foundation for the 'Multiverse' theory. This theory states that we are living in, not just one universe, but an infinite number, many of them overlapping with ours.

There is an anthropic principle that states that we see the universe the way it is, because if it were different we would not be here to observe it. Each of us would then appear to create our own journey through our own universe in our own space-time - all caused by our own observations. We shall come back to this later on before we get too carried away with the implications of it and how it relates to our time cone model.

6.8 To observe causes a collapse !

The next oddity follows on from the last and also concerns the act of observation. When a source, like light, behaves like waves it has various frequencies depending on the wavelength. This can be described by a mathematical term called the 'wave function'. This is a way of describing the position. As it is also like a particle, it too has a probability of being in several positions. In this case they are called possible alternate state vectors. This probability of several possible state vectors is also referred to as a density matrix.

We can now imagine that, in this quantum world, many possible futures can exist, as long as it is before any measurement that takes place (As in our future light cone). Each of these light waves travel unencountered in a form of density matrix. It is only when we actually attempt to make an observation of any of the particles, or a measurement of the path of the wave, that the quantum world collapses into our real classical world. **This is called the collapse of the wave function.** (Sometimes referred to as Reduction)

Erwin Shrödinger, an Austrian physicist was the first person to explain this 'collapse' best. He was the first to find the solution to mathematically describe the wave as a wave function. He invented a 'thought' experiment that describes the problem. He suggested that a live cat be put in a box containing a radioactive source, along with hammer, a glass flask of deadly poisonous fumes and a device that released the hammer and broke the flask if radioactive decay was measured using a Geiger counter. The radioactive source would be known to have a 50% chance of decaying within the time limit of a minute. The whole box would be sealed and switched on. After one minute it would be switched off again. That now means that the radioactive decay has either occurred, in which case the hammer smashed the glass and the cat was dead from poisoning, or that no radioactive decay had taken place. In each case there was a 50:50 chance of either occurring. The burning question was which was the case? Was the cat alive or dead?

The cat at this stage (with the lid unopened) is said to be in both quantum states of dead and alive at the same time. It is not until the lid of the box is opened do we observe the reality. Then one of the two possible worlds collapses from the quantum world into our classical one. This again gives us the indication that it is our act of observation that creates this collapse.

This analogy was taken a stage further by Hungarian physicist Eugene Wigner (1902-1995) who was concerned about what actually causes the collapse of the wave function. He suggested that instead of putting a cat in the box you put a human. This human would then be aware of whether or not they were dead after the one-minute experiment. They would also be aware before anyone else opened the lid and collapsed their wave function. In fact, the human in the box would collapse their own wave function prior to an outsider opening the box. It is clear then that we, as individuals making our own observations and independent of anyone else, create our own reality. Wigner claimed that *the consciousness of the observer makes the difference* and that the consciousness is what brings about the collapse. We will look at this more closely in chapter 10 when looking at that subject in the context of how the brain might work and the role quantum entanglement has to play.

In summary each of us observes independently of others and our own consciousness plays a part. The act of observation (one sufficient to find the path) collapses one of the quantum worlds into our reality. There are an infinite number of quantum worlds each with varying degrees of probability. The nature and the way we choose to observe one of these worlds will assist in choosing the reality we wish to collapse.

6.9 Something out of nothing

Physicists have shown that space (the actual space between the stars, planets and galaxies) cannot be 'empty'. All the gravitational and electromagnetic fields cannot add up and equal zero. The reason being that as soon as this precise value is attached to it, there would have to also be a rate of change of exactly the same amount (zero). This defies Heisenberg's uncertainty principle that says you can never know both qualities at the same time. To overcome this problem, physicists state that there must be a minimum amount of uncertainty. They call this uncertainty a quantum fluctuation. Empty space is therefore, considered to be filled with pairs of particles and their antiparticles. These are constantly being created, live very briefly and then annihilate each other. Energy, in this way, is therefore, thought to have been 'borrowed' from the fields (mentioned above). Due to the very short lifespan, of living and dying, these particles have a large degree of uncertainty. After their short time of life, they return back to the 'nothingness' of empty space. The next thing to remember is Einstein's famous equation ($E = MC^2$). This shows that a relationship exists between mass and energy and in theory a particle with a mass could be created out of energy.

The next step is to realise that energy cannot be created out of nothing unless, in this case, each pair of particle and anti particle has an opposite charge. One would have positive energy; the other negative. They would also have opposite spins, for example one spinning clockwise; the other anti clockwise.

One fact that seems to support the theory that particles have antiparticles arises when you imagine a real electron particle in space surrounded by pairs of virtual particles that are appearing and disappearing. Because of the negative charge of the real electron and the positive charge of the virtual positrons (positive anti-electron particles), there is an attraction. The electrons are then said to be 'dressed' with a coat of virtual positrons around it. When two speeding electrons are accelerated toward each other, as in a particle accelerator like C.E.R.N. the European centre for nuclear research in Switzerland, the two electrons eject their 'coats'. This increases their repulsion (two negatives being forced together) by a measurable and predictable amount. This has now been observed experimentally so we can go on to say that this theory seems to have been upheld. The reason for mentioning about these pairs of particles will become more obvious in the next section.

The creation of these virtual particles became important in the understanding of force over a distance. Virtual photons and the exchange of these is now pictured as the method by which the electromagnetic force works and quite possibly the gravitational force.

6.10 Non-Locality

Non-locality is perhaps one of the strangest phenomena to come out of looking at quantum systems. It started with Einstein being uncomfortable with Heisenburg's uncertainty principle. He, along with Boris Podolsky and Nathan Rosen devised an imaginary experiment that attempted to show that you could measure both the position and momentum of a particle. They suggested that a pair of particles could exist as one, with the spins cancelling each other out and leaving a total spin of zero. Their total momentum would be zero and there would be no external forces acting on them. The two particles could be exploded apart with each now having to have the same momentum because of the explosion from the same starting point. If the first particle had its momentum measured then the second would have to have the same figure, even though it had not been directly measured. You could then measure the position of the second particle and instantaneously know both its position and momentum at the same time. This now defied the uncertainty principle!

Niels Bohr argued subsequently that the two particles were still part of the same system and were in a way still connected!

The problem continues if you measure the spin of one of the particles. Whatever it is, the other must be the opposite because of the law of equal and opposite reactions. This then means that after having made the measurement of spin on one particle (and collapsed its wave function), we have some advance knowledge of the other one. If the particles were moving apart for a long period of time before measurement, then, irrespective of the distance, we would be getting this information about the second particle instantaneously. This now defies the theory that nothing travels faster than the speed of light. In this case the information that has instantly come to you, could have come from a particle that was the other side of the universe!

This was proved later in an experiment done by Alain Aspect in Paris 1982, and John Clauser at Berkeley in 1978. Their experiment was done using photons and polarising filters.

Particles like photons don't appear to be localised, they appear to have a connection across the universe where distance and time is not a concern. The choice of how to measure a particle initially, and therefore a method of causing an initial desired result (How we choose to observe things creates the reality we want) will give us knowledge of certain values in the corresponding particle before they are measured at all. This is what is termed as non-locality. The quantum entanglement mentioned earlier in 6.6, where two particles meet and interact with each other causing path information to be known, can now be seen as being in the same non-local state as is mentioned in this section. They are forever part of the same system.

The universe has therefore been described as a collection of particles that are bound together as part of many systems. These systems connect the observer and the observed in a manner that has been described as holistic. This is taken to mean that we are all part of the 'whole'.

This, faster than light, information that can be transmitted instantaneously between two points can lead us to some interesting possibilities. We can choose how we observe one series of transmitted particles, thereby collapsing the wave function to produce the reality we want, and thereby sending information of a specific nature to another point (where the corresponding series of particles are) at a speed that is instant. This could be the basis for a method by which information could be conveyed outside the normal constraints as seen in our 'classical' world.

We shall see later on that time slows down the nearer you get to the speed of light. Information that travels faster would therefore appear to have to be free from the constraints of time. In other words information could be sent or received from the past or the future within our own space-time.

This strange observation of information coming and going from either the past or the future can also be found in another quantum theory.

In the last section we discussed particles and their antiparticles. These virtual particles, which only last for a fraction of time, have a charge and spin. The occurrence of these pairs with their charge and spin, together with Feynman's 'sum over histories' now allows scientists to make further deductions.

An antiparticle, spinning anticlockwise and moving from A to B, can (because the laws of science are not different whatever method you choose to measure time) also be viewed as an ordinary particle moving backward in time from B to A. Particles that are therefore created in empty space could be termed as being on a circular route within space time. The particle would travel briefly forward in space-time and the antiparticle would travel backward in time.

Scientists are happy to consider that this would seem to allow for the possibility of time travel albeit on a microscopic 'quantum' scale only. When these pairs of particles are put next to a body that emits a gravitational field, like a black hole, one can produce observable effects of time travel.

This unfortunately is not allowed to happen on the macroscopic scale because the normal laws of physics still apply in the 'classical' world.

So it would appear at the moment that time travel on macroscopic level is not going to be possible. On a quantum scale however it would seem that information could be passed from the future to the present and then to the past or back again. It is only at the present though, that reality occurs. It is our own act of measurement with our external senses that 'collapses the wave function' and causes the quantum world to become classical. How this might actually happen is covered in a chapter ten.

Richard Feynman's ideas that particles pass through all points at once (like a wave does) leads to the implications that there are many options for the future. Two approaches have been determined from these thoughts. Firstly, that there is a consistent history and secondly that there are alternative histories. The latter would appear to hold true on a microscopic scale with each history having its own probability, whilst the former would appear to be true on a macroscopic scale.

Now we are back to probabilities of futures and histories it takes us back to the light cone model we looked at in chapter two and it's time we looked at how the scientists view them.

6.11 Light Cones

Aristotle and Newton believed in the concept of absolute time (time was the same for everyone). However the realisation that the speed of light was both finite and constant began a revolution in thought. This was that space and time were not independent of each other. Things that move closer to the speed of light are subject to the phenomenon that time slows down the nearer you get to that speed.

It would appear that each observer must have his own measure of time. Therefore if each observer had an internal clock, it might not necessarily agree with other observer's clocks.

To measure an event (something that happens at a point in space and a point in time) observers will assign it a time and a position. However if the observers themselves are moving relative to each other, they will not be assigning similar measurements to the same event. In the theory of relativity, distance is now defined in terms of time and the speed of light at the same time. This requires us to now think of redefining events in terms of space-time. The fact that the speed of light is the same, whatever the source, has now also been confirmed by accurate measurements.

Now that we use space-time as one co-ordinate in describing an event (the others being our normal three dimensional co-ordinates), we can progress to using light cones as a model.

An event occurring in the present (diagram 1 – page 40) would have a past and future light cone. Any events happening from after that point are things that can be reached from the present by particles or waves travelling at or below the speed of light. Anything lying within the past light cone can only reach the present as long as those particles/waves are travelling within the speed of light.

We have used just this same concept of a light cone to help establish what is possible in our own futures in previous chapters. The present would be a point in space-time that represents where we start.

Any other event would have its own past and future light cone. One can then go on to imagine several of these cones put together in one area and all uniformly the same in shape and orientation. This is called Minkowski space after Herman Minkowski, Einstein's Maths professor. This is a situation where gravity must be absent. However it is because of gravity that light cones become non-uniform and, as such, are known as 'tilted'. Nothing else known in physics can affect light cones in this way. This again makes gravity very different from all the other forces. Gravity, because of this, has been described as the distortion by mass of space-time. A mass (at the present point in diagram 1 & at the tip of the light cone) would distort, in its own way, its journey through space-time. This must even occur whatever the size or density of the mass. This would even include something as small as electrons, although the amount of tilt arising in that cone would be extremely small.

6.12 Relativity

Einstein, in 1915, proposed his general theory of relativity. He suggested that gravity was not a force like other forces because space-time itself was warped. It was warped because of the distribution of mass and energy within it. Masses like the Earth actually follow a straight line in 4-D space-time. By moving in four dimensions it means that a 3-D object is moving in a time dimension as well, which makes it 4-D. It only appears to us that it is moving on a curved orbit around the sun. However the mass of the sun distorts our view. This is even more so for Mercury, the smallest planet near to the sun. Deviations from the predicted orbit of this planet have since confirmed Einstein's general theory.

Another prediction of this theory has also been measured. This is that time slows nearer a large mass. Two accurate clocks showed this at the top and bottom of a tower. The clock at the base of the tower (nearer the mass of the earth) ran slower. This again showed the end of Newton's 'absolute time'.

All this places tremendous emphasis on the role of the observer. Each of us has our own measure of time and our own future time cone and our own frame of reality. The only thing that affects our journey through space-time is gravity. Where we are with respect to masses that distort space-time will determine our future light cone and its possible direction. Gravity can therefore tilt light cones and thus affect our future options.

6.13 Expanding space

On the macroscopic scale, things are also not always what they appear to be. When we observe the universe through a telescope, light from the distant stars enters into our eyes. Light is made up of several frequencies of waves, some visible, some invisible. They can range from microwaves to x-ray waves and from infra-red waves to ultra-violet waves and gamma waves. By analysing what we see in a spectrometer we can glean various bits of information about the stars. When you hear an ambulance or a police car pass by with its siren going you hear a change in pitch in the tone of the sound as the vehicle travels past you and then away. This is called the Doppler effect. It can be measured and the speed of the vehicle can be worked out. The same is true for light waves as it is for sound waves. The infra-red light is shifted in the same manner and it can be measured to determine the speed and direction of a star.

When these calculations are done, the strange result is that all the stars are 'red shifting' away from us. It is as though we are exactly in the centre of the universe. The red shift also tells us that the furthest stars that we see are travelling away from us at the fastest rate. Edwin Hubble the American astronomer first published this fact in 1929. The Russian physicist Alexander Friedman made two assumptions that were later proved to be true. The first was that the universe would be the same whichever way you looked. The second was that wherever you were as the observer, including being in another galaxy millions of light years from earth, you would experience the same red shift and conclude that everything was expanding away from you. It would appear that wherever the observer was – would be the centre of their universe.

The fact that the universe is expanding seems strange when you consider that the most influential force is gravity. Gravity is an attractive force and it would seem to imply that at some point in the future the universe would slow down its expansion and begin to collapse. Some astrologers used to call this 'The big crunch'. However studies of Supernova's (stars that come to the end of their life and allow gravity to collapse them into new astronomical features called white dwarfs) have now collaborated the theory that the universe will continue to expand. It has now been shown that gravity has both an 'attractive' nature and also a 'repulsive' nature. Galaxies also seem to be pushing apart from one another. This two-way nature would appear to agree with the concept that graviton particles or gravitational waves are sent out from the centre of gravity of a mass, whilst retaining an overall attraction back toward that same centre.

In 1965 Arno Penzias and Robert Wilson, from the Bell laboratories in the U.S.A, made a major discovery. This was the occurrence in space of a background radiation with a microwave frequency. This was considered to be evidence of the remains of the original heat from the 'Big Bang' that was supposed to have started everything. In 1992 the cosmic background explorer (COBE) satellite later measured this radiation. The results showed a great uniformity in the radiation that seemed to support an initial big bang theory. However there were some density variations in some areas that are now called 'ripples in space'. These ripples, along with the more obvious variations like galaxies, collapsed stars and black holes, don't seem to point to an initial big bang inflationary theory. Instead a new inflationary theory, originating in Russia, seemed to explain many of these features. The latest self-reproducing inflationary universe theory comes from Prof. Andrei Lande of Stanford University, California. This shows that the Big Bang was actually part of the overall inflationary process and allowed different regions to develop separately with possibly different properties. (One for example could allow an area for the popular theory of superstrings. In this theory string-like features are the building blocks of the universe as opposed to particles and worlds with more than four dimensions probably exist!). The explanation for the variations found in the universe is supposedly due to the quantum fluctuations mentioned earlier in this chapter in 6.9. These fluctuations are frozen and stretched out as the rapid inflation occurs. These then do not disappear but go to build up the density of an area that could later go on to form galaxies. These areas would obviously affect the distribution of matter in the universe and as such gravity would add to the overall effect.

The end result is that, with this latest theory, we could now consider the universe to evolve in a series of bangs creating bubbles of expanding space, each branching out, like a tree, from a previous one. The universe appears to be both chaotic and uniform in nature and also expanding in some areas and stationary in others. From these quantum fluctuations new regions will continue to form in some areas of the universe. This self-reproducing nature would appear to be similar to life itself. It has even been suggested that our own consciousness and acts of observing are in some way connected to this ongoing cycle!

6.14 Measuring Gravity

Following on from the strange features that we find in the 'classical' world, there appear to be huge difficulties in actually measuring gravity itself!

As has all ready been mentioned, the graviton particle has yet to be proved or observed. It has also been mentioned that particles behave like waves and these gravity waves have not been observed yet either. Many scientists are now in a race to build gravitational wave detectors that might detect ripples in space-time. So far none have been detected.

The problem continues when measuring the effect of gravity to any degree of accuracy. Geologists use gravimeters to identify areas underneath the ground that vary in density. They are essentially spring balances that are exceptionally sensitive. One of their uses is in understanding how the molten rock under volcanoes is moving. Mount Etna has many gravity survey stations that allow geologists to map the complex underground system of channels of magma. The different densities of rock cause small variations in gravitational pull. As the magma moves around, the gravity contour map changes. This potentially allows them to predict in advance where the next eruption might come from. Dr David Smith at N.A.S.A.'s Goddard space flight centre has sent gravimeters into space to measure gravitational features beneath the oceans. From that distance variations in rock densities can be detected far down into the earth's mantle. The higher the spacecraft, the less the surface features like mountains affect the measurements. They have already identified the changing convection currents deep within the mantle. These are huge currents, similar to those found in water, of molten rock that move around beneath us. They in turn move the surface plates of oceanic and continental crust. The movements of these are responsible for earthquakes and volcanoes.

With such a dynamic system of a moving mass, it is perhaps easier to understand how measuring gravity might be difficult. The problem being that as soon as something is measured, it has changed again.

This however has not stopped independent scientists like Gabe Luther. At a laboratory in Los Alamos, New Mexico he has spent many years trying to obtain an accurate measurement of the gravitational constant. They call it looking for Big G. Scientists are exact in their knowledge of many fundamental numbers to eight decimal places. With Big G, they disagree after only three!

They are up against severe problems. If you walk into a room, as a mass yourself, you subtly distort the curvature of space-time, pulling everything gently toward you. One day Luther came back to his lab only to find that his measurement was suddenly very different from before. After much consternation and searching it was found that a ton of books had been moved in overnight into an office two stories above his laboratory and that had made the readings different!

Physicists around the world even dispute the best methods and best apparatus to use. Some are now so sensitive that they can also measure seismic activity. This enables them to detect earthquakes and even the size of the surf the other side of the world!

6.15 Summary

Of the many interesting phenomena that have been mentioned so far in this chapter, it is important to summarise a few of more salient parts in order to progress with our quest. The following information will suffice for now and all will become clearer as you read through the remaining chapters.

1. There are four known forces in the universe. The strong force, the weak force inside atoms, the electromagnetic force and the gravitational force. The first three all have clearly defined particles that carry force. The gravitational force only has a theoretical particle, the graviton, and this has still not been actually detected.

2. Particles are strange in that they can also behave like waves (eg. radio and light waves). Gravitational waves have also not yet been detected.

3. Quantum gravity, the idea that gravity does have some small particle of force, is assumed by many to exist at the smallest scale of size possible in the universe – Planks length.

4. Gravity is the distortion of space-time by mass. The most obvious example is a black hole where there is so much gravity that everything (including light) is distorted around it, but distortion will also occur in a tiny way with particles the size of electrons.

5. The actual measurement of gravity's value is extremely controversial and not one that people can agree upon as it seems to vary so much due to the many variables that affect the measurement process.

6. The act of a measurement (like just trying to observe it) of the path of a particle itself is enough to collapse all the possible quantum worlds (future light cone) into reality and into the classical world of reality. What was first uncertain becomes certain. The consciousness of the observer is an important feature that assists in creating this collapse.

7. Each observer has their own measurement of time and creates their own reality with their own individual observation.

8. The way we make a measurement can determine the reality of our choice. If we want to measure a particle, we will find a particle. If we set out to measure a wave, we will encounter a wave.

9. It would appear that we, as individuals, seem to be at the centre of the universe from whichever standpoint we care to choose.

10. Space is not empty. Quantum fluctuations create particles and anti particles from borrowing energy from the electromagnetic and gravitational fields. This allows force over a distance to occur (eg. the force that exists between earth and the moon.) With anti particles and particles moving in circular routes, time travel, on a microscopic level only, would appear to be possible.

11. A pair of particles can be made to behave in a 'non-local' manner. This seems to allow information to travel faster than the speed of light. This requires the system and the observer to be connected in some way, possibly over huge distances of space.

12. The concept that particles travel through all points, like a wave, implies that there are many paths and options for the future. Probability for each path will partially determine the likely outcome. This could be portrayed on our time cone model that we looked at in previous chapters. We, as a mass ourselves, can consider ourselves to be at the centre of our light/time cone model in our current reality. This we create with our own observations with our external senses. We have many possible future quantum paths open to us, each with their own probability, and all existing outside our own concept of space-time reality. Our light cone and its tilt of direction can only be affected by gravity in some way.

13. Gravity has a two-way nature, yet it is an 'attractive' force. Objects of mass are pulled towards one another's centre of gravity, yet particles or waves are emitted away from those centres. If you were to imagine two masses like the earth and the moon, then you can imagine the interaction that now occurs between them with respect to each other's gravitational waves or graviton particles.

In chapter eight we shall begin to look more closely at the mind, the way it is programmed, confused and used. What we can learn from this will give us vital information in order for us to proceed on towards the link we are fast approaching.

CHAPTER SEVEN

AN INVITATION TO TRADE

We walked on, side by side, in silence. Long shadows from the mountains in the west fell over Invercarrie leaving it in the dark. As we descended, the orange glow to our left faded and a cold chill settled about us.

"We must make a plan." Says Angus abruptly, breaking the silence.

"What do you mean, we?" I react slightly startled by his decision to join me in my mission to rescue Mairi, "This is my problem. I don't want to get you involved or to put you in any danger." I reply, not looking up from watching the trail we were on. Darkness now made it less easy to see the now steep and winding path and there was lots of loose gravel that made it slippery underfoot.

"It's too late, Fionn. I became involved long before we met. There's something I should have faced up to years ago. Destiny has finally run its course... besides, I can be of help to you. You know no one here and I have some good friends we can call upon."

"Thanks," I say after a moments thought, "It'll be good to have your company a little longer. What do you suggest we do first?" I ask, relenting a little more.

"There's an Inn here, run by an old acquaintance of Dougie and I." His front foot slides a little, but a well-placed staff stops him from falling.

"Would that be a man named Leag?" I interrupt, now stopping to take more care in descending behind him. "Dugald said he might know where to find you."

"Aye, that's the man, though I doubt he'd of been much use to you if you'd asked about me. For his own safety, I told him little." He pauses at another steep part of the path. "We'll stay there tonight and catch up on news and old times. In the meantime let's discuss what you're going to do." Having got down it, he turns, gives me a sideways glance and waits for me.

"I was going to go and introduce myself to the Aes Dana tomorrow morning and request an examination to become an Anruth." I reply after a moments thought on how best to tackle the mixture of rocks and boulders now below me. "I suppose I would then be expected to meet with Callum Beg... at which time I could confront him with the theft and abduction of Mairi...."

"... but you have no proof of his involvement yet." He interrupts and then pauses, waiting for me to get down beside him, "That course of action would only serve to strengthen his hand. Haven't you any other ideas?"

"No... other than looking for Domnhuil Dubh and finding out where he might be keeping Mairi." I answer, feeling slightly downcast as I listen to my rather weak sounding ideas.

"Well, that's more the right idea." He encourages and turns to start walking again, "We need to first get as much information as possible, without giving too much away. What's most important to you in all of this?"

"I have to find my sister, everything else can wait." I reply, not needing to think about his question.

"I would have to agree with that and if it's Domnhuill Dubh you suspect, it'll be nay problem finding him. Finding out what he's done with her and where she might be though, is another matter." He shakes his head in thought.

"I'll have to try and loosen some tongues then." I half suggest as an option, turning to him and putting a determined face on.

"It would nay be good to under estimate Black Donald, Fionn, he has as many friends as enemies." He adds with an air of caution and by way of offering an indirect answer to my idea.

"I appreciate your words, but I'm going to have to stir things a little in order to get the information I need. What are your plans?" I say changing the topic purposely as I was short on information myself with which I could answer his questions.

"I'll be seeking an audience with Callum Beg as well. It'll be best to do so after yours, that will give me enough time to catch up on all the allegiances that now exist within the inner circle at the Aes Dana. I need to find out what he's up to and how strong he has become." He stops talking and we continue to walk in silence, both wanting time to think about our coming action.

As we reached the outskirts of the settlement, I could see some ploughed fields and an occasional croft but what really amazed me was the extent of the felled ground. The area must have once been deep forest but had now been reduced to a mass of stumps amid waterlogged ground. Our boots sucked noisily through it as we trudged across towards a large embankment.

Nearing this earth and stone rampart, made complete by a wooden palisade on top, I couldn't help but wonder at the time and effort it must have taken to build as it surrounded the whole of Invercarrie. It was the biggest settlement I had ever seen and its size was beginning to diminish my confidence. How was I, on my own, really going to accomplish all that was expected of me.

I was jolted out of my thoughts when I noticed that a few people were staring at us. As I smiled at them and about to greet them, they looked away without any form of acknowledgement being given in return.

"Is that normal around here Angus?" I ask, whom I saw was also aware of their actions. "On the islands, everyone rushes to meet a stranger to be the first to offer them food and shelter."

"Around these parts people are much more wary of strangers, for reasons you can probably guess. They mean well and, once they know you, they are all the more friendly and hospitable."

"How do they ever meet anyone new with that behaviour though?" I ask. "And how can they ever achieve any progress without the exchange of information and ideas or even just talking with other folk?" I continue.

"They don't, is the short answer. Their fear is restricting them. Of course there are the few cases when meetings are inevitable but more often than not they keep within their own kin." Replies Angus.

We eventually reached the large wooden East gate. It was set within part of the stone ramparts and on a slight rise. Above it was a small wooden guard tower.

Angus stops and turns to me just a few paces away and whispers. "Listen. If either of us has a problem here and has to leave suddenly, but still needs to give the other some important news, there's an animal pen to the North of here. It'll be full of cattle this time of year, but warm. It's owned by a farmer that I know well. If you mention my name, he'll let you stay there. You can't miss the pen, it's off to the side of the road next to a couple of grain pits. I'll meet you there or leave word for you, if either of us goes missing in the town or if there is no message, I'll think the worst."

"Do you really think that's necessary?" I state.

"Absolutely. In this place people disappear without trace. On the surface it may appear at times to be friendly and happy, but underneath there's also an evil seam of malice and murder." He warns with a deadly serious tone to his voice.

The giant, two man high, wooden gates took on a menacing appearance as his words sunk in and I found myself thinking about what manner of sin must lie beyond. They opened as we got there and an arm ushered us forward.

"What's your business and where are you heading this time of day?" Comes a gruff voice.

"We're staying with Leag, at the Bridge." Growls back Angus, his tone like that of a cornered bear. I turned and stared at him as his voice had changed completely. From being quiet, it had become commanding, full of assurance and booming with authority. We were let through. Nothing more was said, just a grim stare from the screwn up face of the gatekeeper as though he was struggling to remember our faces either from his murky past or for his future memory. Inside, the place there seemed utter confusion. The main track, if it could be called that, ran down toward the river. It was muddy, half frozen solid and there were large puddles of dirty water and brownish slush. In no particular order there were several wattle and daub round houses off to the sides, some with decaying thatch; others with little more than a lump of turf on top. They were scattered all around and the paths between them led both everywhere and nowhere. A dank fishy smell, mingled with the smoke from evening fires, hung in the air. It made breathing in a less than pleasant experience in the now fading light.

"This is one of the better areas." Comments Angus.

I shudder to think what the rest might be like and I briefly wonder why people would want to live here. Not choosing to spend time thinking about it, I follow on just to his side and behind him.

"Over there is the queen's palace." He says pointing to a large circular wall on the left. I glance up but see little as the stonework is too high.

As we entered further, we walked out into an open, roughly square area. The fishy smell was far stronger now and the calls of seagulls could be heard coming from the right over at the docks. I could see at least three full size currachs moored along the harbour wall, each a hive of activity.

"That's it," says Angus, interrupting my curiosity, "there's the Bridge Inn in front of us."

I turned my roving eyes back to the point of his attention and followed him toward the door of a large dun. Its boulder walls, with timbers above them, gave it more height than the surrounding buildings and the noise from inside also singled the place out as somewhere people liked to frequent.

Angus disappeared inside and I was about to follow when I caught sight of the first few planks of the bridge over the river Carrie. Distracted by this, I went over and up on to it. It was an incredible piece of craftsmanship. Over forty large wooden supports had been put down, some sunk in mud; others held in place by huge rocks. The river itself was over thirty paces wide and flowed deep and fast in the middle.

I now stood in the centre looking around me and soaking it all in, allowing my senses to familiarise themselves with their new experiences.

"Fionn, lad. Come on. There'll be time enough for looking around tomorrow, besides it gets to be less safe on your own the later it is." Calls Angus from the end of the bridge. I took a deep breath of the fresher salty, sea air that was here and turned to join him. In my mind I was thinking of the many new things I could see and do now I'd arrived.

The inside of the Bridge Inn was much like the one in Drummorchy, except that it was even bigger, noisier and filled with even more people. Only a few showed any interest in our arrival; others just glanced up then returned to their drinks. I followed Angus over to a long bar at the far end. Behind it was a wall of casks and a small, rotund, bearded man who looked as though he would have a problem reaching up to the highest of his barrels. He lifted his slightly balding head and stared quizzically at Angus from under thick bushy red eyebrows. Moments later a broad smile filled his face as the recognition dawned upon him.

"Angus!" He booms, holding his arms wide. It attracts the attention of his nearest customers.

"Leag, it's good to see you after all this time," Smiles Angus, reaching over the bar to greet him. They hug each other three times from one cheek to the other.

"We all heard that you'd gone to the Otherworld long ago. There was talk of murder, you and Dougie were wanted for plotting against the King, there were loads of stories going round. How are you now and what have you been doing all this time? Never mind answering now have something to eat and drink. It's on me..."

"Leag... Leag, you don't change do you. It is really good to see you again." Sighs Angus smiling, "But first let me introduce you to Fionn. He's spent the last seven years being trained by Dougie, he'll be able to answer your many questions and maybe he'll even tell you a few stories."

"Fionn." He grasps my arm with two massive hands and matching forearms and shakes it whilst continuing to speak. "Any friend of Angus and Dougie is a friend of mine."

His words were spoken fast with an accent I hadn't heard before. Pleasingly, they ouzed sincerity and his warmth was infectious. Soon we were seated in his own room at the back with a meal of crofter's broth, oatmeal bread and crowdie together with a large ale. The fresh neaps, leeks and carrots were a pure joy after the last couple of days and the crowdie was of a strength and taste of soft cheese I'd never come across before.

After we'd finished, Leag joined us and we talked about old and recent events which was music to the ears of a man like him. He would take much pleasure himself in retelling them to his regulars thereby ensuring good trade for some time to come. As he was a friend of both Angus and Dugald, I also mentioned the raid on the broch and of Mairi's abduction. I thought it best not to mention the helm.

"Leag." I begin, after what I thought was a reasonable amount of time. "Can you help me?" I ask.

"If I can. What do you need to know? There's little that goes on in these parts that I don't get to hear of. Do you need an audience with the queen? I can arrange that." He stops as he sees my hands raised up to quieten him in the kindest possible way.

"No, that's not necessary thanks, what I need to know is more about Callum Beg and Dumnhuill Dubh. Can you tell me of any connection and what they are both up to?" I whisper, anxious not to let any bystanders hear.

He falls silent for a moment and turns to Angus.

"Your young friend treads a dangerous path, and one which may not be that long if he is not more careful." He warns in a voice that is now both deeper, slower and more quiet.

"Fionn." He continues, "I'll tell you all I can, as you're a friend of Angus here, but I don't want to know the reasons." He pauses then carries on in a sombre tone. "Black Donald is into everything around here, he's even said to have spies in the palace. A while ago now he was even given the authority to run the city guard. This I believe was given to him because of pressure on the palace by Beg. There's no visible link between the two, no one has even seen them together. The only time he's ever on his own is when he goes hunting with his falcon, otherwise he's normally found with his cronies at the 'Selkie', an inn the other side of the river. Beg, on the other hand, is rarely seen outside the great hall of the Aes Dana. He used to make regular trips across to visit queen Irnan and her son, but nowadays they come to him."

"What do folk think of that?" I ask.

"Well there's still some that are loyal to the crown, probably the majority, but many are scared of the power that Beg now wields. Secretly they don't like what they see, but things could be a lot worse for them so they keep quiet. No one speaks out against him any more, they all know too many people that have simply disappeared. In the cases that I know of, the evidence definitely points to the 'Dubh', but there is nothing to tie them together. Besides there's no one around now who could stand up to them both. They can virtually get away with anything they want." He shrugs, with a gesture of despair.

"Has Domnhuill Dubh been away recently?" I probe him some more.

"Every now and again he disappears for a few days. He has a Broch on the North coast headland. I don't know anyone who's been up there, least ways returned to tell the tale. If he has your sister, she'll be there. Finding her is not the problem though, it'll be getting her safe return. You'll need to find something he wants more. You might then persuade him to make an exchange."

"Thanks. I don't suppose you know what they both might want or what their plans might be?" I ask tentatively.

"I have no idea what else the 'Dubn' wants, he appears to have anything and everything he wants. As for Beg, well my guess is as good as yours. However," He leans a little closer, "I can't imagine he'll be too happy handing over the control to the queen's son at the end of the year."

"Why does he have to do that?" I ask. Leag again looks at Angus who says.

"At the age of sixteen, he can take the crown as his father decreed.

Callum Beg must relinquish all power to him then as he promised he would on his father's death bed."

"When will that be exactly?" I enquire, my concern barely concealed and my voice rising.

"Shortly after Samhain, in the middle of Seed fall." Interrupts Leag, "It'll be a good time for me with all the festivals and celebrations." He smiles, rubbing his hands in a form of expectation.

"One last question, if I may?" I ask, "What is it that seems to give Callum Beg this control over people?"

"You haven't told him!" He turns to Angus sounding slightly incredulous.

"I have mentioned a little, but I've been away and have not really been convinced by the stories I'd heard." He replies, his right arm waving a mild gesture of dismissal.

"Be convinced dear friend. He has demons from the Otherworld as companions who are at his command to carry out his every whim. Ther's folk who've seen kin die the most gruesome of ways, limbs torn off one at a time and eaten while they watched and before they died. They say he now spends more than half his time the other side learning from the gods. His powers can make you turn and strike your best friend, he can make you see things that others can't. In short he is an extremely dangerous man. If indeed he can still be called a man." He looks around, worried that he might have been overheard.

Angus and I look at each other, both of us knew how stories could exaggerate the truth after time, we also knew of the ways of Ollamphs and how they wielded their considerable influence. However, it was not the warning that worried me, it was the extent to which it was believed by Leag. He seemed a sensible enough fellow, something must have occurred to affect him like this.

"Leag, you sound as though you have experienced or witnessed some of the things you say." I pause not wanting to cause Leag discomfort after his kind hospitality but still needing to know as much as possible. "Can we ask what was it?" I continue, trying to emphasise my genuine concern.

After a lengthy wait, whilst he appeared to be trying to remember something without the associated pain, he replied.

"Not long ago during the Cold Time, I had a dream. It was no ordinary dream as I felt that I was wide awake. I was visited in the dream by a demon. A demon of the most grotesque nature. I can even now smell the evil reeking off of his green slimy skin." He screws his face up as though to block it out still and then spits behind into a wooden bucket. "He commanded me to go to Callum Beg and to tell him everything he wanted to know. All the while this thing was sitting on my chest breathing into my face and prodding me in the neck with its long nails. I still had the marks next morning! Anyway I went along to the Aes Dana right away. They were even expecting me! I was questioned for hours about whether I knew where this person was. I couldn't answer though as I'd never heard of the man. After a few hours he let me go, the strange thing was that I couldn't remember the name of the person he had wanted to know. I don't even know what I told him. It was the worst experience of my life."

"That's very compelling indeed." Remarks Angus, "What do you think Fionn?"

"I believe him," I reply candidly, "I believe that is exactly what he saw and experienced, what it all means though, I am not sure."

"I think that's enough for tonight, its getting late." Sighs Angus rising off his chair. "You'll need a good sleep tonight, we'll talk again tomorrow before you set out. I'm going to stay up a little longer with Leag as there is still something I want to go over with him."

Leag and I both rise and he takes me up some wooden steps in the corner to a room above. "There are furs and bundles of woven cloth over in the corner, you're welcome to use what you wish. Sleep well my friend."

"Thanks." I reply slightly nervously, my mind not having yet forgotten his visiting demon.

I settled down and checked my belongings in the light of a flickering candle that he had given me. Handling them again brought back memories of my family and of the life I had left on the Island. Pangs of yearning and anxiety welled up inside me again. I lay back experiencing all sorts of emotions as I ran through the events of the day in my mind, sorting them into areas for future recall. What was difficult to sort, or to even assimilate, was the variety of feelings. They had been both exhilarating and scary all throughout the day. Controlling my fears, accepting them and overcoming them was now very necessary if I was to accomplish the task now at hand.

It was on that task that I now focused my thoughts. How was I going to proceed next without failing dismally and being found headless in some ditch? Or even found at all?

I woke the next morning with chinks of light streaming through the upright wooden planks that walled the room. There were several others staying and they lay all about the place, some were snoring, some were already getting up. Angus was not among them. I collected my things and carefully stepped between the bodies as I made my way to the steps.

Below, I found Angus and Leag talking over a bowl of porridge. I joined them and we chatted and relaxed whilst exchanging views on the weather. After eating Angus turned to me.

"Fionn, I'm going to suggest that we part company this morning, I'll find you if I've anything to tell you. I think it may be best not to be seen together for reasons I'm sure you can guess at." He stops to check my reaction.

"Fine, I understand," I say, "It's a good idea." I reply, not really sounding convinced as he had been very helpful to me.

"Before you head off this morning there are one or two pieces of advice I'd like to give you. They may come in useful later on in your test. They attach a great deal of importance to the rituals surrounding the sacred groves. Remember them well. They'll also concentrate on the grammar. Your knowledge of Oghams seemed sound, but if you like we can run through the secret language of the poets. Would you like me to go through one or two of these things?"

"I'd really appreciate it, Angus. Thanks." I reply gratefully.

We talked till mid morning, then I rose, thanked him again and left. I made my way toward the bridge, through the crowds of traders. People everywhere seemed to be tugging at my clothes and trying to catch my attention. I was offered vegetables, fruit, some of which I'd never seen before and all sorts of live animals. Even on the open sided bridge, business was being done from off of the passing carts. I managed to squeeze by, nearly falling off the edge in the process, and headed for the large building directly in front of the bridge the other side.

I stood outside and looked at the giant doors. I'd imagined this moment thousands of times, how it might look, feel and what my thoughts would be. I took the chance to match the reality with my dreams and then knocked. The door opened just wide enough to leave a gap to look through and a stern voice from inside spoke.

"Who calls on the Aes Dana?"

"My name is Fionn mac Donal of the Clan Donal from the Isle of Siegg. I seek an audience with the members of the inner Council." I reply cordially and politely, but inside I begin to feel smaller in the face of such imposing administration. I immediately banished the weak thought and listened more intently.

"For what reason do you call?" The voice asked again with the same strict tone that I now guessed was supposed to intimidate on purpose.

"I wish to become an Anruth and to practice my art throughout the land." I give the formal response I'd been told to.

"And why would that be?" Came the third question, and one designed to be off putting.

"I wish to share a great gift and give pleasure to all." I reply with an intentional forcefulness that came easily due to the practice I had put in.

"Well said, Fionn mac Donal of the clan Donal. Wait here." Comes an honest sounding reply.

I am ushered in and told to stand just inside the closed door. The oldish figure of a man, dressed in long dark robes, then hobbled off through another door to the right. I took the chance to look around the room, it was small and dark and the walls were covered in a dark red cloth with a pattern that was indiscernible in the little light that there was. I stood waiting patiently, wondering if this, in its own way, was the beginning of the test.

After what seemed an eternity, he returned.

"Please follow me." He now says tonelessly.

I did so dutifully and was led into another antechamber. This time there were candles and torches on the wall and seated under the light were three Ollamphs. All were easily distinguished by their tuigens, their cloaks of feathers, and their personal gold branches complete with tiny bells. These they rested on a large oak table in front of them. With no seats for me, I was left to stand in front of the two women and one man. The woman in the centre spoke first.

"This is a surprise indeed, Fionn mac Donal of the clan Donal." She says in a deliberately slow, high-pitched, rasping, bird-like voice. "We were not aware of any schools on the isle of Siegg. With whom, may we ask, did you study?"

The question had ended on an even stricter note and showed more than a hint of curiosity. I knew I had begun to gain a little control. The trick now was not to let them feel that or know that I had noticed it.

"I had the good fortune to study with a master seannachie, a man whose skills go unmatched. He goes by the name of Dugald mac Pheig of no set clan." I stop to watch what reaction there might be.

"Dugald mac Pheig, you say." She answers, again in the same high-pitched tone.

She was good, there was no sign of surprise in her voice, nor also any sign of being impressed or unimpressed.

"It was our understanding that the person you talk of has been dead these years. Dugald was indeed someone we all knew well, tell us does he still wear the mark of the Grebe?"

It was like I had just been punched in the stomach, a question designed to throw me off guard and gain back control, a lesser trained student would have flinched and possibly stuttered the next few words. However, I had been prepared well and instantly knew it as a trick question for which she was undoubtedly listening to the way I would respond as well as the answer itself. Dugald had never worn his Tuigen, it had been left behind in his haste to leave the very place I was now standing. I had no idea of its feathers, rosettes or their origin. I did know, though, that Dugald had the fox as his totem.

"At stay-home time the grebes are forced into hiding by the hungry fox." I say calmly and deliberately, resisting the urge to curl my lips. The double meaning behind my words was designed to win back some standing in front of the other two Ollamphs who had, up to now, remained silent. The woman in the centre did no more than raise an eyebrow to my riposte as if she had suddenly allowed herself some personal curiosity as to my presence here.

"Fionn." Starts the eldest of them all. He wore the feathers of a swan, edged with those of a mallard. Although he didn't seem to be in charge here, he was clearly acknowledged by the others as the most senior. "How did you come to meet with Dugald?"

"It was both his misfortune and my fortune that his boat was blown near to the rocks at Donal Broch. His currach was damaged and he was unable to continue his journey, so we gave him shelter and in return he stayed and repaid his debt by way of training me." I reply.

"How can you expect to become Anruth, by sharing the experiences of only one other?" The other woman immediately asks. "Surely in order to be able to present to us an all round knowledge, it would be better to have had a variety of teachings."

"I stand before you ready to receive whatever tests you wish to give me and prepared to willingly accept any judgement you make at the end. I wish to become Anruth no matter how long it takes or when it will be." I answer mixing pride and humility as best as I thought was prudently possible.

"Well said, young Fionn." States the male Ollamph, who then looks round for support amongst his two colleagues. They look briefly at one another and then turn back to me.

"Tomorrow, mid morning, be here and ready or be gone." Says the Ollamph in the centre. "Now, would you like me to show you the great hall before you go?" Her voice changes instantly to one of charm and friendliness and I feel her sincerity and smile.

"Aye I'd like that. Thanks." I answer honestly.

She rose and took up her large golden branch. It had several smaller branches leading off of it and each had a small fingernail sized silver bell on at the twig end. They all jingled in unison and continued to do so as she walked past me and beckoned for me to follow.

I walked behind her, through yet another door on the sidewall and came out into a huge, roughly circular room. The roof was held up by great pillars of stone set in a circle near the middle and a dry stonewall around the sides. Huge oak timbers were supported on top of these and these in turn were covered in reeds. In the centre of the roof, inside the stone circle, there was a large round opening that allowed the light, and any other of the elements, to come in. The floor was made up of large slabs of flat stone, patterns of cobbles and dried earth. A gouged out drain ran from the centre to the edge. What caught my eye first though, was a colossal altar of rock. It lay dead center in the whole arena right under the gap in the roof. Its hand smoothed surface inclined toward one end, whilst the other waist high. If you stood on top of it, you still couldn't reach the thatch above with a spear.

There was no one about except the two of us and she took hold of my elbow and walked beside me over to the centre.

"This has been here for hundreds of years Fionn." She slowly rubs the altar with the back of her fingers then looks straight up into my eyes. "In the days when sacrificial rites were practiced, thousands were slaughtered on this very slab. Nowadays we use it to mark the changing seasons, holding ceremonies under the sun and the stars." She pauses briefly and turns to me. "And also for young aspiring Anruth's." Her face flickers into a quick smile. "I am sure Dugald will have told you how the test is done. This is where you will show us your gift and talents, standing on the altar stone."

Her smile returns more fully, followed by an inquiring look.

"Let's hope the weather holds good," I say looking up at the sky, copying her expression.

We walk on and around in silence. I wanted to familiarise myself with the surroundings in order to better mentally prepare myself for my coming task. I needed to have an accurate picture in my mind of how I would look and feel and sound whilst telling my stories and giving my answers. If I could accomplish this mental preparation sufficiently well, then I could draw upon it as experience when the actual time came. It would be as though it wasn't really the first time and therefore hopefully sound better for those listening.

We stopped at another large door that opened into the original chamber in which I had first waited. She stayed back and left me to be ushered out by the same old man. I turned around, but she had disappeared. The old man grunted lightly at my surprise and went to open the main door.

It was late morning and there was no sign of any decreased activity outside. People were still jostling about carrying their wares. I hardly noticed them though as I was still congratulating myself at having successfully overcome my first task. I started off in no particular direction, wandering as my fancy took me, my happiness gradually being overcome by the immediacy of my other problems, not least the whereabouts of my sister.

It wasn't long before I found myself right in front of an inn. I looked up at the sign to see a picture of a beautiful fish-like maiden, a selkie. A selkie I knew well to be a creature that was not all that it appeared to be. A seal most of the time, except when it decided to come ashore in search of young men. It would then take on the appearance of a lovely maiden in order to unwittingly seduce them back to its lair.

I stood outside wondering what it too might be hiding. A quick glance inside showed it to be empty, so I left deciding to take the bull by the horns, or the selkie by its fins, that very evening. That overall impression was enough to shake me finally out of my reverie and now with a more determined stride, I set out back toward the market. I decided to start there by questioning the sailors about the currachs that had come and gone over the last ten days.

I reached the docks after much pushing and shoving. The area was full of traders and goods being laden onto and off the currachs. As the main port on the East coast, many vessels were heading South to the lowlands and a few would even be travelling further across the waters. Wondering where to start, I spied Ruadh standing on the bows of his boat sorting out his lines.

"Hi!" I call out as I get closer to him, "How are you?"

He eventually sees me standing on the pier amidst the crowd and I notice some look of surprise on his face.

"Can I come on board?" I ask tentatively.

"Sure you can, if you mind where you put your feet." He replies, with a grin.

I climb on board, remembering the first time I had done so.

"What happened to you in Drummorchy?" He asks, with genuine interest. "I waited as long as I could with the tides beginning to turn."

"I'm sorry if I held you up or inconvenienced you Ruadh. I can nay explain to you what my reasons were for not joining you. I just had a gut feeling to travel on foot. It was not that I did nay care to sail with you again." I offer as a reply, not intending to offend the man.

"It's not me you inconvenienced lad, but you sure as did upset Fiacal. He said he'd go and fetch you, but even he didn't return in time. He must be fuming still." He mutters the last few words and shakes his head as though trying to warn me.

So Fiacal had been following me, my senses were right. I would have to watch out for him, he might well lead me to what I needed to know. Somehow it didn't seem as easy as it sounded.

"Ruadh, I'm trying to find the whereabouts of my sister. Do you know who around here would have been sailing the islands, these last few days?" I ask hopefully, not really sure how else I could ask such a question when it could lead to both a delicate and dangerous response.

"It's a brave man that asks questions around here, I'd be very careful who you talk to. As I know a little of you though, I'll tell you this. There are only five people that know these shores well enough to take a craft safely through the islands, and only four currach's. Two are down South right now, the third's mine and the fourth belongs to Domnhuil Dubh."

"Thanks," I say, "Who are the skippers that know the waters that have been around recently?"

"Recently." He stops to consider, scratching the back of his head, "Well there's myself, Connor and Eber."

"Where could I find them?" I ask, beginning to feel awkward for putting yet another question to him.

"Connor's over there." He nods in a direction over my shoulder, "As for Eber, your best chance is in the evening at the Selkie."

"Thanks," I say, turning to leave, "I'll buy you a drink tonight at the

Bridge for your time."

"That'd be grand but I'll be off before then, another time." He chuckles at my offer and returns to his ropes.

I was just about to disembark, when another thought struck me and I turned back to him.

"If I was in a hurry and wanted to keep things secret, is there anywhere else along these shores I could land a boat that size?"

"None that I know of." He calls back.

I clambered back onto the harbour, still chewing his words over in my mind. My eyes though were soon distracted by the variety of produce on the stalls, in particular one stall that had every type of herb I had ever seen and then some.

"Tonics, Elixirs, Balms, Cure Alls. I've got the lot." Comes the cry of a wizened vendor, "Come closer sir," he calls to me, "let me show you something special, a stolen recipe from the yearlong fights. It'll give you and your partner intense pleasure for many nights. Or perhaps it's something a little more sinister you are searching after?" He says more quietly, "I can supply you with anything you care to name that will either make someone sad or bring them joy and laughter."

"I have no need for these things," I reply, "I confess to just being mildly curious for I've kept bees myself and I'm used to stings." I answer him mimicking his rhyming banter whilst adding a cautionary note.

"No need! Indeed! In deed, know need!" He continues gleefully having now attracted my attention.

"Steal a closer look my friend, there's much a man like you could choose to use. What course in life do you follow, for what e're it is, I can send you forth fitter for it on the 'morrow." He follows me as I walk past, holding out various ointments and balms for me to see and smell.

This was clearly no ordinary man and he had truly managed to grab my interest. I decided to pursue the coincidence further.

"Tomorrow, I shall become an Anruth. Tell me how can you help and be sure to make it the truth?" I continue in his own choice and style.

He looks at me and his smile fades into seriousness and then quickly back to joy as he searches through his belongings in a large hessian sack and finds what he is looking for.

"This, my travelling teller of tales, will soothe your throat in times of toil." He holds up a small phial of greenish liquid and waves it before my eyes. "Take it twice to ease your troubles. T'is one bar, bar none to buy this prize. How says you poet are you for it?" He stops and stares into my eyes in silence.

"I've no need at a price like that, my voice works well and that is that." I reply, not really liking my last line.

"Don't decide too soon, like an ignorant buffoon. I'll add in this... to seal our tryst." He produces a leather purse with a drawstring. Undoing it, he tips onto his hand a white powdery substance." Sprinkle this in the drinks of those who would see you dead, and their world will begin to appear all yellow and green, blue and red." He dances around while speaking his last words and for a frail old man he is surprisingly nimble on his feet. I wasn't really sure what he meant by that, but I had the feeling that I was meant to make this purchase.

I took out my own bag, carefully concealed under my skin jacket, and paid the man a small bar of iron. Our exchanges made, I was on my way and he scurried back to behind his stall.

I looked around the other stalls on the side of the docks and in the square in front of the Bridge. There was no one that looked as interesting, nor any that might have been able to help. Those that I had summoned up the courage to ask had ignored me and returned to their business. I had, however, managed to learn from Connor that no one fitting Mairi's description had come into port in the days in question. This either meant that she hadn't been brought ashore here or that they had somehow managed to do so without anyone noticing. I suspected that the latter would have been too risky.

I was extremely tired and hungry by the end of the afternoon, so I returned to the inn. Leag made me a cup of hot water scented with chamomile and spearmint leaves and set about preparing a meal of wild boar roasted on a spit over a birch and bog-myrtle fire. It was the on menu for his regulars that night and by the time it was ready, my appetite was raging with all the aromas coming from it.

By the time I had finished feasting, amidst the interruptions of questions from Leag about Dugald, it was well past early evening and now time to go to the Selkie inn.

Travelling around outside at night in the dark was definitely not for the fainthearted. There were more shadows than light. The only light that there was escaped from around the cracks around the entrances to the houses. It was also a cloudy night with a light drizzle, so there was no night sky either. I fumbled my way back over the river, past the Aes Dana and on towards the Selkie. Outside I could hear the sounds of a drunken crowd. I went over my plan again. My first approach would be to ask for Eber. I'd made up a story as to my reasons for looking for him, whatever happened after that I'd have to play by ear. It didn't seem much of plan now I was standing outside. I took a deep breath and firmly grasped the door handle and stepped inside in a manner as determined as was possible under the circumstances.

Such was the state of those inside, I wasn't noticed until I'd reached the bar. Even then, it was only after several loud calls that I managed to attract the attention of the barman.

"Get me a jug of ale, you earless excuse for an innkeeper." I demand, putting on the air of what I thought would be a typical customer of his.

He looks at me coolly and I eyeball him right back. After a moment of mind searching by the both of us, his face broadens into a toothy grin. His looks were certainly not his strong point, indeed it was probably difficult to tell what that might have been. He returned with a tankard frothing at the brim. I took a long swig and turned around resting my elbow on the bar. The room was roughly triangular in a rounded sort of way with two other exits, one behind the bar and the other on the third side. It was filled with wooden tables and chairs, all of which were taken. There was sparse decoration about the place, probably because of the fights and potential breakage's, but still it retained a warm sort of atmosphere.

The exit to the other room was nothing more than an archway. Standing in the middle of it, overlooking both rooms was a huge giant of a man, a good head and a half higher than myself. I presumed that this other room was for more private functions and preferred regulars. His job was probably to see that the wrong people didn't pass by him. I had my first problem.

I tried moving about the room in order to look past the man mountain, it was busy and definitely the place to be. There was live entertainment, in the form of dancers and players, and waitress service. I resolved to try my luck and walked up to the human door.

"I've come to see Eber." I state loudly looking upwards.

"He's not here." The reply booms over my head, "If you're not asked to enter, you drink out there!" He continues, not condescending to look at me.

"I don't think you heard me correctly," I go on slightly softer and almost silently.

"What did you say?" He booms above the noise going on behind him.

"I said you didn't hear me correctly," I shout out, directing my voice in the direction of his left ear. He winces at the sudden pain in his head. "I didn't ask for your permission to enter." I continue. At this he visibly relaxes, "I asked to see Eber. Do you know where I can find him?" I now say as politely as was possible yet still loud enough to be heard.

"He'll be in later on." He answers steadfastly before turning to ignore me.

With little choice for the moment, I waited leaning against the wall. Half way through my drink, the door opened and the epitome of a seafaring man entered and made his way straight toward the inner sanctum. I headed him off before he got there.

"Eber!" I interrupt his thoughts in a way that sounds as though he is an old friend of mine.

"Who wants to know?" Comes the surprised, yet non-committal response.

"I was given your name by a local fisherman. He says you're the best around these parts for a special trip to the Islands."

"Could be. What's the destination?" He visibly warmed to the obvious flattery as people are so very oft to do.

"Bestol." I say, trying to sound as furtive as I can by leaning in toward him as I mention the name.

"You can't land there and there's nothing but rock. Why would anyone want to go there?" Confusion and curiosity now becoming apparent in his voice.

"That I can nay tell you right now, but it needs a big vessel and a skipper with a cool head. I know of a secret place there that we can land as long as the skipper can get through the reefs. Could you do it?"

"Possibly, if the price was right." He asks, now almost fully hooked.

"Let's talk over drink," I say. "After you." I add, pointing past the Athack look-alike and smiling up at him.

We were let in and I followed him over to what appeared to be his usual table where we were served instantly by a young girl, dressed like the rest of the dancers in a short red and green plaid wrap. I smiled at her and asked for two of the local ales. As she disappeared, I took a casual look around at each person seated around the room. I recognised no one, but it wouldn't have been difficult not to identify Domnhuill Dubh. He sat at the table nearest the dancers with two of his men either side of him. Dressed in a black skin jacket and trousers, a thick gold torque around his neck and heavy silver armbraces and bracelets, he was obviously also a man of substantial wealth. I watched as he pulled his hands back across his long black, over dyed, hair and arranged his ponytail. My blood began to race as I scrutinized his face. There were signs of recent scars. I took a little pleasure in thinking that they may well have been caused by my father.

"So you know the 'Dubh'," Eber guesses as he sees me looking.

"By reputation only." I answer, trying to come across as none too interested as I can. "This is the first time I've seen him. I've just come up from Drummorchy yesterday." I manage to continue with as calm a voice as I can muster. Inside I was seething with anger.

"When would you want to go?" He switches back to business.

The drinks arrive, another of the dancers doubling as a waitress, carefully places them on our table. I thank her in a kind tone that is returned with sincere smile. She was obviously used to far less courtesy.

"In ten days time. The problem though is not when, nor is it why, it's more one of if you can help."

"What do you mean?" He says quickly. I can sense this was taken personally, but it needed to be done in order to gain his full commitment and to extract the information I needed.

"My problem," I go on, "is not getting there and picking up the particular cargo, so much as getting it back without anyone knowing about it. I would need somewhere equally secret, if you know what I mean. I'm not even sure such a place exists. I can't take it straight into Drummorchy and there's nowhere nearer that would be safe."

"Such a place may exist." He hints. "But it would be as equally dangerous as your place in Bestol. Either way makes this expensive." A gleam in his eye appears at his last words. He rests his head in the palm of his hand and his elbow on the table and looks at me in an inquiring way.

"What would your price be?" I say, pleased at learning of the possibility of secret landing place near here.

"Three gold bars." He replies quickly, trying to make the price sound believable by keeping still and not changing the direction of his gaze.

"Three," I feign surprise, "The cargo itself is not worth that, let alone the profit in it." I add.

"If it's that important to you, you'll find a way." He replies stubbornly.

"Make it two and you've a deal." I offer holding out my hand.

He looks at it, and then takes it and begins to shake with a business like firmness. "I need to check a few things first, if all's fine, I'll agree to two gold one silver and five iron."

"Two gold, one silver and no iron," I reply, feeling his grip strengthen around my fingers.

"Done." He smiles, and we let go our grasps.

At that moment a shriek, followed by a slap, caused all of us in the room to look up. The waitress that had served us was being jostled around and man-handled by one of Domnhuill Dubh's men, the other two were laughing at her attempts to break free. Needing no further excuse and acting on gut feeling, I rose out of my chair and went over.

"Take your hands off of her." I call out sternly. The stunned amazement on his face at my interference distracts him and the girl struggles free.

"By the blood of wounded bull, who dares to address me so." The man demands, still sat down but now giving me a piercing look that tried to kill me on its own.

"No, No!" Cries the girl. "Don't Gruach. He doesn't know." Interrupts the girl who is trying to now keep between us. As he struggles to get up, she puts a hand on his shoulder to try to stop him.

"Get off wench!" He shouts trying to rise but obviously also the worse for wear for drinking.

"I am sorry my lady if I have offended you and your friend," I say, "I was under the impression that you needed some help. If you change your mind, I would gladly bury him under the bull he so eloquently talks of." This, as I intend, incenses the man further. Apoplectic with rage, his face reddens, his eyes bulge and he manages to stagger to his feet.

"Sit down, Gruach." Orders Domnhuill. "Won't you join us, my bold young man, I'd like to know more of the likes of a man who would approach us in such a manner." He reels the words out, like a person used to control and being obeyed. This was no light request.

"My thanks and a thousand pardons if I have offended you. I am used to seeing women treated with much more care. You get far further that way, would you not agree?" I try sounding him out.

"You're new around here." He purposely ignores my words, "Where are you from?"

"He's just in from Drummorchy." Says Eber, now behind me. "He's after my services to pick up some cargo on Bestol."

"Bestol, you say. There's little of value on that accursed rock. What's you're game?" Barks Domnhuill, his face beginning to sneer as he stares down at the table in front of him. He toys with a dirk on it, spinning it around in circles, thinking about Eber's explanation and waiting for me to reply.

I stare ahead at the angry oaf who has now sat down again. Looking straight into his eyes, I lower my voice and utter, "If your friend doesn't calm down, I'll twist his arms around his back and tie them to his feet." On hearing this, Gruach visibly winces and I can see his the veins in his temples beginning to throb.

"There'll be no need, he does as I say." Replies Domnhuill. "Now tell us what's your business?" Impatience now straining inside him.

"I'm looking for someone?" I find I enjoy seeing the anger rise up within and hope that it might make him drop his guard and say something he'd normally not.

"Who?" He continues, now fully irked. Everyone is now looking at me. Eber and the girl are still standing and the three others are seated. I look around at each of them studying them carefully for their possible strengths and weaknesses. I turn to the girl.

"Are you with these men in some way?" It was a carefully designed question. I needed to take control away from the 'Dubh' and, at the same time, buy myself some time to think how next to handle the situation. She looks at me with disbelief, but also, I would wager, a little admiration. Then she looks over to Domnhuill for some approval, he nods back at her.

"In a way yes, I am. The 'Dubh' has been good to me, he treats me well and took me in after my folks were murdered." She stops, obviously unsure if she had said too much.

"I ask because I am looking for a girl, not unlike yourself, " I pause, deciding to proceed boldly, "recently my sister was taken, I have reason to believe she may have been brought here to Invercarrie first, possibly then to Bestol." I add. "Her name is Mairi. "This has the desired effect and I notice Domnhuill sit up a touch. Before he could speak though, we are all interrupted by an angry voice coming from someone entering the room at pace.

"I've looked all over, and if he is here, I can't find him." Shouts the man who has just walked in. He stops in front of the table. We all look up and I turn around to face him. It was Fiacal.

"That's him!" He cries out, pointing at me. I force a smile.

"It's good to see you again." I start, "I am exceptionally sorry you missed your boat journey on account of me." I say, hoping to distract him in order to get to my feet. A hand on my shoulder forces me back down.

"You were looking for me, now why was that?" I ask, trying to feign innocence, but fast realising things had got out of hand.

"If you are who we think you are, you're either very brave or very stupid." Says Domnhuill with a deep, scowling voice barely louder than a whisper.

"My name is Fionn mac Donal of the clan Donal," I utter with closed teeth, "I was told that you might know of the whereabouts of my sister. Have you a problem, with my asking you that?"

"Are you asking or accusing?" He sneers back at me.

"Only the scum off a sow's belly would run away from an old man with the odds of three to one. Cowards and curs are names too good for men who would stoop to having to abduct their women. Obviously they're too ugly to get them to come willingly." I finish my tirade, casting an accusing eye solely at Gruach who finds it too much to bear.

He jumps to his feet and the table and drinks go flying. With arms flailing, Eber and the girl are knocked aside in his attempt to get to me. It was what I was waiting for and intended.

"You need to be sent back to cleaning cattle pens, where you belong, you clumsy excuse for peasant." I exclaim loudly, rising and stepping backwards to move the chair out of the way. I notice Fiacal stepping toward me and I turn to face him as well.

"Let Gruach have his fun, Fiacal." Commands Domnhuill.

The large, muscled bulk throws a punch to my belly. I slide forwards and to his side, grab onto his arm and help it on its way and then yank it sharply downwards. With the extra momentum he continues out of control onto the top of the nearby table. It too gets sent flying and with it Gruach sprawls to the floor.

He picks himself up and, returning to his former ire, launches himself at me again. This time he reaches with both hands for my neck. I grab one and twist around so my back faces him. I then drop to one knee whilst casting him forward and over my head. This time he falls badly, his landing broken poorly by the unfortunate position of a sturdy chair.

I look around at the others. Fiacal is itching to join in and is already fingering his dirk. Gruach rises up, more slowly this time but not from thought or care, rather on account of his now damaged left leg. Again he lurches at me, desperation and shame etched on his face. This time a simple strike to his face causes him to defend his eyes with a hand. It is his mistake because he misses seeing my knee rising into his abdomen. He drops like a stone, clutching his chest and gasping for breath.

I turn back to the others. The 'Dubn' is on his feet.

He was not a large man, but what he lacked in size he made up with his presence. His whole persona exuded confidence mixed with evil and malice and he wasn't smiling. By now everyone in the pub had stopped what they were doing and were crowded round to watch. Surrounded on all sides, I began to think I had seriously misjudged things. They all grabbed me at once, there was little point in defending, if I took my almost definite beating with honour, they just might not kill me. I took one more chance.

"I have a meeting with Callum Beg in the morning, I'd hate to upset him by not turning up." I chance.

I notice a momentary hesitation on Domnhuill's face. He must have somehow known about my visit there that morning. To anyone else and coming from anyone else, it would not have been believable or even important enough to sway any decision.

He decided not to speak and instead drove a full on punch to my gut. Even tensing my muscles it hurt and doubled me up. I catch him holding his wrist out of the corner of my eye. I was right, it had hurt him too, but it had only succeeded in making him decide to kick me instead. A poorly aimed foot struck me on the side of my bottom and I just managed to pivot around in time. I sank to one knee. He bent down, grabbed my hair, pulled back my head and whispered in my ear.

"If you are not out of Invercarrie by tomorrow afternoon, on some corricle back to where you came, I'll find you and you'll be dead as soon as we step outside the city walls. Do I make myself clear Fionn mac Donal of the clan Donal." His low and threatening voice steels into silence, only broken by the noise of a spit hitting me on my neck.

I managed a nod and was then chucked unceremoniously outside onto the dirty wet slush. Waiting till I was left alone and after they had returned inside, I picked myself up. My wet and dirty clothes stuck to me and I immediately started to shiver. Whether it was just the cold or the near escape that I had, I couldn't tell, either way I slowly made my way back to the Bridge Inn. I mulled over the things I had learned from the encounter, all in all it had been worth the pain even though I'd probably come close to going missing myself.

I went upstairs, first checking to see if Angus had been in. He hadn't, so I decided to get some sleep. As I lay down, I pondered the ordeal I would have to endure in front of the inner council of the Aes Dana tomorrow. I wondered how the other initiates might have spent their last night's preparation, certainly none like I had. Still, I was exhausted and would probably sleep better than they had.

I was right, I awoke feeling better than I had felt for many of the previous mornings. My hip still ached from the night before, but I was alive. After a breakfast of oatmeal, I set out.

I was led into the great hall where nine Ollamphs each greeted me in person. Many asked after Dugald and several wished me luck. Callum Beg was not among them. I was surprised at how disappointed I was about that, until the lady that had seen me the day before, came up to me to say that if I passed this initial phase, I would be interviewed in person by the Ard Ollamph. I was asked questions on every subject and then even on some I didn't know. My knowledge of grammar was tested to its limits, as was the rituals at the sacred groves. Each time, I acquitted myself sufficiently well to proceed to the next part. The last exam was the telling of a story of my own choice in its entirety. I had decided to recount some of the more awesome events that Cuchulainn, the champion warrior, had encountered in his life. I started from the point he had decided to become a warrior and had gone to train with the warrior-princess Scathac in the land of shadows. I went on to include his epic journey across the great sea to the Otherworld in his serpent headed currach. I told of the time he spent there as a king, with his regal tuigen made up of such strange plumes, to the many people who were so different to himself. I concluded with his return and of the many beautiful objects he brought back. Some of these had now been lost forever; others were still with us and used in current ceremonies.

It was received well and at the end it felt as if even nature was on my side as the sun went behind the clouds as I finished speaking. It added to the effect in the great hall as it coincided with me telling of the hero's death. It was a good omen and unanimously they agreed that Dugald had taught me well.

I was asked to wait as they filed out into one of the rooms on the side. What seemed like a year later, they returned to invite me to go on to have an audience with Callum Beg. Again I was asked to wait.

This time I was led through to an ante-chamber and told that Callum Beg would call for me when he was ready.

I sat down on a stool that had been placed centrally and faced a wall covered in dark brown drapes. On them were embroidered pictures of stars, demons and animals of all shapes and sizes. A solitary, thick candle lit up each corner of the room. Feeling slightly disoriented, I got up and paced around. Dugald had warned me that the Ard Ollamph might want to meet with me alone, if I passed the first part of the audition. If that were the case, it was anyone's guess what might happen. It was probably filled with ritual. I readied myself as best I could for whatever might come.

After only a few moments the door opened and the smallish figure of a man entered. His gaunt face was partially hidden by his long, slightly greyish, brown hair. It hung straight down around his face and shoulders and from the side all you could see was his bent and crooked nose. He was wearing the full regalia of an Ard Ollamph complete with full-length golden branch studded with jewels and gold and silver bells. As he walked over he shook it gently and the most beautiful sounds came from the rings and chimes.

"Congratulations Fionn." His voice was warm and welcoming. "Only a few reach as far as you have today, you must be feeling happy and pleased."

He reached me and with a frail wiry hand he leant forward to touch my shoulder. "Can you come with me? That's good." He continues as I rise. "Come along into my room. Will you carry this with you?" He points to the large candlestand I had been looking at earlier."

"Of course." I say, picking it up and bringing it into his room. I take a moment to look around. It wasn't decorated ornately, the walls were now covered in black drapes and against the far wall there was a long bench with a large number of strange looking objects set in no particular order. What was perhaps a little strange was the number of lit candles that were all around the room. They were on the walls, hanging suspended from the ceiling and also on stands. Because of them, the room was exceptionally bright. What he wanted another one for, left me curious for I had no idea. There were also two wooden chairs, each with soft cushions, one at the side by the bench; the other in the centre.

"I would like you to take a seat as I talk to you." He beckons with his hand for me to sit down. "I am going to talk to you about a lot of things, it won't be about any more tests, that is not what you want." His voice seems kind and I begin to wonder whether this can be the same man that everyone has talked to me about.

He takes the candlestand from me and lights the candle whilst keeping his back to me. "Can you sit down and place your hands on your lap."

I do so, wondering what was coming next. In my awareness, I sense his enormous presence, a huge charisma emanating from his body and with it there were no signs of animosity or hatred, just interest.

"You must be very tired from your ordeal, let me get you something that will help you relax." He says soothingly. I have to admit that this was not what I expected, nevertheless I am grateful and say, "That would be nice, thank you."

He turns to go over to the corner and in doing so knocks one of the suspended candles a little, it begins to sway slowly from side to side. I watch it and become aware of a deep chanting sound coming from another of the rooms. I listen to it and try to guess what ceremony is being performed. He returns with a bowl of water that has some herbs sprinkled on the top. I knew most herbs and could recognise the chamomile, but not the others. He brings it to his lips and takes a sip. "Hmmm. Lovely just right. Try this Fionn. Smell the water first, it will make you relax more."

I reach forward and the smell wafts up and hits me. It has a wonderful heady aroma of the type that invites those even with no thirst. I take a small sip first, then a large gulp. I hadn't realised how dry my throat had become after all that talking.

"As I talk, and I can do so comfortably, I wish that you will listen to me comfortably as I talk to you about a bird." My curiosity perks up even more.

"Close your eyes and imagine you are a bird flying high over the glens." He goes on in a melodic way.

"Picture in your mind the things you can see, the fields and crofts, the feelings, the sounds of the wind currents and the other birds in the air... Listen to me and you will feel better... you are flying high now, high above the clouds.... Listen to me and wonder what you can learn...

I know that you are wondering whether to fly higher or lower and I wonder whether you are aware of a strange sensation."

I strain with all my senses to seek it out and begin to smell the perfumed water again. Its familiarity was warming.

"Imagine that you are now flying down, sinking lower and lower towards the ground. The lower you go the more relaxed you become... As you sit there, listening to the sound of my voice, you will relax more and more... As you fly lower you are heading for a beautiful warm light... As you open your eyes you will see a light."

I open my eyes to see the swaying candle. "Staring at the candle," he goes on, "will make your eyes tired, smelling the water will make you relax."

I was indeed extremely relaxed and fully aware of everything he was saying to me.

"How soon will you realise that you are sitting here comfortably, listening to the sound of my voice and you are becoming tired and sleepy and relaxed as quickly or as slowly as your mind wants you to... As you close your eyes again, you will feel relaxed and happy to go to sleep."

I feel like I am asleep, yet I can hear every word he says.

"You can hear every word that I say and you are happy to talk to me about a lot of things. You will remember all that I tell you when you wake up... and... whenever you want to enter my room again you will go into this same relaxing sleep. Now that you are here and have passed and become an Anruth, what are you going to do and how can I help you?"

I feel compelled to answer. I want to answer him because he has helped me. I have passed.

"I am looking for my sister Mairi." I say.

"Anything else?" He goes on calmly.

"I am going North to meet a man named Lugh." I say, not sure if I should have said it. The effect of the words though, is enough to make Callum Beg cough. It checks me slightly.

"Do you know where he is?" The question comes and I am both trying and trying not to answer it. It is then I realise that something is not quite right and I remember to start to recite mentally the lorica Angus told me.

"Do you know where he is?" The question comes again. I continue concentrating on the lorica.

"Fionn." He starts again. "You are awake, you do not remember the things that I have asked or said."

It was a statement but I answered.

"No." And I am sure he is right about something.

"Congratulations, young Fionn. You have passed your final ritual." His words seem clipped and were delivered quickly, this time there was no feeling behind them. He disappears behind one of the black drapes and comes out with a new tuigen. Follow me. I get up slightly disorientated with things and wondering about the ritual he had referred to.

We go out of his room and back into the great hall. This time all of the Ollamphs are standing up and in a semicircle. We pass each in turn and all of them praise me individually. My mind is spinning at the pace of it all. The next moment, I am at the altar stone and they are helping me on with the tuigen. It is made from the feathers and skin of swans and ducks. The neck down to just below the shoulder was made from the blue of the mallard and below that, the white of the swan. As they all gathered around me, they shook their branches, happy that another was joining their order.

Whilst the tiny bells rung out, Callum Beg approached and presented me with a branch with little silver bells, the insignia of my new rank. Joy and satisfaction coursed through me and I wished that my family and friends, in particular Dugald, could have been here to see me.

As the applause continued, I turned and took out the blue and orange feathers and arranged them into a small rosette. Then with a little care, I inserted them into the white section at chest level. I would sew them on more securely later. As I turned around in front of them again, I heard one or two gasps. I had to admit that it was a good feeling.

After many further conversations with each and all of them, although not with Callum Beg, who seemed to have disappeared, it was time to leave. I had wanted to speak some more with the Ard Ollamph, as something at the back of my mind was troubling me. But it was now late afternoon and I hadn't eaten, so I made my way back to the Bridge Inn, very aware of the looks and wide passage I was getting from the passers by. As soon as I entered the inn, I sensed something wasn't quite right. There was a group of people over at the bar discussing something in earnest. As I shut the door, they looked over. In the middle was Conal Brus. I walked quickly toward him and he and I met in the middle of the room.

"Fionn, they've taken Niamh." He says with both anger and desperation.

"Who has?" I blurt out, alarmed at the news.

"I believe it was Fiacal. Come, let me tell you of events that happened after you left."

He led me back over to the bar. Colin Oig was there, in all his finery, along with two other men. Conal introduced me to them. One was Jamie mac Lean, the other was his son Euan. It was to Jamie's house that Niamh had been going to stay at whilst she was in Comrie.

I was told quickly what had happened. After I had left Drummorchy, Fiacal had stolen a horse and chased after Niamh and I. Losing me, he had followed her to Comrie. Not finding me there, he had decided to abduct her, presumably to question her as to my whereabouts. Since then, she had been missing. Jamie had sent Euan back to Conal Brus and had followed Fiacal as best he could all the way to Invercarrie. Conal had come up straightaway and had arrived this afternoon. His first thought was to link up with Colin Oig to find out what he could about Fiacal's whereabouts.

Through being told all this, my mouth was open wide in shock. I couldn't believe that all this had happened on account of myself. I had posed no threat to anyone, least ways not yet, and I wasn't even known about on the mainland. The only connection at all seemed to be the piece of the crown helm.

"This is terrible." I cry out, having managed to catch my breath. "Conal. I am extremely sorry to have put your daughter to such a risk, if I had known or even thought more clearly, I would never have agreed to her coming with me. I will do anything you want in order to get her back safely."

"Thank you Fionn, but I too am to blame. There's no point in trying to change the past, we need to look toward changing this situation as soon as possible." Says Conal stoically. "Have you seen anything or anyone since you've been here Fionn?" He asks.

"I was at the Selkie last night..." I began.

"Are you mad," chips in Leag from behind the bar, "after everything you told me. What happened?" Curiosity getting the better of him.

"....as I was going to say," I look at Leag, who nods back at me, "I went to the Selkie to find more about Domnhuill Dubn and the whereabouts of my sister. It was a mistake I know and I've the bruises to show for it. However, it confirmed to me that they were involved in taking her. Also something I said to Domnhuill made him stop to consider what he was doing, which made me to guess that he must have had some contact with Callum Beg. Your friend," I say turning to Colin Oig in a half accusing way, "Fiacal was also there."

"I have no friends, only business acquaintances" He replies, cordially. "What Fiacal does outside of my trading, is of no concern to me, unless it can lead towards earning me a bar or two, speaking of which I believe it is my turn to speak." He proceeds now with his hands held together and waist high as I had seen him do before, "I believe I may be of help to you after all. If Domnhuill Dubn has Mairi and Niamh, I have known him in the past to be persuaded to swap stolen goods for bars."

"You would condone his actions, by mediating in such a trade!" I exclaim, looking him straight in the eyes then turning to the others for support.

"Not at all, I never take sides in these issues, nor does it help to get too involved. I always try and find an outcome suitable to all sides. If it is, I get paid my fee. In this case, it would appear that you want the safe return of your women. What I can do for you is find out if this is possible and what price it might be."

"Do what it takes." Growls Conal Brus, "I'll pay what is necessary."

"In that case I shall proceed to make enquiries. You understand though that any arrangement that is made, is done without prejudice. There can be no further action taken on either side."

"But that means they'll get away with it. I can't let the matter rest there." I shout out.

"They've been getting away with this for ages, there's little anyone can do about it." mutters Leag.

"That is your prerogative of course, but you will have to do it without the help of anyone else, including appealing to the Queen." States Colin Oig with finality.

I am left without words and with little choice but to go along with what Colin Oig has suggested. I'd come to dislike him for the relish he seemed to be taking with his disinterested stance. I look at each of the others in turn, hoping to sense some sort of support for my feelings. However, they all appeared to be resigned to the situation and happy he was there helping them.

Colin Oig got up and headed for the door. We all returned to the bar where Leag has put drinks before us and huddled together into a small group. Conversation was easily overheard and there were probably spies everywhere. Some of us chose to stand, while others sat on stools and leant against the wide wooden bartop. It was a while before any of us spoke. They asked me about my day at the Aes Dana and I told them. Even repeating it didn't lift my spirits. We were still talking well into our evening meal when they asked me about my interview with Callum Beg. Up until then, I hadn't really considered it much. I had been so taken up in the joys of actually attaining Anruth status.

"What exactly happened when you met him?" Jamie asks. "Is he really the monster people think he is?"

I pause to consider my answer, realising that probably only a few people have seen him at all lately and even fewer actually having had an audience with him. I think back to the moments in his room and realise that there was little in my mind that I could recall.

"I have to say that I found him to be disturbingly friendly. He was not at all what I expected, he asked about me and how I felt I did in the examination."

"That can't have been the same person I met." Interrupts Leag. "The Callum Beg I met was anything but friendly and nice. Are you sure you met the same person?"

"Absolutely, however I had to undergo some ritual I had not come across before. He carried it out in his room, but the funny thing is I can't remember anything about it."

As I was now talking to them trying to remember, a flashback of flying in the air comes to me, "I remember something about flying in the air above the clouds with him, looking down at the ground." I stop talking and look up from my thoughts. They were all staring at me aghast. Euan and Jamie even pulled back a little in the chairs.

"You worry me." Says Conal at last. "I don't think I really want to know any more." He stops what he is saying and finishes his food in silence, as did the others.

I am left alone to my thoughts, aware of the distance I had placed inadvertently between myself and my friends. I would have to be more careful in future. I had forgotten how the ordinary folk think of those gifted in the arts. Much was still beyond their capacity to take in and understand certain things, just as it appeared to be to me now, but on yet a higher level still again.

Colin Oig returned later on in the night. Wasting no time, he called us to gather round him. "I've got good news and not so good news." He starts. "Firstly, they are happy to make Fiacal exchange Niamh in return for two bars of silver. Domnhuill has personally guaranteed it and that's good enough with me. How say you on that?"

"I'll pay of course." Says Conal, "Is she unharmed?" We all sense his personal angst behind the question.

"She is unharmed and will be with you tomorrow." He replies in a reassuring tone and then turns to face me. "They have asked Fionn to go to the North gate in the morning with the bars." All eyes are now on me.

"I'll do it." I say quickly. "What about Mairi?"

"That's the not so good news." Colin continues, "They won't admit to holding any woman against their will in the name of Mairi." He stops and looks down at his feet, knowing his words would not be to my liking and not wanting to look me directly in the eyes.

"I don't believe it." I call out.

"Wait a minute, Fionn." Colin holds up an arm to calm me down. "All is not lost here. In this case, I believe that they want you, yourself, to ask them. Perhaps to give them some more identification on your sister." He tries to suggest.

"What tricks are they playing at?" I shout out. "They know full well they have her!" I turn to all the others in turn looking for some support to my accusation. In each case I received a reluctant shrug back.

"It's a dangerous game they play, Fionn." Answers Leag, reaching across and placing his hand on my shoulder. "They won't admit openly to anything that might not pay them enough." His voice has a cautionary tone to it.

"Leag's right Fionn," goes on Colin, "if they are not admitting they have Mairi, then there must be another reason worth more to them. In this case, more than just money."

"But what? What on earth could that be?" I say exasperated.

"I have no idea and I couldn't even guess. I am sorry. I have done my best." Sighs Colin, putting his hands on his hips. "Conal, I'll not be charging my usual fee for this negotiation, you can buy me one of your drinks when next I'm at Drummorchy instead." He ends with an offer that can uphold the pride and honour of both men.

"That's good of you Colin. I appreciate all that you've done here for Fionn and I tonight." His tone holds none of its usual richness and I can see the fatigue all over his face.

"Think nothing of it."

We all talked some more about what I was to do the next morning and then went upstairs to get some sleep. Colin Oig left to go to back to his own place. Once again, I found myself reviewing the days events last thing at night. This time, even though I was extremely tired, I took a long time to fall asleep. I wasn't looking forward to the next day.

In the early hours, I awoke. The weather had taken a turn for the worse. It had got colder because of a vicious North wind. It howled through the cracks of the planks along the sides of the sleeping room. None of the others were awake yet, so I crept downstairs. Leag was up though and I wondered if he'd even had a chance to go to bed from working late last night. We ate some porridge together and drank mugs of hot milk flavoured with dried bilberries. It was good to feel the warmth inside my belly.

As the others came down to eat, I said my goodbyes and paid Leag for his hospitality. I wasn't sure what was going to happen, but I wanted to pay any dues to the friends I had recently made.

The North gate was taking the full blast of the icy wind and I sheltered behind it. The gatekeeper looked as miserable as a ewe that had lost her lambs to a wolf and he showed no desire in talking. I couldn't blame him though, he must have been even colder than I was having spent the night here.

I watched as his replacement trudged over from the distant horizon outside the gates, leaving a trail of footprints behind him in the drifting snow. As he got closer, I could see the warmth from his heavy breathing escape into the air like a tiny cloud. It was not a morning to be out for long and there looked to be more heavy snow on the way. It wasn't until he got up close to me that I recognised him. The bulk that was Gruach loomed over me. He stared down and grinned stupidly at me.

"You're to come with us." He bellows against the sound of the wind.

"Us!" I thought, turning to see the frozen gatekeeper who was now grinning as well. There was little else to do but follow and we proceeded out of the gates and retraced Gruach's steps back outside of the town. Heads down and into the wind, the cold bit into our faces. As I walked, I considered the more positive side. If it had been warm, they might well have had the energy for a fight and two against one were not really good odds.

Over the brow of a small rise, I could at last see where we were heading. It was a Broch on the edge of the cliffs. The water was about thirty paces beneath us and, looking at the waves breaking against the rocks below, it made me feel even colder. Why anyone wanted to build a broch here I had no idea.

It was a new circular stone building that had a large entrance half-way up, reachable by twenty wooden steps. Inside there was a stone stairway around the sides in between the outer wall and the inner wall. It led to both an upstairs chamber and a downstairs cellar. On one side there was a large stone fireplace and in it a large fire was beginning to crackle into its fullest flames.

There were several people in the huge room. All of them were near the fire. Amongst them I could see Niamh. I unwound the wrap I had circled about my head and neck and immediately made my way over to her. Her initial joy at seeing me turned into a look of sadness straight-away.

"Niamh, are you alright?" I hold her by both arms and look into her eyes. She lowers hers.

"I'm fine, I'm so sorry I've caused you this problem." She looks up again.

"Don't be silly lass, It's me who should apologise to you." I reply guiltily.

She puts her arms around my waist and pulls me toward her, hugging me as hard as she can. My arms are left dangling in the air to my sides and I slowly bring my arms up and place them onto her back and hug her back. It feels good and comfortable and I leave them there.

"Enough of that!" Comes a voice obviously used to being obeyed. The vast frame of an old woman, who was more used to eating for two, comes over to us. We pull apart like two chastened children that have been found guilty of picking at the scraps before a meal.

"You've brought the silver bars!" She orders, her statement thinly disguised as a question.

"They're here." I reply getting them out. "Now let us go."

"The girl goes, you don't!" She commands again, waving her arm in some signal.

"What trickery is this?" I demand back, "What are you playing this time?" I move towards her, twisting my shoulder to the side and dislodging the groping arm of a guard in the process.

"This is no game, laddie." She growls in a voice most men would be proud of and comes forward to confront my own approach. She looks up into my eyes with the wild look of a cook that's had her food rejected. I hear Gruach chuckling a few paces away. "I've orders to keep you here and let the girl go. It appears you didn't heed a warning given to you some two nights ago."

She was wrong, I remembered the words spoken by the 'Dubh' word for word.

"You'll only be staying a short while," she cackles, turning her back on me and walking away, "tak'im down boys."

Two oafs move in beside me. "A moment, if you please, to say my goodbyes." I ask.

She stops to consider my request for a while. "As it's the last time you'll see her, I suppose that'll be alright." She waddles off cackling still and collapses into the seat next to the fire.

Her words had seemed more ominous than I would have cared for, but I was glad of a few moments with Niamh. We walked together to the far side of the room for what little privacy we could get.

"Fionn." She began, her voice filling with dread that chokes her next words. She stops for a moment and reaches up and places her palm on the side of my face, "What's going to happen?" She asks finally, her voice now sounding very scared.

"Have no fear, lassie. I've a long life ahead of me and we've not yet had that dance we spoke of. I'll return as soon as I can." I say as reassuringly as possible, for my benefit as well as hers. "What can you tell me about this place?" I whisper, aware of all the eyes and ears upon us on the other side of the room.

"They keep people downstairs in the cellar. This is the first time I have been allowed up. It was horrible, cold and dirty Fionn." Both her hands move round to the front of my cloak and she grips the edges to it. "Please try to take care of yourself."

"Do you know of anyone else down there or were you alone?" I ask, hopefully.

"There is one other girl Fionn." She whispers back. "It's your sister Mairi. We talked for ages through the night. We couldn't see each other but I told her that I had met you and that you were looking for her. She's a lovely person Fionn, I'd really like to know her better."

My heart sighed with the relief. I'd eventually found out where my sister was.

"Niamh, I am sure they will take you back safely now, tell Conal what you told me. Tell him not to worry about Mairi and I, but ask him to send word to my father. Will you do that for me?"

"Of course, Fionn. Please take care." She starts to cry and I hold her to me again and this time our cheeks touch. I feel her moist tears against my skin and it tickles in a delightfully sensuous way. For a moment, I was a world away from here in a land of continual joy.

"That's enough. Tak 'im down now." Comes the order again.

Two burly young men grabbed each of my arms and began to walk me downstairs. I had a fleeting thought that I could throw them both down in front of me, possibly killing them, and then try to make my escape with Niamh. It was instantly followed by the more rational thought that there would probably be too many of them who would suddenly appear from upstairs or elsewhere. I had little choice for the moment but to comply. I turned and looked back at Niamh and we exchanged a final, almost futile glance.

Down in the cellar, it felt nearly as cold as it did outside. I was thrown into a cell. The floor and walls were stone and the door was thick oak wood with a small metal grille half way up. Gruach followed us down and came up to the grille.

"Tonight, when Domnhuill returns, you will die." He smiles, letting it fade into his toothy grin, "If you're lucky you may get a choice. Death by air, by water, by fire or by earth. If you're really fortunate, we'll just take you're head off." He laughs loudly at his words. I looked at him as he continued laughing.

It was not a time for answering so I fixed him the stare of a man with confidence. It was a stare that came from some form of deep knowing. His laughter began to die down and soon he just backed away from me, uncomfortable with my refusal to give in to fear. When he got to the stairs he turned his back on me, trampled up the steps heavily and was gone. I was alone.

CHAPTER EIGHT

THE POWER OF THE MIND

The main aim behind this chapter is to present a sufficient level of basic information about the mind and the brain, to mention some of its more dramatic associated effects and to begin to look at some of the connections common to all the subjects covered so far. Scientists are only now just beginning to understand some of the amazing facts and functions about these areas, and many of the recent revelations have led researchers very close to answering a few of the major questions left in life. We shall see from looking at a few of these developments, how the brain and the mind appear to work.

We need to cover and discuss current theories on consciousness along with certain aspects on specific areas of the brain. The subjects of hypnosis and language patterns will also be covered along with the latest research on dreams and their related phenomena. The chapter will conclude with some examples of the power of the brain and will aim at leaving a positive message that connects up with the earlier chapter on success. This whole section will be briefly summarised before introducing chapter ten, which will aim at connecting the mind with the physics already discussed earlier in chapter six.

To begin with, we must try to get some agreement on word definitions. Many words that are used these days tend to have differing definitions and connotations. Even when we use words in everyday speech, we translate what we hear being said by channelling them through our own perceptions. One example is the word 'scrambling'. Some readers will now be thinking of eggs; others motorbikes; some clambering around on all fours and a few are encoding information. Even when we use sentences to describe something, there can be misconceptions. This most often occurs in the classroom when the teachers are writing down comments from the students. The words they write down will generally be theirs, having made a quick translation of the comments they are hearing. This inevitably leads to misunderstanding and wrong perceptions.

In geology, two terms have been half jokingly assigned to people describing rocks. They refer to the methods people use when naming them. On the one hand you have the 'lumper's and on the other there are the 'splitter's. The former will generalise and group many rocks under one heading; the latter will aim to specialise and define to the n'th degree with the use of longer and longer nouns that fewer and fewer people understand. In truth neither side is wrong. Rocks, due to their very formation, all vary from one another in some percentage of composition and texture and specialists need to distinguish between them when communicating with one another. However we need to be able to communicate efficiently with larger numbers of people if we are seeking to influence them. In this case more generic terms are needed as long as there can be some agreement with their definition. Specialising, by its very nature, leads to less disagreements with definitions, but also leads to excluding large sections of the community from understanding.

In this book, I would like to be able to appeal to large numbers of people and for this reason I need to generalise. This, in no way, means that I am underestimating the complexity of the subjects, nor do I seek to give the impression that I am providing answers to some of the controversial issues. I am merely trying to convey information that will allow a baseline of knowledge to be built from which we can progress to the next section.

8.1 Consciousness

Some of the few major questions left in life surround that of consciousness. Why and how does it arise? How does it fit in with nature and physics? Can it be explained by physical laws? Answering these questions has been the realm of scientists and philosophers for many years and, as you might imagine, has led to many arguments and controversy. To define consciousness is understandably not easy but we must try to go as far as we can in this direction in order for us to progress a little further.

Initially the philosopher Rene Descartes adopted what is now termed a 'dualistic' approach to the problem. He considered the mind and the physical brain to be two separate entities with some separate 'realm' for the 'mental substance'. More recent theories suggest that all can be explained by just physical action. This, more 'reductive' approach, says that all the small-scale activities that go on, will eventually explain the large-scale actions that are encountered. This 'bottom up' approach to finding out about consciousness is put together with a 'top down' one. The latter investigates by analysing the larger, measurable activities (like brain patterns) with a view to the same objective of coming to an overall understanding of consciousness. Although there have recently been strong cases put forward for 'dualism', notably David Chalmers' 'naturalistic' version, I tend to favour the alternative because this allows for the possibility that quantum mechanics has some role to play in bringing about consciousness. I will go into this aspect much deeper in chapter ten. Nevertheless, most people now agree that quantum mechanics plays some role and the argument now centres on the amount.

Descartes first got people thinking about the brain as though it were a machine. This mechanistic approach allowed scientists to gradually build up a picture of what was going on. Evidence came mainly from two areas. Firstly from injuries to the brain and the effects they had on the patients and more recently from advances in technology. These include the use of Magnetic Resonance Imaging (M.R.I.), Positron Emission Topography (P.E.T. Scans), Electroencephalography (E.E.G. machines) along with various others as well.

It is generally taken that consciousness is a natural phenomena and, as a term, it can be split into two areas – Phenomenal and Psychological. Every mental property is either one of these or a mixture. The phenomenal is characterised by the way the mind feels and experiences things; the psychological is characterised by what the mind does and the actions it takes in response to the phenomenal. How we perceive things is also psychological. Our cognitive systems, which are those that are sensitive to external environmental stimuli are taken to be natural phenomena. This would include the actual conscious experience of what is being perceived.

For the purposes of this book, we are only interested in the phenomenal side of consciousness, and the way it may operate. Daniel Dennett, author of 'Consciousness Explained', says that to explain consciousness you need to explain functional phenomena (reportability and control) and that we must look to this area for answers. He goes on to say that the mind works with no central H.Q. or control centre but has multiple channels of activity all working simultaneously to influence the outcome. This concept has been given added strength with Rita Carter's book 'Mapping the Brain'. I will outline a few of the relevant details, for instance where the brain houses consciousness, later on. But first, I need to continue further with the definition of consciousness.

For my purposes, I wish to take consciousness as awareness, a knowing about something and an ability to report on ones mental state, or cognitive capacity. I am aware of the argument that there is a connection between consciousness and awareness as there also is in their underlying structures. I would also agree that this is only a component of consciousness and not perhaps a complete description, as is also the connection between consciousness and the physical processes that occur in the brain. However as I mentioned earlier, I need to start with something from which we can generally agree upon before proceeding.

To define things a little bit further, I would like to go on and say that when we are asleep, we are unaware and therefore not conscious (albeit our minds are still working). There would also appear to be levels of consciousness. One example might occur when we are learning to drive a car. At first we don't even know if we can or can't do whatever is necessary and we are unconsciously incompetent. Once we start to get in we become consciously incompetent. After a while most of us become consciously competent. Finally, we develop the ability to converse with others, listen to the radio and read directions whilst driving. Our gear shifting takes place naturally and instinctively. This could be termed unconsciously competent (Even though we are still conscious of something else at the time).

To take our conscious experiences further, we can catalogue them into visual, auditory, tactile, olfactory and taste. These are all external observations, which have an important relevance when looking back at chapter six. In that chapter it was mentioned that the process of observation collapsed the 'quantum' world into the 'classical' world. This is the actual creation of reality as we experience it.

This initial experience has been termed a first order judgement. An example is 'I see (external sense) a blue van' (This corresponds to the same external senses mentioned in chapters two and four). A second order judgement would be the sensation – 'I have a blue sensation and I am aware of that sensation'. A third order judgement would be a deeper recollection of the experience later on.

These second order judgements could also be deemed to be similar to our 'internal' senses (These are also the same senses talked about in chapter four). One can close ones eyes and shut out external stimuli and we can still recreate the image of a blue van in our minds. One can make up sounds and with a little effort one can make up feelings. With a little extra mental stimulation, one can even recollect smells and tastes and experience them as though they are real.

We can even look at a brain scan to see what areas are working when we do these things. The response to the external stimuli of seeing and hearing a van would be similar to that of reading (seeing and internally hearing the words). The visual cortex is active at the back of the brain and the auditory cortex at the side. If we are thinking about the words when we are reading, an area called 'Broca's area' in the frontal lobes becomes active. It is not alone, as there is also widespread activity in various patterns all over the brain depending on the intensity and area of activity. When we switch off the external activity (like shutting our eyes) and just revert to thinking, only the frontal lobes exhibit activity.

8.2 Thinking

Thinking involves recollecting, imagining and self-awareness. This reflecting or creating is a bringing together of memories, pictures and sounds. Whereas the processing of the sensory information is done unconsciously, in the respective regions of the brain, thought processing is done consciously in the frontal lobes. It also requires attention, which is a mixture of arousal, focus and orientation. This alertness and awareness can be measured in intensity. The sleepier the brain, the less activity is seen in the frontal lobe region. The ability for this part of the brain to focus and increase in intensity (by a flood of neurotransmitters) is important. A specific group of neurons, found at the top of the brainstem, controls the level of activity in the brain. When they are stimulated and release the neurotransmitters dopamine and noradrenaline, the prefrontal lobe in particular is activated. The stimulation of this group of neurons in this area also creates alpha brain waves (electrical activity within a certain band of Hertz).

This is commonly associated with alertness and other activities that we will encounter later on. As thinking involves memory to a greater or lesser extent, it is important to briefly explain the current theories on memory. (See diagram 5)

8.3 Memory

Memory can be split into long term and short term. The short term operates to serve the long term. It doesn't, as was originally thought, operate like a computer with 'bits' stored in specific areas on a hard disc. Instead, the entire cortex plays a role. P.E.T. scans show many different areas of small activity working in patterns in a hugely complex manner. It would appear that the brain is more of a tuning system, tuning into our memories when we wish to recall them. This is similar to Jung's concept of the collective unconscious and his 'interconnectedness' of all memories. If we want to remember something for the long term, we know it is far easier to recall an image. An image is made up of many aspects and will therefore have a fuller pattern etched into our minds (This image may well be inaccurate with each recall, but the overall impression is remembered). It is far easier to recall than a series of numbers over a long period of time. An example to try is to remember your very first telephone number (as long as it's not your current one). It would have been etched in your short-term memory at the time of current use, but will probably be a much hazier memory than the image you will be able to recall of the place you were living in at the time.

The short-term memory, also known as the implicit memory, has been found to only be able to hold a small amount of data at a time, whilst the long term, or explicit memory can cope with huge amounts of data.

It was Donald Hebb in 1940 who first discovered the connection at the cellular level. A brain cell, with its many dendrites and axons branching off it, provides the main passage for channelling information in the brain. Hebb identified the fact that the connections, between the cells and the synapses of other cells, strengthened each time they were used. The patterns, created with the firing of the neurons, showed strong and weak links. Where there were strong links, memory would be recalled with ease. This fact corresponds well with experiences

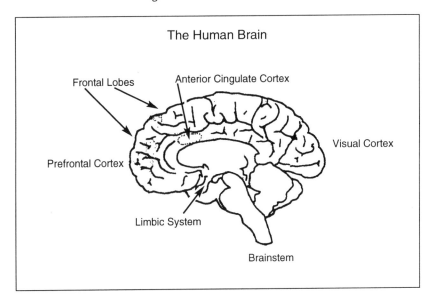

Diagram 5 – The human brain

found when teaching animals tricks. Pavlov showed this in his now famous experiments with dogs. (Although some would argue that the dogs were successful at training Pavlov!)

Our long-term memory is not anything like as exact as our short term memory. Due to the complexity of its storage mechanism, it is not always retrieved as exactly as we would like. Over time this gets worse. We develop a gradual mutation of the facts each time we make a recollection. An area of fantasy is added that builds the picture as a whole, till eventually it can become quite different. However, it still comes across to the recollector as true. This is just one of the ways that we find that the mind can create its own concept of what was real. Compulsive liars have a real problem with this!

Another well-known area that assists to create images is our eyes. They have blind spots where there is an absence of light sensitive cells at the back of the retina where the optic nerve joins the eye. If we look with one eye closed, we might expect to see a dark patch corresponding to the area of view that is not picked up in the open eye due to the absence of cells. We obviously don't have a dark patch as what happens is the mind makes up what it imagines to be real and glosses over the whole area with data picked up from the surrounding cells. The blind spot still exists and magicians sometimes use it to their advantage when they do sleight of hand tricks in front of our eyes. We will cover this conundrum of fantasy mixed with reality and the minds influence on this area later on in this chapter.

There are specific areas of the brain that are important to get to know in a little more detail. They are described as follows:-

8.4 Cells

It's the cells in the brain that create the activity. About one in every ten of the several billion cells are neurons and these are able to carry an electrical signal from one cell to another. There are two types of peripheral nerve cell, the sensory and the motor. The 'sensory' carries impulses from the sense organs in the body to the brain and the 'motor' carry instructions from the brain to the body. As well as there being an enormous number of neurons in the brain, there are many thousands of connections with each one. Each neuron connects up with its neighbours by using branch-like tendrils. These branches are either axons, for conducting information, or dendrites for receiving information. Where they meet, there is a gap called a synapse. These gaps fill with chemicals, called neurotransmitters, when the cell is activated. These activations take place at around 500 times a second and thousands occur simultaneously. An interesting fact to note is the speed that this information travels is at odds with the reaction times of our bodies, so the brain has some mechanism that slows things down for us to be able to handle it. (See diagram 6)

8.5 Frontal lobes and Cerebral blood pressure.

The frontal lobes found in the front of the brain are the areas that house 'consciousness'. It is the place where ideas are formed and where plans and thoughts are created. It is also the site that has evolved most during recent human evolution. Animals have a less developed region, which might give us an indication that they have lower levels, or amounts, of consciousness and it might also suggest that they fit into more of a genetic role in life. This would possibly be because they have lesser use and control over their inner senses. The more developed the species, the

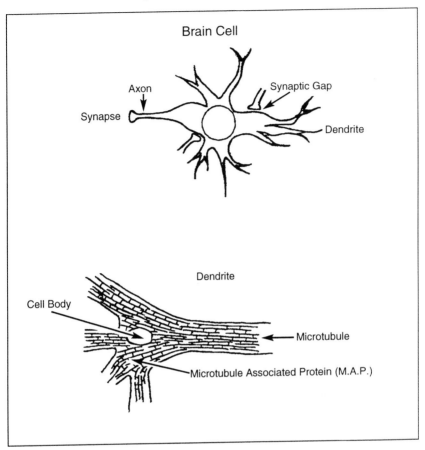

Diagram 6 – Brain cell and Dendrite

more they might be able to use their inner senses for activities like hunting and feeding.

The frontal lobes are also the supposed 'home' of the elusive 'third eye' that mystics talk about. Right at the front of this area is the pre-frontal cortex. This is the area that springs to life when we think. It is also the region where we have the conscious perception of emotion and where we have our ability to attend and to focus. A reduction in the role that this area plays, leads to a more dream-like state of mind and being less in touch with reality. When we dream at night, there is a marked decrease of activity in this area. There is also a direct comparison with the amount of activity seen in this area of the brain, with the quality of consciousness. This increased activity in this region also coincides with an increase in blood flow and blood pressure. Localised pressures within the brain may have important implications when it comes to consciousness.

Our bodies have varying amounts of stress throughout the day and our blood pressure rises and falls accordingly. However the brain is very sensitive to pressure changes and needs to have constant cerebral flow. Severe cases of changes of pressure in the brain lead to problems like Ischemia or stroke. The brain is protected from the large variations of pressure that are seen in the rest of the body by having a precise mechanism of autoregulation. It is so sensitive that when you wiggle your toes, the neurons in the cerebral cortex controlling that movement receive a greater amount of blood supply than their neighbours. This fine control is assisted by the Arterioles. These are the blood vessels that feed the capilliaries in the required area. They change the diameter of their walls and let more or less blood through. This in turn increases or decreases the pressure. The centre of the brain that controls this is in the Medulla. This is found in the Brain stem and is regulated by groups of neurons designed especially for this.

The Medulla is also the area where we find the Brain Blood Barrier (B.B.B.), another mechanism designed to stabilise the blood within the brain. However there are some regions in the brain that lack their own B.B.B. These organs, like part of the hypothalamus, the pineal gland and the pituitary gland, are regions in the brain that coordinate the activities of regulating blood pressure and fluid balance. With all these organs and their activities involved in regulating a very pressure sensitive area, it is perhaps surprising to know that scientists today know very little as to why we have these changes in blood pressure. In today's modern environment where there is far less need for our innate flight or fight reactions to stressful situations, we can only wonder at what other needs our minds and bodies must have for such a precise mechanism for localised control over blood pressure and flow. One possible answer to this question is given in chapter 12.

The short term working memory is also located in the prefrontal cortex, this is where the ideas are manipulated and held in 'mind'. An important feature is that without certain parts working, it can lead to a source of amnesia with no reference to space or time. Past events also appear to be less specific and appear vague. This means that this area is heavily involved in our grasp of reality as we observe it or as we 'collapse' it into our own consciousness. As one would expect this region has also got connections with almost all other areas of the brain, but interestingly has an especially strong link to the limbic system.

8.6 Limbic system

The limbic system is made up of the hippocampus, thalamus, hypothalamus, amygdala and the pineal gland. It is here that emotions are generated. The emotions are more than just feelings, they are also deep ingrained survival mechanisms or instincts. They provide a very necessary function that allows us to adapt and fit in with our environment.

The hippocampus is an area essential to the laying down of long-term memory, the hypothalamus adjusts the body to balance with the environment. The amygdala is the place where fear is both registered and generated and the thalamus is a sort of relay station for sending information to the right area of the body.

The way it might work is like this:- The frontal lobes have a capacity to feel emotion. As the only conscious area, it will perceive the need for a specific type of emotion when its senses are alerted to something. It sends a message down its neuronal connection to the limbic system. The limbic system then sends messages out to the body (via the hypothalamus and thalamus) to make the necessary changes (fight or flight possibly). Neurotransmitters are released and hormones (like adrenaline) are pumped out. The heartbeat and blood pressures are changed accordingly and a message is sent back to the frontal cortex saying that there is an emotional response.

This two-way link with the conscious part of the brain is important because it binds the conscious area with the unconscious area. The key to this link would appear to be the emotional messages that are sent back and forth. If we take an emotion like joy, there are two ways we can react, we can purposely make up a smile or we can smile in a joyous way that just comes naturally from within us. The first is initiated from the frontal lobes and the conscious mind and it produces certain effects. It uses a specific set of muscles in the face and particular neuron pathways and circuits. The second smile comes via the limbic system is created in a different way and from along different routes. This type of smile, unlike the other, has a very real effect and can also be felt by others as do all the emotions that arise this way. This is important because one of the reasons we have emotions is to influence others. The stronger direction, interestingly enough, is the route back to the cortex from the limbic system.

It is generally considered by most scientists that there are four basic emotions and, like colours, they can be mixed to give all the others that we find. They are disgust, fear, anger and love. These correspond with our basic expressions, except that love is substituted for happiness and sadness. The way the brain is composed shows that, of all the systems transmitting information, the one for sending out emotions is favoured most. It is also the one that is most dominant. However, it is still programmed by the conscious mind in an area in the prefrontal cortex called the ventromedial cortex. We can consciously make a choice, using this area, as to whether or not to send positive or negative thought signals down to the emotional generator (the limbic system). The amygdala can create negative fears for us with whatever intensity we desire. It is interesting to note that in depressive people the ventromedial cortex is almost dead, showing little or no activity.

In sales training there is an expression 'action dispels fear'. It refers to a way of sustaining prospecting activity in the face of the two commonest fears mentioned in chapter two, the fear of failure and the fear of rejection. The saying holds true if we want to avoid being depressed. Keeping the frontal lobes active with non-emotional tasks suppresses the amygdala from flooding the system with negative emotions. A rush of pleasure could then be allowed (This introduces the neurotransmitter dopamine into the brain) from the limbic system. This chemical stimulates and excites the mind and gives the emotional feeling of pleasure.

8.7 To summarise so far:–

We have only one region of the brain (in our frontal lobes) that seems to hold our consciousness. We seem to be able to vary the intensity of use of this area at will, depending on the amount of attention given. A region inside this area can decide what emotions to call for from its emotion control centre. The connections between this region and the limbic system (where the emotions are generated) are very dense. This is also the main connection between the conscious mind and the unconscious mind. Our emotions, and control over them, would appear to be extremely important in this link. The prefrontal cortex also handles our thoughts and 'inner' sounds and our 'inner' visualising and also those conscious feelings we choose to have. It houses our ability to discern between space and time. It has a language centre that allows us to program other regions with our thoughts. In the centre of our brain, the limbic system houses our basic urges and desires and also makes automatic responses to external stimuli. The whole brain is required to feed the frontal lobes information in order for full consciousness to emerge. The visual images seen through the eyes and the sounds that we hear, all come to the frontal lobes via the representative parts of the brain.

The information coming from the environment is first picked up by what is termed our 'external senses'. In our conscious mind, we also register these same external stimuli but we also have the ability to manipulate the senses here. This is referred to as using our 'inner senses'. Shutting our eyes and recollecting our holiday experiences, the feel of the sun on our faces, the taste of the seawater the first time we swim in the sea, are all created using these inner senses.

Now that we know a little more about the 'hardware' side and how the brain and mind appear to work, we can look at some of the related phenomena and how we can use this information.

8.8 Zen

The Art of Zen is said to be purely devoted to liberating the human potential of the mind. The following saying by Zen master Linzi relates well to our senses. We first perceive through external stimuli entering our minds, then secondly we can create perceptions in our conscious mind.

"The six subnormal faculties of the enlightened are the ability to enter the realm of form without being confused by the form, to enter the realm of sound without being confused by sound, to enter the realm of scent without being confused by scent, to enter the realm of flavour without being confused by flavour, to enter the realm of feeling without being confused by feeling, to enter the world of phenomena without being confused by phenomena."

This sixth sense has sometimes been referred to as proprioception. It is the bodies awareness of its position, posture and equilibrium and involves an integration of many sensory inputs from throughout the brain.

What the Zen master is alluding to is that the ability to use our inner senses, whilst not being disturbed by the information coming in from our outer senses, will lead an individual to an enlightened state of mind. The extreme relevance of this will be revealed slowly as we proceed throughout this book.

8.9 Neuro-Linguistic Programming

The teaching of the use of these same inner senses can be found in several applications today. One of these is found in the techniques seen in Neuro-Linguistic Programming. This N.L.P.T.M. has been called the art and science of personal excellence. It was developed by John Grindler, a professor of linguistics at the University of California, and Richard Bandler, a mathematician and computer scientist. They built a model for effective communication, personal change and learning and as a tool it has a value to everyone seeking to improve and enhance their lives. It helps to create more individual choice and ultimately more freedom. The name of the model is explained as follows: - Neuro, is based on the neurons and the way they work in the brain; Linguistic, is the part language plays in our thoughts, behaviour and communication; and programming, refers to how we program ourselves to do certain things. In summary N.L.P.T.M. deals with the way we filter, through our senses, the external experiences down into our internal perceptions. It goes on to look at how we use those same inner senses in order to achieve the results we desire.

Before coming up with their concept of N.L.P.T.M., Richard Bandler and John Grindler interviewed several successful people and three top therapists and analysed their methods to obtain models of how they achieved their success. They were Fritz Perls, the founder of Gestalt Therapy, Virginia Satir, an extraordinarily successful family therapist and a well-known hypnotherapist Milton H. Erickson M.D. An analysis of their methods revealed several insights into the way language, and in particular the patterns used within language, played a part in programming minds. In their experience humans do not operate directly upon the world but rather they operate through a created representation of what they believe the world to be. Depending on a person's beliefs, they will create, through their individual perceptions, a worldview of their own. Humans create a different model of the world in three ways.

Firstly some of what they experience is deleted (remember long term memory problems). This is due to excessive amounts of data that enters each sensory input. This is done unconsciously. If we take an example of this experience, like scoring a goal in a football match, it enters and is registered in our minds in a way that approximates what happened. Due to the large amount of information we are experiencing at the time of scoring, the brain only takes the amount that it wants to register the whole experience.

Secondly, we distort the information we get from our external senses when we use our inner senses to imagine or think about it. To continue with the goal scoring analogy, it would be like remembering the event at a later date. Each time we recall the experience our emphasis on different parts of the overall event changes. The goal becomes better than it perhaps actually was. The goalkeeper's efforts might well also become more valiant every time the story is retold. All these changes can quite easily take place on the subconscious level without the person even being aware of them.

Thirdly, we generalise using the information stored in our memories to allow us to operate in our view of the world. Once we have scored our first goal it becomes part of our experience bank and the next time we find ourselves in a similar position, perhaps when the ball is crossed from the corner near enough to head it into the goal, we draw upon our general experience in this area to assist us in our actions. The brain makes certain assumptions as to the process of goal scoring by the model it has just begun to build up. This model is later improved and enhanced upon each time we try to score a goal and forms a generalisation on goal scoring.

Each of these three ways enables us, as individuals, to create our own representation of the world we live in. This can be put to good use when we seek to influence, persuade and communicate. If we can first understand the methods by which people create their worldviews, then we can use the same methods to communicate with them in a far more accurate way than anyone else can.

This concept of seek first to understand, then to be understood is certainly not new. However it takes us to a new, deeper level of understanding if we use some of the methods seen in the N.L.P.[T.M.] model.

In our M.10 sales training courses, we ask people to imagine a scenario where the people in Britain speak, not just one or two languages, but over a hundred different languages with no individual one dominant. Not only do they speak differently but they also have cultural differences and act and behave in a variety of ways. The task is to recognise a persons particular language, habits etc. and speak to them in their own tongue and in the same manner. Everyone knows of the difficulty involved in translating foreign languages and that the advantages in communicating and influencing, lie with those people who happen to be bilingual. If you want those same advantages, when you wish to influence someone, then you must learn the techniques and master all the 'languages'. Luckily this isn't the reality as all you have to discover are just a few of a person's patterns. This will suffice in giving you a definite advantage, when it comes to influence, over a person who doesn't know them. Aside from helping to understand how to influence others, N.L.P.[T.M.] provides an excellent method of understanding the patterns of the 'great' people in life. As we all have the same neurology as these people we can all learn their qualities and be and behave like them. N.L.P.[T.M.] can help you emulate these people, not just with their language patterns, but with all their subjective patterns as well. This enables all of us to learn and succeed, in all areas, far faster than was possible previously and it provides an extremely hopeful picture for the future.

8.10 Influence

These days everyone is a salesperson: like them or loathe them, you are one or have to be one. Whether you have a product to sell, a service, an idea or even a lesson, you need to be able to communicate. If you want to influence them (to get them to buy from you or to buy your ideas or just even to get them to do something for you), then you must learn the techniques. Some of the greatest influential speeches ever made by politicians are laced with influential language patterns and are based on the principles of hypnosis. Perhaps the best-known example is Martin Luther King's speech where he says 'I have a dream'. That is, perhaps, why it was also one the speeches that had the most impact on the American people.

If we are to break down influence into its components, we arrive at three parts. The first is the words we use, the second is the way we speak them, our intonation and general voice quality, and lastly our physiology, or body language. The latter is by far the most persuasive of the three, with the least effective being words alone. Take a moment to think back to when you were listening to your teachers at school. Who was the most influential and why? Was it what they said or the way they said it that made you remember most easily? What kind of body movement was there and how fast did they speak?

If no one teacher stood out for you, maybe there was someone else you met that has had a huge influence upon you. It is even possible to be influenced by someone you have only seen on television. Whoever it was, the principles and components of influence remain the same.

The next question to ask ourselves is: – What are the effects of this influence today? For some people whole careers have been built on the influence of someone from their past (and not always the right one for them!). If we are to truthfully answer this question, we begin to see many things in ourselves that are actually products of other people.

If we take time out to listen to other people's conversations (the chat radio stations are excellent for this), we can begin to recognise patterns in the language used. At its most basic level there are the much-repeated phrases. These are used as a matter of recourse to many arguments and debates when the art of listening has been all but lost. The words are said, but the meaning behind them is lost and is not conveyed. This is partially because the listener is thinking of their own point of view and partially because the speaker doesn't themselves have the full grasp of the meaning behind them. Political and religious dogma are two of the best examples. Followers of a particular party will often repeat phrases that their leader may have made to them. These same phrases are said again and again as a form of 'hammer and nail' approach to persuasion.

This shows a very basic, and to some degree effective, form of programming of our minds (As purchasers of goods we would consider this pressured selling). From childhood we inwardly digest all that our external senses pick up. Our brains are, at that age, similar to non-programmed computers, and are eager to soak up information. As we grow, the information comes in and we program and reprogram ourselves into a more and more complex system. Eventually we become who we are today by virtue of all the programming of our minds (both good and bad) from the external stimuli around us (which includes the interaction from those around that influence us) and also from any reprogramming that we choose to do ourselves. This latter statement refers to our ability to consciously analyse our external stimuli and to decide what action we may wish to take. This would therefore require the use of our inner senses.

8.11 Language Patterns

Taking language patterns a little further on down the path of complexity, we can identify different areas that we all commonly use. These areas are also representative of our earlier programming and are based on phrases with which we are most comfortable and their underlying structures. If we are able to find out the patterns for a particular individual, it would give us a huge advantage if we wished to influence them. Hypnotists use this same principle in order to assist their subjects.

One of the initial exponents of the use of language as a way of categorising people was Rodger Bailey. He developed the language and behavioural profile (L.A.B. profile) from a set of patterns called meta-programs, which were first identified with N.L.P.T.M. by Bandler and Grindler. These meta-programs are the same as the filters we use when we use our perceptions to make up our own view of the world. Bailey developed well designed questions that, when answered, would reveal personality patterns. This was seen in the way, or the structure, that the question was answered, rather than the words that were used.

Once an individuals patterns are established, specific and appropriate language can then be used that will be far more influential. This can be seen more distinctly when using exactly the wrong language for a person who uses an opposite pattern. An undoubtedly poor response would result and the feeling of the two of you having little in common would be perceived on both sides.

An example of this is the internal /external pattern. This assists in determining where someone gets their motivation from. People with an internal pattern get their motivation from within themselves. They gather in information, then decide upon it themselves. External people will want to consider other peoples opinions and require outside feedback and references. To influence each personality, you need to match up their required forms of motivation. It is useless and extremely unproductive to offer an 'internal' person loads of references saying, "Talk to these people, they'll tell you how good my services will be for your company." The 'internal' will just dismiss the statement and probably you too, whilst an external would be more than happy with the comment. Using a common language between people also shows another important aspect of communication and influence. People like people like themselves. The desire to be 'liked' very often manifests itself in a form of mirroring, where one partner begins, unconsciously to mirror the other. This is most often seen with body language. They say imitation is the greatest form of flattery for a good reason. The person being copied feels respected and is being listened to and tends toward liking the flatterer (albeit this is most often at an unconscious level). This leads to a creation of rapport. This mirroring is another initial technique seen used by hypnotists. They look to first mirroring, then pacing their clients in their endeavours to lead and suggest to them. I will go into this further in a little more detail later in the chapter.

There are many useful profiles that can be found in people. Using them all in conjunction with the other components of influence add up to a very powerful set of methods that can enable someone to reprogram a persons mind and alter the way they think and act. This can be a very beneficial tool which is why N.L.P.T.M. is used with increasing success in the field of therapy.

8.12 Belief & Influence

The most powerful tool of influence is universally recognised to be belief. When you believe what you are doing or offering is far more valuable than that which you are asking for in return then extreme influence can be achieved. Beliveing the opposite leads to the consequences seen by Gerald Ratner, as was mentioned in chapter 4. Once the word was out that he considered his jewellery 'junk', hundreds of people believed it too and demanded their money back.

If you manage to conjure up sufficient belief in something, then it can become infectious. Many new age religions have sprung up around highly influential people, purely because of the amount of belief that was created. People with belief come across as passionate people. The way they talk is filled with gesticulation and fervour. They display excellent vocal qualities and body language, both of the other two components of influence.

In our own minds we have core belief systems (In our frontal lobes). Our beliefs (inner senses of feeling) have been built up over the years, instilled in us by those people that have influenced us (whether we let them or not). Influencing people is therefore a way of getting someone to change their inner senses to those that are in accordance with the person doing the influencing. Communicating straight through to someone's inner senses, going straight through all their filter systems is what is necessary and this is exactly what the hypnotist aims to do. They, of course, have the permission of the subjects before they start.

What if, however, we choose not to be influenced. How can we close ourselves off to someone who is seeking to persuade us one way or another? We all have the ability to close our minds and become stubborn. In doing this, we are always party to our own point of view and no one else's (something also heard a lot on 'chat radio' stations). However, if we wish to progress in this world, we need to open up our minds to new information, allow it to pass through our filters and adapt our beliefs accordingly. This can only be done whilst actively listening. This entails the shutting down of our internal voices, thoughts and images (our inner senses) and tuning in to the external stimuli of our choice. We are fortunate to have evolved a system that enables us to sift out the background noise from that which we are fixing our attention upon. This is not so for those people with poor hearing and who have to use an aid, they have the added problem of not being able to discern particular voices above any others. To them all the voices all appear to blend together and this can be exceptionally frustrating in a crowded room.

If we apply ourselves to the principles of active listening, along with a sufficient amount of curiosity, then our minds can become open to further information. This seems a simple enough exercise and one that should be second nature. It is not, however, the situation we come across when we initially train salespeople. Many of them find it hard to do this to begin with and it takes some time before they get back into the right habit. The art of listening appears sadly to be dying amongst people today, as is the whole art of communicating effectively.

During the last ten years of my life, I have been fortunate to learn about sales and communication techniques and the art of asking open questions. These are questions that cannot be answered with a 'yes' or 'no' answer. In a salespersons quest to find out what is wanted, these open questions need to be asked in order to open up the mind of the customer. This exercise has the knock on effect of opening up the mind of the salesperson. Also during this period, I was also fortunate to meet many different people from all walks of life and business. This combination of meeting new people and finding out about them, along with keeping an open mind, allowed me to pick up a huge amount of information not normally accessible to the average person. This, along with the useful coincidences that I mentioned in an earlier chapter, assisted me greatly when it came to combining all my thoughts at the beginning of writing this book.

For those of you who are unsure of where you are heading in life, it is suggested that getting out and meeting more people, keeping an open mind and preparing to be influenced will get you far further toward your answers than by doing the opposite.

In summary, the power of belief is extreme and it is limitless. An unbelievable amount of belief in what you do can lead to unbelievable things being done. Nurture it and it will grow. Be careful what you say, think, feel, hear and do for they can all affect your levels of belief. If you want to achieve great things, start building the belief that you can in steady easily believable stages. We shall see later on in the book just what has been done and can be done using the power of this inner feeling.

8.13 Hypnosis

I need to return now to hypnosis and to some of its mysteries in order to begin to explain more of the possible things that the mind can do. The supposition I wish to make here is that self hypnosis and hypnosis are similar but for the fact that someone else is giving the commands. All that is possible under normal hypnosis should therefore, under the right conditions, be possible with self-hypnosis. Hypnotists will be the first to tell you of the many levels of hypnosis. The mildest form (which itself could be open to some debate) can be seen in advertising and marketing. In its base description, it is an attempt to persuade people to act differently to what they are currently doing. This is done to get people to either buy a new product or else to continue to buy the same product in preference to all their competitors.

This is little different to the hypnosis done in hypnotherapy. Using the techniques of mirroring, language patterns, deep structures, pacing and leading, the hypnotist will, through suggestions, change a client's internal referencing systems and core beliefs. This is done more precisely than the generalised ways used within advertising because of the one to one nature of the work.

Companies, in their marketing strategies, are suggesting to their customers that they can create a pleasurable association between them and their product or service. The more successful they are, the more money they make. This association with the mind's pleasure centre is crucial if influence is desired. At its basic level it is similar to Donald Hebb's neuron pathway linking up the pleasure centre with the belief system and its memory. The stronger this link; the more likely the influence it will have. The reason adverts are so often repeated, is that it strengthens the new neuron pathway. Eventually, we find ourselves going down the aisles of the supermarkets, for example, picking items up and placing them in the shopping trolley without going through a conscious questioning process of whether of not we ought to buy it or another brand. We pick the brand that has a strong association of pleasure with our internal belief systems.

On a full analysis of the techniques that advertisers use, it can be seen that they are all similar to the techniques that the hypnotist uses. Hypnosis has often also been termed the power of suggestion, with self-hypnosis being nothing more than self- suggestion.

You may remember that subliminal advertising was banned in most countries due to its effectiveness at passing through the customers external senses and conscious control centre straight into the emotional centre and back, reprogramming the inner senses belief systems along the way. It was felt that this powerful method was unfair as the individual lacked any control of the situation.

Proof that subliminal messages work was once seen in Oxford street, London. Retailers had huge problems with shoplifters and would try anything to reduce this happening. They played tapes of music with a subliminal message (A message at a sound level just below that of conscious hearing) saying 'shoplifters will be prosecuted'. Each time they tried this, shoplifting was reduced by around 30%. (As this experiment was not that tightly constrained, it is possible that other variables were at work to produce this outcome. As we have seen belief and expectation are powerful modifiers of results. If the shopkeepers were aware of the experiment and had belief in its ability to work, then they could have quite easily influenced the resulting drop in shoplifting in some way. Either way it shows the use of the inner senses affecting an outcome)

However, because the hypnotist's client is an agreeable and willing participant, and the suggestion is more exact, a deeper level of hypnosis can be entered. It is within these deeper levels that we encounter more interesting phenomena.

The best-known phenomenon is perhaps the one where the subject can feel no pain. This was particularly useful in the earlier days when there were no anaesthetics. Two hundred years ago Franz Mesmer practiced the art, later called Mesmerism and the origin of the word 'mesmerised', for the benefit of surgical operations. Dentists today sometimes teach a form of self-hypnosis as an alternative to a pain killing injection. This self-suggestion that there is no pain has also enabled top athletes to push their endurance levels higher and higher. It takes them through their pain barriers with a minimum discomfort. (This is not necessarily recommended as the pain is there for a reason and training beyond the barrier will almost definitely start doing some damage to the body).

Another interesting feature of being hypnotised can be seen on the shows stage hypnotists put on for their audiences. Easily susceptible and suggestible people are chosen from the audience and are asked to perform certain activities whilst hypnotised. In the majority of cases, people were found to have talents that they could not display when they were not hypnotised. They would sing with far better voices or act with far greater abilities than beforehand. This would appear to be similar to the benefits that athletes or performers aspire towards in their 'psyching themselves up' before a race or show. The only difference is that in the one case the hypnotist would have control over the situations and in the other the individual themselves had the control.

The control of body functions has been carefully documented by the medical profession whilst under the individual's own control. There is plenty of evidence to show that a person can, with self-suggestion, lower or increase their heart rate. Biathletes do this in order to shoot more accurately after having done an exhausting cross-country skiing course. Some subjects have been recorded controlling their blood pressure and gastric secretions using this form of biofeedback. You can test this for yourselves if you have access to a heart rate monitor. Once you have put it on and measured your resting heart rate, remember back to a time when you were enjoying yourself, when you were laughing and relaxed. Relive the experience as vividly as you can, recalling the sounds and feelings at the time. Once you have done this for about a minute, check your heart rate again. It will, in almost all cases, have slowed down. You have now just managed to exert some control over your bodily functions (albeit in an indirect way). Whilst not perhaps true self-suggestion, it should indicate to you that manipulation of the body by the mind (Biofeedback) does indeed work and that when the methods of self hypnosis are fully applied, greater things could result.

Free air divers have taken this concept to extreme levels. They compete to swim down as deep as they can with one breath of air and also for the longest they can hold their breath underwater. The record depth is around 100 meters and the record time is over 7 minutes! This they can only achieve by being able to reduce their heart rate to below 20 beats per minute. The average resting rate is around 70. Their oxygen blood levels fall from a normal 98% down to below 70%. All their natural survival mechanisms try to kick in to get them to breathe, but to reach their targets they must overcome these urges. (Apparently it gets easier after 2 minutes!). It is interesting to note that in order to do well they must not get stressed as that increases their adrenaline levels and heart rate and with higher heart rates their oxygen supplies are eaten into too quickly. Medical scientists have measured their brain waves whilst they hold their breaths and found a much higher number of Alpha frequency waves, signifying the extreme levels of focus and relaxation. All those that compete in the sport are the first to agree upon the one fact that the winner is the one who controls their mind the best. This is the same in all sports at the top level of competition as was previously also mentioned in chapter four. Further clues as to how they achieve their particular outcomes are uncovered when they are asked what they think of when they are diving. Some imagine that they become like a fish and that their environment is quite natural to them, others think of dissolving into the water and becoming at one, or at peace, with the water. This visualization is critical to their performances and provides us with important clues to achieving success in whatever field we are working.

To look at this in more detail, we must analyse more of the effects of stress on the body. When the body reacts to stress, the hypothalamus (The brains major control centre) sends information out to the adrenal glands to release the stress hormones adrenaline, noradrenaline and cortisol into the bloodstream. Glucose is shifted to the muscle cells from the liver. The heart rate increases and circulation is re-routed. The blood vessels serving the muscles and brain dilate whilst the others contract. This allows more oxygen to feed the muscles and, as in the case of the divers, it quickly eats into the oxygen supplies.

Stress can therefore be seen to alter the blood pressure from one region to another, thus creating density fluctuations throughout the body. The brain naturally also shows these density variations.

Stress, as was discussed in chapter two, is attained through choice. Individuals can choose whether or not they wish to be stressed and what they wish to think about and what to visualise. By following this reasoning, people can choose (albeit indirectly) which part of their brain receives higher densities of blood.

This has particular relevance when we get to chapter ten. The message here is that stress, whether you choose it to be positive or negative in its effect, plays a part in the connection between mind and body. If we go back to our model of time cones with the two ends of the spectrum of a genetic path and an aspired path, we can again note that stress partly determines the chosen path and now we can see the way it affects the mind-body relationship.

8.14 The Zone for enhanced Sporting Excellence

This mind-body relationship is well explained in an excellent book by John Douillard called Body, Mind and Sport. Once a professional athlete, he now teaches the mind-body principles to people all over the world. Top athletes like Tennis players Martina Navratilova and Billie Jean King have followed his advice and all have reported an increase in their abilities because of it.

The secret lies in reaching 'The Zone', an elusive exercise high. Athletes talk of entering into a place where there are no thoughts and the crowd disappears into a moment of perfection, a total harmony of mind and body. People talk of being in the zone when they just know beforehand when everything is going to work just as they expect. This could be before a basketball throw, a throw of a dart, a hit of a golf ball or a baseball. In each case (you may have experienced this once or twice yourself) the sports person knew just after the release that the ball was going in, or that it was the perfect strike.

John Douillard teaches a way that allows anyone to reach the zone and to benefit from it and also allows people to reach it far more often. It is based on the principles and ancient teachings of Ayurveda.

The Zone is also referred to in teachings from China and Japan, but the oldest references are found in India, the land of Veda. This is the same origin for what was later to become the modern day martial arts. According to some writings recently found at a Shaolin temple, the messages from the Vedic culture became the forerunner to Zen Buddhism, Kung Fu and Tai Chi. The clear message from all these is that the mind and body are inseparable.

The Zone has also been referred to by many other names, 'peak experience', 'flow state', 'altered state', however, it is not the same as the 'runners high'. This is a state brought on by pain and exhaustion and the release of endorphins, enkephalons and other substances into the bloodstream by the brain. The zone requires the absence of pain. Roger Bannister summed this up when commenting about the run when he broke the four-minute mile barrier. "We seemed to be going so slowly... I was relaxing so much that my mind seemed almost detached from my body. There was no strain. There was no pain. Only a great unity of movement and aim. The world seemed to stand still or not even exist."

A tribe of native Mexicans called the Tarahumara Indians were found to have extraordinary running abilities. They seemed to be able to run for vast distances without any perceived effort. When scientists measured their performance, they had below average heartbeats and lower blood pressures at the end of the run than at the beginning. This they achieved by entering into 'the zone'.

John Douillard took brain wave pattern readings on some of the athletes that followed his teachings. He found that when they were in the zone, they had a much greater number of Alpha brain waves. Their heart rates were on average lower than normal athletes and their breathing rate was much lower at a steady 13-14 breaths per minute.

One of the keys to recreating the zone quickly and frequently, is to breathe correctly. When we enter this world, we breathe through our noses and eat with our mouths. Every land animal that runs uses their noses to breathe through, even when they are exhausted. Just look at the nostrils of a horse next time you see one running. The only exception is when they are overheated and, because they lose heat through their tongues, they pant through the mouth to cool themselves down. However, due to nasal congestion when we have a cold, or later on in life through too great a dairy fat diet, we are forced to learn to breathe through our mouths. With correct, deep, diaphramatic breathing, that generally has to be re-learnt over time, we can begin to enhance the mind body connection. The reason that this may be so is that the nose, through its olfactory sensors, has a more direct link with the brain. A breath through the mouth goes straight to the lungs without being picked up by such sensitive sensors. This is just one example of the many mysteries of how our mind works and its connection with our bodies. Currently people around the world are working to enhance this connection because they know it both exists and is beneficial to them. In our quest we also need to look further, in the same direction they are, to reveal some of its secrets. This we will do in chapter twelve when we cover martial arts in more detail.

8.15 Deep level Hypnosis

With greater levels of hypnosis we can look at more amazing phenomena. The hypnotist can alter the intensity of the suggestion and the subject can alter the degree of acceptance in order to give more dramatic effects. On the stage, subjects can appear to hallucinate and see things the audience cannot. These can range from seeing aliens landing to seeing people naked when looking through a pair of glasses. The latter is one I myself have tried out at a cabaret evening amongst a large group of windsurfing friends who were all on holiday. I once hypnotised a lady who found great delight at seeing everyone naked when looking through a pair of dark glasses. What was strange was that she could also see correctly skin imperfections and other markings on the bodies. This real effect is mirrored in other experiences. Under hypnosis people have been able to hold their hands above a live flame. They, as mentioned before, have experienced no pain, but also in this case no blister. The subjects had been told that there would be no pain and no blister.

This experiment was duplicated with a hot metal rod and, when touched, there was no pain felt and no blister (when there definitely ought to have been!). The same experiment was repeated with a cold bar and the same subject was told that there would be pain and he would have a blister if he touched the bar. He did so (somehow persuaded?), it was painful and it did raise a blister that was on the finger long after the hypnotic effect had been stopped. (The mind creating a new reality!)

Another similar, but opposite example (in that there are no blisters afterwards) and one perhaps known to more people, is that of the firewalk experience. Many self-discovery workshops use this as a means of ridding people of their fears and inhibitions. Contrary to popular belief, those candidates that walk over the hot coals do so at a normal walking pace for a length of over ten meters. Beforehand they undergo an intense 'psyching up' motivational session. This session has distinct similarities to hypnosis.

Only when people believe that they can walk over the coals without getting burnt feet, do they start to cross. Needless to say nearly all reach the other side without a blister in sight. Quite the opposite is the case when you accidentally step on a hot coal with bare feet. Being totally unprepared for the event, the pain and the heat causes the foot considerable damage. It has since been proved that if you lengthen the distance of the fire, even greater amounts of personal belief are required. This reaches a point when it becomes impossible to walk further than the limits of the strengths of your beliefs.

However all this raises an important point. It would appear that a person that has reached this 'hypnotic state' is able to alter their reality by using their mind. To those members of an audience who had been hypnotised to see aliens landing in spacecraft, it was a very real occurrence and their reactions to it were also very real. However it was not a true collective experience (it involved other members of the audience) and as such was not real to many other people. The blister, however, was a personal experience peculiar to the subject themselves. This was an area that they, internally, had much greater control over, as it affected only themselves and therefore they were able to change a normally expected reality to one they were actually concentrating on. This observation by the subject collapsed all the possible outcomes to the one that he had been led towards, with his inner observations, by the hypnotist. This was not the case with the audience where only a few members were hypnotised into seeing aliens. Of all the possible future outcomes, the probabilities of this really happening were just too small. Despite all the concentrations of their inner senses, it would have quickly fallen outside the future time cone and missed the reality of the present.

If the blister experiment had been done without the lead of the hypnotist but by the individual themselves then it should also have the same outcome. However the level of intensity of self-hypnosis would need to be far greater (than the normal lower levels generally seen) in order to cause the same effect. This is because it is currently easier for a hypnotist to attain these deeper levels than an individual. However, it is not at all beyond the bounds of possibility as it has been evidenced by many superhuman feats.

The outcome of all this is that an individual, with sufficient powers of self-suggestion, could cause and create the reality of their own choice (as long as it was personal to them). This is remarkably similar to how successful people attain their goals and this has already covered in chapter four.

At this point people may say that there is nothing special about hypnosis and that it is something quite ordinary. There are two schools of thought as to what hypnosis actually is. On the one hand there are the 'state theorists' who argue that hypnosis can induce a special state of focused concentration, and on the other hand there are those that say hypnosis is nothing more than everyday levels of suggestibility and imagination. It is possible that both are right depending on the intensity of the hypnosis. However, what is more important is in understanding the implications of how it works and what we can learn from the subject as a whole.

The first thing to note is that everyone can be hypnotised to some extent and only a few people are highly susceptible. The second thing is that it is much harder to be hypnotised if you do not wish to be. As individuals we have a choice. The next thing to note is that this is a very real phenomenon and although there were fakers in the past, the effects are measurable (what they do not yet prove is which one of the above schools of thought are right).

At the Imperial College of medicine in London, neuropsychologist John Gruzelier and his colleagues have been working on analysing hypnosis in more detail, hoping to answer some of the controversial questions. What they have definitely found out is the importance of mental focusing. In the early stages of the induction routine, you have to be able to shut out all the external senses to the exclusion of the hypnotist's voice. People who are easily hypnotisable can quickly ignore sounds and train themselves to focus on the words of the hypnotist. These effects can be seen on brain P.E.T. scans. (Whether they correlate to trance states or just deep levels of concentration and relaxation with ordinary mental and physical changes remains to be seen another day. In our case, which of the two sides is correct is not actually important).

If we take a closer look at particular features seen on P.E.T. scans done on people that are hypnotised, we find more interesting information that correlates well with what we already know.

The anterior cingulate cortex, the area of the brain that indicates focus and attention shows increased blood flow due to the intense focusing. The deeper the intensity of focus, and therefore level of hypnosis, the more increased the blood flow and blood pressure around the region. This change in pressure again has a high degree of relevance as we shall see in chapter ten.

The colour centre of the brain, back in the visual cortex, responds under hypnosis when subjects are told that they are colour blind or can see colours that do not exist. Blood flow, and by association blood pressure and density in the region, either falls in this area when no colours are perceived seen, or rises when they are.

In the frontal lobes blood pressure increases when subjects respond to suggestions. This is, in part, because they are using their inner senses more (for example their thoughts). Subjects also show a complete loss of the track of time when they are hypnotised. This goes hand in hand with their loss of interest in the actual, external world and as they begin to treat the products of their imagination as real and believable.

This question of reality, and that which is real to one person might not be to another, will become clearer as we progress on through the book. What is clear is that only that which is personal to the individual, like the blisters, can later enter into everyone's perception of reality. For those real-like hallucinations, that involve more than one individual, then clearly we must all first experience them similarly in an enhanced, focused 'state' before they 'collapse' into our universal reality. Before we can understand how that might happen, we must add one more dimension that will be covered later on.

Proceeding to look a little further into the power of the mind, we should take a look at some of those people that have different experiences from the normal. Dr Sheryl C. Wilson & Dr Theodore X. Barber from Cushing hospital, Framingham, Massachussetts, U.S.A. made an in depth study of 27 fantasy prone women. These women were analysed as normal in all other ways of life except for their ability to fantasise. They were tested along with 25 normal women with no special abilities to fantasise to give the test added meaning and strength.

These ladies all said that they had the ability since birth. Many had so called 'friends' that no one else could see and most of them reported that they preferred living in their fantasy world to the real world. They all said that they experienced their fantasies as real events. Sometimes they would become the characters they had read about in books, overiding their previous character. One lady thought she was leading a lamb in a meadow when she suddenly 'awoke' to find that she was walking down a street filled with traffic. The experiments that were carried out on the women showed that the fantasy prone women had much more vivid imaginations and that they relived their memories with not just sights, but sounds, tactile feelings and emotions. Many of them also had a near perfect auditory memory. They also appeared to have above average psychic abilities, doing better in telepathy tests than the baseline group of women. All of them were far more susceptible to being hypnotised. Two thirds of them could have their fantasies with the same intensity whether their eyes were open or shut. All of them had exhibited an easy control over their bodily functions like heart rate and blood pressure.

These women all showed remarkable similarities in what was required to become hypnotised. However, they could do this on their own, in their own time and at their own desire. As to how successful they were in their chosen fields still depended on their physical, practical planning and goal setting abilities.

What we can learn from the studies of these women is that if we apply the same intensity of inner senses to our goals as they do (like the vividness of their imagination), then we can progress far more quickly toward 'collapsing' the future outcome and creating our chosen new reality. We have already seen that the inner sense of belief plays a major role in influence and success and when we look at applying heightened levels of intensity to all of the senses, we might well begin to expect that the mind can produce some extraordinary feats. I shall go into some of these later on in this chapter.

There is a medical condition that has been known also to simulate the experiences of the fantasy prone women. There is a form of epilepsy, known as narcolepsy. This, sometimes chronic brain disorder affects about 1 in 30,000 people. Sufferers suddenly fall into a dream state of sleep known as R.E.M. (rapid eye movement) sleep. It can occur for anything up to 30 minutes and is often accompanied by loss of muscle control and loss of the concept of time. Researchers at the Stanford university centre for narcolepsy have found that outbursts coincide with increased intensity of emotions. On some occasions, they have been known to continue what they were doing in an automotive fashion (The commonest example is a continuation of writing). A few extreme cases involve people who slip into a completely different reality. When they 'awake' they can be doing something completely different to where they find themselves, similar to the lady leading the lamb in the meadow whilst on the main street. They too, find it difficult to determine between their dream images and reality.

Thus it would all appear to back up the concept that it's the intensity of the inner senses that helps to bring about reality. To bring about the reality of choice, then a degree of direction is also required. Only then, and as long as it's personal to ourselves, would it appear that we could have ultimate control over our destiny. To find more about this direction we must proceed onwards with our quest.

8.16 Post Hypnotic Suggestion and programming the mind

One of the more amusing applications of stage hypnosis is the ability to leave a suggestion inside someone's mind. Even when audience members return to their seats and have full consciousness, a trigger (like a whistle) can bring about a change in behaviour. Then, whatever the hypnotist has suggested to them, they end up doing. This experience for them is a very real one.

This technique has been used, sometimes quite effectively, to help people overcome their fears or to stop habits they don't want, like smoking. All that has been used is the hypnotist's language, which is spoken to their subjects in their heightened levels of sensitivity and suggestibility. Their brains are then far more receptive to the new programming.

All this shows is how much we are a product of how our minds have been programmed and how easily we, or someone else, can change those programs. We have seen that these are made up of several parts, like core beliefs, and that they are mainly manipulated by language. There are many people in the world with many different languages and if you have ever tried translating one language to another, you will find it is not an exact art. Many words don't have exactly the same meaning and connotation when translated. As our thoughts are conducted in our own language, the way we all program our minds throughout the world will be slightly different from one another. This is probably one reason that we have cultural differences between countries. We ought to look at this concept in order to find out if we can learn something useful for the future.

The English language is very noun oriented, we like to name things and describe objects. This gives us a very fixed notion of the world about us. Niels Bohr, the Danish physicist, referred to this type of language as 'classical' in nature. The definite position and speed of electrons are talked about as though they are both known. As we have already learnt in chapter six, this is not the case (Heisenburg's uncertainty principle). To be able to describe them with more exact meaning, and hence fit in with a more apt 'quantum' worldview, we must look for another approach. Bohr went on to say that our 'classical' way of thinking restricted us in understanding the quantum world. We still consider that the electron possesses a position and speed and that it has a reality of its own, independent of any observer. Our materialistic, noun based language, which talks of objectives and realities, is common to the European languages.

David Bohm, the late professor of Theoretical physics at Birkbeck College, took this further and suggested that a verb-based language might better serve to describe events at the quantum level. In his book, Wholeness and the Implicate Order, he describes a language based on processes and activity. Bohm argued that this hypothetical language would be far better adapted to enfolding and unfolding matter and thoughts, feelings and emotions. What he did not know until shortly before he died, was that this type of language already existed among the native American Indians. The Algonquin family languages of the Cree, Mic Mac, Cheyenne, Blackfoot and several others all place emphasis on verbs and reflect in them a reality of transformation and change. Algonquin people are concerned with the animation of all things and they have a widespread use of verbs, some with hundreds of variations of endings. Their language uses sounds and rhythms to give meanings to the way things occur and the interrelationships that exist. Needless to say it is extremely hard for any accurate translation to a European language, as there is no dictionary that could cope.

One example is the word 'autumn', when used it does not automatically bring to mind a specific image that is the same for all of us. However, the American word, more heavily influenced by the Native Americans, is 'Fall'. This word more easily conjures up in everyone's minds, the actual falling of the leaves from the trees. But even the use of this 'verb' has been corrupted and is now used as a noun in American sentences.

8.17 Cultures

If we are programmed by our thoughts and beliefs from within our conscious mind (whether by ourselves or someone else), and our actions are a consequence of those programmes, then the type of language we use must play an important part in those actions. Cultures across Europe differ to some degree, but only marginally compared to the culture divide between the indigenous American Indians and ourselves.

If we are looking for indications as to how the mind works, we need to note the differences between ourselves and the American Indians and listen to what they themselves say about their language and how it helps them.

1. They consider language not just as a vehicle for communication, but also a living thing that is a link with the universe.

2. It is not a language designed for objects, but for entering the realm of the world. They maintain that objects exist, not in themselves, but in their relationships with other things.

3. They say that certain words have great power and can only be uttered with sufficient people around to contain the energy that lies within them. This is because to say something releases great energy that enters into the surrounding energy of the universe.

4. They consider speaking to be a positive action that can bring about change.

5. They have a vast amount of words that vividly and accurately describe processes, often with relationship to a particular place.

6. They don't categorise in their thoughts like we do. We have categories like fish and birds, they only refer to the processes of animation that are taking place in the water and the air.

7. Even their perception of time and space are not separated in their language like we separate the past, present and future.

As you can see there are vast differences in the way they use language from the way we do. Their interrelatedness with nature is also well documented and they are well known for their exceptional, if not a little peculiar, healing abilities that are still a mystery to ourselves in the west. This goes along hand in hand with many other feats that seem amazing to us, but with which they take for granted and as natural. They don't talk about knowledge, but more of a 'coming-to-knowing'. This appears to be a form of tuning into a source of information by accessing and forming a relationship with the surrounding energy fields.

8.18 Conclusion

The American Indians appear to use the many qualities of the inner senses like their vividness and intensity in order to achieve what they want (collapse into reality), and also as an access to a form of universal 'energy' force. The structure of their language more accurately suits and describes the 'quantum' world than ours does.

If we return to our model of the time cone, they appear to have found a way to tune into the 'quantum' worlds of the past and future cones in a way that assists them in creating their reality of choice. With our 'noun constrained' language we would find it harder to program ourselves with the same level of attunement. The fact that they also do not separate space and time, also reinforces this as they see things in a more holistic manner. The fact that they are reluctant to use certain words, shows us that they are aware to some degree that a form of observation will create reality, and one they might not want.

Of everything we have so far learnt about the mind, and about the complete and intense use of all the inner senses to achieve (collapse) the outcome we personally want, we have now come across the first reference to a 'force' or 'energy'. It would appear that it has a highly relevant role and is intimately connected with ourselves, our relationships with others and the universe as a whole. This will be looked at more closely in the next chapters, but we still need to look in further detail at some of the other interesting and relevant features found associated with our minds.

8.19 Dreams

An analysis of dreams and their related features may allow us to find out more about how the mind works. What appears to occur in the mind when we are asleep, may give us a clue as to what could also occur when we are awake. The implication being that the mechanisms that are at work within the brain when it is asleep must also be potentially able to work when it is awake.

I mentioned at the beginning of the chapter that our minds are not conscious whilst we are asleep and this is backed up by the fact that there is little or no activity in the prefrontal cortex at the time. The brain has two recognisable patterns of sleep. Non R.E.M. (Rapid Eye

Movement) sleep and R.E.M. sleep. During R.E.M. sleep, the brain dreams and the visual cortex shows signs of increased levels of activity. Nightmares are identified when the brain activity centres on the amygdala (fear) region in the limbic system. The brain waves are predominantly of theta wavelength. This type of sleep shows much in common with psychosis. People suffering from delusions or bizarre thoughts show brain patterns that are similar to this form of sleep. This is caused because the conscious region of the brain is shut down and cannot organise things. People who live in a delusional world, similar to the fantasy prone world, do so in such a powerful way that reality cannot break through.

The deeper sleep, with no R.E.M., has more delta wavelength brainwaves ($^1/_2$ to 2 cycles per second). There is less activity in the limbic region and almost none in the frontal lobes.

Sleep can be further divided into more stages but at this stage it doesn't serve to assist us on our journey. What is interesting to us, is that part of sleep where we have dreams. An analysis of the mystery of these dreams is what we must next look into.

8.20 Dream Research & Dream Telepathy

Much of the initial research into dreams was carried out at the Moses Maimonides medical centre at the state university of New York from 1962 to the early 1970's. Here they investigated the possibility of telepathic dreams and the ability for dreams to predict the future. They chose a person who had declared that they had an ability to receive information telepathically whilst asleep. This was tested in laboratory conditions using a 'sender' who spent the night awake trying to send images of a picture that had been given to him in a sealed envelope. Only when the subject was asleep in another part of the building, was the person allowed to open the envelope and start 'sending' their visual image of the picture. The experiment was a success, with the subject being able to describe accurately the picture when waking first thing in the morning. Numerous other experiments were carried out along strict guidelines, including one done on a massive scale that included the rock band 'The Grateful Dead'. They assisted in the experiment to see if the message that was sent might be stronger if more than one person was the sender. Their 2000 strong audience assisted and a picture, chosen at random, was shown to the audience. It was another success and the subject, Malcolm Bessent was able to identify four out of the six pictures shown.

The scientific community ignored the evidence for this dream telepathy up until 1995 when Dr Dean Radin, a statistician and a director of the Consciousness research laboratories from the university of Navada, looked into the data from the Maimonides centre. He recalculated the statistics and found that the probability of it just being chance was 75 million to one against. It would appear that telepathy does seem able to occur when we dream. This does not prove conclusively that it could also occur when we are awake and conscious, but it does mean that there is some mechanism within the mind that allows it to work.

Dr Cathy Dalton of the department of Psychology at the University of Edinburgh has done similar experiments more recently and again results are shown to have exceeded that of chance. Her experiments were also more geared to finding out why telepathy might be more special in dreams. She used methods to cut out the external senses in order to see if it helped results. It appeared that when this was done, there was a greater match up with the target data that had been transmitted by the 'sender'.

One of the methods used to test telepathy is the use of the 'Ganzfeld' state. The state is designed to minimise all external stimuli so that the inner senses of the subject can be more receptive to telepathic messages. The musical sound of flowing water is played through headphones and a red light is shone at the eyes that are covered up. In this state, messages are sent and received and then measured for their accuracy. An interesting feature that came from the answers was that they were more often than not describing something happening rather than the specific item that the sender was envisaging.

If telepathy has a higher chance of success when the messages that are being sent are actions, rather than things, then this too has a connection with the quantum world. We have already seen that the quantum world can be described far more suitably by using a verb based language. This, perhaps, gives us a clue as to how we might be able to operate more effectively at a telepathic level. It might also give us clue as to where the explanation for telepathy and other related subjects like clairvoyance might be found and how they might work. They would have to be at the quantum level of the brains operations. We will look further into this intriguing idea in chapter ten.

The results of all the experiments show that there is a significant probability that telepathy is possible whilst we are asleep. As to whether it might be possible when we are awake is another matter. We ought to be able to accept that a mechanism of some sorts is there to be used, but we are at the mercy of all the translations that occur between the non-conscious sleeping mind and the conscious mind. The additional information coming in via all our external senses will add to this problem. If we are to attain more than the flashes of occasional telepathy that sometimes occur when we are conscious, then we must find a way around these problems.

8.21 Native American Indians and Dreams

This problem with the translation from the sub conscious to the conscious is similar to the translation of verb-based life and language of the Native American Indians into our noun oriented language. The translations between the two are not straightforward. If the 'sender' is transmitting their image of a noun (which in itself is subject to misconceptions and connotations), and the projection can only take place effectively as a verb (or as something that is being done), then the receiver, (who is only receiving the message of something occurring), can only provide that as an answer (or only guess at what noun it might refer to).

Dreams play an extremely important aspect of life amongst the American Indians. The Indians, with their varied rituals, display a far greater imagination and inward intensity than that of the modern man. This is partly because of their attention to their dreams from an early age. They consider dreams to be messages from beyond, warnings, prophecies and revelations. Some tribes, like the Iroquois, hold a dream festival where everyone gets together to discuss old and new dreams and then look at their possible meanings. They then follow the meanings in their everyday life and consider them vital to any success or undertaking. The Mojave also believed in the existence of 'The great dream'. 'A dream that was dreamed in the womb, forgotten in childhood and if lucky was recaptured in youth.' This dream would be the ruling dream of a person's life, a dream that would bestow upon the holder great insight and wisdom, a dream that would give direction to their journey through life. This is similar to the concept of a vocational path in life. Dreams would give them the ability to heal, have courage, be creative and it's because of these attributes that they were actively encouraged. Several enhancement techniques were used to increase their capacity to dream. They would stay extreme lengths of time in sweat lodges, sit in caves or on mountain tops. C.G.Jung in his travels regarded that the enlightenment that the Indians sought through their dreams was similar to his 'cosmological meaningfulness'.

8.22 Out of Body Experiences

Dr Charles Tart, Professor of Consciousness Studies at the university of Nevada, ran a sleep laboratory in 1966 to study out of body experiences whilst asleep. They found a young girl claiming to have these experiences every time she went to sleep. She was able to fall asleep and rise up, out of her body, and look down at herself. This awareness is also termed lucidity and is a rare occurrence amongst people. Lucid dreamers are able to control their dreams and dream with a remarkable vividness. In this case, under laboratory conditions, she was placed in a room with a tall ceiling. There was only a bed and a shelf far out or reach. Her entire sleep was video taped and her brain waves were monitored. On the shelf, a different five digit random number was revealed each night and placed next to a clock after she had fallen asleep. After three nights, she was able to wake in the morning and tell the scientists the exact number and time of her out of body experience. At the point she left her body and rose up to a position to where she could look down from above the shelf and read both the number and the time, she had an unusual amount of alpha brain wave activity. This is something rarely seen in sleep.

The experiment again only proves that the brain has a mechanism that allows this to happen. It does not include the possibility of it happening whilst we are conscious, but again it does give us an insight into the nature of what might be necessary. This appearance of alpha brainwaves is commonly found in many psychic people, like healers, as they conduct their business and it would appear to have relevance.

8.23 Remote Viewing

Similar to the girls experience whilst dreaming, remote viewing is the ability to picture something far away from you, that you had no prior knowledge of. The difference is that the conscious mind is involved as the subject is not asleep. If we accept that the mind can do this while asleep, then we ought to be able to accept the possibility of it doing the same whilst awake. This is something the American military looked at very seriously due to its obvious military applications. Tests involving remote viewers were done on many occasions, sufficiently so to prove statistically that they were factually correct and that it does work. However, it was also something that still had complete misses as viewers came up with the wrong picture.

This appears to me to further support the view that the mind has an ability to do amazing things, especially when not confused by the conscious mind. It would appear that the transmission of correct information is a two-stage process. Firstly the reception of the right information at the non conscious level, then the relaying of that information back up to the conscious level. It is that last stage where the external stimuli confuse the issue. As individuals we distort and confuse the information with all the barriers we put up in terms of our perceptions. If we can clear these, with sufficient focus and attention, then we might be able to train our minds to be able to accomplish these feats at will, or at least to a better ability like some people around us already have. Fortunately the path to doing just this already exists. By programming our minds with the correct suggestions, we can instruct it to do exactly what we want.

Some of us may have had or heard others speak of 'out of body' experiences when there was a life or death situation. People report that moments before an event, like an accident, they saw themselves from high above the scene looking down. I knew a chaplain that said, in complete honesty, that this had happened to him microseconds before a car crash. He said that he saw the whole thing briefly from above and seconds later he was back in the car again. Patients in the operating theatre have sometimes talked of similar recollections whilst being operated on. I mention these things to cause the reader to consider that these experiences are more common than is generally accepted and a large number of people already accept them as real. They don't need to have this type of phenomena proved to them because they've all witnessed it themselves.

8.24 Dreams of the future

Lucid dreaming has also been associated with the 'ability' to foretell the future and other supernatural feats. The dreamer's awareness of dreaming has enabled researchers to communicate with them whilst having the dream. This has enabled scientists to learn far more about the subject and is ideal for testing psychic activity. Stephen Kapit uses dream forecasting to determine the U.S. Stockmarket activity. He put specific advice he learned from his dreams onto the internet and currently 94% of the people who have followed his advice have made money. He says he has vivid, unforgettable dreams and that later on the images return in real life.

Chris Robinson saw terrorists planning an attack in a hotel in Cheltenham in the U.K. in his dream. He reported this to the police and later on the place was raided and the terrorists and their weapons were captured. He later went on to use his ability to assist police as a 'dream detective' with several successes.

These examples do not prove clairvoyance can exist in the conscious mind, but do however, show that it is possible in the sleeping mind. This also though, does not rule out the possibility of conscious clairvoyance.

Many of us may have had personal experiences of vivid dreams, often about something catastrophic like air or motor crashes, only to find that when we awake the event actually occurred somewhere in the world. Of course these cannot be proved by some kind of recreation of the events under laboratory testing conditions, but that doesn't mean they didn't or couldn't happen. All I wish to do is to draw attention to the fact that the mind has a way of working that sometimes allows these things to occur.

Some of you might be now asking how is it possible that you can know what is going to happen in the future. The only answer that can be given is that we, ourselves, seem to have created our concept of past, present and future from out of our own consciousness and by the observation of our surroundings with our senses. This awareness of space-time is individual to ourselves and by no means should be a golden rule for everything encountered in the universe. Indeed, in physics we have already shown in chapter six that not everything appears to be what it originally seems. This appears to be especially so in the case of space-time. The quantum world does not appear to recognise the same rules and provides reasonable possibilities for faster than light travel and because of that, the concept of space existing with space-time being just another dimension, is quite feasible. Being able to work outside of this dimension would leave room for the possibility to know about the many pasts and futures.

8.25 Creative Dreaming

The question now is whether or not there is anything between the 'conscious' and the 'sleeping mind' that suggests that if one can do something, the other can as well. One area that might show this is in the area of creativity. It is well known that dreams inspire creativity and problem solving. Floyd Ragsdale, a chief engineer for Dupont in Richmond, Virginia dreamed he was inside a piece of machinery at work that was repeatedly going wrong and failing. In his dream he noticed the hoses acting strangely when the machine was running. When he was awake, he remembered the dream and suggested inserting a spring to reinforce the hoses. The hoses were normally out of sight and could not be seen when the machine was switched on, so the suggestion could not have been made beforehand as the engineers hadn't even identified them as the source of the problem. Needless to say the solution worked and went on to save the company millions of dollars.

Paul McCartney says he dreamed the tune of 'Yesterday', which he later wrote down when awake. Many other artists have likewise mentioned the same thing, only wishing that they could have come up with as brilliant a song too. This is perhaps not that surprising as the mind appears to continue to work on whilst we sleep. This ability for the mind to continue to work while we are doing something else can be evidenced whilst we are awake as well. The best example is doing the crossword puzzle. If you don't finish it at the first attempt, like most people, you are often left with clues that you are sure you know the answer to. However your mind has gone blank and no matter how hard you try, no answer comes. Leaving the puzzle at that point and doing something else quite unrelated for half an hour may be the only option. How often have you then returned to the puzzle later on, only to find the answers suddenly spring to mind? (An interesting continuation along this theme is found in the range of puzzles that can be bought that involve removing a rope from a piece of twisted metal, or a ring off of a seemingly endless circle of rope. They are all possible and come with solutions, however what I have found is that if one continues to say that the puzzle is impossible in one's mind, then an answer is never forthcoming. It is only when one has sufficient belief that it is possible, that ideas to try certain moves come into one's mind.)

This period of alternative activity has allowed the mind to go to work on your question in an unconscious manner. This is like the mind when it's being creative or like problem solving whilst being asleep and unconscious. The same parts of the brain must operate, only in one of the cases you are fully conscious.

This might suggest that whatever the mind can achieve whilst asleep, it can also achieve whilst you are conscious. The trick would appear to be to program it the correct way to come up with answers. This would certainly make the brain and the mind an extremely power-ful and useful tool if it could be activated at will. But there is already evidence that the mind is an extremely powerful entity and if we accept that, then it takes little extra persuasion to accept the possibility of telepathy and clairvoyance and a whole host of other Extra Sensory Perceptions.

8.26 The placebo effect

The placebo effect is well known. It was originally developed as a test to test the effectiveness of drugs. Subjects were given pills to cure some ailment like a headache. Half the pills might be a new drug; the other half nothing more than coated sugar. The subjects would not know about the test as the pills were made to look alike. The results became known as the placebo effect as headaches appeared to miraculously dis-appear amongst the subjects who had only taken sugar pills. The only explanation is that their belief systems worked some way to provide the expected solution, in this case the absence of pain in the head. Placebo effects are not just seen with painkillers, but in all other forms of drugs and treatments. A classic study done by Charlotte Feinmann of the University college of London, found that 30% of patients treated with ultrasound therapy after dental surgery significantly improved even though the machine was switched off at the time.

This placebo effect has an interesting cultural difference. In Germany the effect can be as high as 70%, while in America it is closer to 40%.

It is an embarrassing fact for the medical profession that a third of all patients get better whatever treatments they are given. Beliefs and expectations have even been shown to affect the time of ones death. American researcher David Phillips found that 20% of a selection of famous people died shortly after their birthdays, compared with the norm of 3%. This was presumably the desire to celebrate their life's achievement one last time. Among Jewish populations, the death rate drops by 30% just before Passover, because of peoples desire to have one final celebration.

New light has been thrown on the placebo effect by a new medical discipline called psycho neuro immunology (P.N.I.). This is the study of how a persons mental state can affect their immune system. In one study Dr Hugh Baker from Westminster Hospital, London found that first year medical students were more likely to fall ill than second year. This was traced to confidence levels and anxiety.

At the common cold clinic in Salisbury, Dr Sheldon Cohen has shown that only 20% of people exposed to the virus actually became infected and of these only 25% developed symptoms. The efficiency of the body's immune system plays a big part in determining whether or not you could get infected by a virus. The immune system has been shown to depend largely on mental factors like how good you feel, how in control you feel and how positive your approach to life is. All these mental factors play a part in whether of not you are susceptible to illnesses. If you allow negative stress to affect you then you will succumb far more easily to ailments. Nowadays people in the medical profession accept that up to 80% of all illnesses are psychosomatic. That is to say that 80% of peoples problems would be non existent or controllable themselves, if they adopted the right mental approach.

Beliefs, expectations and the right mental approach to life do not, at first, seem to explain the results of an experiment done by Dr Tony Scofield and Dr David Hodges, lecturers in animal physiology at Wye college, London. They looked at the effects 'Healers' had on plant seeds and conducted an experiment with Geoff Boltwood, a healer from Ealing in London, to determine if he could affect the rate at which cress seeds could germinate. The experiment was repeated six times in a double blind manner, with some of the seeds made sick with salt water, and they found that on five occasions there was a highly significant difference in the rate at which they grew. The tests involved the healer holding the seeds in his hand and directing healing thoughts at them. Scientists have since derided the results due to the lack of a scientific explanation. However Dr Benor, author of many books on the subject of 'Healing' has since duplicated the results of the experiment as well as conducting many others involving healers. Large scale clinically controlled trials have yet to be done using healers, principally because of the costs, but this does not mean that something must be influencing the results and showing a healing effect. The healers themselves refer to an energy. This may well be assisted with above average amounts of belief.

This 'energy medicine' is found in many societies around the world, including that of the native American Indians. We will look at this 'energy' in more detail in chapter twelve as it is integral to our quest.

8.27 Summary

We have seen that the concept of consciousness and the unconscious might be explicable at the quantum level of matter if we take a 'reductionist' approach. What is occurring in our frontal lobes is a mechanism that is creating our conscious view of the real world from out of the quantum world. It appears that the use of our 'inner' senses gives us control over what we would like to happen. The greater intensity of focus, vividness, belief and thought gives us a greater power of control and the ability to do even more extraordinary things. We can also self-program ourselves with the language we choose in order to make further achievements. Language itself would also appear to have a connection with the quantum world in that a descriptive verb based one more accurately defines things in it. The effectiveness of this programming will have great relevance on how we envisage the quantum world interacting with the brain and how events might collapse into everyday reality. It is this subject that we will pursue next in chapter ten.

In many instances of psychic phenomena the concept of time seems to disappear and the only connection with time in the brain is found in the frontal lobes. When these are used, while we are conscious, we have a good sense of space and time. When that part of the brain is inactive we lose track of it.

Our mind can control our bodily functions. These include our blood flow and blood pressure. We can also alter the pressure densities within our body, including the very specific parts of the brain that we are using. Stress can initiate these actions. Positive stress leads to pressures where we need them, in the particular parts of the mind we are using, and where we are in control through the use of our inner senses. Negative stress leads to similar pressures but in the wrong parts of the brain for any personal benefit. In these cases we are either externally led and feel we have little control over things or we are overstepping the amount of stress that is healthy for our bodies and therefore producing strain.

If we develop a harmonious mind body relationship we can attune ourselves more easily to the use of the inner senses and that will also assist in creating the reality of our choice. When putting all these things into effect, it appears that something else is required to finally add the last piece of the jigsaw puzzle. This has been referred to by some sources as a form of 'Energy'.

In the model that we are following, we can now imagine the vast number of possibilities open to us in our future cone. Everything that can be done in the quantum world and in the subconscious exists in this realm. We also now know that the method for steering ourselves to the reality we want lies within the use of, and the way we use, our inner senses. They can literally channel the path that we want into our present reality and classical world. Our journey through space-time seems to hold the clue as to how we make the final collapse into that world of our present, near the tip of the cone, and this is what we must now look at in more detail.

In chapter ten we will also look at the role of pressure in the brain and why it may well be a necessary part of the overall procedure. We will also cover the current thoughts that some of the scientific community have had on where and how consciousness might exist within the brain. This takes us down to the sub-microscopic quantum scale of matter in a 'bottom up' approach to finding out more about the mind and its link with physics. Once this has been established, we will be able to proceed on to the final part of our quest to find a link between Modern science and Ancient Earth and Human Energies.

CHAPTER NINE

A WAY TO DESTINY

I leant against the far wall in silence, casting a thoughtful eye around my new surroundings. The broch had been built recently as the thick bronze bars in the middle of the door still had their shine to them. A solitary flickering candle the other side of it provided the only light. The floor was solid stone and seemed to be the same rock as the cliffs. That ruled out any form of digging, even if I had anything to dig with. At first glance, there didn't seem any way out. I slipped slowly down against the wall till I was on my haunches. Things were not looking good. I could feel a bed of old straw with my left hand. It was damp, my heart sank into deeper despair.

Alone with my thoughts, I stared down in silence trying to fight back my fears and rising despondency. To have come all this way, having found my sister and then to fail was an overpowering feeling. I thought of my father and brother and wondered what they would have done. Neither, I was sure, would have ended up in a position as bad as this.

The more I thought of my family, the worse I felt. Everything that I had done up to now was looking like it was going to be worthless, all that training would have been for nothing. I began to reflect on things that I had done, wishing that events had been different. I thought of Dugald and Angus and asked myself what they might do in my situation.

As soon as I thought about that, I remembered Angus telling me about the cauldrons of inspiration. A ray of hope shone out from deep within me and eased the strain inside my stomach. If I had any chance of survival, I had better start remembering the things that I had learnt. I needed inspiration badly, but there was no way I was going to receive any in my present sad state. I needed to fill my mind and heart with joy and thoughts of happiness.

Knowing that and doing it were two completely different things. I started by thinking about all the good things that had happened recently. My sister was alive, that was extremely good news. I'd passed and become an Anruth, something I'd wanted for many years, which was also good. I'd met some good friends and learnt many new things and with that had come a sense of excitement I'd not really experienced being isolated on the island of Siegg.

I was feeling better already, so I spent some time reliving the most enjoyable periods of time that I had recently had. I started off remembering my run down the scree slope. After a few moments, I was feeling better, but still without any answers to my predicament.

Then I remembered the kingfisher. Why had that happened? Was his death really a portent for my own after all. My heart sank again. Angus had said that that was unlikely and had gone on to say that I would meet with Lugh.

Lugh. This mystical man of legends. Thinking about him somehow gave me a lot more hope. In fact, somewhere deep inside me, I knew that one thing was true, I would be meeting with him. If that was the case, there was no way I was going to die just yet, which meant one thing, I was going to get out of this place.

Reflecting on all these things made me feel far better, a power surged within me and expectation and belief began to grow.

I was shaken out of my reverie by a knock at the door. I got up and looked through the grille. Outside there was a woman with a bowl of broth. I'd forgotten about food, but now looking at it, I knew I was famished. She turned to look at me and both of us registered a little surprise. It was the same girl that had been the waitress at the Selkie.

"You again." She starts, stepping back half a pace. "What are you doing here?" Realising it was a daft question, she quickly adds "I mean, how did you end up here?"

"I came to rescue my sister and Niamh." I reply, "How did you end up here?" I ask back, smiling through the grille.

"I live here, Domnhuill's my step father..." She pauses, presumably waiting for some usual reaction. I look at her blankly, not showing any understanding, so she continues, "I only work at the Selkie on their busy nights."

"I see. Did you not mind what they were doing with you two nights ago?" I enquire, now with a little genuine concern to my voice.

"They were only playing, Domnhuill would have seen I was

alright." She smiles at my concern and twists her hips slightly one way then the other whilst still looking me in the eye.

"It's not the way to handle a girl where I come from." I offer, in some way trying to win her prolonged attention.

"And what way would that be Fionn mac Donal from the clan Donal? What way would an islander handle a girl like me?" she pirouettes playfully around with one hand holding the hem of her plaid skirt, the other balancing the bowl.

She was not an unpretty little woman who dressed in a way that showed more skin than I'd ever seen on any Island woman. Her white top must have left her cold whenever she left the hearth of a fire. She exhibited beneath it the slender figure of a dancer. I wondered whether or not there was something here I might be able to exploit that would make her want to help me get out of here.

"If I could only step out there with you lass, It'd be a pleasure to show you." I flirt back, hoping it might work to my advantage.

She stops and her smile disappears. "Sorry, I can nay do that, but I haven't thanked you properly for coming to my aid that night. Come here." Her playful voice switches to a more serious tone.

I lean towards the grille that she unlocks and swings open. There is just enough room for me to stick my head out. She lifts the bowl up and offers it to my lips. Just as I am about to sip, she pulls it back down.

"Close your eyes," she says, "let me feed you."

"Why?" I answer, my confusion apparent.

"Because I say so and it's my game." She scolds mildly with mock selfishness.

I had no option as the smell was making me even hungrier and I was completely at her mercy. I closed my eyes and could feel the heat from the bowl as it got closer. I opened my mouth slightly and waited. In an instant she'd pressed her lips against mine and was giving me a passion filled kiss. Completely taken aback, I opened my eyes. Her spare hand was around my neck. There was no escape. All I could do was look at the hair on the side of her head that swept around a small dainty ear. Her eyes were closed and I could smell her sweetness. It was not at all unpleasant, it was just that I felt awkward being so helpless.

She pulled back quickly, after what seemed like an eternity but was really only the briefest of moments. At least she was still smiling.

"Here eat up." She continues, as though nothing had passed between us.

"I don't even know your name," I half protest and smiling back at her.

"Igrainne." She pronounces quickly and as if it was unimportant. She lifts the bowl to my lips again.

This time I hesitate, but looking deep into her eyes I chance another go.

"It tastes almost as good as you." I say after the first sip, "Did you make it?"

I was not good at this and it sounded very contrived. Nevertheless it appeared to have an effect. "Fionn, you are a one to be saying such things. It's certainly a shame you had to come back. Come finish this quickly and if I've time, and I can, I'll pop down again. I've a mind to hear more about the men from where you're from." The genuine interest behind her voice, mixed with a little cheek, cheers me as it appears I might be getting somewhere.

I drank the broth thankfully and as soon as I had finished, she spun around and skipped off to the stairway and ran up two at a time. At the top, she stopped, looked round over her shoulder and straight into my eyes giving me a big smile. She then dropped her gaze down to the side of her legs, turned and disappeared.

I was left a little dazed by all that had happened and immediately set about thinking how best I could use this new turn of events to my advantage.

I also began to wonder where they were keeping Mairi. There was no one in the cells either side of me. I sat down again, this time feeling much better. To keep my composure and joyous mood, I began to retrace my favourite times. The more vividly I recalled events, the better I felt and soon, in my mind, I was far away from the cell.

Later that day, I heard more people coming back down. I got up quickly just in time to see Mairi being led back into the cell next to me.

"Mairi!" I shout out, "It's Fionn, how are you?" I call again, rushing up to put my face against the grille to look out and see how she was.

"Fionn!... Fionn! Och it's guid to hear a familiar voice." She tries to come over to me, but is restricted by her guard. "Are you well, brother? What? How? ..." She fumbles out, her mind too full of questions to ask just one.

"Aye. I'm fine Mairi and glad now I've found you're alive and well."

"What about Father?" She asks in a concerned way, now having come face to face with me just outside my cell.

"He's going to be fine too. He sent me to find you and bring you back." I reply, my words failing at little at the end at the seeming futility of my situation.

"Well you've found me well enough, but I d'nay ken how we're going to get out of here and get back. Things are a bit dire to say the least." She replies in her slightly sarcastic but affectionate, sisterly way.

"Talk in the cells all you like, but you've to get in now." Comes the gruff voice of the guard as he directs her towards the open door to her cell.

He locks her in the one to the right of me and disappears upstairs. I wait for a moment until he's gone.

"Have they treated you well here?" I ask, my lips pressed between the metal of the grille.

"Not bad, I have to say, Fionn. They let me out during the day when Domnhuill Dubh is not here."

"That's good. Do you know why they did this yet, and what they've in mind for you?" I ask, masking my concern lest she detects I know more than I wish to say.

"No. And I don't think I want to know. All they said was that I'd be here at least half a year, after that no one would talk about it." She pauses and there is a moment's silence between us. "Fionn, the word up there is that they intend to dispose of you tomorrow morning. What's going on, what have you done to them?"

"I seem to have upset them, mainly because I wouldn't give up looking for you. That and probably embarrassing them at the Selkie inn two nights back." I reply.

"But why have they done all this?" She asks in an exasperated manner.

I go on to explain all the events that led on from the attack up till now. I also mentioned the crown helm and Callum Beg's involvement but I decided it best to leave out what he might have in mind for her.

"I understand all that, but why did they ta'e me?" She persists.

"I think it was for some later bargaining power, just in case they needed it. Also you might have just been in the wrong place at the wrong time."

The moment I'd finished saying that, I knew it had sounded a weak response and that she deserved better. However she seemed to accept the idea.

I continued to question her about everything that she knew and what the routines were at this place. She answered all my questions as best she could but she had obviously been kept in the dark about anything important.

Then after a break of contemplative silence she says to me. "Niamh seems like a nice lass, you made quite an impression with her."

"Really." I reply, reddening and thankful that she couldn't see my face. "What makes you say that?" I realise I am forced into replying by her continued silence.

"The way she talked of you. I liked her. We only had a short time together and we cheered each other up a lot by talking about you mostly." She stopped, obviously trying to provoke some sort of response from me.

After trying carefully to think how to reply and with words failing me, I started to say something when we were interrupted. Igrainne had appeared at the top of the stairs and quickly ran down and over to me.

"Listen." She starts in earnest, "Domnhuill's just got back, he's in a foul mood and wants to see you. If I were you, I wouldn't make him worse. You don't want to know what he's like when he has a rage."

I wanted to ask what it was like, part of me felt like finding out for myself; the other tended to err on the side of caution and to find out why he wanted to talk to me at all.

"I'll do my best Igrainne, but only for you." I add hoping that it might make some difference later on. I follow her up the steep stairs, trying hard not to look at her legs that are right in front of me.

"Good luck, Fionn and please be careful." Calls Mairi, who I can now also see pressed up against the grille.

"I'll be fine." I say reassuringly, turning back and waving at her not to worry.

We ascend into warmth and light and the thick trapdoor that covers the top of the stairs is put back down again after we reach the top. They obviously didn't want the cold creeping up into the room. Domnhuill Dubh was sitting with his legs up on a stool in front of the fire. I could hear the others talking upstairs. Igrainne joined them and I was left alone with him. I watched him looking into the light, obviously in deep thought. Shadows flickered all around the circular room playing on the whitened stonewalls. There was a quiet mumbling of voices from above. Everyone was quite probably intent on hearing what was going to happen and were whispering amongst themselves.

As nothing was, I ventured closer to the hearth, seeping in the warmth gratefully. I stood staring into the flames, copying his gaze and trying to anticipate his thoughts and actions.

"In the short time that I've come to know you," he begins in a slow and measured way, "you've managed to cause me more trouble than any other person I've ever had the pleasure to kill." He pauses, but not I suspect for me to say anything. "I've never seen Fiacal so disturbed, nor Gruagh with such a blood fury. To the extent that they're now both arguing over who can sever your head first. Tell me, what is it that makes you such a special pain in the back side?" His voice quickens as he snaps the last words out at me. His head turns and our eyes meet for the second time.

"You came and took from us what is rightfully ours. I'll not rest till I see them returned." I answer slowly, holding his stare and using every effort to retain my calm.

"That rest will come to you sooner than you think. There are things afoot here that are far more important than you. We needed what you had, you weren't using them, we took them, so I don't see your problem."

"Who exactly do you mean by 'we'?" I ask, curious to see if he would confirm any link with Callum Beg. It wasn't a good move.

"You're not in a position to ask questions," he rises to his feet and takes one step toward me, "and especially not one to get any answers." He snarls and his hand lashes out to grab my throat. Standing a good foot taller than him, I manage to step back just in time and catch his wrist. I see his other hand reach for his Dirk in his belt, then stop. As if he had changed his mind, he relaxes and twists away leaving his back to me. I let his arm pull away as he turns.

"I brought you up here to tell you what we are going to do with your sister. I want you to die knowing how pathetic your rescue attempts have been and knowing that she will suffer horribly as she is split right down the middle, then her guts will be pulled out as she takes her last few breaths." He chuckles at the thought and turns back to face me. "What have you to say now you worthless sack of words?" His voice rises and I notice it has gone silent upstairs.

"By Senchan's breath of damnation, you dare to challenge me with words." I burst out, wanting to come across with dignity, fearlessness and power. "All those that you lie with will go barren, your cows will run dry, you shall live in eternal fear of all animals that stalk the night and your destiny will be to die painfully amidst their throng. May your dreams be filled with the wails of the sidhe and your waking thoughts filled with terror." I continue, with the words for the threats springing intuitively to mind. I begin to circle him, fixing his stare with my eyes narrowed.

"You dare to threaten to sacrifice my sister, daughter of Donal mac Donal, defender of the great armies of the South, friend of Amairgin Whitehair and countless Kings, and think you can escape without retribution. I command that my geas become real and that forever more your life will become filled with the same misery as the lost souls of the misshapen Formorii."

I stop, standing still between him and the fire, facing him square on. My dark silhouette menacing, I lower both my outstretched arms and end my curse. There is a moment's silence that I sense is one of uncertainty. After which he roars into a deep laughter and collapses into his chair. I stand still, maintaining an aura of deadly calm. His laughter eventually stops as he sees it is having no effect on me.

"Take him away." He bellows. "I give you your life for this one night for amusing me with that outburst of cows' dung. Any other time, I might have enjoyed exchanging oaths with such a worthy adversary of words. When the cock crows on the morn, your last glimpse of this world will be without your body and your head will be sent back to your island kin."

The same two oafs that had earlier that day taken me down to the cells, had now appeared having come down from above. They moved quickly to my side. I left with a smile on my face and strode over to the door in the floor that led down to the cells. Igrainne lifted it up and I winked as I passed. She followed me down leaving the other two up by the door. Once at the bottom and, as she was opening the door, she turned to me.

"Thanks." She says quietly, touching me on my upper arm in a familiar gesture.

"What do you mean?" I gasp, perplexed. I turn to face her fully and as I do her other hand reaches up and gently takes hold of my other arm.

"For not upsetting him and making him laugh." She replies earnestly, looking deep into my eyes and moving up onto tiptoe.

"I didn't try to," I say, "I meant everything I said." Now feeling slightly confused and awkward with her advances both verbally and physically.

"You stood up to him," she goes on, "he likes and respects that. He takes no pleasure in killing someone he has no respect for." She brings her heaving chest now firmly against mine, drawing my gaze with the movement and causing my head to lower.

"That's very reassuring Igrainne." I say playfully looking back up into her eyes, realising that my chance was near to coming.

"Listen very carefully to what I am about to say Fionn." There was a serious tone to her voice, yet with almost a slight stutter. "I'm not going to lock the door, I don't know why yet. Just wait a quarterday till it gets dark then come up. Everyone will be up top except a guard. Wait till you see me come down for ale. The outer door is not locked, you can escape while I distract the guard."

"Why are you doing this? and what about my sister Mairi?" My excitement rises at the chance that I am getting but not wanting to leave my sister behind too. She forcibly pulls back away from me, almost pushing me back against the wall behind me and I wonder what it is that I have done or said to have been on the receiving end of such a change in attiitude. She smiles wickedly back at me, knowing she has me confused.

"You'll have to leave her for now, she'll be fine. Just remember you'll owe me for this." She holds up her index finger and shakes it in front of me until I nod my consent.

"Won't they know it was you that didn't lock me in?" I add as an afterthought.

"Here take this knife, you'll have some time to scrape away the wood on the outside of the grille. They'll wonder how you ever did it, but no one will blame me." She says, breathing a little faster, her chest rising and falling at quite a rate now. "I'll lock the door with you on the outside, they'll think you've managed to squeeze through the small hole. That should confuse them plenty." She finishes with a short laugh.

"I will indeed owe you my life for this and I don't yet know how but someday I will repay you. "I reply, taking the knife.

Without warning, she flung her arms around my neck and again pressed her full body against mine. She sank her teeth into my lips and the slight pain it gave me was strangely pleasurable. Now I could also look into her eyes and I saw that they were glistening with an intense passion. Just as I began to react back, she pulled away, leaving a taste of wild redberries on my tongue. Saying nothing, she reversed away from me with a fierce smile covering her whole face. Then she turned and ran up the steps and was gone.

"I don't think I know you, is this really my brother Fionn!" My sister teases half in jest, half in actual amazement.

"Mairi!" I am bought to my senses, my mind still reeling by the recent turn of events.

"What is this side of you that I have not seen after all these years?" She probes with the drive of a woman who is closing in on a new juicy piece of gossip and scandal.

"To be sure, Mairi. I have no idea what it is or indeed what you are on about. It is plainly clear that the woman Igrainne is slightly the worse for the ills of the mind. Why else would she allow me to escape. Hush now or they'll be down to see what's up!" I try to refrain her from pursuing her delight at seeing my embarrassment by moving up near to the door of her cell to stop her from calling out.

"Why indeed, if it was not to be with you later, my innocent brother." She now whispers directly into my face from the other side of the grille. "Can you not see she enjoys playing with you, just enough to distract you of your thoughts of Niamh." She continues in her own playful manner.

"Enough, Mairi. My mind is not ready for all these woman's words. I have to think." My patience is wearing a little. "We'll talk more later. I have to get on."

I set about the hard oak with the knife, chiselling the metal bars out bit by bit. It was sacrilege that they had used oak in the first place, but they probably didn't care.

It was a full quarterday that had passed before I had finished with the bars and had formed a plan that I was happy with. I went over to Mairi's cell and we talked some more about life on the island. I meant to cheer her and to lift her spirits for the coming days she would be alone for at least now we had a chance.

"Mairi. I have to go and get some help. If you come with me now they'll find us easily. I have a feeling you'll be fine for a while here. I promise I'll come back to get you out as soon as I can, though it might not be for a couple of moons. If I break my gease may the skies fall upon me, may the seas drown me and may the earth rise up and swallow me. I will get you back home safely."

"You're a good brother, Fionn. Donal would be more than proud of you now. Go safely and take care." She reaches her hands out through between the bars and I take them in mine in a tender clasp.

"I can handle myself now Mairi, d'nay worry yourself."

"T'is the women I mean, Fionn." She says mischievously.

"Be off with you." I joke with her and turn to quietly slip up the steps.

The door at the top was shut but not locked. I lifted it up a touch and felt the warmth hit me full in the face. Looking around, I could see the one guard over at the fire and Igrainne standing next to him in a seductive manner. She could certainly appear to be a truly spellbinding woman when she wanted and I wondered what her role was and what future she had decided upon.

I noticed her look my way and then move slowly toward the guard. Taking this as a sign, I came up and out as silently as possible. The hinge made a sound like an angry crow and I thought the whole broch would hear. I froze for a moment before continuing. Once out, I stepped lightly along toward the inner porch. On a stone shelf next to it stood a flagon of ale and six tankards. I slipped out of the room into the long anteroom that led to the door outside. Luckily my bag was there. I slipped it over my shoulder and was about to leave when an afterthought struck me. I rummaged inside and found the small package of white powder that I had bought two days ago. Sticking my arm back inside, I emptied its contents into the flagon of ale. It fizzed a little, then disappeared. Whatever it did, it could only help and with a bit of luck hinder any that might come after me.

Outside it was bitterly cold and dark. Thankfully it wasn't wet and raining, but a layer of fresh snow lay ankle deep all around. There were footprints leading down the steps, so I went down backwards and set off in the same manner heading back to Invercarrie.

After a few hundred paces the snow had thinned out and had drifted to the side, so I turned and broke into a stealthy run. I had decided to make for the place Angus and I had chosen earlier and after a period of hard running, I came to the main road. I turned North on a hunch that the animal pens and grain pits were further out of town. It was a lucky guess.

The large pits to the side of the road were nearly empty, a sign of a long winter. I went round between them, destroying my tracks with a frozen branch of holly. The pens were full of highland cattle as Angus had said. I moved closer, only suddenly to see the light of a small fire. It was well shielded and could not have been seen from the road. I approached cautiously, the last thing I wanted to do was to stumble across more problems. I had been warm running and even though I'd been careful not to break into a sweat, I was chilling fast. As I got closer, I could feel the heat of the flames on my face and hear the crackle of the sticks as they burnt.

"Come out, whoever you are." Calls a familiar voice.

"Angus, it's Fionn." I say bursting out and rushing to fall on my knees in front of the fire. "It's good to hear you again," I go on, warming my hands, "Where are you, show yourself?"

There's a moments panic in me as I think I have been fooled, but no sooner had I thought that, he pops out from behind a feeder box.

"I could see you coming well away laddie. You'd do well to cover those eyes another time. The fire reflects well in them. Look away as you approach and you might live longer."

"Thanks," I say gratefully, "Do you happen on having some food with you? I would nay ordinarily ask, but I had to leave in a hurry."

He set about preparing me some oatmeal, whilst I told him all that I had happened since we'd last met.

"Here." He says passing the warm bowl to me, adding a mixture of dried berries on the way. I stir them together with a wooden spoon and finish it all in silence. By the time I had finished, he had some hot, herbal water for me. We squatted down next to the fire and began talk.

"You'd make a good woman," I say jokingly, "And I'll be ever thankful for it." We laugh together and lapse into a sigh, gazing silently into the embers of the fire.

"It's I who will have to thank you one day." He starts off again mysteriously, "I must give you some news now which has great importance for you." He shifts uncomfortably on his haunches to face me more squarely.

"That sounds ominous." I say clutching my drink with both hands and sitting back into a comfortable listening position. We fall silent as we hear the cattle moving restlessly in the next stall.

"It was no one." Angus says after a few moments, "It might be that they aren't used to fires at night beside them." He goes on and I nod in agreement. "When I left you, I went to see someone I thought I could trust. A member of the inner council at the Aes Dana. I stayed with her for two nights reliving our pasts. Eventually I got round to asking about Callum Beg and his connections amongst the other Ollamphs. Unfortunately, they were deeper than I suspected. They have all been corrupted completely by him and are now all totally behind him. As soon as I mentioned the Crown helm, she took me straight to where it was." He pauses for a moment between each bit of information, wanting time to think clearly about what he was saying. "There was only one piece missing. She then tried to get me to join them again and told me about their plans. I soon realised that I had been told too much to back out without them killing me, so I decided to pretend to go along with them." He pauses, now fully deep in thought.

"Fionn, your arrival here has caused many people some severe pains in the head." He begins again, in the same intermitted manner. "It was completely unexpected. At first they were not sure what to do. In the end they allowed you to go through with the initiation tests, not expecting in a hundred suns that you'd be good enough to pass. Well done, by the way."

"Anyway." He continues, "Callum Beg wants the whole crown helm to add weight to his master plan. He aims to become King himself, before Queen Irnan can proclaim her son to be of an age to take it himself."

"What!" I say shocked, putting my drink down beside me. "How can he get away with that?"

"He intends to have a Tarb Feis at Samhain. He can't obviously conduct the ritual sacrifice of the bulls himself as well as devine that the entrails proclaim him king. He needs someone well respected to carry out the ceremony. That's one reason why he's been searching for Lugh and when you came along, saying you were on your way to meet him, things went crazy. That one thing probably saved your life."

"But where does the crown helm fit in?" I ask, now rising to my feet and starting to pace in circles around the fire.

"When the people are told that Callum Beg will be their king, many might object. By taking the precaution to announce to them that he has the completed Crown Helm, he will swing the remaining doubters onto his side, then no one will be able to stop him." He stops and looks up at me.

"But he hasn't got the complete helm. He hasn't found the last piece." I reason.

"That's the other reason for finding Lugh, he apparently has the last part of it."

At that last disclosure, I stopped pacing and stood still looking at Angus through the flickering light of the fire. All this information was almost too much for me to take in. I wondered what would be next.

"Where did you fit in to all of this?" I ask him, wanting more to hear the way he answered the question rather than the reply itself.

"Originally Beg wanted me out the way until he had won over all the other Ollamphs. Later he wanted to force me to assist him to find all the parts of the helm and then to find Lugh. That last part includes you. They intend to follow you in order to find him." He peers closely back at me to assess my reaction.

It was as he expected. I was stunned into momentary silence by his revelation, trying to assess exactly what it all meant.

"That's going to be hard now." I state openly, thinking of how I'd recently marred their plans. "I doubt that they'll notice I've gone till the morning when I was due to be killed."

"Your escape has probably saved Domnhuill Duhb's neck as well. If he'd taken your head, there'd be no one to find Lugh." Adds Angus, with a little amused grunt.

I return to sitting down next to him and picked up a stick lying half out of the fire. I used it to prod the embers and enjoyed watching the collapse of the burning logs down into its centre. The flames immediately grew with the advent of fresh wood now amongst them.

"Are you really sure I'll be able to find the man? If Callum Beg has been looking for him all these years and not found him, he can't be that easy to get to." I ask, just a little apprehensive at the enormity of the task ahead of me.

"I saw it myself and there's nay doubt about it, you will find him. I am sure he can be found, if he wants to be found. Which is why none of Callum Beg's cronies have managed it yet." He picks up one of the unburnt logs that has rolled off to the side after my disturbance and tosses it into the middle. The fresh sap catches the heat and it hisses and crackles.

The gesture and whole scene was not lost on me as I notice the look on his face as the wood starts to burn. He was definitely enjoying the thought that it was Beg that was burning amid the flames and not just a branch of birch.

"But once I've found him, what then? Will he be able to change things and help us, all on his own?" I distract him.

He sighs deeply before answering me. "There's nay doubting he is an extraordinary man, just as there is nay doubt that events will unravel themselves in their own good time. They'll be more than enough answers then. Meantime, you must be sure to set off early. You'll need a healthy start, if they're not going to find you and catch up with you."

"Where do you suggest I start?"

"You should make your way up to Killiecraigie, the folk up there would more likely know of dolmens and where they might be. One note of caution though, the further North you go, the more they are still believers in the Cult of the Dead. It was the Cult that probably put up the stones in the first place. Even if they didn't, they certainly used them." He stops enigmatically and begins to get out his sleeping bundle of furs and plaid. Whilst arranging them next to the fire he continues.

"I'd also take far more care when you walk around there. They are strange folk and altogether more bloodcrazed than the Southerners. However, I'm beginning to have my doubts about that now as well. I suspect Callum Beg is resurrecting the Cult down here." He warns, stopping his nightly preparations to look at me directly when speaking his last words.

"How can you tell that?" I ask, now getting my own furs out.

"The Cult used to use the same place that the Aes Dana now stands. Those stones were probably erected by them as well. You yourself saw the sacrificial stone in the centre. Callum Beg spent a lot of time there studying its strange carvings. It's my belief he is behind the disappearances and the recent sacrifices. He would choose to rule with the power of fear and bringing back the sacrifice of the bulls would be a start to it all. It could well be that he has your sister kept back for just such an occasion as well."

I blank out his last words and instead ask him in a concerned way. "What will you do?"

"I'll go back and try and throw them off your trail as best I can. I'll also find Conal and the others and confirm to them about where your sister is being kept. When you get back to Invercarrie, check here for any messages from me. If I find out anything significant, I'll leave a crafty ogham for you here." He chuckles at the thought.

We talked a little longer as we lay next to the fire and he told me of a few secrets on leaving the city without being seen and also about the road North. Words between us drifted slowly further and further apart and eventually we fell asleep.

My internal awareness awoke me when I wanted, just before dawn. There was no time for food and we parted wishing each other well.

When the sun came up, I was well past the farm and travelling off to

241

the side of the road in the Glencannick forest. The trees, which were mainly spruce, fir and silver birch, ran right up along the coast. There was little undergrowth, so the going was fair. What stopped me from going faster was the occasional drift of snow covering the burns that fed the sea. On numerous times, I found myself floundering on all fours, covered in the stuff, as I fell in again and again. Eventually, wet and cold, I decided I was far enough away to chance journeying on the track.

Having taken this decision, I made good speed. The next settlement was Dun Carlabhagh. Angus had told me they were just a group of farmers, normally a days journey from Invercarrie. I was hoping to be there around midday. Everyone travelling would generally stop there for the night, but I had decided not to endanger them with any knowledge of my passing. I had also been told of a Boar's leap to the West, upstream of the Dun in the Gleann Sgurr. My mind wondered what new physical feat I would have to endure to overcome this obstacle.

I needn't have worried. Having left the track well before the Dun, I circled round, till I came to the river. It was wide and deep, but further up I could see some shallow rapids. Walking up to them, I noticed several sties with sows and boar running wild. I could cross at that point and did so, mindful of the slippery, algae green boulders under the water. I'd seen no one and had presumed that no one had seen me, so it was with a lot more confidence that I set off for the next settlement. The scenery was the same as before, but now the sun had been hidden by cloud that was descending ever lower.

The seas were calm and grey and with only a light breeze, the languid crash of the waves on the shore was all that broke the silence on my journey. I'd been prepared to avoid anyone I came across, as it was no one seemed to have ventured out to travel that day. I spent my time going over recent events and trying to come up with some solution to release Mairi. The fact that I was proceeding North in search of Lugh, the legendary Samildanach, hadn't escaped my thoughts either. It seemed to be inextricably bound up with everything that was going on and yet it felt like I was losing control. Instead of making decisions based on my thoughts, I was merely reacting to the will of others. If I was to succeed, I would need to change that.

The sun was about to go down and I could both see and hear the Rougie falls in the distance. The land had risen slowly and there were small cliffs down to the beach. The waters here ran straight over the hard dark rock and fell far down to the sands below. A lone falcon circled overhead and swooped down to perch on a dead, lightning struck, tree. I watched it as it cast it's keen eye over its new surroundings. As I walked by, not fifteen paces away, it took off flying South-West and over the forest.

As I neared the huts that stood either side of the banks at the top of the falls, I noticed signs of evening activity. Before I was seen, I waded through the undergrowth that ran along the side of the trees and continued on, within the wood, to intersect the river further upstream. I decided to stop somewhere there and get some sleep. I had been travelling hard all day and had covered a distance done normally in a day and a half and all I'd eaten was a trail mix of nuts and dried berries that Angus had given me. I'd enough oats for the morning but nothing for tonight. I'd have to sleep away any hunger pains. As I looked for an area to light a fire and bed down for the night, the air shook with thunder and moments later the rain came down, heavily and noisily. Even under the cover of trees, I was getting soaked. I trudged on, trying to look on the bright side of things. I was still alive and there was still hope.

When I reached the river there was only a little light left in the day. I stopped to look around for a place to build a fire and as I did so I heard the sound of music drifting out of the silence. Drawn like a moth to a candle, I tried seeking it out. It came from a large timber sided round house right in the middle of a clearing just higher up the river. Wooden pipes, a drum and a hand harp were all being played in a tuneful melody. I stood still and listened until I began to shiver.

With the weather turning even worse, I was becoming desperate for good shelter, but I also had no desire to endanger innocent people with problems of my own. I was exhausted from the day's travelling, frozen, hungry and now drenched. On much reflection, I felt that I really had no option but to ask here for some hospitality.

Curiosity had also got the better of me and I approached quietly to where I could listen better. I now squatted down less than ten paces away, letting my mind wander with the sounds and the beat. Every now and again it would stop and start off with a different tune. My hunger was soon forgotten, along with any danger, I crept up to a crack in the timber wall where some wattle had fallen away. I thought it best to check things out first. It was needless to walk into more difficulties. These were new lands to me and the folk were unknown.

Crouching down and feeling extremely guilty, I peeked in. The sight I saw startled me backwards and I toppled over with my feet and arms left dangling skyward. I gingerly approached again, if only to check that my eyes hadn't been playing tricks with me. Inside there were definitely three women, all dancing around in circles and playing musical instruments. That, in itself, was not too extraordinary, but what was really compelling was the fact that they were all next to naked. All that they wore were thin, sleeveless, almost see through, tunics that only came down to the top of their behinds. The fronts were open down the middle to their belly buttons. Each also had a thin leather belt that seemed to have pouches hanging from the sides.

I watched, drawn by their completely relaxed motions. Each woman was different and moved separately, yet they were all shapely and attractive. The older one had slightly grey hair, whilst the others had blond and brown. I guessed that they were mother and daughters, but I could have easily been wrong. What was really fascinating to me was their air of peacefulness and harmony. The serenity of it all was seeping through the walls and beginning to intoxicate me with its power.

How was I now going to be able to approach and knock on the door, knowing what I had seen inside. If I did and was allowed in, what then? Would I be safe from them? I'd heard talk of such activities before from tales told. Events surrounding such as these either ended up happily or badly for the adventurer. Which was it to be for me?

I got up, determined at least not to be caught in such an uninvited position, and went round to the door. Events had brought me here, so I decided to trust to fate. It was customary to give hospitality to travellers, so I put aside any feelings of awkwardness and fear and knocked.

I knocked twice, immediately regretted it and knocked a third time. Three was a lucky number and these were superstitious times.

The blond girl answered the door and in a manner quite unashamed of her near nakedness.

"Please do come in." Her voice is gentle and still full of the tones of her music. "Cold and wet evening coming, miserable outside, welcoming in, pleasure for all." She turns and steps, still half dancing to the music, to the other side of the door allowing me room to enter.

"My immense gratitude for your kind hospitality," I say, wondering what new manner of speech this was and clearly unsure of where to rest my gaze.

I enter and they take my cloak and lead me to the hearth of their fire. As custom dictates, they offer me food and drink. "Eat, Drink. Banish your thirst and hunger with us. Warm fire, sit relax." Half sings the grey haired lady, appearing now with a dark gown that covers her from head to toe.

"I have nothing to offer in return." I reply politely.

"Strange for one who likes to use words." She says smiling at me and casting a glance at my cloak of feathers.

She spins around and returns to the centre of the room where the others are still gyrating their bodies in tune to the music they are playing. The three of them continue their movements, I watch and eat at the same time.

I looked around at their wooden hut. Like all of them, it had a ceiling that rose pointedly in the centre. Long wooden beams stretched across and up to the top and hanging from the walls were many animal skins and body parts. The light came from nine massive candles, situated around the edge of the room. It wasn't completely circular inside as one segment was walled off. This stone section housed the fire I was sitting next to. In the far end there was a wooden door that was shut. I presumed that that was where they probably slept. There was a pleasant odour of pine from the timbers, mingled with the slight smokiness from the burning beech logs. After such a long and difficult day, I began remember my tiredness. Through closing eyes, I watched them dance around a large circle in the centre of the room. All the time they carefully avoided stepping onto or over the line and I wondered about its importance along with the carefully laid pattern of the flagstones.

The beat from their music began to match the pace of my own heart and I started to feel light headed. I finished the last mouthful of food as my eyes closed over. As soon as that happened, everything stopped.

"Sleeping, tiredness, sorry." Comes three soft voices. I open my eyes to see all three of them bending over my slumped body. I close them again immediately as all I can see are their heaving and panting chests. They show no acknowledgment of my visual distress, staying as they are.

"Come with us, the heat is ready." Comes a voice. I look up again as they are helping me to my feet. I wonder what they mean, but am to weak to resist. We move toward the closed door of stretched hide, which opens before me. As it does a gentle heat rushes out to greet me. They quickly usher me inside, bringing a candle in with them.

In the dimmer light, I could see a huge bed of furs in a strangely semi circular room. In the centre there was a large flat stone embedded in the dried earth. The walls here were made of poles of willow threaded with hazel and more skins.

"Sit, relax, let the warmth enter in." Says the blonde haired girl, as she sits down on the furs. "Take these skins off of you." She continues. I am too tired to resist and several arms disrobe me of everything but my leggings. These I resist their attempts to dislodge and they simply return to their rituals.

Barefooted, I watch as they joined hands and sit cross-legged on the earth around the central stone. Slowly and carefully they pull a large stone from the wall. It had been shaped to provide a ring that they had tied a length of rope twine around. With all of them pulling on it, they drag the whole fire from the other room into the middle of this one. The heat suddenly increases intensely.

"Drink much, here." Says the blonde girl again, passing me a large drinking sac. "We will sweat well tonight."

"What are you doing? What is this place?" I stutter out in my disorientation.

"Drink deep, it cools and refreshes." She takes back the sac, gulps down several mouthfuls and passes it back to me. This time I gratefully sip. Mercifully it is only mountain water and my fears begin to subside. The water wakens me a little and my mind feels up to thinking about my current circumstances.

I looked around and got the feeling that this particular room was designed specifically for retaining heat. There were no gaps in the walls as they'd sealed the hole where they had pulled the fire through. Even the door seemed tightly shut.

It was getting hotter, yet it felt cooler lower down where they were. I joined them on the floor, sighing as the colder air allowed me to breathe more easily. I turned to look at them and they smiled back at me. They were warm sincere smiles that made me feel a little guilty for not completely trusting their motives initially. I returned to watching them complete their rituals. They seemed to take great care in placing large, smooth stones in the middle of the fire, then followed by handfuls of fresh herbs. The mixture of different smells, the smokiness and the heat all combined to make me feel dizzy and light headed. After a while they splashed water onto the hot stones and clouds of steam rose into the air and my body began to sweat profusely. I squirmed as I was getting distinctly uncomfortable in my skin leggings. The others had already completely disrobed, but I resisted the compulsion to do likewise. I was still not prepared yet to completely disregard my own principles. However as I attuned to this new temperature, my sleepiness returned and I was soon fast asleep.

I awoke with an intense throbbing pain in the temples of my brain. Holding my head in my hands, I sat up and looked around. I was still in the same room, lying on the furs. I was also naked. The pain behind my eyes mixed with images of a recent dream. I tried to recall them but the hurt was too great. All I could recollect was that it was an extremely intense dream.

My body was sticky from all the sweat and I ached for a long cool drink. Not finding any of my clothes, I was forced into wrapping a fur about my person. I decided that my best course of action was to take a dip in the river outside and it was there that I headed, hoping that the weather was not too inclement.

There was no one in the hut so I continued on. The door was open and it was sunny outside, a smile escaped from my lips as I slowly stepped outside. It felt good to have survived so far.

The river pooled over at the far bank and looked to be about waist deep. I took a deep breath, waded in and then plunged beneath its crystal clear waters. I drank greedily then stood up throwing my hair back. This was not a time to stay in for long, so I went straight back to the side. As I came out two of the women appeared from around the other side of the hut. This time, it was they that had the advantage. They were wearing full-length plaid wraps. There were red, green, black and brown lines and patches all fitted together in a seemingly random manner. It made for a colourful sight in the early sunlight, but all things considered an imposing one for a naked man.

"Good morning." I call out, rising out of the waters and quickly grabbing the fur I'd left on the grass.

"How are you feeling friend of our friends, enemy of our enemies." Says the older of the two, moving around so that we stood together in a small circle.

"I'm feeling a lot better now thank you." I lie, as my head is still sore albeit numbed slightly with cold. However, I am more than a little confused by their words along, with many other things around here.

"Could you explain what happened last night and what you mean now?" I ask, showing my bewilderment.

"Last night was a time for dreams and answers to questions. You came to us with many of all three. We expected you sooner, so we started without you, I hope you didn't mind."

"Mind. I had no idea." I say, even more befuddled and moving my fur about in a feeble attempt to cover my total nakedness.

"There is much you don't know, nor ever will. We each play a part in the whole. Ours is now to assist you on your way and give you time to reach your goal." She answers in a way that seems practiced and rehearsed but also one that is full of smiles.

"How do you know so much?" I inquire, my awe in these women growing by the moment. I make a move to return to their hut and they follow beside me.

"Oh we don't. We have only just found out a little ourselves." Replies the elder of them.

"What else can you tell me and how can I repay you?" I go on. "And by the way, where did you put my clothes?" I beg of them, my desperation now more than obvious on my face.

No sooner had I said that, than the younger girl disappeared off around behind the hut.

"There is nothing you can do to repay us now, but succeed in what you do and that will be comfort enough for us. As to what else we know, all we can tell you is that Lugh is expecting to see you." She dips her head down at the end and averts her eyes for the first time since I left the water. She senses my relief.

"How can you know that?" I say by way of more of a statement than a question.

We now stopped and stood in a patch of sunlight just away from of the door. From nowhere she seemed to have produced a dry piece of fine cloth which she now held in her right hand. I looked at it, expecting to be given it. Instead of that she moved around to my side and reached out to dry my back. Her touch jolted me and the pleasure that filled my mind was broken by her renewed conversation.

"You are not yet ready to find him, there is something else that has to be done before he will allow you near." Her circular drying movements were widening down the length of my back.

"What's that?" I try to concentrate, but the enjoyment of the massage leaves me short of words.

"I have no direct answer to that, but a clue I can give to you, that may or may not be relevant, is that your dream last night holds a key."

The information she seemed to know about me was awesome. However, any thoughts I might have had on the subject were soon interrupted by the younger girl arriving holding my clothes. All three of us stared at them without moving. Eventually I took them from her, along with the cloth that had been used to dry my back. The rest of my wet body I wanted to dry myself, although I'd given up on getting any privacy to do so.

"If I could only remember what it was." I carry on about my dream. "You don't happen to know that as well by any chance, you seem to know everything." Regretting my innocent sarcasm as soon as I finish dressing and realising the pressure I had put myself under.

"It will come to you in time." She resigns, showing no concern over my remarks. "Come now let us eat and send you on your way. We will meet again soon enough." She adds on a happy note.

I follow them back inside where there is a cauldron of porridge and wild berries on the boil. I was going to ask where the young blond girl had gone, when seeming to sense my thoughts, the older woman says, "We have a pony for you to use, I have sent for her and she will be with us shortly."

"That is indeed far more than I can really accept. Thank you but no." I say, spooning up a large mouthful of the steaming food.

"No is not an option, we insist that you take her. She will find her own way back." The younger girl insists and reaches over and touches me lightly on my forearm as she finishes.

"If I accept, you must tell me why you are willing to help me so much." I remonstrate with them.

"We had a collective dream last night."

"Not everything comes to us in dreams." They each take it in turns to talk to me. When one finishes a sentence; the other starts.

"Reasons and answers appear in their own good time."

"What is important is to act on what is learnt." My head turns from one to the other to listen.

"We understand the importance of assisting you and can only guess at the reason." The spoon that I have been holding is still half way from my mouth.

"Now eat up. I suggest you try and make Killiecraigie by nightfall. They are a strange folk up there, but they probably think that of us." The elder woman finishes and I could tell she was now of a mood to say no more.

I ate my fill pondering her last words. Since I had come to the mainland, most of the people I had met seemed strange. She was probably right.

Outside stood a beautiful white pony, it stamped its front foot and whisked its tail as if it was acknowledging me. I sensed that it looked forward to a good run and that it would be an agreeable companion. I climbed up and turned to say my goodbyes. The blonde girl had still not returned so I waited a while, but they bade me farewell and said they would send on my regards. I left with mixed emotions but altogether enriched by my latest experiences.

We set off and went into a canter once the other side of the river. My pony seemed to know the way I was heading and the girls had given me good details so we were soon out of the Glencannick forest. It was still sunny, but at this time of the year I knew the weather could turn at any moment. We joined up with the North road and made good pace toward Craigielachie. The two peaks of Carn Sgulain and Ben Craigie towered above me to the West. The slopes looked steep and rocky. Ahead lay Glenesk and after crossing that, we would come to the huge Achentoul forest. Angus had warned me about what I would come across along my way North and had advised me, for no reason he could give, to at all costs try and avoid that place.

We passed through Craigielachie that consisted of a few crofts, half buried under earth. Those people that saw us coming seemed to disappear quickly back into their holes. I thought little of it and was thankful there had been no delay. We were making good time. Killiecraigie was a full two days ride from Invercarrie, or a three-day walk. I reckoned we'd be there early, soon after midday.

The sea stretched out to the East and my mind set to wondering about what lay across the waters and which way it really was to reach the Otherworld. Its greyness didn't give any clues away so I gave it up as I had done countless times before. The Achentoul forest was now on my left. It didn't look any different from the previous forests and was certainly not an imposing sight but, as I had recently learnt, first impressions can sometimes be deceptive.

Throughout the day, I had also been constantly vexed at trying to remember the dream that I had had. The more I tried to recall it, the more it eluded me. It wasn't till now though, after I'd just given up trying, that a flash of it came straight into my mind. The memory was one of flying through the air like a bird. It had felt strangely familiar and very intense, yet I had obviously never flown before. Nothing else came to me, so I was now left pondering its meaning. If there was one thing I had just learnt from the three women, it was to pay much more heed to my dreams. Just how to do that escaped me for now, but, just as other things seemed to jump into my life, I fully expected that some under-standing would be forthcoming.

In the distance I could see a small boy sitting on the side of the road. He was squatting down and holding his head in his hands. As I got nearer, I could also hear the sound of deep sobbing. I slipped off of my pony and walked slowly over to him. I judged him to be only about five years old and he reminded me of the youngsters back at Donal Broch, but for the fact he was wearing a small silver torque around his neck.

"What's the matter lad?" I ask, squatting down two paces away from him. He looks up at me and sniffs back some tears.

"I was out hunting and I've lost my father's favourite spear over the edge there." He points to the side of the track that drops down to the rocks below. His chest starts heaving as he is about to cry again.

"That's nay reason to fass yo'self lad. Hunting you say and what may I ask was someone your size hunting?" I ask, purposely changing the subject a little.

"Wild boar." He replies, his eyes widening. I could see a small flame of passion stir within him.

"That's a mighty fine prey for you to be stalking. You must be good as I've not seen any around here and I have it on good authority that when a good hunter goes in search of wild boar, the boar all go to ground. They can all sense the danger."

He looks at me, wondering whether to believe me or not. I nod a lit-tle as if to give my words extra credibility and he begins to smile.

"Come now," I say, "Show me where it went over the edge. Perhaps I can get down and retrieve it. Then we'll see if we can get it back before your father knows it's gone."

He gets up grinning and I realise that I had guessed right about him not having his father's permission.

He goes and points over the edge. About thirty feet below I can see it lying on the rocks, just a couple of paces from the incoming tide. My pony neighs and steps back away from the drop.

"Hold her for me." I say to the boy, "What's your name?"

"Brynn."

251

"Well Brynn, you take care of her while I nip down here. When I get back up you can show me the way to Killiecraigie."

I looked over the edge. It was a steepish climb but there looked to be a few holds and the rock was firm. I slid over the edge on my stomach and found a ledge with my feet and in a short while I was back on top again along with the spear.

"Thanks. Thanks." He shouts out, jumping up and down as I give him the weapon. He begins to dance around in a small victory circle letting out small whoops of joy all the while clutching the shaft tightly as if his life depended upon it.

"Now, perhaps you can show me the way." I interrupt him. "Why don't you ride, while I tell you a story to pass the time on our journey." I suggest as an added incentive.

At this he leapt up and down and thanked me profusely again and again and I realise that I have made a firm friend in the young lad. It wasn't long before we reached the outskirts of his settlement. It was situated on grassland, back from a small bay. The beach was almost definitely the nearest possible landing place for any currachs north of Invercarrie. There were none there now and there were very few people to be seen. All of the buildings were made of the local dark grey stone and were sunk into the sand. Earth and sand was also half mounded up around the walls and the roofs were turfed. If you hadn't been looking for it or noticed the small circle of stones helping to make them watertight, you could have quite easily missed it.

We entered the village with Brynn calling out to all his friends. He wanted them all to see him riding the white pony. Gradually people began to appear from out of the holes to their homes and, as soon as they saw Brynn, they ran over. I noticed that the older folk were all wearing silver torques and several had similar armbraces as well. My first thought was that they must find the metal locally and that it was their main form of trade, but there seemed no sign of any works in the area. Apart from the silver, many of them had more tattoos than skin visible on their bodies. It produced a particularly sinister effect when the light behind them and as they moved in and out of the shadows. I considered the possibility that it was strong sign that the cult was alive and thriving up here.

Once the initial introductions were out of the way, I was invited to stay with Bynn's folk. Their home was near the centre of a maze of tunnels, all of which required an extreme bending at the waist in order to pass through. At the end of one of the passageways, we came out into a large room that left me with enough space to stretch up into a standing position. The walls were all ringed with stone and had lintels capping them that held up a clay and turf roof. Several large stone piers came out from the sidewalls each making a dark and private alcove in between. It was from within these that most of the stained faces peered out at me, eyes glinting from the light of the central fire.

In return for their kind offer of food and drink, I told them a story of Cuchulainn and his journey to the fabled Isle of Emain Abhlach. At the end, I asked if there was anyone here that knew the inland areas well and they told me that the only one would be their local Anruth. After that, they plied me with questions on many subjects till the early hours. I went to sleep exhausted, but more than content with my new profession. I decided to visit their local man of knowledge in the morning.

I awoke to the sound of the children playing in the centre of the room. As soon as they saw I was not asleep they ran over to get me up and lead me outside. It was as well they did, as there was no way I could have found my own way through the maze. Outside, the weather had turned worse again. It was cold, windy and wet, but not cold enough for snow down at this level. I learnt that their Anruth could see me after midday, so I tended to my pony in their stone built stables and was helped by the many children that seemed happy to just follow me around. Brynn of course was in charge as a sort of self-styled leader and the main point of contact between them with myself. During lunch with all of them in the stables, I told their favourite stories about the sidhe. There seemed to be no end to their desire in listening to the many tales. The more horrible and shocking, the more they liked them and asked for more. In the end I had to send them away and went to meet their Anruth.

He lived in a separate block to the side of the main settlement that looked like a mound of its own. It too was covered in long grasses, now blown nearly flat in the increasing wind. There was a storm coming.

I entered on all fours, this passageway was just too low for me to bend at the waist and still proceed. As I entered his abode, I looked up. He sat opposite, facing me, my eyes were the same height as his feet. It was a position he had obviously designed in the past in order to create sufficient deference amongst his visitors. He was a bulky looking man, well draped with a dark brown plaid and straightaway I imagined the difficulty he must have in entering or leaving his home.

"Please get up my fellow learned friend." He starts in a light apologetic note. "I am sorry about the entrance, I keep meaning to change things, but as you would know it has its advantages. My name is Uther."

"Thanks." I say rising up and moving toward the offered seat next to him. "It's good of you to see me."

"Not at all, I like to keep in touch with outside events, especially those down South. Tell me, if you will, what's been going on?" He turns slightly to eye me better in the candlelight, still cautious as to the reasons behind my presence.

I sat down on a raised flagstone amidst a variety of strange objects and bones that I moved to one side and went through all the current events that I was aware of. I realised that it was a rather thinly disguised attempt on his part to try and work out my feelings and to whom my allegiances lay. So with that in mind, I gave him as much information as I could, in a manner that supported all forms of view. At the end he got up and walked around in small circles with his hand on his chin, as though in deep thought.

"Fionn." He starts. "You are an exceptional teller of tales, as indeed all our youth are saying." He pauses, and I wonder whether his play on words is masking a vague insult, "You have quickly become their friend and that makes you a friend of mine, whatever brings you up here. Thank you for your news and I offer my congratulations on becoming an Anruth like myself. Tell me though, what is your question of me, for I too have one for you?" He fixes me with a beady stare, tightens his lips and furrows his eyebrows.

"Uther," I begin, ignoring his facial expression, "I have been asking if anyone around here knew the inland areas well. People told me that you might be able to help. I am looking for a dolmen of three large stones that stands on the rise of a small hill somewhere in this northern region. Do you know of such a place?" I end openly.

"I know of such a place, why is it important to you?" He replies, unable now to disguise his curiosity.

"A friend of mine had a dream that I was to meet someone at this place. I believe it was an important dream." I say, not willing to expound much more but keeping his eye contact. He relaxes a little, seeming to accept my answer as genuine.

"I've found over the years that it is very important to follow ones dreams, especially when you are young, so I'll tell you where I think you can find this place. There is an old path that used to run across the mountains to Finlarich Broch on loch Dubh. It takes a good four days travelling to reach it. On the final way down, past Ben Affon and Carn Eilrig you'll come to a wee loch just inside the Kildamorie forest. Instead of following the path downstream, travel west up the hill through the trees. When you reach the top there is a clearing. You'll find the Dolmen there. As you are probably aware it's one of the most secret places. I'm only telling you its location because I am well aware of the power of dreams and as an Anruth you will be aware of the correct ceremonies to proceed with once you are there."

"It's very good of you to tell me these things, I appreciate your help." I say, humbly. "You said earlier you had a question for me?"

"Indeed I do." He leans back on his seat and stretches. Afterwards he bends forwards again and asks in a semi-puzzled tone of voice. "Are you aware you have been followed here?"

My face and my mouth both register my shock. "No." I stutter out, my mind instantly wondering how Domnhuill Dubh could have found and caught up with me so soon.

"Perhaps you might be able to answer my next question, before I tell you more." He proceeds quizzically.

I look up and nod for him to continue. "Who might they be, do you think and why do you suppose they are following and not trying to catch up with you?" His tone is now more authoritarian and one that is demanding honesty in answering.

There was little I could do but inform Uther of the difficulty I had with Domhuill Dubh and his men. I told him about Mairi, and the raid on the Broch. However I decided it prudent not to mention details about Callum Beg, the Crown helm and my search for Lugh.

"As to why they are following me, I can only assume they are waiting for me to lead them to the Dolmen. I told them a story about retrieving some gold that was buried there many years ago by my father. I said I would have used it to help buy my sister's freedom. They must have believed my story and were checking up on me maybe hoping to take the gold for themselves. As it is we expect to return and rescue her just as soon as my father is better. In the meantime I'm up here looking for this Dolmen as I am sure, because of the dream, that there is some reason it is connected to all this. I just don't know in what way yet." I shrug my shoulders at the end in genuine uncertainty.

"I have to say Fionn, that your last account makes for much more interesting listening than the first." He chuckles. "Oh my, what demonic times we live in." He stops and turns to smile at me, then busies himself looking for something amongst his possessions.

"Here we are." He pulls out a long horn, raises it to his lips and lets out three long blasts. The ensuing noise causes me to quickly cover my ears with my hands, but I wasn't fast enough to avoid the momentary deafness afterwards.

Shortly, three large warriors squeeze through the entrance one after the other and are standing next to me. Each carried a long sword across their backs.

"Those men you spotted earlier hiding in the woods." Uther remarks to them. "They're up to no good with young Fionn here."

I looked at the three and watched as their faces turned to deep grins.

"You know how I dislike cowardly behaviour, even more so when people are being so unfriendly by not being forthcoming. I think the time has come to teach those curs a lesson." Growls Uther in a tone that seems tinged with an element of enjoyment.

"Fionn, you'll be wanting these I expect." gleams one of the men, handing me a sword and a wooden targe. I take it and nod, my mind blanked at the speed that events seem to turn. Another slaps me on the back and I am shaken to my full senses again.

"Come, let's go before the storm hits." Says the third, just as enthusiastically as the others.

Before I have really stopped to think about my reaction to what was happening, we had gone outside and had run around to the other side of their village. Disappearing into another one of their holes, they helped me out of my clothes and on with some weapons. They themselves adorned their bodies with gold and silver torques and armlets, and began to colour the rest of their skin with a mixture of brown, red and green paints. There appeared to be no backing out of what might lie ahead of me. To show my disinclination to fighting would be disrespectful to them in the light of their hospitality, friendliness, assistance and support. I had to fit in with their customs. Any other action didn't even warrant thinking about, which would have hard anyway as my mind was all ready a whirl at having been followed and found so soon after my escape.

Out we went and straight into a crowd of all those that were left in the village. Cheering us, they parted to allow us through. We walked on toward the outskirts and back along the North road to where my adversaries had been seen. Urging them all on from behind was Uther, who was letting out short bursts on his horn interspersed with loud incantations shouted out in some strange language I'd never come across before. The sea wind was cold enough with my skins on, but now, with only a wrap around my waist, I was freezing. I worked hard to put the pain out of my mind by concentrating on the coming confrontation. My thoughts flashed back to my early memories training with my father. I was never as good a swordsman as him or even my brother, but I had a good grasp of the basic moves. This would be the first time my abilities would really be put to the test. The other three looked to have the confidence that can only have come from many previous successful fights. This was highly evident looking at their scarred semi-naked bodies.

My wooden leather covered shield felt light and comfortable. My sword was plain, but at least it was iron and that gave me a little comfort.

Fifty paces away from the edge of the dread Achentoul forest, still in sight of the village, we stopped on the edge of the track.

"Is it cowards that hide in the wood or is it the ugliness of your faces that shames you into not having the courtesy of asking for hospitality?" Calls one of my colleagues.

This was my problem and I didn't like the feeling of hiding behind someone I hardly knew, so I moved to the front.

"My name is Fionn mac Donal of the clan Donal." I call out loudly and slowly. "If you've a quarrel with me, show yourself or forever be damned to a life as a yellow bellied runt of a sick sow."

There is a rustle in the undergrowth and striding out into the open came Domnhuill Dubh, Gruach and the guard that had been distracted by Igrainne. All three were hastily preparing themselves for a fight whilst trying to retain some air of dignity.

"Damn you, son of Donal. You have a nerve to think you can get away with threatening me and calling me a coward in front of my friends. I am Domnhuill Dubh of the clan Dubh. Commander of the Queen's guard, champion of thousands of fights, severer of hundreds of heads, father to fifty sons and master to no one but myself. Today you shall taste my sword and your tongue slit from end to end. Yours will be the third head on the end of my spear by the end of today. Taking Niamh's and Mairi's heads will be nothing to compare with the pleasure I'm going to have in taking yours."

It was a good opening cry from him, none of which I believed, and I knew I had to make my reply appear stronger than his. I also needed it to sink in and have a visible effect on Domnhuill if I was to retain the support of my newly found friends. I could sense they were warming to him and obviously respected this sort of bravado.

"What's wrong with you, son of Dubh, you're not looking anything like your true self. It's not like the commander of the queen's guard, or fearless champion, to hide in the bushes. From the look of you, none of you appears to have had any sleep either." I gamble on the fact that a night out in the forest would be cold and uncomfortable and I recognise the opportunity to reinforce my earlier curses to him. "Perhaps your dreams are not now to your liking after the geas I have cast upon you. Tell me, you three pathetic excuses for men, did the animals in these woods of Achentoul keep you awake with fear last night."

The memory of my curse touched a chord deep inside him and all three visibly flinched at my last words. It was all that I needed. Sensing that they had lost this round of words, they charged. Letting out screams behind me, I was nearly overtaken by my three comrades in arms. Swords and shields raised high and swinging, all seven of us rushed towards each other. I could hear Uther's horn just above the yells. The black figure of Domnhuill Dubh advanced toward me. The figure of a falcon on top of his helmet flapped as its black wings went up and down with every pace he took. At full speed we met. Our swords and shields clashed with no thought of style or finesse, just the intention of knocking each other over.

We bounced and rebounded off to the sides and all of us spaced out and began to circle one another. Gruach for his sheer size grinning happily at having attracted two opponents. His oversized battleaxe swung in a wide arc slicing a corner off of a shield.

I parried two quick side slashes with my shield and feinted a stab in between them. Not following up my feint was designed to throw him off my train of thought. Unpredictability could be my advantage. A thrust to my head, I allowed through my defence so I could side step him and attack his flank.

Now closer to him, I lifted the hilt of my sword up into his chin and caught him a glancing blow.

He returned my blow with an icy stare of pure hatred and let out another scream combined with a strike to my stomach. Twisting aside to avoid this, I noticed it turn into an intended feint and didn't manage to escape his real strike to my thigh. A sensation similar to hundred bee stings cut into me and I felt blood pouring down my leg. With no time to look, I parried the next two attacks with my shield and sword and chose to leave my good leg in front to help maintain an attacking stance.

The guard let out a cry, he had been hit in his shield arm and it now hung limply by his side. Gruach backed nearer him to give him what defence he could. His two opponents took turns stepping in to attack him after each swing of his axe. He had wounded both of them, with what must have been close to life ending blows to their torso's, and their blood ran freely.

Domnhuill Dubh came on again. This time he charged hoping my leg wouldn't stand firm. I allowed him to come onto me and stabbed at his foot. The weight of his charge knocked me back and my back leg gave way. At the same instant my sword connected with his ankle and dug deep. We both fell over backwards. He floundered awkwardly, dropped his shield and clutched his foot. With my training, I carried on rolling and came back up onto my feet. Unfortunately my shield didn't come too as the strap broke under the pressure of my weight. Seeing me advance upon him, he pulled out his dirk with his free hand and knelt up. I reached for mine and walked towards him.

"You know we let you escape!" He sneers from the ground. The words catch me off guard.

"What?" I say, regretting opening my mouth immediately afterwards. It was just the chance he needed and he managed to stand up.

"Igrainne was acting under my orders, you fool. You didn't really think you could get away from us that easily did you?" He continued pressing home an area he now felt that gave him most advantage.

It wasn't a question I was about to answer with words, so I replied by going in for a strike. Now we both had our dirks out, the fight had changed. Getting in close was far more perilous. He parried me easily and we exchanged a few more blows, each of us moving less fluidly and favouring our good legs.

The guard went down and his last gurgling breath was followed by a shrieking victory call. It was enough to distract Domnhuill and Gruach. I launched a vicious strike diagonally down onto his shoulder and came in under his arm with my dirk. With his concentration lost momentarily, he was caught off guard. However, his quick reactions saved his life as my knife only went skin deep into his stomach before he twisted and parried it with his own.

His face registered the intense pain and his hand moved to clutch his chest. Gruach saw him step backwards and moved quickly to his side. Together the two backed away from us with Gruach slightly in front. My fellow friends were nursing too many axe wounds to follow up their retreat too hastily and they looked to me for guidance. My instincts told me we should finish them off, but my guess was also that it would still be far from easy. In the end I decided that I now had an overall edge over him, though I had to admit he was by far in the way a better fighter and that I had been lucky today.

"Go back and live life as a beaten man, let your dreams become more vivid with fear until you put right that which you have done wrong." I call out leaving them to go.

"We'll meet again soon enough. Just remember, I have your sister and you have just condemned her to live the last few months of life in misery. Next time I will able to kill you and you will not be allowed to escape from me again." He yells out with increasing loudness as he distances himself from us.

His final words made me wonder whether he wanted me dead or not. After all he had been following me for a reason. Tonight not now, was not the time to dwell upon the subject.

Cheers went up from around all those that had come to watch. These people obviously liked a good fight and loved to show respect where it was due. There were calls for a feast and the four of us were carried all the way back to the village. It was now that I really began to feel the cold. Up above them all, I caught the full force of the wind on my near naked body. My leg was stained with my own blood and with every bouncing step, a little more seeped out.

I noticed Uther out of the corner of my eye, at the back of the throng. He wandered over to the dead guard and severed the head with what looked like a sacrificial knife. He then put it into a large hessian sack, tossed it over his shoulder and followed on behind.

Angus's warning about the Cult immediately ran into my mind. I felt though, that I had nothing to fear from these strange people. Indeed, I thought that they now almost considered me to be one of them.

A wild boar was split in half lengthways and roasted on a spit in the centre of a large communal room that seemed to be at the centre of the maze of tunnels and passageways. We all sat around the open log fire in expectation. Our exploits has created a magnificent hunger and the sight of the gently darkening meat made our mouths water like springs. The four of us had been given the best places and our wounds were being tended to with wild herb compresses and poultices by some of the womenfolk.

A large pitcher of ale was being passed around and had come by the four of us several times. I was glad of its pain relieving properties and its internal warmth was matched beautifully with the heat from the flames. The sense of being alive, the passion of the day, the joy of winning and the feeling of new and shared friendship made this a moment to savour and with it came the urge to tell the greatest of stories. Having held them all spellbound both before and after eating our fill, I clothed myself and undid my roll of furs to bed down for the night. Before I was asleep though, Uther came up to me.

"Fionn, Your prolonged stay here would be of concern to me." He begins, his voice carrying a sombre tone. "In the short time you have been with us, you have affected all our lives for ever. Much as I would like you to stay and share more of your time and knowledge with us, I think it best that you go early in the morning. Your enemies will undoubtedly return and we must prepare for them. Many will die for you and I must find a way to limit that number if we are to continue to live here at all."

"I understand Uther. Is there something I can do to help?" I offer, my heart heavy with his words.

"No. You have played your part. Time will tell the rest of the story. I hope you find what you are looking for and that it is worth the price we all will have to pay."

With that he turned away and walked off without looking back. I contemplated his words for a while before closing my eyes and committing the day's events and feelings to memory. It would be good to relive them as vividly as possible in the future as and when they were needed. Sleep came easily afterwards.

The next day I was woken by Brynn. Still tired from the yesterday's events, I rubbed my eyes and managed a smile. I had dreamt strangely during the night and his interruption caused me to forget all about it. Nevertheless, I thought, if it was important to know, the dream would come again and I would have another chance at interpreting it.

"Fionn, come quickly. It's lovely outside." He cries jubilantly, beckoning me repeatedly with his hand.

I rose shakily, my body reminding me of yesterday's efforts with aches and pains all over. I checked my leg, it looked fine and only felt sore, so I covered up the wound with the poultice again and got to my feet.

Outside Brynn had been right. The sky was a deep clear blue on one side and on the other the reddish sun shone low over the sea that was dazzling in its reflected light. Together we were drawn down to the beach. We walked in silence taking in deep fresh breaths of the cold still air. On the sand, we took off our foot skins and went barefoot down to the water. The feeling of wet sand between my toes reminded me of my youth on the beaches of Siegg and the memory lightened my spirits and made me feel good all over.

The water was freezing as it lapped at our feet. No matter how inviting it appeared, and no matter how much you knew it was cold, it was always a shock. The encroaching numbness soon took away its pain and we walked on side-by-side, ankle deep in the light surf.

After some light conversation I broke the news to him that I was leaving that morning. He understood but was still unhappy. To cheer him up I suggested that he accompany me for the first part of the journey up to the forest. That and the promise of a short story made him return to his former happiness.

We strolled back to the stables and readied the white pony. I said my goodbyes to Brynn's parents and my fellow comrades at arms and set out.

It wasn't long before we got to the edge of the Achentoul forest. At that point, my pony refused to go any further. No amount of coaxing could make it continue. For whatever reasons this place had in obtaining its reputation, they seemed to have been carried through into the whole animal kingdom. I had no option but to brave whatever they might be and so continued to spend as long as I could trying to coax my pony forward. It was to no avail and in the end I decided it best for Brynn to take her back with him and send her on her way back down the North road. I was sure she could find her own way back from there. Thinking about it later, it was probably for the best as I was unsure what obstacles I was going to come across in the coming days.

It was a tearful Brynn that left me, even after I had given him my word that I would return again one day. It was with those happy thoughts that I left on foot and made my way along the old path to Finlarich Broch.

The trees either side of me stretched over the narrow path and at times it became quite dark. I had been told that the path vaguely followed the river that flowed down from Loch Divach, although since I had entered the forest I had neither seen nor heard it.

I was steadily rising up a gentle gradient all the time, but could see little in front or behind me. The locals at Killiecraigie had said that they had used the lower reaches of the path for hunting trips as there were many herds of wild boar in the forest. A few had gone up as far as the loch, but none had had reason to travel further. Trade with Finlarich was now done through Invercarrie as the routes were a lot safer and wider the other way. I could see why now as, at times, the path all but disappeared. It continued like this for most of the day. My leg ached but the fresh poultice that had been applied was helping considerably. I decided against stopping for a rest as it might begin to seize up and stiffen, so I continued onwards. I munched on a trail mix of dried fruit and thin strips of cold boar meat while I walked and decided to try and make for the loch before dark.

Later on in the afternoon, the path came to what I presumed to be a tributary of the river. I crossed and found that I was soon walking along the side of a fast flowing burn. This joined the main river and the path widened and led onto a grassy bank. With no clear signs of where to go next, I presumed that following it upstream would lead me to the loch. The scenery was much more pleasant now and there were signs of activity all about me. I could see fish swimming in the water and insects skating over the calmer areas of its surface. Even the birdcalls were more evident. Having seen no evidence whatsoever of any foreboding, I wondered what indeed it might be that had created the fear that most people seemed consumed by when they mentioned this forest. Putting the despondent thoughts aside I pressed on.

Ahead of me the river cascaded down some rapids. With no other option, I clambered up the side using my hands. The grass was wet and icy in places and at the top of the rapids, the river had bulged into a large pool. However, it didn't look big enough to be Loch Divach so I kept on. What followed was a series of pools with small waterfalls each sufficiently large enough to require me to use some thought as to how to overcome them.

At last I arrived at the top and was met with the awe-inspiring sight of the Loch. Its dark waters gave it a menacing appearance that was enhanced by the fact that the whole area was in shadow. The sun had

now gone down behind Ben Affon, but there was still more than sufficient light as the sky was cloudless. This vast secluded loch of water
was surrounded on all sides by trees save for a wee area of grass half
way along on the Northern side. I headed for it, determined to make it
an area to bed down for the night.

On reaching it, I saw that there was an obvious place to pitch my
belongings and there was plenty of evidence to suggest that others
before me thought so as well. It was situated between the loch and a
small feeder burn that gave it both security and convenience. There was
also plenty of old wood around for a fire. Having got one going, I got
out my small cauldron to heat some water. I chose the burn, rather than
the loch, to fill it and squatted down to scoop up some water. No sooner
was the cauldron in the water than I spied a Kingfisher out of the corner
of my eye.

It sat on a branch overhanging the water and was looking down into
it. By some weird association, I looked across the other side half
expecting to see another boulder. There wasn't one. Leaving the cauldron hanging from my hand and still in the water, I just gazed at him. I
closed all thoughts from my mind and I just stayed as still as I could.
Moments later he turned his head, looked at me, then turned away again
and swooped off.

He flew upstream and landed on another branch the other side. I
pulled out the cauldron and sat it down next to me. Keeping my eye on
the bird, I crept along the bank as best I could with all the bushes that
were at the waters edge. I crouched down again when I was opposite
him. As I did he flew off again and perched on a small outcrop of rock
in the middle of the burn some way upstream.

I followed him this way, without really knowing why, watching him
flit from one branch to the next. The burn was joined by others and at
times I waded across just to keep him in sight. This continued until we
both reached a small pond. I knew he had landed the other side somewhere, but try as I may I had completely lost sight of him. I listened out
for his now familiar call but heard nothing. Looking all around the
pond, I could find no other water running into it and guessed that it
must have been fed by an underground spring. The whole area was
peaceful and quiet and as I gradually gave up my search, I began to
notice how beautiful it all was. The water was dark, yet totally clear and
I bent down on one knee to see my reflection in its mirror calm surface.
I watched myself for a while trying to recognise the man before me.

Somehow it didn't seem like me. I had come a long way in a short time.

Right in the middle of my thoughts, my attention was instantly broken by the sudden appearance of the reflection of the face of an old man. I spun around to find a grey-haired, bearded man smiling down at me. My surprise made me nearly fall back into the water. He stepped back, as though aware of his effect. I slowly stood up and looked at him, unsure of what expression to make. I looked more closely at him. He wore a full-length light grey cloak and held a long staff. At the end was a golden branch with many small gold and silver bells hanging off of the many ends. Of the many thoughts I could have had, I wondered how he had approached me so quietly without the sound of a single bell ringing. He reached out a frail hand and touched my shoulder.

"I'm sorry to have startled you like that, sometimes I forget how quiet I try to be." He says in a voice that carries melody, charm and even a little humour.

"That's quite alright." I reply, "I was just a little surprised to find anyone up here. I had just expected that I would be on my own."

"That's strange indeed," he says playing with his beard with his free hand. "I thought that you were looking for me. My name is Lugh."

The Eastern Hinterland

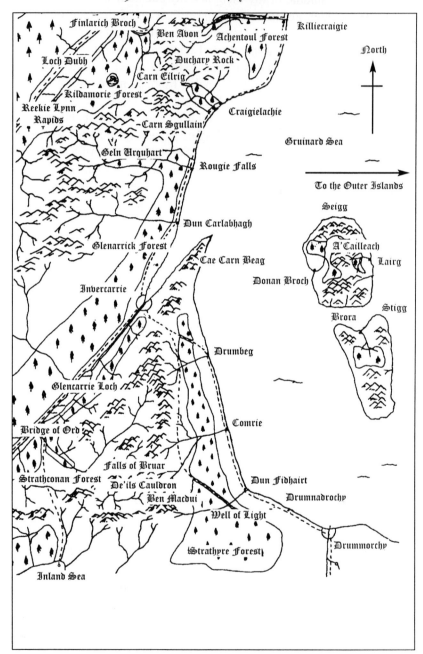

CHAPTER TEN

CONSCIOUSNESS WITHIN THE BRAIN

In this chapter we are going to look at some of the current research that is going on with regard to consciousness and how the mind might work at the microscopic scale. What is important in our overall quest is to note the role that gravity might play in bringing about reality as we know it.

This chapter follows the 'reductionist' approach to consciousness (as opposed to the 'dualist') where the attempt is to explain everything that happens in the mind and the brain by the reasoning from what is seen to occur from the 'bottom up' and 'top down'. The 'top down' approach covers psychological phenomena and other measurable features in the brain, whereas the 'bottom up' approach tries to start with possible phenomena at the smallest of scales and then proceeds to work upwards towards some connection between the two. This chapter will look at the latest research on the latter.

It has been shown that the quantum world could be regarded as the collective unconscious and that the answers to all things, quite possibly, lie in this world, only outside of our concept of time. In chapter six we saw that trying to measure things on a quantum scale immediately collapsed their 'wave function' and they became part of the 'classical' world. This measurement, or even one just sufficient to find the path information of any particle (as in Rempe's experiment mentioned in 6.6), is what happens when we use our external senses to observe the objects around about us. By observing them, it can be said that we are collapsing them into our reality.

If this is the case, then we must look at what actions are going on in the brain when this occurs and we must also look at what might be going on when we use our inner senses. There must also be some method that allows us to turn our inner senses into the reality we want as we have seen that this is possible when looking at the principles of success and hypnosis.

But if we were to successfully argue that this whole phenomenon of consciousness could be explained by a 'reductive' approach, then it ought to be possible to build machines that could compute, as we do, in a similar way.

Roger Penrose in his book 'Shadows of the Mind' sets out an argument that there can be 'appropriate physical actions in the brain that will bring about an awareness, but that this physical action cannot be properly simulated computationally.' This argument suggests that we can go a long way to simulate the processes in the brain, and indeed people are already working to produce 'quantum computers' which will come close to this, but that there will always be something that we can't reproduce.

The element, he goes on to say, that appears to escape being explained by physical processes is that of our 'free will'. Our actions of free will still appear to be neither completely random nor deterministic. Sometimes our thoughts and action are deterministic and logical and at other times, they are not. This last point could be described as being similar to acting on impulse or instinct.

It would appear that there are three areas to consider when looking at the ways our brains and minds might work. Firstly the method of the external stimuli coming in via our external senses causing a reduction from the quantum world to the classical. Secondly, the method of operation in the brain that allows our internal senses to think, visualise and be conscious. And lastly, a method that allows us to seem to have the free will to take our thoughts and visions in the direction we wish them to take and to create the reality of our choice that is personal to ourselves.

We shall see in this chapter that gravity has a major part to play in the functioning of the mind. However, we must also remind ourselves that very little is really known about this force. On the large scale, all we can really measure is the effects of gravity and on the small scale we have yet to measure gravity waves or particles. We have even seen how difficult it is to obtain a constant value that everyone can agree upon. In chapter six we also looked at the concept of quantum gravity and its particle, the graviton, which has still yet to be proved to exist beyond doubt. We have stated that it probably only exists at or below Plank's scale, the smallest scale at which things can be separate from each other. For quantum gravity to exist at this size, it may be further assumed that it is also part of the intrinsic make up of the universe. It is

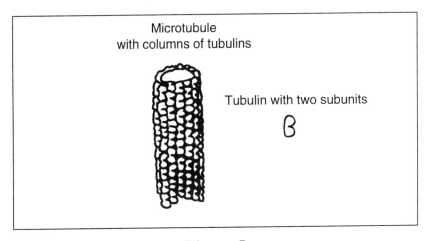

Microtubule
with columns of tubulins

Tubulin with two subunits

Diagram 7

quantum gravity that has recently been shown to have a connection with the way the mind might work and this is the area we will now look into in further detail. Firstly though, we need to understand more about the working parts of certain areas of the brain and to try and see where the quantum world might be able to reside within it.

10.1 Microtubules

For the quantum world to exist, or operate within the brain, then some mechanism that avoids its instantaneous 'collapse' must be operating somewhere. Just by being in contact with the sides of some vessel would be similar to an external sensory touch and, as such, would be a disturbance. This would not allow the quantum world to remain indeterminate and uncertain because an observation of sorts would have occurred at the point of disturbance. Reduction would then take place and the quantum world would collapse into the classical world.

The places now considered by Prof. Stuart Hameroff and Sir Roger Penrose to have the qualities of maintaining an undisturbed quantum world are in the microtubules inside the neuronal cells. We have previously looked at the cells called neurons in the brain and the way that they transmit information amongst their millions of connections, and it is inside these that we find microtubules. They are small, hollow cylindrical tubes about 25 nanometers on the outside and 14 nanometers on the inside and they can be as long a few millimetres. (See diagram 7). Microtubules are found in all cells however they differ in neuronal cells in that they are mainly parallel whilst in others they are radial

Neuronal cells are held in shape by a cytoskeleton. This is a thin filament of protein and microtubules are a part of its structure. The walls of the tubes themselves are made up of interlocking, hourglass shaped units called tubulins. Each tubulin has a subunit called a dimer. These tubulin dimers can exist as one of two forms that correspond to their state of electrical polarisation. These electrical states are influenced by the neighbouring tubulin dimers to the extent that it is possible for 'electrical' messages to be sent down the length of the walls of the microtubules. It is in this way that information is transmitted along their lengths. The pattern of these signals and their strength and uniformity become important when we look at what is happening in the mind.

Before we go on to discussing what happens within the microtubules, it is worth mentioning that there are unicellular organisms like amoeba's and paramecium that also have a cytoskeleton and microtubules. They behave amazingly in ways that even allows them to learn from their past experiences. Each cell would appear to have its own nervous system. Some of the earliest life forms in fossil history, called Eukaryotes, are cells that have cytoskeletons. Eukaryotic cells are found in all animals and almost all plants on this planet today. The evolution of mankind and microtubules are therefore inextricably linked. The main difference between now and then is the number of neuronal cells. The earliest organisms and the paramecium have very few and there are vast numbers in the brains of humans.

If it is assumed that each cell has its own nervous system, the next question to ask is whether or not it has its own consciousness. Before answering that, we must return to the reason the microtubules are hollow and what might be occurring within them.

10.2 Quantum Coherence

It has been suggested that something called quantum coherence might exist within the microtubules. This is a state where all the particles involved participate collectively in the same state. A large number of particles would behave as a whole and the wave function that describes them would hold on a large scale. This is something that we can already see exists in other areas of science. The phenomena of 'superconductivity' and 'superfluidity' have been shown to have something that is called Böse-Einstein condensation. This can occur if there is sufficiently high energy levels and high dielectric properties. The action inside of a laser is typical of a Böse-Einstein condensate. The atoms inside are excited in such a way that when a certain energy level is reached, a burst of coherent energy is stimulated. This moves back and forth within the laser until all the atoms are coupled together. At the point when there is total coherence, the photons of light are emitted.

David Peat, in his book Blackfoot Physics, notes that all this is similar to the Native American Indians concept of 'subtle' energy. This energy is not referring to the physical energy that a body has, but one that combines the cells, the organs, other biological processes, and the informational activity all into a coherent whole. Any illnesses that a person might have would show up in an incomplete 'subtle' energy and could be detected by the medicine man.

He goes on to say that this concept also has its similarities in homeopathic medicine. Homeopathists state that by repeatedly diluting their medicine, they introduce 'subtle' information from the active molecules of the medicine into the water. This information is then, supposedly, passed on to the patient's body when the medicine is ingested. This may seem a little farfetched but it is important to remember that water itself still contains some mysteries to our scientists. Water is made of oxygen and hydrogen in molecules of H_2O, but physicists and chemists cannot agree on how these molecules are arranged together. We know that there is a weak force called the hydrogen bond, which attracts the hydrogen atom from one molecule to an oxygen atom from another molecule. This allows for some self-organisation of molecules amongst themselves, but it is the overall result after this that produces the disagreement. It has been suggested that whatever complex arrangement results, any slight change (maybe leading to a reorientation of its geometrical structure) could introduce some message or signature that a body might later be able to read and benefit from.

It is important to consider the nature of water, because the interiors of the microtubules are empty save for the occurrence within them of water. (Some molecules are found to travel down the microtubules and it has been suggested that these conduits have a multi functional purpose). The nature of this water may well have some relevance in light of what has just been mentioned. The water exists in part, if not in whole, in an ordered (or vicinal) state. This is to say that there are also no dissolved ions within it. So it could quite possibly be pure enough, and ordered enough, to allow for a form of quantum coherence. If this is the case then it might well be possible for the interior state of the tube to remain unentangled with its environment (i.e. not being disturbed by it) for sufficient time to allow the quantum world to exist inside the brain. Biologists have also found that 'ordered' water also exists for a short way around the outside of the microtubules. This may be acting like some kind of shield as well and would be guarding the inside from disturbances sufficient to cause a 'collapse'.

However it has been argued by some, that this is a relatively useless theory due to the size of each microtubule. To be a good theory, and to perhaps differentiate us more substantially from unicellular organisms, the internal quantum world must be able to bridge the gaps between all the microtubules and operate in a collective manner. This would require information travelling, in a quantum state, past the synaptic gaps at the end of each neuron and into the next microtubule. A simple connection across the gap can be ruled out as its neuronal firing, with each electrical message, is clearly a sufficient enough disturbance to the environment to reduce the quantum to the classical. The interesting explanation that has been put forward so far, is the argument of non-locality as seen in chapter 6.10. This would effectively mean that everything that was occurring inside the microtubules was part of the same system. This adds a holistic nature to the argument that has also been recognised by David Bohm in his work with implicate, or enfolded, orders. David Bohm argued that reality was not just an interaction of material things, but a process he called the 'Holomovement'.

The holistic argument says that the things we observe with our external senses are explicate forms and exist with an underlying implicate order. Each object contains the whole and even in the objects parts of the whole still exists.

This is not completely strange, as we can observe the same effects with holograms. If you had a photographic plate with a holographic image that had been imprinted onto it, you could see the impression of a three dimensional image. If you broke that plate into several pieces, you might think that the image would also be broken up. In fact, you can still see the whole image in each of its broken parts!

David Bohm's ideas were shown to have some connection with the indigenous science of the Native American Indians. They too believed in a similar occurrence to the way life exists in their relationships to the world around them.

The current thoughts, therefore, are that there is a distinct possibility that the quantum world can exist inside the brain and that microtubules are the most likely place for it to reside. The conditions found within these tubes are thought to be suitable so as not to allow collapse to occur due to the entanglement with its environment.

If this is the case, then we must then look at what happens when collapse does occur. Originally it was thought that as soon as something was observed, it reduced (collapsed) into the classical world. This was looked at in chapter 6.8, but it doesn't explain everything, including how our inner senses might operate.

10.3 Reduction

Our external senses receive a huge amount of information that comes from all the observations we make around us. This direct observation of large-scale classical objects and events, immediately causes a reduction in the regions of the brain that receive the information. Reality is then created, personal to ourselves. The fact that reality already exists is down to other people and animals making observations and also the interaction of all the particles of matter disturbing the environment sufficiently to cause collapse by itself.

These two things, observation and environmental disturbance, both cause the reduction from the quantum to the classical and both occur in a similar manner. The only difference is that with observation, the reality becomes personal.

What is of interest to us in our search for a link is what Sir Roger Penrose first suggested when looking at what must be involved in this reduction. He looked at the action of observation from the point of view that it must involve one mass meeting another mass. This has been likened to a photon of light hitting a mirror. In the brain, one of these masses would play the role of the environment, like the walls of the tubes; the other would come from the stimuli entering the brain. The question he asked was how much of a movement of a mass need there be, when the observation takes place, for a reduction to occur. He deduced that the answer depended either upon the mass of the objects or whether the distance moved was far enough. What was even more important was that, as each of the two objects have a mass, they must also have their own gravitational field. This is arguably very small, but it has been shown to be sufficient to make a discernible difference.

At the moment of collision, there is a significant difference seen down at the smallest unit of scale-Planck's Scale (10^{-35}cms). Roger Penrose argued that down at Planck's scale there is actually a displacement (quantum superposition) of mass from itself for a sufficient length of time for reduction to occur. These 'space-time separations' are extremely unstable and lead to two superposed states occurring. These two states are like two tiny black holes, in that they each distort and curve space-time in opposite directions (due to the gravitational masses of the separated mass itself).

This is the way that reduction is now deemed to occur and it also seems dependent upon mass, size, density and gravitational energy. Bigger things reduce more quickly and with larger amounts of energies there is a shorter period of time that these superposed states can exist.

Although this reduction is a random procedure, it is still regarded as highly controversial by some physicists, however it is now accepted to be real by most of them and also the forerunner to explaining Objective Reduction.

10.4 Objective Reduction

If reduction is the method that explains how our external senses assist in creating our reality, then objective reduction is an extension to that theory that has been put forward to explain how our inner senses might appear to work.

If there is insufficient mass or energy for reduction to take place immediately, and 'space-time separations' haven't reached a critical degree of separation, then there is a period of time beforehand that could be regarded as when we think or use our inner senses. It is in this period, while there is a build up of gravitational energy, that pre-conscious processing in the mind is said to occur. The system shows a developing superposition of states, whilst still maintaining a form of quantum coherence. (This mental processing would be similar to when successful people use their inner senses to hold in their minds an image of the future that they want. The microtubules used in this incidence would hold the image and that quantum world future.) This process has been said to occur in the walls of the microtubules, where each tubulin dimer transmits a sequence of electrical charges with its fluctuating dipoles. Each tubulin is supposed to be able to exist in each of the two superposed states and, along with its neighbours, can simulate a sequence of patterns down the length of the microtubule. When the patterns become sufficiently large enough, then a form of objective reduction occurs. This threshold has also been shown to be dependant on and related to quantum gravity.

This process of patterns of activity running down the length of the microtubules is the supposed method in bringing about consciousness. Normal reduction is not occurring because of this, perhaps because of insufficient disturbance from the environment, but objective reduction is reached by a self-collapse induced by reaching this gravity threshold. This process is said to be occurring when we are thinking consciously. Obviously, if we are also awake and using our external senses then normal reduction is occurring at the same time.

As has been already mentioned, Roger Penrose successfully argues in his book 'Shadows of the Mind' that there must be an element in this process that cannot be produced by pure calculation or computation. This 'non computable' factor is said to be our own free will and the choice as to what, and when, we want to think and visualise. Our consciousness can now be considered to be made up of two factors firstly, the non-computable and secondly the computable.

We can only try to study what might be computable and we must look at what might explain consciousness on that basis. Basic organisms do not have sufficient numbers of microtubles to be able to co-ordinate patterns and retain a large-scale coherence over a long enough period of time, so it is accepted that if they have any consciousness at all it is minimal. However, with increasing numbers of microtubules, it can be argued that there is an increasing amount of consciousness and that some animals are as conscious as we are. There are many experiences that could back this up and one only need study the activities within a herd of elephants to see high degrees of emotions and presumably therefore, conscious activity.

10.5 Orchestrated Reduction

Inside the brain the objective reduction process can occur several times and in several places giving rise to what has been termed a 'stream of consciousness' or 'cascades of objective reduction'. The uniformity of these over large areas is said to be because they have been 'orchestrated' by interconnections between the microtubules. These links are termed M.A.P.'s (microtubule associated proteins) and it has been further suggested that these assist in tuning all the microtubules so that they can all act together. This would correspond with a heightened sense of awareness or increased consciousness. Their role undoubtedly controls the degree and type of consciousness. It would also appear to be able to allow the intensity of the experience to be adjusted by increasing the number of connections in certain areas.

All the above-mentioned methods of reduction can be used to explain normal experience, heightened experience, an altered state and dreaming. There is, however, another area to cover and the model needs to explain this as well. In earlier chapters we saw that the internal senses could be used to bring about a specific reality. The chapter on success showed that if we become inner directed, we can reach the goals we want and in chapter eight we saw that the mind could be confused into believing something that later turned out to be real (blisters on the hand ch. 8.15). If we accept these as possible, then we must look to explain how they might occur with the models that have been put forward. Something extra is needed in the model of objective and orchestrated reduction in order for it to have an impact on creating reality for ourselves. At the moment we know we need all the microtubules working together, with the assistance of the M.A.P.'s, in order to create an intense inner experience. We also need to add the non-computable element of free will. However something else is also required.

10.6 Self-Induced Reduction

We have seen that gravity could play a major role in inducing the final collapse into reality, as witnessed by our external senses, so we must look further into this area to see if we can find an explanation. To find the possible answer, we must first look at what happens when we become unconscious.

The two best-known methods at arriving at an unconsciousness state is firstly with anaesthetics and secondly by being knocked on the head. One of the strange things that I have learnt since researching into these subjects is that the medical profession has no real idea how anaesthetics work! What is even more worrying is that chemicals with completely different compositions, even inert gases (xenon), can bring about unconsciousness and they are still unsure why this is the case. Whatever is occurring, the result is to completely inhibit microtubule activity. One experiment that has been done is to subject an anaesthetised tadpole to varying degrees of atmospheric pressure. It was found that with increased pressure, the tadpole can recover consciousness. Pressure would then appear to have some role to play.

Microtubules have been said to behave in ways similar to waveguides. Waveguides are tubes that are used to shield internal messages that are being sent from any outside interference. They are most often used in the aircraft industry to avoid important signals being interfered with by others in order to provide a smooth control over an aircraft. One small but important feature of waveguides is the pressure difference between the inside and the outside. With sufficient differential pressure, a more unaffected message can be transmitted. This might be the same principle operating with microtubules. Any increase or decrease in pressure might alter the pressure differential between the inside and the outside of the hollow tube and thus cause or allow environmental disturbance.

This is a possibility that is backed up by the effects of a blow to the head. The shock wave of pressure sent into the brain could assist to alter the working operation of all microtubule activity. If the punch was of sufficient strength then a knock out could occur giving rise to unconsciousness. Obviously many other things like the electrical activity of the brain are also affected with a blow to the head and this plays a major role in bringing about unconsciousness.

If pressure plays some role in disturbing the environment, causing quantum entanglement and collapse, then we must look at ways this might occur in the brain that could also be influenced by our own will. In chapter eight we saw that, when we used our minds, the specific areas of the brain we were using, registered changes in blood flow. These areas would also show changes in blood pressure and effectively become more or less dense. We have already seen that a particle of mass has a density and its own gravitational field, so we could easily deduce that these regions of the brain could have their own brief quantum gravity effect by having differing regions of differing gravitational fields based on all the changing pressures and densities.

We know that quantum gravity seems to play an integral role in bringing about reduction, orchestrated and objective reduction, therefore it might also indicate that gravity from a more external source can cause some form of self-induced reduction. This could well be the extra difference that is required in order for the internal senses to bring about actual reality. By taking this argument further, we can say that by using our inner senses in certain ways, we can gravitationally influence the parts of the brain we wish to. This would be by just thinking the right thoughts and visualising the right images. This has important implications when we come to look at chapter 12.

If we are to accept that gravity from an external source, such as blood pressure fluctuations from differing brain regions, can effect reduction, then we must also look at the possibility of the influence of gravity's affect on the mind from other areas.

10.7 The end for Astronauts?

Going down this train of thought, we ought to first look at whether or not there are any other affects on the mind in connection with gravity. An environment like outer space is where there is near zero gravity (The gravitational attraction between the celestial bodies must mean that a small amount of gravitational field exists between them). If there were differences there, it might give us some further clues. We should also look at the influences of nature around us, in particular the effects of mountains and valleys. The intense variations in density and gravity could well have some effect on the way we interact with our reality. The position of the sun and the moon and other celestial gravitational influences might also show some influence.

However, we might only be able to recognise their effects on the mind if we were actually in the process of trying to create our own reality by being internally directed, and using our inner senses, rather than externally led. Several experiments could be devised for astronauts that might be able to test this theory. Their ability to be hypnotised in space might well be affected with the lack of gravity. Of the reports I was able to obtain from communication with astronauts, it was mentioned that the intensity of their dreams was greater than normal. This could have been just due to the excitement of their occupation or possibly, with less external gravitational influence, the inner senses they used in their dream sleep were able to be more active under their own self collapse gravity thresholds.

This can be contrasted to the apparent effects on the mind found in deep level mining. As a geologist working at depths of 7000 feet below surface (roughly 2000 feet below sea level in that specific area), I had, on many occasions, to walk for up to an hour to get to the developing ends of the mine. During these periods, often accompanied by times of extreme silence and darkness, I used to let my mind wander into an open state of awareness. My memory of these events is still, to this day, distinct. The intensity of all my senses was acute and highly focused. I could easily create and recall images, feelings and thoughts in ways that seemed to me to be very real.

Out in space however there is good evidence that a near zero gravity environment can affect the mind in an opposite manner. Dr Chris Flynn, a N.A.S.A. psychiatrist has said that we know that people can get depressed, anxious and bored when in space. Russian cosmonauts on the Mir space station often complained of depression and said that it was common amongst all the inhabitants. It is important to remember that astronauts are rigidly psychologically screened before being allowed into space, because of problems such as these, and all of them did not exhibit these psychological conditions whilst on Earth. The question that has to be asked is whether or not astronauts have less control over all their inner feelings because of the lack of gravity in their environment. Questions must also be asked about their other inner senses, like visualising and thinking. When they are not conscious and asleep, there does appear to be some difference as has been mentioned above, so some connection seems to be going on. The mind seems to require sufficient amounts of gravity in order to function effectively. This is not that strange a requirement because we have evolved within the gravitational environment of the planet and it would be natural for our brains to have adapted to the prevailing conditions. Is it then also possible that varying levels of gravity (or observation of types ie. particles or waves) can allow us to produce states of mind that can accomplish incredible mental feats? Would higher amounts of gravity, exerted on an openly aware mind, allow it to achieve even greater things by collapsing the reality that is wanted? Does the minds link with gravity jeopardise future long-term flights in space? There are many questions that would appear to need answering.

Astronaut Edgar Mitchell, on board Apollo 14, conducted an interesting experiment in space that sheds a little more light on our future in space. Only four other people on Earth knew of the experiment as it was testing psychic abilities (To advertise the fact that he was going to do these experiments would have left him open to much criticism). In his book 'The Way of the Explorer' he mentions how it was done and the results. Every night in space, without his fellow astronauts knowing, he arranged five Zener Cards in a sequence on his clipboard. These cards with different symbols on were then 'transmitted' mentally to the four people back on Earth. These four people then tried to attune themselves to the sequence that had been arranged for each night and record their thoughts.

The results of the experiment were statistically significant in that they showed a successful match on more occasions than could be put down to just chance. The question that has to be asked is whether or not people are able to be more 'psychic' in an environment where there is little or no gravity. Are they in a closer connection with the holistic 'Quantum' world?

This is not a question that is new by any means and many people have pondered the possibilities of what life might be like in space and its affects on the human mind. Dr Timothy Leary, a pioneering psychologist, ex Harvard professor and writer, has always maintained that mankind's future exists in Space Migration and that it would help us evolve as individuals. He maintained that this environment would allow us to eventually program our nervous systems for any function that we would wish. Much of his life's work was about understanding the human mind and his work gave rise to what he called the eight neurological circuits. These circuits describe the mental states of evolution that individuals could aspire to. He felt that the highest four circuits could be more easily attained by more people when living in space. It is for this reason he felt that our future lay in that direction. The highest circuit he describes as the 'non-local quantum' circuit. That life however, because of the evolution, would be vastly different from that which we know now. One reason for this could well be that of the impact on the mind of living in a near zero gravity environment. For any readers wishing to know more about Dr. Leary's ideas it is suggested that they read the books by Robert Anton Wilson, in particular 'Prometheus Rising'.

All this leads us to presume that gravity and the mind are intimately connected and that it plays an important part in creating our realities and our connection with the quantum world. It doesn't however provide us with the answer to everything. The one area that still eludes modern day thinking is that of how free will operates. What is it that allows us the ability to make decisions and choices?

10.8 Free Will

Some might argue that with such a huge amount of potential gravitational influences on the mind, what was previously described as free will, is not really so at all. All the effects are almost certainly non-computable, but also not random or deterministic. However, I think there is still an argument for non-computability on the grounds that in the case of all the evidence that could be presented, there is nothing that accounts for the 'I'. The actual decision-making is still done by an individual, but now, quite possibly, with a lot more external influences than was previously thought.

I want to point out that I have only offered this additional model of self-induced reduction as a method for assisting in the creation of reality from a starting position of using ones inner senses, rather than as an alternative model to show the understanding of how consciousness might arise. The difference being that there is a requirement upon the individual to have a willingness to want the inner senses to become reality. Only with this focus and intensity would the conditions begin to become right for the environment to become entangled within the microtubles in the similar way that normal reduction works with the stimuli from the external senses.

To increase the focus and intensity one need only look at finding a method of creating greater coherence, over a larger area or increasing the gravitational influence. The possibilities of doing this, and that our ancestors actually did this, will be looked at more closely in chapter 12.

CHAPTER ELEVEN

ILLUSIONS AND CIRCLES

"Lugh!" I exclaim and stutter, "But... how did you know who and where I was, and that I was looking for you?"

"Come." He smiles, then turns to the side and places his arm behind me and continues. "There is plenty of time for questions and answers later. Let's get something to eat and drink before nightfall. I am sure I saw your fire not far away."

He gently nudges me to set off in front of him, and he follows just a little to the side and behind. My mind was again trying rapidly to keep up with the pace of events and had resorted to a sort of numb blankness. As if reading my lack of thoughts, he continues on talking in a soft, slightly melodic tone.

"As to how I came to be here, and how I found you, they are not exactly questions that I can fully answer. Firstly, I don't really know you at all, so looking for you is not really true. I was looking for someone, yes, but all I sensed, was that it was someone who was looking for me." He places his hand up onto my nearest shoulder from behind as he speaks and I can feel the light grasp through my leathers.

"But how did you even know that?" I ask, searching to comprehend things as much as I can, "And how did you know to come to that pool?"

"There are things in life that just don't conform to the common way. Those things come from deep within and can be said to be a form of knowing without knowing or a seeing without seeing. I think of it as touching a universal source of knowledge that sits outside of land and time as we witness it. By following and trusting your instincts, you lay yourself open to its gifts. In many ways, it's how you come to be here too. By the way, I don't wish to appear rude, but how do you come to be here?"

His last question jolted me fully back to reality and that I had quite forgotten my manners. "Oh! My apologies. My name is Fionn mac Donal, of the clan Donal from the Isle of Siegg. I'm sorry for my forgetfulness." He waves a hand in the air as though to say that it was of no matter and for me to continue.

"I guess that the reason I am here now is directly down to a man I've only recently met, Angus Og. He said that he'd met you once and that you might be able to help me. Other than that, there's a great many reasons as to how I've found myself here."

"Well, then," He breaks in, "I'd love to hear all about it after we eat. Let's get things sorted first. I'm famished, it's been a long day." He lengthens his stride and is soon walking by my side towards my camp.

We soon got back to my fire, which was thankfully still burning well. I added some more wood and put the water on to boil. We then added mixed herbs, dried vegetables and fungi from both our packs and stirred up a hot broth. This we drank from our bowls and added to it with some griddled bannocks that we'd roasted over some embers we had dragged out from the centre of the fire. Having eaten our fill, we leant back on our elbows and stared into the fire. It was then that I began to go over recent events.

He listened attentively to all that I said, probing occasionally with short questions just to get the detail he wanted. I finished my story at the point when I'd been looking for the kingfisher and had looked up at him. He leant back on the ground and stared up at the stars. Sensing it was best not to talk just yet, I just waited in silence watching him deep in thought. He was a gentle old man with a face that was etched with lines, his cheeks were reddened from what must have been years of being out in the elements. His deep blue eyes were the only sign left of youth. Their intense gaze seemed to show all the emotions he wished, just on their own. The light from the stars and the fire danced within them and his presence seemed to grow larger and larger.

After what seemed an eternity, he sat up, breathed deeply through his nose and then exhaled slowly. Yet again, I began to feel the space between us converge as his size appeared to expand. He adjusted his legs nimbly and now knelt beside me and held out his hand. I reached over and took it and felt a surge of energy rush through me. I was left with a tingling sensation along my arm, a warm glow in my stomach and a growing smile. Looking over the now calm loch and sitting next to the fire, I felt the most comfortable I'd ever been since leaving Donan broch.

"Fionn." He begins, "There is so much to do in so little time. I hardly know where it's best to begin. Perhaps I should ask you first what you would like me to try to do for you. Is there anything specifically on your mind?"

His question takes me by surprise a little as I was wondering what he had been thinking about and had thought that he was about to offer me some revelation. However, the one thing that had been puzzling me was the omen, so I decided to ask him about that.

"Lugh, I was hoping that you might be able to tell me more about the omen that I saw. Angus received a vision of you and I at a dolmen near here and that I should try and find you as you might be able to give me a fuller explanation. What does it all mean?" I ask.

"Well, Angus was right to say that the death of the kingfisher did not denote your own demise and he was also right in saying that it showed a change was on its way. As to why you should see a kingfisher, there is in fact a relevance I can only say that you will become more aware of over the years. A spirit guide takes whatever form is necessary and most meaningful. One thing you will come to know is that time has no place where the spirit lies. However for now, what I can tell you, which is of utmost importance, is this. The kingfisher is showing you the way to go. Just like you followed him up to the pool not long ago and found me, he is your guide. In many ways you and him are eternally linked. You are him and he is you."

"I'm not sure I understand you." I interrupt, unconsciously leaving my jaw wide open and feeling a mild stupor coming on.

"Most spirit guides are there to help their chosen partners with their decisions in life. They consult them in one form or another in order to receive some assistance. Yours, however, has chosen to appear almost at its own will in order to give you guidance. The reason for this, I think, is that you are closely following your vocational path through life and that you have a destiny of universal importance."

"But what could that possibly be?" I blurt out, with the reverberations of a deep shock beginning to shake my insides around which was strangely similar to the feeling I'd had crossing the Gruinard Sea on the currach.

"That is not for me to tell you, even if I could fully answer the question. Having said that though, I believe that it was in both our destinies that we should meet. Just as events have brought you here, similar strange events of great significance have led me back here today. I feel that if you continue to follow your instincts and look further at exploring all your coincidences, the answer to that question will come to you in the fullness of time. What I can tell you though is that I believe you are destined to become a man whose power and influence will upset many, but will bring happiness to many more. How it all turns out though, is up to you."

"Could this dream that I have been trying to remember have something to do with all of this?" I ask tentatively, not sure I really want to know the answer yet in case it comes out as equally stomach churning as the last.

"Almost definitely. Dreams can have tremendous importance. As with all these things though, it is their interpretation that is crucial and so often it is done wrong as people only see what they want to see." He replies, his voice now raised slightly and sounding less grave and more excited.

"You mentioned that events brought you here, what do you think the reasons are behind that?" I ask.

"That is something that I have been trying to discover just now, along with your omen. Angus said he saw you and I at a dolmen. I think I know the one he means. If that was the case, we are still some way away from it. This implies we should be spending some time together. If that is so, then it can only mean that we have much to share in the way of knowledge and information. You have already been good enough to tell me of recent events at Invercarrie, so now it's my turn to talk."

With that, he reached into the folds of his robe and pulled out a small bundle. This he carefully unwrapped and brought out a small metal object, the like of which I'd never seen before, nor could I guess at its purpose.

"This is the fourth, and smallest piece, of the crown helm. It is the interlocking piece that holds the rest together, which is why it appears different from the other three." He holds it up in the firelight and, as he does, it appears to take on a magical quality. Passing it to me, he continues, "I met Callum Beg many years ago."

He had my keen attention beforehand, but now even my ears were beginning to bend forward.

"Before Angus or Dugald had known him at the Aes Dana. It was I that had mentioned the existence of the Crown helm to him in the first place. He knows that I have this piece and I've been aware for some time that he has been looking for me in order to obtain it. Up until now, even I myself did not know where the other three parts had been kept. It would appear that Callum Beg has nearly succeeded in his wild quest."

"But he hasn't got all four pieces yet." I declare.

"No, but now he has three, it won't be long before he gives up trying to get the fourth and makes a close enough imitation. He could guess at its shape and mechanism and no one would be any the wiser." He says.

"What do you think we should do?" I ask with a note of alarm.

"I think that the time has come to stop all these ridiculous stories that I hear about the 'Samildanach'. Since I've been away, the truth appears to have been completely distorted and it's time people should see that I am real, like they are. By doing that, I should force Callum Beg's hand." He finishes and we both stare across the water and remain silent.

"But what I don't understand," I begin after a while, "is how he thought he could get you to proclaim him king after the sacrifice of the bulls. Surely he would have known that you wouldn't have agreed to it."

"Indeed, It's something that's been puzzling me too. I'm sure though, that he has his plans as indeed we must too." He contemplates his last words yet allows no concern to show on his face and I wonder how he manages to remain so calm.

"What do you suggest?" I enquire, after watching him gaze for a few moments in silence.

"The first thing to do is to start with you. Come and kneel next to me like this." His words were now faster and edged with purpose.

I move over closer to him and kneel as he had been doing since he had sat up. "Place your hands in your lap and breathe in slowly through your nose." I do so. "Now match your rhythm with mine." I find that harder, but I manage to slow it down till we are breathing in harmony. "Now empty your mind of all thoughts."

This was much more difficult. The more I tried, the more some things kept popping back in. Flashes of the past and people I had met recently all entered into my mind.

"Relax," says Lugh, "Forget about those people, you'll see them again soon enough." My surprise makes him chuckle as he seems to be able to read my thoughts at will. "It will get easier," he continues, "so try by first of all substituting those thoughts with ones about your body. Listen to your heart beating."

There is a moment's silence as I begin to hear my heart pump my blood around my body. After a while it sounds and feels like two waves rushing away from each other and back again each slightly apart from the other. The more I listen, the louder it seems.

"Now look into the fire. Pick one spot deep in the orange glowing embers and stare at it, yet at the same time be aware of what is happening around you. Now, using your mind, bring that spot closer and closer to your stomach and then into the very middle of your body. Now let the spot turn slowly round and round and every time it turns it gets a little smaller."

I did so and found that the thoughts had gone and were not really replaced by anything that I could describe. It was a sort of nothingness. As if sensing I had reached the state of mind he had wanted me to, he goes on. "Now open up and feel happy. Let joy enter into your heart for no other reason than that you are glad to be alive. Let this feeling join up with the feeling of being part of everything living. Become one with everything around you."

After what could have been a few moments or a few years, I felt a tap on my shoulder. Suddenly, all my senses appeared to be working loudly. I felt refreshed and invigorated.

"What did you feel?" He asks.

"A sort of connection with everything which seemed to be giving me energy, as well as taking some of mine."

"That's good. What else?" He prompts me.

"It was as though there was no time at all... just a being at 'one' with everything."

"That's good for a first effort." He praises in a kind voice, "We'll practice some more tomorrow."

"But what does it all mean?" I enquire, "And why are you teaching me these things?"

"I think that one of the reasons we have met up with each other is for me to help you discover certain things that will be important for you in your quest in life. I'm getting on in years now and my time has nearly come. It will be good for someone, such as yourself, to learn some of the secret ways, if not for yourself, then for someone else you can pass them on to." He suggests finally and then pauses in thought. I remain quiet for a while.

"I just seem to be full of questions at the moment." I break the silence, "What did you get me to do a moment ago anyway?"

"That was just the beginning step of a long journey. It is a place you can go anytime to clear your head or to refresh your mind. It is also the starting point from which to base all future work with your mind. You will need to learn to access that state quickly and at any time and in any place. The importance of that last word will become clearer as we go on. Tonight however, it's getting late and we'd best get some deep sleep."

After that we talked a little more of plans for the next day and we agreed that I should return with him to a place nearby that he used when in these parts. The clear starry night made it crisp and cold so I threw some more wood on the fire to keep burning well into the morning. We then wrapped up well in our sleeping furs and settled down for the night. My mind was still full of questions and the only way I could stop it overloading was to go through the events of the day. Sleep came easily afterwards.

The next morning the weather was fine. The skies were a deep blue and we were woken by the dawn chorus from the birds in the trees around us. I built the fire back up and put some water on to boil. Having break fasted, we packed the few things we had and began to walk.

Now that I had found Lugh, I had half hoped to be returning to Invercarrie to rescue my sister. The fact that I was heading in the opposite direction distressed me slightly as I was unsure of what was going to happen next. Meeting with Lugh was obviously important, but half of me expected that we would have both gone straightaway back down to the broch where she was held. Now it appeared that he felt that it was necessary to teach me something beforehand. After all the learning I had done in the last seven years, I wondered if it would ever end.

We rounded the end of the loch, having skirted around its edge, and were now moving steadily up the glen keeping the river to our left. We were on a narrow path that wound in and around moss-covered boulders and tree trunks. In places the sunlight just penetrated through the thick branches of the trees and the occasional beam of light made the water sparkle as it ran over rapids. The result left a dappled, shadowy effect along the small track.

"Lugh," I start, hopefully, "I have to say that I've got some doubt as to what I really should be doing?"

"That's very possible," he replies, "perhaps you'd like to explain what you mean in more detail."

"Well. I am still very concerned about the safety of my sister and the fact that I seem to be no nearer in rescuing her."

"That's understandable, anyone in your position would be highly concerned. However, what makes you say that you are no nearer to rescuing her. From what you've told me, you have done a great deal. Have you not?" He asks back.

I stop to think about it and he's right. "It's just that I don't feel I'm getting closer to achieving what I need to do." I go on.

"That's as in many things in life, Fionn. It would appear that to go forward we must also go back. At times like that you must stop and look at the big picture and trust in your intuition. You have to look at how you have got where you already are. Did everything run smoothly and logically? How much came from coincidences? Only when your mind is closed to its inner senses and open only to being led by others will you find yourself straying from your vocation in life. Explore the coincidences that surround you. Ask yourself why and for what meaning do they occur and when you have the answers to those questions you will be able to expel doubt more easily."

"So, what you mean is that I should not worry about her as I have already taken steps to ensure her safety, and that now, because I have met you, I should explore the reason why it has relevance to my role in life and even my sisters life."

"Precisely." He utters crisply. "How do you now feel about your earlier concern?"

"Better." I reply truthfully, "But perhaps you can enlighten me as to what you think as to our meeting, from your point of view?"

"That's a fair question and one that requires answering now. I must first start by telling you about the Otherworld as it concerns that and a meeting I had with Callum Beg over there."

"What?" I blurt out, my attention almost straining a muscle as my head twists round to look at him. The hairs on the back of my neck start sticking out and beginning tickle me. "What happened?" I say after a moment, my mind failing to come up with any other words.

"I thought that might interest you." He smiles, "It was the first time I went over. It was only a short visit, not like my last one which took me away for several years."

"How many times have you been?" I ask with the curiosity of a small boy that still slightly too shocked to ask anything else.

"In actuality, just twice."

"But how did you go? Was it by a mound of the sidhe, or a trip over the sea?" I ask, now excited but still highly confused as I was sure that the Otherworld was just a place of myths and legends and not actually real.

"Fionn, there is something you need to know. Something that Dugald either doesn't know himself or for his own reasons decided not to tell you." He looks round for somewhere to sit down and sees a medium sized boulder just off to the left of the track.

"What's that?" I ask, curiosity raging inside me.

Before answering, he walks across to the large stone, turns and sits down and leans lightly on his branch and begins to talk. "The Otherworld is a very real place. The stories you tell of the heroes in our legends visiting it make the place out to be some kind of magical land where incredible things happen. The sidhe, through the many stories told again and again, have become a people who are looked at with suspicion. They are said to have strange abilities and there are many different types. Is that not so?"

"Yes, that's what people like to hear when we tell them. They all love the mystery that surrounds the Otherworld, to say nothing of all the gods that are said to inhabit the place." I reply moving across to stand nearer to him.

"You're right, they love the stories, but these stories are now only thinly related to the truth." He gazes out past me looking down the glen we had just come up.

"Well, what is the truth?" I ask, almost impatiently.

"You remember Cuchulainn and his travels?" He turns back to face me.

"Of course." I reply, not realising it wasn't really a proper question.

"He was among the first to visit the Otherworld. It is a land many days sailing over the sea to the West, a huge place with many different peoples. Some have even been brought back to these shores. They are people very similar to us, except that they are on the whole smaller, which is why they are often called the 'little folk', and browner of skin, which is why they are sometimes called 'brownies'." He stops on the path and turns to look at me to see that I am still following him both physically and mentally. My mouth is agape in the desire to know more, so he continues.

"Cuchulainn first arrived dressed in full tuigen. He was an adventurous fili just like you, yet this was many years ago now, even long before me. The first the folk over there saw of him was standing in the bows of his boat, the feathers on his cloak blowing in the wind. The figurehead of a giant serpent at the front was an imposing sight to them and, as he looked so different, they thought of him as a god. The fact that he was covered in feathers made them think he could fly. They called him Kukulkan and Gucumatz, which meant feathered serpent as they could never get the pronounciation of his name quite right. They worshipped him and he brought peace to their lands. In return he was adorned with gold and many things that are found over there but not here."

"What else is different about the place?" I ask inquisitively.

"The birds have many coloured feathers, the fruits of the trees are completely different, as is much of their food. The way they speak is not the same and communication takes time. Gold and coloured jewels are abundant and the sun shines nearly all the time. There are many things that are different, too many to talk of now. I just want you to know that it was as real as this land and the people as real as us and they're not without their own problems too."

"What do you mean?" Now fully immersed in his revelations to even remember my own problems.

"Have you ever wondered where the Cult of the Dead might have originated?" He pauses to wait for me to answer and check on the way he is going.

"I thought that it had started in a land way to the south and came to us first on the North shores." I say.

"Well yes." He says after what seems an eternity. He casts his eyes to the left and right as if trying to recall a memory from long ago and fit it into what he is now looking at. Only when he seems to have made up his mind does he speak again. The waiting consumes me with anticipation. "That much I would agree with you, however before that, I believe it came from the Otherworld. When Cuchulain arrived, many years even before I was born, sacrifice was common. He changed all that, but after his death, it slowly reappeared. The leaders believed that to control and have power over their people, they must create fear. With fear they can get people to believe collectively anything that they want. It is a powerful tool as you will come to understand."

"Is this where Callum Beg got his ideas from do you think?" I ask.

"When I met him over there, it was purely accidental. I had travelled separately from an Island off of the west coast on a large currach, clad in bronze. He had somehow come over from the lands to the South. It was not a good meeting. He had gone over in search of knowledge, like myself, but had been influenced by what he had seen accomplished with such power of control over others. He learnt how to manipulate others with just the spoken word and how to instill fear into large numbers of people. Any appearance of one of us from our land is treated with awe by the sidhe and we were often treated like a god, because of Cuchulain. My turning up interrupted Callum Beg and his relationship with them as I instantly disassociated myself from him and what they were doing."

"What were they doing?"

"All the typical cult things like sacrificing young women and children, severing heads, reading entrails to devine the future and generally controlling their peoples every moment of the day. Much of which we've also seen over here." He hangs his head at the thought.

"What did you do?" I squat down so I can study his face, wanting to know as much as possible from him.

"I stood up to them by inviting them to try to manipulate me. Obviously it didn't work." He shakes his head and what despair there might have been in his voice vanishes as quickly as it was hinted at. "The result was that it divided the people into two groups. That was when he left, but only after he had heard of the existence of the Crown Helm. You see it was over there that it had been made."

"So Callum Beg returned to Invercarrie, hoping to find it and recreate his own 'Cult of the Dead' over here." I add.

"That would appear to be the case." He surmises.

"How can we stop him though?" I ask in earnest.

"I'm glad you said 'we'." He rises and heads back to the track. "It brings us back to your original question about what you feel you ought to be doing. Do you feel that you should now be returning to Invercarrie to retrieve your sister or finding out what we can possibly do to restrict Callum Beg's activities?"

"From what you have just said, it would appear that the two are inextricably linked and that there really is no choice." I reply following behind him.

"I would have to agree with you, whole heartedly." He finishes and strides on ahead with an air of determination about him.

"I've just one more question for now." I call after him quickening my step, "Why do people say that they can reach the Otherworld at these mounds and at the sacred places with the stones?"

"All will be revealed in good time Fionn. Our next stop is an ancient forest not far away, you'll find out more when we get there."

We walked onwards and slowly upwards. We'd left the main path some way back and now progress was slower as we had to negotiate more of nature herself. Fallen trees, bogs and boulder piles all had to be rounded and gradually we came to a sheltered part of the glen that had obviously rarely been seen or touched by another human. Giant twisted oaks of a nature that I'd never encountered before were matched in size by giant elms and beech trees. Their roots all intertwined in a manner that matted the forest floor together in some sort of pre-agreed harmony. There was a stillness about the place that looked as though nothing had changed there for many hundreds of years, which it quite possibly hadn't.

"Fionn, choose somewhere to try that exercise I showed you last night." Lugh's voice interrupts the tranquillity.

I looked slowly around wondering where might be best, when a stray thought came into my memory. It was the time I was on the boat with Ruadh. In that moment, I remembered his words about looking for that which was out of the ordinary. Almost instantly, I found myself staring at a particular aged oak. Its trunk had split half way up and it lower branches were now bent over and resting on the earth below. In the middle of the split there was a huge nest of loose sticks and twigs. I decided that it was a perfect spot to practice and climbed up.

"That's a good choice." Says Lugh, nodding in agreement.

I settled into the routine I had been shown and soon found the state Lugh had talked about. This time though it felt slightly different. The energy around me seemed to be mobile. It was not only there and fuelling me, it was also more vibrant than I had experienced before. I stayed a while until Lugh called me.

"What does it feel like here?" He asks in a gentle, quieter voice.

"A little different from before." I whisper back afraid of disturbing the tranquillity.

"In what way?" He asks again.

I told him what I felt and he seemed pleased but wouldn't be pressed on reasons why just yet. Again I would have to wait and discover for myself.

"Come, we have to reach Duchary Rock before it gets dark. We'll visit here again, for there's a lot that can be learnt from the energies of this place."

After having eaten a light snack, and tarried awhile admiring the beauty of the place, we set off. It wasn't long until we'd climbed up out of the tree line and were heading towards a small lone mountain. It wasn't the highest peak in the area, but it was the only one that was isolated from the others, not being part of a range. The landscape had changed now. There were no bushes or trees, just short grass and large, rounded, flat boulders and bare rock. These were often covered in green and white lichens and due to their size, gave shelter to lone patches of heather. Looking all around me there were white patches of snow and a few darker areas of earth, which had been open to the sun for longer. It was a beautiful sight, but not somewhere that was too hospitable. Lugh had said that he had supplies for a long cold season stocked in a cave there and that he used to use the place as a home many years ago. It was there that we were going to stay for a while, whilst he taught me what was possible when you harnessed the energies I had just experienced. We were also, somehow, going to collect information that would enable us to form a plan to bring down Callum Beg.

The cave was near the summit and nicely sheltered on the south side of the rock. At this height, nearly everything was snow covered and the tracks of several animals lay everywhere. We checked them for signs of bear and wolf outside the front, found none, but still entered carefully.

Just inside the entrance had been built up with a dry stonewall with an opening one end. On entering, I was immediately struck by an old musky smell that could only have meant that it had been home in the past to a variety of animals. Fortunately there were none here now.

We made ourselves as comfortable as was possible and lit a fire with the wood we had carried up with us. The warmth soon both eased my limbs and the constant throbbing from my wounded leg. I checked it over after carefully removing the poultice.

"What have you there?" Says Lugh, catching sight of it.

"I got stabbed two days ago, in the fight with Domnhuill Dubh that I told you about."

"You never mentioned your wound." He chides me in a sterner voice.

"I didn't think it necessary, it's on the mend now." I say, trying to play down its importance.

"Let's have a look at it." He comes over and kneels down next to me and peels back the poultice.

"Hmm. This needs further attention, it's got some dirt in." He fetches some water and pours it over the wound. The coldness and the pain makes me gasp." Lie back a moment." He orders in a way that is without question. I do so and feel him place the palm of his hands over the area. Almost immediately there is a tingling sensation that grows into a warmth. "Feel the warmth coming from my hands, the warmer it gets, the more the muscles will knit themselves together and repair themselves. Picture in your mind the sides healing together. Can you feel the area becoming warmer?"

"Yes." I reply, as I had to accept that I did.

"Good, then you will know it is repairing itself." Moments pass as the warmth spreads and intensifies. "Soon you will know that there is no wound as it will be completely repaired. As the warmth goes away, the work will be done and there will be no wound. Would you like that?"

"Of course." I reply again.

"How much?" He persists.

It sounded a stupid question but I answered anyway, "It matters greatly to me. I know how dangerous open wounds can be."

"Good, then believe that it will disappear as soon as the warmth disappears. The more you believe, the more the warmth will go away and the repair done. Can you feel it become less warm."

"Yes, slightly."

"What do you think is happening?" He goes on.

"Well the wound is healing itself together."

"What else?"

"The skin is forming over the surface again."

"As the area gets cooler, is there any sign of the wound now?"

"No, not at all." I imagine in my mind.

"Can you feel any warmth from my hands now?"

"No, none at all." I say searching for any sign at all.

"And your wound has healed completely?"

"Yes." I reply strangely, yet in an assured way.

"Sit up and have a look then." He concludes in a confident manner.

I sat up and looked down at my leg. There was no sign of a wound at all.

"That's amazing!" I exclaim, "How did you do that?"

"Well to begin with, it wasn't just me, you helped as well."

"How could I have helped?" I remark perplexed.

"It is all down to the power of suggestion. That, as well as some earth energy. Suggestion is merely a manner of talking that enables you to persuade someone to believe something. I will teach you the basics as it will be important for you to use a form of self-suggestion in order to achieve certain things. Think of it as just a tool that confuses the mind into thinking different things. If it's done with the use of earth energies, you can also change reality itself, as in the case of your wound. You already use many of the principles when you tell your stories, probably without knowing it."

"That's incredible." I answer. That could mean almost anything is achievable." I state.

"Quite possibly." Says Lugh, now smiling.

I get up and try walking around on my leg. It seems as good as new.

"I wish I'd mentioned it earlier now, it might have saved me some pain on the walk up here."

"Try that exercise again up here." He says, changing the subject, "I'd like to hear your thoughts on what differences there might be."

"Sure, if you like." I reply enthusiastically, my mind filled with all the possibilities that this newfound knowledge might lead to.

I knelt down next to the fire and repeated the exercise for the third time and found that reaching the state this time was much easier. Lugh had also reminded me of the three cauldrons that Angus has told me about and that by keeping all of them upturned it would greatly assist me. Even with this in mind, I was unprepared for the surge of energy that came into me once I reached the state. After only a few moments I felt giddy and light-headed as my whole body seemed to become invigorated.

"How was it this time? Did you notice any difference?" He says, now grinning from the opposite side of small stone hearth.

"You knew it would be like that." I reply, half mockingly. "How come it was that much more powerful and that there seemed to be so much more energy around?"

"Why do you think there was?" He questions back.

"The only difference I can think of is that we are much higher up. Does that have any importance?"

"Very much so Fionn, but where do you think that these energies might come from?" I thought about it for a while and remembered the energies in the forest that seemed slightly different.

"I would guess that they come from everything around us. Some things and some places appear to give off more, or different, energies than others." I venture.

"Right." He explains, "Everything and everyone gives out energy and receives energy in a form of a constant universal relationship. Only by becoming attuned to it, can we begin to recognise the patterns and their benefits. Where do you think the largest energies come from?" He asks.

"I suppose from the largest things." I guess.

"And what would they be?" He prompts me with another question.

"The Earth itself, then the Sun and the Moon." I go on with rising interest and understanding.

"Precisely Fionn. After a while you get to recognise areas and times when and where there are greater energy levels than others. Up at the tops of mountains is one such place. The Earth's energies seem to be channelled and become more dense and powerful on the more pronounced areas like Duchary Rock here..."

"... And for that reason it made it easier for me to access them." I interrupt.

"Yes." He answers quickly," However, even though they appear to come from the Earth, you must remember that they also come from the sun and the moon and even you and I. Everything exists as a series or relationships where this energy appears to be a form of universal power and link."

"How can it then be used for any good and how does it affect us?" I go on.

"You've already seen how it differed slightly in the ancient forest, it also differs slightly in humans.

It's as though our own interaction distorts it slightly and the way we act and think distorts it in different ways. Do you remember the story of Cormac's Cup, I would imagine Dugald would have almost definitely taught you that one."

"Yes of course." I reply.

"Remember the well of wisdom and the fountain of knowledge and the five streams that flowed from it, that only the learned people drink from."

"Yes," I say.

"Well, the streams refer to the five senses through which knowledge is learnt. To learn you must drink from all the streams and the fountain from which they come from. It is the same with learning to harness the universal energies. Some will only ever aspire to using the energies particular to their own bodies, for true power you must first open up to the universal, then learn to project it through you."

"But how is that done?" I interrupt eagerly.

"By using all your inner senses. Your inner words are your thoughts. Your inner sights are your dreams and visualisations. Your inner feelings are your beliefs and desires. I have just told you about the power of suggestion. You must learn to use the same techniques of self-suggestion along with your inner senses to project and receive things along the same lines of energy you have just witnessed. To do this successfully and with even greater power, you have to shut out your external senses and access even greater levels of power. This can, however, only be done with repeated mental practice. Do you think you are up to it?"

"I am willing to start," I answer, "I know I can do it." I add trying to sound more positive.

"Good. We'll start with your first experience now. It's time we found out more about Callum Beg and what he's been up to." He gets up and moves swiftly round to my side of the fire and kneels down next to me.

I cast him a curious look, which he noticed and returned with a wry smile. He did not initially come across as a man that was forthcoming by nature, so I waited in silence as a sign for him to go on and explain a bit more. I got the feeling that everything would be covered in the fullness of time and at a pace that was outside both our control.

"One thing I have to warn you of," he begins after having made some mental preparations of his own, "is to not show any signs of emotion. Don't be afraid of what will happen, just keep hold of my hand at all times."

We knelt together and reached the same state again. He held my hand again as he had the first time and I followed his every instruction to become calm and relaxed. Having done this, I felt the power surge out from him as well as the surroundings and then a tremendous feeling of serenity as we seemed to lift up out of our bodies in our minds. We then drifted slowly out of the cave, hovering in the air above the footsteps we had only just made a little earlier. Looking back in, I could see our bodies kneeling side by side as if in deep meditation.

Higher and higher we rose, our hands still held together. There was no cold and we could only hear the sounds we wished to hear. Evening was coming and the sun was an orange glow low on the horizon. With the skies still clear, I could see large distances across lands I didn't even know the names of. This high, I could see over the Gruinard Sea and to the islands of Siegg, Stig and Bestol. As we travelled south to Invercarrie at a speed faster than that of any bird, I recalled my journey North that I had made only days ago. Soon the Broch where Miari was held came into view. Part of me wanted to dive down and see she was still alright and for a moment we almost started to go in that direction until I heard the voice of Lugh in my mind saying not to worry.

Our destination appeared to be the Aes Dana and no sooner did we see it, than we were down through the opening in the middle of the central hall and standing next to the alter stone. The place was empty except for two people arguing in one of the side rooms. It was not one I'd been in before. The door was open, so we drifted inside only to find both Domnhuill Dubh and Callum Beg in a heated rage with one another. We stood still and watched and listened. The room was filled with weapons and blades and other instruments of torture. The two of them were arguing whilst pacing around a central table that was covered in straps and belts. There was also a sinister collection of skulls decorating the walls.

"How could you possibly lose track of one person so many times, you complete imbecile!" Shouts Callum Beg, grabbing a large bronze pestle from its stone mortar and waving it in the air.

"If you'd given us the right information about the man in the first place, one of my best fighters wouldn't be dead now. It's your part of the bargain to give us what we need to know to do your dirty work. You should have told us he had friends up North and that he could fight." Screams Domnhuill Dubh even louder.

"He doesn't know anybody up North, you idiot, he just makes friends easily and how on earth did you let him find you? Didn't I tell you I need him and Lugh alive. Killing him in a fight is the last thing I want." He shouts again, this time picking up one of the skulls in his spare hand and still pacing around the central table.

"It was difficult enough not to kill him. If I had been trying to kill him do you think I would have been hit in the foot! I don't know why you even need him or Lugh now, you've got the main parts of the Crown helm, you can make up the missing bit and no one would be the wiser. We don't even need the girl."

"Of course I need the girl. I have to have an untouched woman that's not from Invercarrie or the mainland if I'm to complete the ritual at Samhain. She's also useful if we ever need to control him. He won't dare to disrupt our plans while we keep her alive." He growls, thinly disguising his contempt at the other man's ignorance.

"We can find another one, nearer the time, this one's showing signs of giving us trouble, her family probably knows where she is by now and it won't be long before they come after her. We either sell her or dispose of her right now." He demands.

"You'll do nay such a thing and I'll not be taking orders from yourself. Just remember who you're talking to." Rasps Callum Beg, and raising both skull and pestle in front of him he begins to knock the one against the other.

The effect it has on Domnhuill Dubh makes him clasp his hands around behind his head, his arms covering his ears. He begins to groan a deep guttural sound and he launches himself toward Callum Beg.

"Stop your evilry Beg or I'll call in my guards." Commands Domnhuill Dubh. It seems to work as he puts down the skull. "You need me," he continues, "let's work out what we need to do to keep to our plan."

"Fine, then return to Killiecraigie and find out if anyone knows where he was headed. Someone there is bound to know. Take forty of your guard and level the place. Put meaning into the name of the place and kill them all if necessary."

"That's sounds good to me, though I want full share of the spoils this time." Barks Domnhuill.

"That's of no interest to me, just find out where he's meeting Lugh, then get there, get them both and the missing piece! I've got to sort out some problems here with Queen Irnan, she wants that blasted son of hers to work with me here in the lead up to his coronation. That's something I need like a snake in my bed and I don't need any more problems like that in the lead up to the end of the year."

"What shall we do with the other girl though, we recaptured her as you suggested?" Reminds Domnhuill almost as an afterthought.

"Was there a problem with that?" He almost sounds concerned, but instead of continuing to talk directly to Domnhuill he goes over to the other side of the little room where, on the table, there are the entrails of some animal. He picks up a slender black glass knife and begins a morbid disection.

"No, we snatched her back during the night after they left Invercarrie." Domnhuill looks over Beg's shoulder, watching him work. There is a visible distaste in the man eyes yet he is drawn in to peer more closely by his morbid curiosity.

My mind began to show signs of concern and my heart nearly missed a beat. Could they possibly be referring to Niamh.

"Good, it's as well to have some extra leverage. Where is she now?" He continues without looking up.

"I thought it best to bring her here, it will be easier for us to deny that we did it. She's locked up in the room next to this." Says Domnhuill, now backing away from Beg and turning to go to the door.

"Hmm." Ponders Callum Beg turning round, his interest rekindled. "That might have been the most sensible thing you've done in a while. Bring her in." He orders.

Domnhuill goes over to the connecting door, opens it and moments later brings a struggling Niamh into the room with a vice like grip around her upper arm. It was too much for me. 'No' I cry out in my mind. Lugh tightens his grip on my hand and I feel his calming presence, but it was too late.

"Silence." Shouts Callum Beg, suddenly feverishly alert and darting glances all around the room.

"We're not alone!" He grabs an amulet from off of a side table, slings it around his neck and slinks his head forward as though hunting out the source of a strange smell.

Domnhuill looks at him strangely, "What on earth do you mean?" He calls fiercely.

"Silence, I said!" He says again, even more forcefully and proceeds to move across the room in large open sweeps as if searching for something he'd lost. "I'll find you. I know you're there!" He shouts hysterically up into the air.

A voice in my head from Lugh tells me it's time to go and for the second time I find myself leaving this woman in circumstances out of my control. The pain surprised me but within moments we were out and up into the evening air. In what seemed like no time at all, we were back in the cave.

"May the Dagda's club strike me down with some more sense, what happened back there?" I ask, having taken a while to fully return to my normal mind. "Why did we have to leave so suddenly?"

"Many reasons, Fionn. Unfortunately your surprise at seeing the young girl there caused too many emotions within you to surface and I couldn't calm you down quick enough."

"Quick enough for what?"

"Quick enough not to be detected by someone as sensitive to these things as Callum Beg is. He immediately sensed your presence, possibly mine too and will now probably have guessed that we heard everything that they were talking about."

"I'm sorry," I say. "Seeing her again threw my mind. I thought she was safe." The worry in my voice is obvious.

"What is her name?" He asks comfortingly, coming over and putting an arm across my shoulder.

"Niamh." The word escapes my lips, still fresh with the memory of her presence the last time I called her name.

"The girl you rode North with from Drummorchy." He presumes correctly, talking about her as if sensing that it was what I needed to do.

"Yes." I reply gingerly, never having before experienced the feelings that were now surfacing from inside me.

"It would appear that you care greatly for her. That's a fine thing, but emotions as strong as that have their place and if you are to help her, then learning to control them becomes imperative."

"That's not going to be easy." I reply.

"No, it's not. At times like that, it helps to immediately focus on the universal energy. Supplant one thought for another, the mind can't hold two thoughts at the same time. We'll learn more about that later so don't worry, it may not look like it, but we've time on our side." He leaves me to go over to the back of the cave.

"Not that much." I remark. "And it still seems there are mountains to climb and what can we do to warn my friends at Killiecraigie "

"I'll take care of that." He replies calmly, "Let's get some food together and rest a while. I'll tell you more about the Otherworld, if you prepare dinner, how about that?" He hands me a cauldron that he has just picked up and points to a pile of wood further at the back of the cave.

"That sounds fair." I agree, moving over to fetch the items in question.

After eating and listening to each other's tales, we discussed plans for the next few days. Lugh suggested that we stayed put for a while, then make our way down to the dolmen for the spring equinox. According to him, this would be my next lesson on from the one I was learning on the mountain top. The movement of the sun and the moon around the earth changed the patterns of energy in predictable ways. At the dolmen it was easier to see and feel this and he wanted me to be able to distinguish between the energies coming from each of the celestial bodies. At the equinox the sun would rise up from behind the horizon precisely in the East and the night and day would be of equal length. All that was left, was to determine the position of the moon and that could be done on the day.

As it was still some days away, I spent my time learning as much as possible. We began by learning to access the universal energy quickly, then projecting it with the inner senses. In doing this I began to hear and send thoughts between the two of us as our own bodies energies met and interacted with each other. At first it was jumbled up, but with more and more practice, and with the learned exclusion of unwanted information, I managed to progress little by little. We even began to send visions to each other and create illusions within the mind of the other. This was followed by the sending and receiving of feelings. Although it was weak and sporadic to begin with, it was a start and I could begin to see its relevance and importance if I was to survive another encounter with Callum Beg.

Two days before the equinox we set off down from the cave and headed West. The dolmen was where Uther had said it would be and both Lugh and I half guessed that there would be a reception waiting for us. If that was to be, we had developed a plan for just such an eventuality.

As we walked up the last few strides of the hill, we kept hidden well inside the Kildamorie forest. We looked cautiously out across the clearing on the top where the Dolmen stood. There were three flattish vertical stones in the centre with one large slab across the top. However, it was a cold and damp mid-afternoon and there was low cloud covering the whole area. The stones loomed out in front of us and looked as though they were completely unsupported by the hidden ground. If anyone was waiting for us up there, we wouldn't have been able to see them either. There was only a little time left and, as sunrise the next day was the time of the equinox, we would have to be up all night making preparations. It was going to be tough in this weather.

Around the edge of the clearing we looked for the heel stone. That was our guide. We may not be able to see the sun in the morning, but as long as we could see that stone, we would know where it was and could focus on the sun's presence. Lugh had told me of the importance of the stones in the last few days. They had been put up many years before by followers of the sun and the cult of the dead. They had recognised the importance of knowing the onset of the seasons in advance in order to predict favourable crop growing times. This gave them a chance to control the people with the impression of their wisdom. They could also feel the energies attached to the sacred places, which is why they chose these areas to put up their stones. The flat slabs were there for their ritual sacrifices. They used them to prostrate their victims flat across the slab before performing their despicable arts.

Several stone circles were built at a later date without these 'altar tables' and there were others that had had them removed. Lugh told me that what had been found afterwards, was that certain stones, if in the right position, could actually help channel the earth energies to a single point. This greatly assisted the attainment of a universal connection. People also built mounds and erected massive megaliths to help enhance this effect and this was the reason that people associated the Otherworld with the mounds of the sidhe. Ancient mystics had used the mounds to travel more easily, in their minds, in order to get to the Otherworld. Stones and mounds were also put up in areas where the energies were strong, but not yet focused sufficiently to be of use to everyone. All of these places had become sacred and many were kept secret still by the Aes Dana even though nearly all of the learned folk had forgotten how to best utilise these energies.

This place was one of them. Only a very few people knew of its existence and of the ceremonies surrounding it.

"Fionn, go underneath and dig up the earth, you'll find a few items I left here long ago, they'll come in useful." Whispers Lugh. "I'll keep watch from over here."

I did so, using my hands and a short digging stick I had fashioned out of wood. It was like looking for buried treasure and my excitement made me work fast. The short visibility because of the dense mists added to the sense of atmosphere. Before long, I had uncovered a bundle of cloth. I picked up one end and lifted it to allow the contents to slide carefully out. What lay in front of me on the fresh soil took my breath away. I turned away to look at Lugh, who was now standing behind me. In my awe, I had not heard him approach. Though now I thought about it, I couldn't ever remember him making much of a noise wherever he went.

"Hand me the crystal and the drum if you will, the sword and the dirk I suggest you secrete about your person. They may come in handy later." He suggests.

I handed him the small, colourless, flawless crystal that was about the size and shape of a plum. Its coolness even in this cold cloud cover made it an irresistible prize and I could only wonder at how it had been made or even its purpose. The drum was the least impressive of the four items, being made from a black wood and a stretched hide from an animal unknown to me, the sword and dirk had been made two of a pair as their hilts were similarly inlaid with red and green stones. I lifted them up carefully and inspected the blades. They were iron, but of a kind I had not encountered before. Lugh had obviously read my thoughts.

"They're not from around here, if you are wondering. I brought them back from the Otherworld. The metal came from the stars many years ago and has been worked again and again with many other metals like gold and silver. That's what gives it its strange hue. I've no idea if they are any good, they were a gift. Perhaps they'll be of use, perhaps not. It will depend on what you believe is possible."

"They will do well, but I hope things don't come to that. There is no way we can defeat Callum Beg or Domnhuill Dubh with force." I state.

"Your right there, lad." He releases a dry smile that raises one corner of his mouth ever so slightly.

"Now come and help me up here will you?"

I got up off my knees and came out from under the big slab and held out my hands to give him a leg up onto the top of it. Once up, he held out his hand and helped pull me up.

We were at least a man's height off of the ground and with the natural rise of the top of the hill, we could just see over the tops of the trees, the rest was obscured by the greyness of the cloud.

We knelt, as we had done so often recently, side by side on top of the cool, flat, grey rock. I couldn't help but wonder at the effort with which the builders must have gone to, in order to get these chosen stones into their final resting position. Lugh had told me that they had come from far away over land and water. Their shapes had taken ages to carve correctly but nothing compared to the time taken in bringing the stones to their final resting place. The rocks had been chosen because of their excessive weight and their crystal alignments. These features needed to contrast well with the local stone.

We waited in silence, remaining in the open 'state' that I had begun to learn was the foundation of all mental feats. As evening drew on, the cloud began to lift and a light breeze soon parted a few of them to reveal the starry night. Our luck had held and the moon soon lit up the sky complete with a frosty ring. With the positions known, we began to focus on their individual energies. As passage was made through the night sky, I began to recognise the changing relationships of the respective energies. Lugh had told me that the periods of greatest effect were felt when there was a conjunction of all three bodies. At times of alignment like these, great events occurred and even though other humans may not be aware of their energies, it still affected them in one way or another.

I could sense the arrival of dawn and adjusted my position to kneel facing East and the heel stone. Visibility had fully returned and the morning glow lit up the entire area.

To the West we could see right over the forest and down to loch Dubh with the Reekie Linn rapids at one end and Finlarich Broch the other. To the North as far as the eye could see were lochs and more lochs. In the East, between the peaks of Ben Avon and Carn Eilrig, we could see right through and over the Achentoul forest to the Sea. This narrow horizon was exactly due East of us and, with the peaks as sights, it was the place we now channelled our thoughts. As the sun would rise, a surge of energy would rush to greet us and it was then that I would, on my own, try to travel in my mind, as I had done before with Lugh.

As sun came up, I centred myself and projected my visions up and out assisted by the its force. The next moment I was up in the air with Lugh beside me, but this time we were separated. With only a thought and a projection, I could move where I wanted to go. I went higher enjoying an unknown freedom that was hard to describe. It was like dreaming an intensely vivid dream, yet also being in control of the dream.

I lowered myself back down and moved around the clearing, still using my mind. I watched a rabbit feeding outside its burrow. As I approached it looked up at me as if sensing my presence yet showing me no fear. I smiled and continued exploring near to the tree when a movement in the bushes caught my eye.

Edging ever closer, my curiosity having got the better of me, I floated above the bush. What I saw caused me to forget everything. I returned to my body on top of the dolmen with the impact and speed of ripe pear being thrown against a stone wall.

Lugh was instantly by my side as I struggled to regain full control of my senses.

"What was it Fionn? What happened to make you lose your concentration?"

"Under the bushes over there." I try to whisper, but it comes out far louder than I intend. "They're here."

No sooner had I said that, and my words presumably heard, than a cry went up and twenty fully armed warriors charged at the dolmen. Lugh immediately stood up and raised his branch high, shaking it slightly. A gentle ringing began. Between his feet lay the crystal and the drum hung by his side. With his free hand he began a light rhythmic beat on the drum. With every step that they came closer his beat got louder and louder. I pulled out the sword and dirk and stood up to face the oncoming mass of bodies. Domnhuill was at the front, his sword waving high in the air. Gruagh was straining to keep up with him, his heavy bulk not as fast, as they ran up the slope. With only thirty paces to go before they reached us, I heard howls coming from behind me. The noise stopped a few from rushing further forward; the others kept on at a pace.

The howls got louder and I looked down beneath me to see hoards of fully-grown wolves leaping out from under and around the dolmen just as Domnhuill and his men reached us. Swords and teeth met in a vicious clash as jaws locked around arms and blades struck flanks of fur and flesh. I parried thrusts that came at me from all sides and kicked at the hands of those men that tried to climb up. Domnhuill hurled abuse after abuse at me, goading me to either come down and fight or demanding that we surrender. Many men fell to the wolves ferociousness and screams were mixed with whimpers as both animals and fallen warriors lay strewn across the grassy field.

With wounds to my legs and feet, I struck out wildly at the nearest bodies that approached me. Several drew back, badly cut to the head and shoulders, and promptly they were jumped upon by more beasts from the pack.

In the end, with only ten of them still standing, they drew back a few paces and drew out their throwing axes and dirks, an ochie dhu was thrown from amongst their midst. Its blade missed me by a finger width but struck Lugh deep in the chest. He went down, falling forward onto his knees, his one hand clutched at the knife the other groped inside his robe. Blood sprang out everywhere. It was obvious to everyone that he had been mortally wounded. From out of his robes he took the fourth piece of the crown helm and held it up for me to take. Just I reached out to grab it, it fell from his weakened, outstretched hand, down onto the grass below. With this final act he fell flat, face down against the slab of rock. There was silence. Domnhuill rushed forward and picked up the golden icon and held it high in the air.

"We have what we wanted and done what we set out to do." He shouts heavy of breath. "Fionn mac Donal of the clan Donal, you and your friend are finished. We have won." He turns and grins wildly at his remaining comrades, shaking the icon up high in front of them.

Shouts went up from his men. Only Gruach, who was limping with a badly mauled leg, wanted to continue to fight. "Enough Gruach, he'll not trouble us anymore. If he does, or even dares show his face near Invercarrie again, he'll lose both his sister and the fair Niamh!"

I was too distraught to say a word and watched as they backed off, helping the few that could walk as they went. I turned to Lugh and saw his body lying in a pool of blood with his gold branch lying next to him. The sight brought me back to reality and I turned to let out a yell at Domnhuill and his men. It was a cry that came from the base of my lungs and was sent forth with all the force of the universal energy that I could muster. The result echoed through trees and valleys for as long as a man can hold their breath. All of them were stopped in their tracks by the sound and could only move on after it had gone. A lone wolf howled after them.

CHAPTER TWELVE

ON HUMAN AND ANCIENT EARTH ENERGIES

It is time to now look at the second of our two subjects and as we do so you will begin to see the Key to the secrets that the Ancients have known about. In this chapter we are going to delve into some of the more intriguing aspects of 'Energy' that have been found within humans and you will be getting the opportunity to discover its effects for yourselves if you follow the experiments. Ancient Earth energies will then be covered with a view to first illustrating some of their similarities to human energy and then to show some of their more amazing phenomena. The latter reveals fascinating new possibilities as to how the ancient peoples of this planet used these energies. Firstly though, much of the evidence for Human Energy stems from work done more recently by Eastern philosophers and this is the area we must start with in order to accumulate the right information to continue of search for the link with modern science.

The three great religions found in the East are Confucianism, Taoism and Buddhism. It is the underlying connections between these three, that have led to Eastern philosophy as it is thought of today. The central concept of a universal energy was integral to Confucianism and Taoism from the very beginning, however Buddhism saw that the control of the mind was initially the path to follow. Although all three have distinct differences, there were sufficient similarities to allow them all to coexist happily and lead to further development. Zen Buddhism, developed in Japan, was one such development. It was mentioned in chapter 8.8 that Zen is devoted to liberating the mind through the use of the inner senses, so we must now look at how this 'energy' has its connection with the inner senses.

This chapter will go on to cover several other subjects in some detail in order to give the reader as much relevant and factual information as is possible. The emphasis will be to show how this 'energy' exists within the different topics and how it is utilised to give the results that are witnessed.

As with science, this subject also has its guardians and with it, secret languages that only initiates are allowed to learn (unfortunately much of this language is also padded out with the jargon of each discipline. This in turn makes it difficult to understand for the lay person). Once these hurdles have been cast aside though, some common ground can be found.

The main principle behind Eastern philosophy is that a universal force, or energy, in some way connects us all together. In China they call it chi, in Japan it's ki. In other countries it is known as prana, num, kundalini and several other names depending on the culture. For the purposes of writing this book, I will refer to it either as ki or chi when using its name, but it can be implied that any of the names are equally correct. Everyone agrees that it is all the same force, but it's from there onwards that the disagreements start. These disagreements have lead to the current separate ways and also happen to coincide with the beginnings of much of the colourful and descriptive language. Language, as we have seen in chapter ten, is the main way of programming the mind to think and act differently and this only perpetuates the separate paths that have been taken in the many eastern disciplines.

You might well think, because of all these differences, that we could not really learn anything or make any conclusions about the overall subject. However, we can find some answers if we look in the area where there is general agreement. Specifically, we need to look at the methods used when this 'energy' is 'tapped' and the way in which it can be used. The similarities with regard to our 'link' then begin to arise. We should also look at the old 'sayings' from some of the most influential 'adepts' in these fields. These wise people have come to know and understand this 'Energy' purely by living with it and developing it within themselves for most of their lives.

At this point, you might say that these sayings are just hearsay and consider them 'inadmissible as evidence' as word of mouth does not provide proof. However, some of the feats that these people have been observed doing, defy common scientific principles. (We will be looking at a few of these and giving you the opportunity to try some in your home later in the chapter). The fact that these feats have been achieved only through the connecting use of this 'energy', really ought to require us to listen with more care as to what these adepts have to say. If we do listen, without pre judging what we hear, and then make our comparisons, we can see some interesting similarities with what western science has been telling us.

For the purposes of this book I shall divide discussing ki into two sections. The first section will be ki and individuals, the second ki and the earth and other celestial bodies. No distinction has ever been mentioned before and I do not intend to give the impression that one exists. It is purely done in order to present the information so that it can be more easily understood. Those people following an Eastern philosophy believe ki to be universal in its nature and it is found within all their different disciplines. Some of the more relevant ones, that base much of their work with the use of ki, are aikido, acupuncture, tai chi and ki gung. We will now look at these in more detail.

12.1 Aikido

Aikido is a purely defensive martial art and contains no violence at all. It has been described as a subtle and sophisticated art and, apart from self-defence, it provides a framework for strengthening the integration of mind and body. It was originally developed by a Japanese man called Morihei Ueshiba from movements found within the arts of sword fighting, ju jitsu and aiki jitsu. Morehei Ueshiba lived in Japan from 1883 to 1969 and in 1903 he joined the army and fought in the Russo-Japanese war of 1904/5. In 1915 he studied aiki jitsu under the grandmaster Takeda Sokaku from the Daito Ryu. Takeda Sokaku was perhaps one of the most famous martial artists he would learn from, before going on to start his own dojo in 1920.

In 1942 he moved away from Tokyo to Iwama and built a school for people to study with him and it was there that he founded the aiki shrine. His descendants still teach his techniques and philosophies at the shrine today. It was here that the art of aikido began. Its literal translation is the 'way of harmony of the spirit'. The training concentrates on developing ki, having a relaxed frame of mind, generating an overall awareness within the body and being in a state of readiness for action without tension.

It relies heavily upon the development of ki and the concentration of that ki at the hara. The hara is a point in the body, just below the abdomen, that is common in all the energy-based disciplines. It also happens to be described by the exponents of these arts as the 'centre of gravity' in your body (This is actually scientifically correct).

As with many of these arts there are rules and principles that, if followed, will allow the student to progress. There are four basic principles that are said to unify mind and body. The first and fourth are principles of the mind; the second and third are principles of the body. When looking at the connection between the two, we learn that the mind leads, moves and controls the body. Before an attacker strikes, it is their mind that decides, in advance of the attack, what their body is going to do. The art in aikido is to be prepared, in advance, by recognising that the attacker's mind has 'moved' first.

Here is a simple experiment that you can do at home in order to see the mind moving the body. Start by holding your hands together with interlocking fingers. Now hold your two index fingers straight out in front, keeping your thumbs crossed. Look keenly at both of the extended fingers and think of them coming together at the fingertips. Do not consciously make any muscle movements to do this action, but just watch as they come together. Now try again from the beginning and do the opposite and think of them staying apart. You should find that in the second instance the fingers remain apart until you start thinking about them coming together. This change over comes exactly at the time your mind changes its thoughts.

There is not thought to be any division between the mind and the body and they are originally said to exist as one. This view does not support the 'dualist's' view of consciousness that we saw in chapter eight but instead lends more weight to the 'reductionist' approach.

The first principle is to keep one point. This refers to the 'hara' mentioned earlier and when one is actively and continually thinking of the one point, one is said to be 'centering' oneself. The effectiveness of this is frequently seen with the ki test exercises that are performed in aikido classes. Just as a muscle that is used and pushed to its limits will strengthen, so will the mind if it is assisted and tested with repeated exercising. One of the delights in aikido is encountered when new students first experience ki and its effects. When a new student discovers what they can do for the first time, the look on their faces is similar to seeing a child discovering the enjoyable taste of ice cream for the first time.

A simple test that can be tried at home with a partner is one based on this concept of keeping one point. Kneel on the floor and lean forwards to rest on your elbows. Lower your head until it hangs and relax your muscles. Now think of a point in your belly and keep focusing on it throughout the test. Your partner should kneel to the side of you and facing you. They should place one hand on your shoulder and the other on your hip and push when you are ready. As they push, keep thinking of your one point and feel and imagine all their energy rushing through your body into that one point. With practice you will be able to stay upright (not pushed over) with greater and greater amounts of shoving from your partner. To test the difference between that and not keeping one point, you should ask to be tested again whilst thinking of something else (like shopping or washing up). This time it will be almost certainly be far easier for you to be toppled over.

The second principle is to keep calm and relaxed. As was mentioned in the previous experiment, it is important to relax. None of the moves in aikido are done using great physical exertion, this makes it popular amongst women as it is a great equaliser of the sexes. I have witnessed many small women throw large men during a simulated attack, much to the amazement of both parties.

The third principle is to keep weight underside. If we relax completely, the weight of each part of our bodies naturally settles at its lowest point. By thinking that parts of our body are either heavy or light and by relaxing completely and remaining calm, we can make those parts of the body seem either heavier or lighter.

One test that shows this well is called 'unraisable body'. The idea behind the test is to either allow people to lift you effortlessly or not all, depending on whether you are thinking heavy or light. By keeping weight underside, relaxing and remaining calm it is almost impossible to be lifted. By thinking of being light, it will be easy for less people to lift you up into the air. To amplify the effects it helps to also concentrate on the central point in the abdomen.

The fourth principle is to extend ki. By keeping 'one point' we are already extending ki. Once we 'centre' ourselves, we can then project ki outwards in whatever direction we choose. In doing this, it allows a flow of ki to come in to our body and then out in the direction we have chosen. We then find we are continually exchanging and interacting with ki.

A good example of extending ki is a test that beginners to aikido are soon taught. It is called unbendable arm. A student will hold out a slightly bent arm that is relaxed. They are asked to keep all four principles in mind and in particular to extend ki out from their 'one point' up, along and out of the end of the arm. The 'tester' will then place one hand face down on top of the bicep; the other underneath the wrist. The idea is to then try to bend the arm at the elbow. If it is performed with tensed up muscles first and without ki, the arm will eventually bend. If done correctly next by extending ki, it will not. What is interesting to note is what the students are asked to think of when performing the extension of ki. After 'centering' on 'one point' the extension is made by visualising a beam of light shining from the centre, up through the body and shoulder and out along the length of the arm like a torch. To make the arm more unbendable (In the beginning students are tested with only a little strength so as to build up their ability), the visualisation/expectation/internal dialogue must be made more intense.

What can often lead to confusion amongst beginners is the fact that it doesn't matter what you visualise, or think of, and many people choose different things, whichever suits them best. This leads us to look more closely at what is being done in order to achieve these results. The only conclusion is that it appears that the mind body connection is being assisted again by the use of the inner senses. If it's the first time that you have tried all of these tests, as has been described, you will undoubtedly be feeling a little perplexed, as are all the newcomers to ki aikido. Questions like "What is happening?" and "How does it work?" are common at this time.

Before we look at answering these questions, we must first look further at what is required to achieve these and even greater phenomena. Along with visualisation and imagination, expectation and one's inner dialogue are also utilised within a concentrating mind. All of these allow us to move ki calmly and naturally to where we wish it to go. The ki tests mentioned above are part of an extensive range of tests that are used in aikido to build a students ability to control ki. The reason for doing these tests is that they form the basis of the defensive aikido moves. The end result is that if they are attacked, rather than using force and strength to defend themselves, they draw in their opponents ki to their 'one point' and then project it out throughout the move. In effect, when they are performing the move, they are visualising a complete flow of ki about themselves and their attackers. This visualisation could be of interacting light beams or waves breaking on the sea-shore.

Whatever works for them will create the desired effect as long as their internal senses are completely activated. This movement of the mind pre-empts the movement of the body and their opponent's body. If you are fortunate enough to have witnessed someone who is well-practiced in the art, you will notice that no amount of strength will help the attacker if you are using ki. This is the power behind aikido as a defensive martial art.

All the moves are carried out in a totally conscious state of mind. However the aikido student does not actually want to be conscious of anything in particular. They seek to initially achieve a state of mind called 'mushin', also known as 'no mind'. This means that the inner senses must also be used in an unthinking manner, rather like the unconscious competence stage of learning mentioned in an earlier chapter.

When students stand and wait for attackers to reach them, they must forget all the techniques they have learned. They must not think of the movements of their opponent, but must be open to the dictates of their unconscious. Mushin indicates a state of alertness, heightened awareness with increased intuitiveness. A master, by doing this, will seek to be aware of what is happening in the mind of their opponent before a strike has come, and will have reacted instinctively just beforehand. In this mode of open mind, the flow of ki is continual and the master becomes an active part of the flow and 'at one' with their opponent. This state of mind has been measured to have a high percentage of alpha brainwaves (a topic which was mentioned in chapter 8) as it is also witnessed occurring in several other disciplines. The difference is that in aikido and other ki based arts, exponents train specifically to enhance this state as they are aware of its importance. Knowing this, we need to look at what other methods they use to strengthen this state of mind and also what they say is actually occurring with regards to ki.

Apart from keeping this particular state of mind, the breathing is also important. We have previously seen this to be so with the free air divers mentioned in chapter 8. In their case, they too needed to achieve a calm and relaxed frame of mind. The connecting principle in these two cases, and in all other related ones, is that whilst breathing is taking place, it must be visualised. The act of visualising the air going in, around the lungs and out, stimulates the ki and controls its flow throughout the body. The ki in turn assists in achieving the desired outcome.

I would recommend to everyone reading this book that they try ki aikido to find out how it can help them in their daily lives. It not only brings a confidence through a knowledge of self defence, but it also provides a framework for life that appears to me to assist in the discovery of your vocational path in life. When you are following your vocation in life the eastern philosophers say that you are living closely with ki. In chapter 4, it was mentioned that to partly achieve one's goals in life, one had to use one's inner senses (The other part was correct planning). This would appear to be a similar message to that which is taught by the Sensei's in aikido today. For those people who would wish to flow and live with ki, there appears to be the distinct possibility of achieving amazing results in your chosen field.

12.2 Acupuncture

Amazing results is the theme we should pursue in the next few sections. Acupuncture is a procedure that has produced results that have defied scientific explanation. It is based on the assumption that ki flows through 'channels' in the human body called meridians. The practice is thought to have started 4000 years ago at the beginning of oriental medical history. Some would argue however that it began even earlier. A frozen body of a stone-age man, discovered recently in the Alps, was found to have lines tattooed on his body in exactly the same positions as modern day acupuncturists state that the meridians lie. These particular lines corresponded to arthritic pain relief treatment and, from an analysis of his bones, that happened to be a condition that the man had been suffering. Whenever the origins, it would appear that human energy has been known about for a long time.

Each meridian is said to be linked to a specific organ within the body and along their length there are points, called Tsubos, where ki can be contacted. It is at these points that needles are placed (or finger pressure in the case of shiatsu) in order to bring about the desired outcome of better health. It must be mentioned that these lines have never been actually measured or seen and at the moment only exist in the mind of the practitioner and their patient. That does not mean they don't exist, nor does it mean that it can't work. It just means that western science hasn't devised a method that can observe them. Some people at this point might disagree with this statement as there are machines available on the market that allow practitioners to find the nodal (surface) points of the meridians. By passing an electric current through the body from one electrode to another, when placed on the nodes, it is possible to find the path of least electrical resistance. These paths would seem to match the meridians and the machines are used to help find where they lie in a person as each individual is slightly different. However, just as a hollow tube can allow water to pass through, it can also be a conduit for other things. Meridians may well allow electricity to pass through more readily, but this does not necessarily mean that they were formed for this purpose. One theory could be that the regions of the body where the meridians lie are denser, or have a mean density, compared to the other areas. Electricity could tend naturally to travel more easily in the denser regions of the body. This could explain why they can be used to determine meridian positions and it can also give us a clue as to why ki also flows in these regions.

Ill health is said to impair the flow of ki. The application of needles or finger pressure appears in many cases to have a well-documented degree of beneficial effects. Perhaps one of the more understated aspects of the application technique, is not so much the position of the needles, but the thoughts in the mind of the practitioner. In experts there is a high amount of care and sensitivity shown throughout the process. This corresponds to the use of the inner senses, as has been mentioned beforehand, and obviously it plays an enormous part in the treatment. If you have any doubt about this try experiencing a massage by someone that would rather be somewhere else and doing something else and compare that with one that is done with loving care. The movements may be the same, but the overall effect is drastically different!

As with aikido, acupuncture practitioners believe in the 'hara', the centre of the body's gravity. It is there they believe that the spiritual force exists. The region must be relaxed so that they can project their energy out from the hara and into their patient in order for them to receive the full benefit of the treatment.

12.3 Chi Gung

Chi gung is the Chinese art of developing energy. This is done for good health, training the mind and to develop what is called the 'internal force'. It has become popular today as an effective means of stress management and general fitness of mind and body. It too has close parallels with aikido and other Eastern philosophies and produces some unbelievable feats and results that confound western medicine and science.

Chi gung has been found to exist in China as long ago as the Shang dynasty (approx 1500 yrs B.C.) but only recently has it acquired its name. The name is a collective term that covers all arts concerned with chi (ki) or energy. Like all of the eastern arts, it is an experience, not solely knowledge, and as such must be practiced. These seemingly impossible feats (some of which are mentioned later) can only be done by someone with a highly developed mind who has had years of practice.

Mencius, the second sage (Confucius being generally recognised as the first sage) explained that a person's will power could control the flow of energy. That and positive visualisation are the main tools that are used by chi gung exponents. Again it is inner feelings and inner seeing that appears to be intimately connected with chi.

There are often many names given to moves within martial arts like Tiger Claw and Iron Head. These are aids for the memory to assist in a clearer picture being built up through visualisation and we have already seen that the clearer and more focused the inner senses, the more effective the results.

Shaolin monks, famous for their kung fu training at their monastery in the Henan province in northern China, practice the techniques of chi gung using these same tools. They manage to take punches to their stomachs without being hurt, they can break bricks without damaging their hands and run great distances without tiring, all from developing their internal force to a high degree. Many of their moves also have these colourful descriptions as has been mentioned above.

Just as with aikido, breathing is tremendously important for the student of chi gung. Deep abdominal breathing, as opposed to the typical western shallow chest breathing, is practiced until it has become a habit. Once this is mastered the visualisation of ki flowing in and out is added. This exercise becomes the foundation for many of the arts seen performed in chi gung.

The following steps are commonly carried out when practicing chi gung for the benefit of relaxation and managing stress. It takes five minutes and if performed accurately and regularly it becomes more and more effective. If you are interested I suggest that you try them out and pass judgement on the exercise afterwards. If not then please continue on to the next section.

1. Lie down somewhere or lean back in a chair placing your arms in a relaxed manner by your sides.

2. Close your eyes and clear your mind of all thoughts and smile. (Clearing your mind of all thoughts requires constant practice).

3. Start taking slow deep breaths (only through your nose) that fill your lungs right down into the abdomen. Picture this happening in your mind. Visualise the air swirl around deep down, then imagine it being exhaled. Exhale completely as though you are fully emptying your lungs.

4. Once you have managed that with total concentration, say to yourself (self-suggestion) that you are going to enjoy a deep relaxation for the next few moments and that you will be fresh and calm afterwards.

5. When you feel that five minutes have gone by, place the palms of your hands over your eyes and gently massage your face. Then acknowledge to yourself that you do feel fresher and calmer. (Self-suggestion again as a route to a preferred reality.)

The similarities between this highly beneficial exercise and that of self-suggestion discussed in chapter 10 are clearly obvious. This connection is mentioned for the purposes of the book and in no way is meant to undervalue the exercise. If we want to feel better, why not try to influence ourselves through the power of suggestion, especially if it works.

Variations on this exercise with different thoughts and visualisations can bring about quite dramatic effects on correcting ill health. The Shanghai second tuberculosis hospital employs chi gung therapy as one of its main methods of curing patients. In experiments done in 1965 on tuberculosis patients that practiced chi gung four times a day for a period of three months, it was found that their diaphragm movement increased from 1.8 mm to 5.88 mm. Their breathing rates dropped from 19.5 times a minute to 15 times and their lung capacity increased from an average of 428.5cc to 561.8cc. What was even more noticeable was that during practice these figures were substantially better. In all cases the patients were cured.

Just as in the hospitals, China has recognised that the benefits of chi gung can help in its schools. Chinese research showed that practice improved the mental faculties like focusing and concentration. In research at Bai Diu En medical university they showed that this occurred for pensioners as well. Further studies at China's science college biophysics research centre showed that practice also delayed senility.

Meditative practices within chi gung have been clearly shown to be highly effective in many areas of life. The most important aspect of the meditation is in keeping the mind empty or focused only on one thought. This action has been measured by western science and also at the Neuroscience department of the Shanghai First medical college in 1962. When a subject has their brain wave activity measured whilst practicing chi gung, two states of mind are identified. When emptying the mind, there is a clear abundance of alpha waves (8 –10 samples per second) over the other waves. When the subject is thinking or visualising, then theta waves (4 – 8 samples per second) are identified as being the most predominant.

Many of the greatest works of mankind have come about as a result of meditation. Inspiration and creativity are highly sought after commodities in today's world, yet they are accessible to all of us through a greater understanding of meditation. Leonardo da Vinci was not only a painter but a scientist and inventor. His flow of ideas used to come to him whilst staring into the embers of a fire. Ideas would just suddenly appear in his mind. Mozart would find inspiration on journeys into the countryside. Sitting in a coach, he would gaze, without thought, out of the window and ideas would come to him.

In each case, the two states of mind mentioned above were being used. Firstly you must attain an alpha state of mind, where you have no conscious thoughts at all. It helps to focus on a spot and just become generally aware of things surrounding that spot rather than the spot itself. Try holding a finger up in front of your eyes. Focus on it and move your hand slowly around in a series of circles. Now let it come to rest in front of your eyes again and keep on being aware of the rest of the room (or where ever you are). This should begin bring you to higher levels of alpha waves. It is the same state of 'mushin' mentioned above in 12.1. If you find yourself thinking about something, dismiss it and try again (It helps if the area you are in is quiet). After a while you will become better at keeping this frame of mind. Combine this exercise with that of the aforementioned breathing exercise and you will manage to focus on the spot with greater ease. Once you have mastered that, gently allow yourself to think about a particular project that you are working on, or problem you wish to solve. Fix your mind only on one aspect and become aware of any flashes of thought or visions that come into your mind. Take note of them, but continue to fix your mind on your one chosen thought. This is allowing the mind to access things on a more subconscious level. This is possibly a place where there is a collective, holistic or universal nature of knowledge. It is also allowing a greater level of theta waves to be generated by the mind.

Afterwards you should note the flashes that came to you and then see if they are relevant or useful. Sometimes they may not be, but others might well prove quite fruitful. If nothing seems to come out of the exercise, then it is suggested that the question you present to your mind be changed. Ones of a more specific nature may be more effective.

Leading on from creativity and inspiration, other even more extraordinary feats have been witnessed (If not yet measured under laboratory conditions). Masters of chi gung have been able to channel chi, similar to the way aikido masters do, in ways that allow them to be telepathic with other people. It is said that they can travel in their mind to distant places and witness events that occur there (Like remote viewing mentioned in chapter 8.24) and relate them back, before the news has reached where they were under normal circumstances. Both of these feats are said to be done using chi.

12.4 Tai Chi

Tai chi has become very popular in the western world as a method for retaining ones health. It is a particularly effective method for relieving stress. Its full name is Tai chi chuan and its literal translation is 'supreme ultimate fist' but the real spirit of the meaning is 'moving harmony'!

Tai chi works on the mind and the body and can often be dismissed by bystanders as being an ineffectual exercise when they see people practice. The reason is because all they see is the physical side, which appears slow and unexhausting, and they miss the importance of the mental side. The slow movements do not appear on the surface to be as good an exercise as a brisk walk or a run, however if done correctly, they have been shown to be beneficial by giving health to huge numbers of people.

The movements are simple to learn, but hard to master. Complete relaxation and the absence of tension is crucial. Once the physical movements are learnt, the mental pictures and the breathing must be added. As with other martial arts, there are names to assist in the exercises like 'Two full moons' and 'Eagle spreads its wings'. These individual exercises are put into a sequence called a 'form'. This is a series of gentle flowing movements that exercises the mind and body extremely efficiently. Again in Tai chi we can see the importance of the use of the inner senses, the attainment of alpha and theta brain waves and the correct breathing techniques.

Tai chi has been seen to cure disorders of the heart, circulation problems, addictions, arthritic conditions, muscle injuries, asthma and nervous disturbances. In each case, the problem is believed to be due to a blockage in chi flow due to the damaging effects of tension within the body. Tai chi seems to unblock the problem and goes on to help cure the patient.

12.5 Energy Relationships.

If you have ever experienced a meeting between you and another person where that other person has been reprimanding you for some error you had made, then it is likely that you are also experiencing a draining effect on your levels of energy. You might well walk away feeling downcast and low, in a manner that will be in complete contrast to how you might have previously felt after a meeting when you have been praised. On both occasions you will have had an energy relationship with that other person.

Either one of you will have been empowered or deflated as energy has been given or taken. Every time you interact with another person some form of energy relationship takes place. At any one time a person could be said to have an energy level from 1 to 10, (The scale is used for comparative purposes rather than any actual measurement of energy) and to move up and down the scale is as simple as changing your mind. Just as the mind controls ki flow, it also controls energy levels. These can taken to be one and the same thing. In James Redfield's book 'The Celestine Prophecy', he writes his personal messages to the reader as 'insights' within the context of a novel. He explains energy relationships as something that exists as soon as we are born and that we seem to be forever struggling to get energy from other people. This selfishness is habitual and is ingrained from early on in childhood due to the energy relationships that we have with our parents and other adults.

Parents can either be 'questioning' or 'aloof' in their communication with children. A parent might constantly ask a child questions in a way that requires the child to have to answer in a long-winded way. In other words unable to just answer with a simple 'yes' or 'no'. This drains the child and results in them resorting to becoming aloof in order to conserve their energy levels. This aloofness only serves to perpetuate the questioning from the parents at their own expense of energy. They require that the child answers in order to stop being drained of energy themselves because of their continual questioning process. Only when a child does fully answer, does the parent begin to feel energy seeping back in, unfortunately this is at the expense of the child's energy. This can happen the other way round as well with a child that is constantly asking an adult questions. When this occurs adults can soon tire of giving answers and then resort to an aloofness of their own.

This can happen on a day-to-day basis and very often it is carried out in a repeated fashion time and time again. This habit forming process can be continued onwards right up into adulthood. In extreme cases, when aloofness and questioning is insufficient to gain the energy wanted, parents and children resort to more violent dramas. The two ends of the spectrum are 'intimidatory' and 'cowering'. This leads to harmful patterns being imprinted upon a person's character. One might be a person who develops a threatening behaviour in unwarranted situations and another might be a feeling of fearfulness for no real reason. In each case it is due to the selfish nature of individuals requiring energy from those that are around them. It has to be said that most people are unaware of these relationships and if they were, and could see the damage it was doing to their children, they would definitely stop.

The answer to these troubles comes firstly in recognising the dramas that are being enacted and secondly by avoiding them. One of the ways that this can be done is to adopt the reverse behaviour and start sending energy to others. This empowerment can be done as easily as changing an attitude of mind. Unfortunately this is not always that easy. In our training at M.10, we teach the understanding and recognition of energy relationships in order to get our clients into a better frame of mind. By learning how to send energy to your potential customers, they will feel more empowered to act, to decide and to want to buy from you. The trick is to think solely about your customer's needs and wants and not to focus on yours. It has become a highly effective sales tool and results in people wanting to see you again and again, which can only mean more and more repeat business. It is a healthy win/win situation that is thoroughly recommended.

I have mentioned energy relationships as they are very real and can be felt by everyone. Chi is the energy that we have all witnessed and felt. If you have done some of the tests mentioned earlier, you will have realised its power even more recently. The use of chi has achieved fantastic results in the fields of health, mind and body but has yet to be successfully identified by western science as anything that is materially tangible. (A good question to ask oneself is why it has still yet to be measured when you consider all the advances that have been made in science recently.) It is because of this, and our search for a link, that we should now look at what some of the experts, who work with chi, have to say about their subject.

12.6 Ki Sayings

Much discussion has gone on between chi gung masters, Taoist priests, Buddhist monks, scientists, physicians and philosophers on the subject of chi. Their thoughts gave rise to four fundamental concepts and they are as follows: – 1. Chi is Energy; 2. Chi has material reality; 3. Chi is the basic 'element' of which everything in the universe is constituted; 4. Chi fills the whole universe and hence is a universal medium.

Koichi Tohei, the founder of the Ki No Kenkyukai school of aikido and one time student of the master Morehei Ueshiba, says of the essence of ki, "We begin with the number one in counting all things. It is impossible that this 'one' can ever be reduced to zero because, just as something cannot be made from nothing, 'one' cannot be made from zero. Ki is like the number one. Ki is formed from infinitely small particles, smaller than an atom. The universal ki condensed becomes to one point in the lower abdomen, which in turn infinitely condensed never becomes zero, but becomes one with the universe. Thus we understand the essence of ki."

He went on to say, "The universe is a limitless circle with a limitless radius. This condensed becomes the one point in the lower abdomen which is the centre of the universe."

How a person comes to have these insights into something as seemingly tenuous as ki appears to be, is extraordinary in itself. However the feats themselves are also extraordinary, so we can only guess or marvel at the intuition that must come to all these wise and practiced individuals.

A Taoist sage once said (before political correctness), "A human being is not isolated. Chi flows through him and circulates through all creation. He experiences all aspects of life as interconnected and interrelated with the vast universe." This is similar to Jung's 'Acausal Connecting Principle' or principle of synchronicity. Living with ki and following the flow could also be deemed to be similar to following our 'vocational' path seen in the time cones. Our coincidences, being signposts that we are on the correct way, are due to this interconnectedness.

To find out more about what these ancient adepts thought about ki we only have to look at a few more commonly held beliefs and sayings.

Zhang Dai, a scientist and chi gung philosopher who lived at the time of the Song dynasty in China more than a thousand years ago said, "The cosmos is like a body of chi. Chi has the properties of yin and yang. When chi is spread out, it permeates all things; when it coalesces it becomes nebulous. When it settles into form it becomes matter. When it disintegrates it returns to its original state." The fact that this was said so long ago might well amaze modern day physicists.

The following are more sayings that help to describe chi and how it fits in with the rest of the universe.

"Chi has gained two meanings, heaven's chi and man's chi."

"The central unity represents the cosmic life force, the ultimate essence of the universe, enveloping it and moving it from within."

"The law of harmony in the universe is held together by the tension between positive and negative forces, yin and yang. Without their constant interplay the universe would collapse."

"Yin and yang are the cement of the manifest world. From the force of the moon in space being balanced by the force of mother earth, through all humans and human organisations, to the maintenance of the structure of the smallest particle by balance and harmony, in all these is seen the play of yin and yang."

It is clear that there is a collective opinion that ki takes on two forms. Firstly, that which is found within humans and secondly, that which is found in matter like the Earth and the moon. It is the same ki and, just as there is an interplay of energy between humans, there is the same between celestial objects.

Here are some more thoughts on the subject of yin and yang chi.

"Yin and yang are the two primordial forces that govern the universe and symbolise harmony."

"Yin and yang merge together into one."

"Chi ascends and descends and moves in all ways, upward is the yang, downward is the yin."

"Man's chi is strongly influenced by the chi of both heaven and earth."

"Chi spirals around inside the earth sometimes down toward its depths, sometimes up to its crust."

It is clear that these ancient beliefs, held true by the wise sages of the past, indicate that chi must both come from the earth, the moon, the sun and other objects in space as well as coming from ourselves. All this chi interacts with each other, but is in fact the same thing only having a different source.

Even western scientists have shared similar views that humans exist in some form of a relationship with the rest of the universe and that some binding force holds us all together. The following sentences were taken from thoughts that Albert Einstein had on the subject.

"A human being is part of the whole called by us the universe, a part limited in space and time. He experiences himself, his thoughts and feelings as something separated from the rest, a kind of optical illusion of his consciousness."

We are left only to consider what material thing chi must relate to in our modern concept of western science. However before pressing on down that road, there is more to find out about the concept of earth's chi.

12.7 Feng Shui

Feng shui literally means 'wind' and 'water' but refers to an art that helps us to locate ourselves in the universe in the most favourable way with regards to chi and our relationship with chi. The forces at work are believed to be responsible for determining health, prosperity and good fortune. Today people spend large amounts of money to have a building surveyed by a feng shui master in order to find out if it will bring them good or bad luck if they live there. Even in the west, planners have consultations before erecting a building. Designers will often have to go back to their drawing boards to re-site a door entrance or reposition a window in order to obtain a more favourable aspect for chi flow. A feng shui priest even first checked out the world trade centre building in New York.

Sometimes when we are looking for a house to live in, we will get a feeling about the place. It won't be something tangible that we can explain, but it's often that gut feeling that either makes you purchase the property or not. The feng shui expert will tell you that it is sensitivity to chi that you have felt and that it was the chi that gave you the good or bad feeling.

Feng shui masters have other roles to play, apart from just recommending whether or not a house may be good to live in, and that is their ability to tap into chi in ways that enhance the less favourable situations that they come across. There are methods they can use that seem to allow the flow of chi to run freely again, therefore bringing the environment into harmony.

On mountains and volcanos, chi (energy) is said to be extremely strong. The Chinese say that a country's feng shui depends upon the position of its rivers and mountains. The mountain peaks take on a special reverence and many temples and shrines can be found on top of them throughout the whole of China. This is due in part to the strength of chi that appears to be found there and the benefits that it can bestow the individual who meditates there. How many times have you climbed a mountain and felt really exhilarated at the top? It's not just felt due to the sense of achievement because you can get a similar feeling if you arrive there via a cable car or chair lift.

In exploring the reason behind this, we must remind ourselves of what is known about the geology of the inside of the earth. Deep down at the centre there is a highly dense core, thought to consist of iron and magnesium. Outside of that there is the inner mantle, then the outer mantle. The surface consists of either thick continental crust or thinner oceanic crust. The whole crust is made up of great slabs of rock called plates. These massive plates move against each other, sometimes descending, sometimes riding up on top of each other and sometimes spreading away from each other. They are able to do this because underneath, in the upper mantle, there is a molten layer of rock that acts like a lubricant. This molten layer, in the upper mantle, has large convection currents that move material up, along and then down depending on temperatures. These currents in turn move the plates above them.

This whole scenario is like a large pan of milk that has been left to cool on the stove. On inspection you will find that there is a skin that has formed on the surface (similar to the plates). If you heat up the milk again, the lower, warmer milk rises to the surface where the skin is; the cooler milk at the top then descends, taking with it the skin.

This whole model is an ever-changing one that has density fluctuations all over the place as pressures increase and decrease within the circulating molten rock. It is with this picture in mind that you must now envisage how the concept of earth's chi fits in. In the sayings above, it states that earth's chi spirals around inside it before reaching the surface (possibly giving rise to the misplaced feeling that the earth must be alive like us in some way). Is it possible that these changes of density might affect the passage of chi? It would only have to be affected in a very small way to give the overall impression that chi has moved substantially due to the numbers of chi particles involved. If density does appear to have some effect then it might also explain why chi seems to be stronger at the top of mountains. In relation to the air surrounding the mountain top, the density difference between the rock and its surroundings would be large and the chi coming from the centre of the earth would travel up within the denser area. This could even allow the chi to appear to intensify as it seems to be channelled up within the rock to the mountain top.

To begin to pursue this concept a little further, we only need look at the earth energies that have been found in the South West of Great Britain.

12.8 A revealing new look at Earth energy lines

The art of 'dowsing' has been used all over the world as a means to finding various things. The commonest and best known is water divining. I have known many scientists who have successfully dowsed for water without understanding how it works and, as a geologist, I too was asked several times to locate water for farmers in the Western Transvaal in South Africa. My only advantage over others was perhaps in knowing the geology of the area and the likelihood of the capacity of the rocks under the ground to hold water. However in many cases you have to be exact in the knowledge of where to drill to intersect water (due to it running in channels as it often does in rocks like limestone). In these cases the best method is to get out your dowsing rods. Anyone who has tried it out and seen that it works (having drilled and hit water) will attest to its accuracy.

The reason it works is said to be due to the sensitivity to water that a dowser appears to have. As our bodies are largely made up of water, it is not perhaps surprising that we are somehow sensitive to it. I am not about to explain how it works and I am only mentioning it because the method of dowsing has also been used to find lines of earth energy. As we ourselves seem to have this energy within us, in our chi, then it might be supposed that we could also be sensitive to the chi around us.

Earth energy lines were once called 'ley lines'. This old term was attributed to Alfred Watkins, a pioneering photographer in the 1920's. He suggested that certain ancient sites fell in an alignment across the U.K. countryside. He called these alignments 'leys'. After much work, all he would conclude was the possibility that these lines were ancient tracks possibly laid down in the neolithic era. Today, the Saxon term for meadows – 'leys', is still used by some to describe lines of earth energy.

There is certainly a big question mark as to whether earth energies do run in lines across the countryside. In some cases, like mountain ridges, it may well seem to be possible, but in others it may also be wishful thinking added with a touch of the power of belief. However, even though there seems to be a question as to whether these energies run in lines, there is little doubt that they occur as they have been successfully dowsed again and again in the same places by separate people at different times and each without the knowledge of the others.

Hamish Miller and Paul Broadhurst investigated and wrote about earth energies across England in their book 'The Sun and the Serpent'. They set out to dowse the reputed energy line called the St Michael alignment. This alignment runs up through the south west of Great Britain and across into East Anglia. It's direction, by coincidence, leads to the position on the horizon where the sun rises on Mayday (This is the same day as the Celtic festival of Beltane).

The following famous sites lie on this line:– St. Michaels Mount (A small island of rock near Penzance), The Cheeswring (A collection of stones on Bodmin Moor), Brentor (Another high peak with a church on top near to Dartmoor), Glastonbury Tor (A well known hill amidst a flat plain) and Avebury (A circle of stones), Burrow Mump (A small hill in isolation similar to Glastonbury Tor with a church ruins on its summit)

When they set out to dowse the line, they sensed some interesting phenomena. Although the overall line appeared to be straight on a national scale, it didn't on a local one. The energy was also sometimes sensed as quite a broad band width and sometimes quite narrow. In some places it disappeared altogether. Hamish Miller also mentions in his later book, 'It's Not Too Late' that the lines appear to reverse in their direction of flow from morning to evening. The subtle nature of these energies seems to be affected by the earth's position in relation to the sun. This is given further strength by his observation of a change in the energies from the norm during a partial eclipse.

The fact that these energies appear to alter with celestial events is of extreme importance. Most notable was the fact that the position of the moon seemed to change the strength of the energies. They also noted that as they continued, the strength of the energies being dowsed increased. Although this could well be down to their increased sensitivity having done so much dowsing! It altogether sounds as though this energy is found everywhere on the surface of the earth but that in some areas there are greater concentrations of it which allows for sensitive people to acknowledge its presence. This sensitivity seems to be assisted by ones inner senses, not least by ones inner feelings like belief and expectation.

The very real line that they had dowsed ran through, or within 500 metres of 63 churches, (the clear majority of which were called St. Michael hence the St.Michael line name). They also discovered another line running almost parallel to the length of the St.Michael Line. These two lines meandered and crossed one another several times across the land with the intersections being found at some notable places like Avebury and Glastonbury. This second line they called the St. Mary line (after over 20 St. Mary churches that were found along it). The St. Michael line seemed to have a solar theme at many of its sites, whilst the St. Mary line was linked to a lunar theme.

These themes were noted from the rituals and ceremonies that were evident in the various places along the way. This they deduced from what was found on sculptures in the buildings and from local tales.

What is of interest to us in our quest is the nature of the relief around the line. Many of these places are situated on areas of relative high ground. This is ground that stands out in height within its local environment. Feng shui has already mentioned that chi is stronger at these points, so it is worth looking more closely at this in relation to the position of the line.

The following series of maps, numbered from 1 to 6, show the areas of high ground relative to their vicinity based on contour levels. The areas shown in the maps stretch from the west side of Dartmoor to east of Taunton and follow the positions of the St. Michael and the St. Mary Energy lines. The St. Michael line is marked with the dashes; the St. Mary the dot dash line.

What is interesting to note is that the lines are not straight and that in most cases they lead from one area of relative high ground to another. There is certainly a positive correlation between the areas of high ground and the energy lines. On reading about how the dowsing took place, many of the definite readings took place on the very same high ground. The fact that there were so many churches and castles on these areas is also of interest.

Castles naturally stood to benefit from a defensive point of view from being on a hill. Churches however, also places of refuge in the middle ages, were more often than not built on auspicious spots. These 'holy' areas might well have seemed closer to heaven, not just in their height but possibly because of the feelings of the place that could be sensed due to the strength or purity of the energies being emitted there. These places would have been known about long before the churches were built and were obvious spots to erect a church as a way of one religion dominating its rivals or at least seeming to get along with them. However, with all the stained glass images inside the churches of saints slaying dragons (a common synonym for lines of energy in both the East and the West), I would guess it was more of the former than the latter.

As all individuals each sense things slightly differently from each other, I would suggest that you take a chance to visit a church that is on top of a hill. The feelings that you can sense in them are distinctly stronger and more harmonious than those that can be found in the modern day churches found in towns in flattish areas. An example of this can be found inside the church at Brentor in Devon. As you walk in you are instantly struck by its intense peacefulness.

Many people have questioned whether or not you can collectively take all these places of energy and call them a line. They have also asked why more lines have not been found. One reason for this, I believe, is due to the geological nature of the area underneath the St.Michael line. The geological map shows several high moors in the South West of Britain, all of which are made of a highly dense igneous rock called granite. Across the rest of England there is a band of chalk, the same

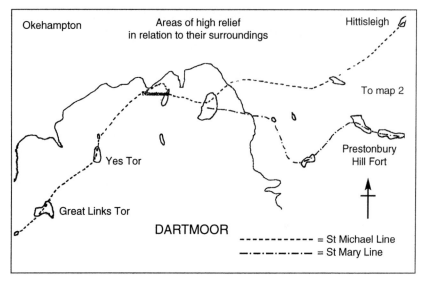

Map 1 – Dartmoor area

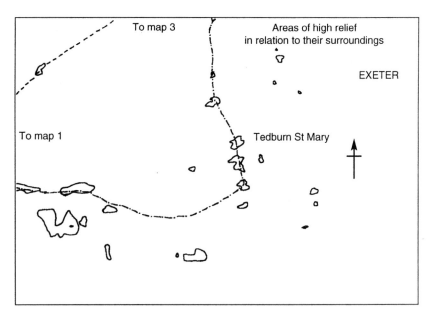

Map 2 – Tedburn St Mary area

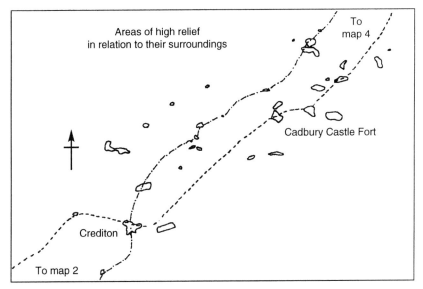

Map 3 – Crediton area

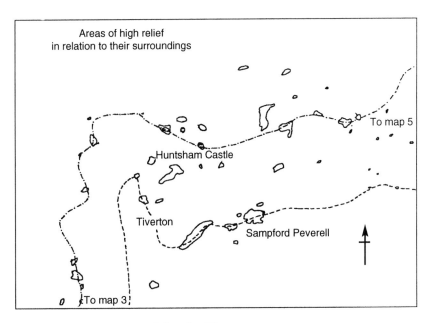

Map 4 – Tiverton area

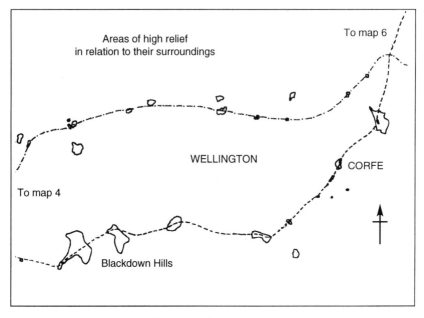

Map 5 – Tiverton area

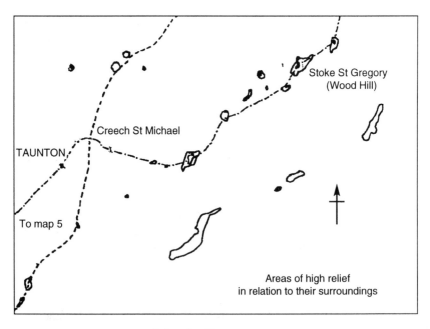

Map 6 – Taunton area

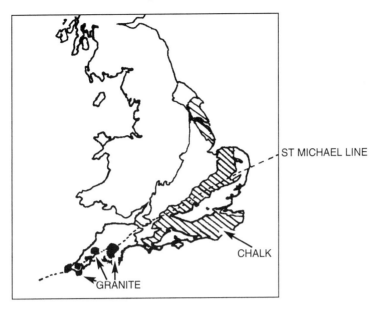

Geological Map of Southern England
Courtesy of British Geological Society

rock that is found at the white cliffs of Dover in the South-East of England. The chalk is nearly always associated with hills due to its hard nature and aversion to fast erosion. These topographical facts alone should explain the positioning of the two lines and a good correlation can be seen on the geological map below. However, what is less well known, is how the granite lies beneath the surface. All the outcrops, like Bodmin moor and Dartmoor, are just pinnacles that come from a massive granite batholith. This is a huge connecting, underground mass of igneous rock that stretches throughout the whole of the south west from the Isles of Scilly right up through Devon and Somerset. This hard, dense rock could possibly, in some way that we will look at later on in this book, help to produce extremely strong chi over the whole area. It could also make it far easier to dowse and identify in this region than perhaps elsewhere. No matter what the surface covering of sedimentary rocks, this stronger chi would appear to come up through them and be more easily sensed at the high points like the local hills.

If you add the geological fact about the high densities of the underlying rocks to the one about the areas of relative high ground and their connection with earth energies, then there is a good case to suggest that an anomaly of a linear nature could be seen to be dowsed all along the south west and up through England.

Dr J. Havelock Fidler, an agricultural research scientist, conducted his own survey of earth energies up in the Applecross Mountains in the North-West highlands of Scotland. Curious to see what he could dowse, he walked all over the area with dowsing rods and ended up with a series of lines that crossed the area. This was investigated more thoroughly and it was found that there was a close correlation between the lines and the geology of the area. It appeared that the earth energies coincided fairly well with the fault zones and even better with the igneous dykes that crossed the area. This appears to strengthen the case for a link up with geological data. Dykes are long, relatively thin, commonly vertical and generally straight igneous intrusions (molten rock forced up along cracks from deep down in the Earth's crust) and they are composed of highly dense material. Although the surrounding rocks in this area are of a high density as well, there is a density difference between them. This could well be a sufficient difference to allow a change in chi to be sensed and therefore give the impression that there was some lineation of earth energy. Other more recent books on ancient earth energies have also made many references to areas of high ground and hard volcanic rocks and their whole association with this phenomena.

It would appear that densities of the underlying rocks play a relevant part in determining the distribution or concentration of chi. The density of an area can be altered fairly easily by human intervention and this leads to interesting possibilities that our ancient ancestors may have known about. One interesting feature along the St.Michael line and St Mary line is the fact that earth mounds have been built on or near to it. Often they are found as coverings for burial chambers, but others, like the one at Silbury hill in Wiltshire (with, after extensive excavation, no evidence of any human burials under it at all), were quite possibly built to try and increase the strength of chi in those areas. The creation of a hill would alter the density of the earth in that region and significantly alter the chi in the area.

If this was the case, another question that immediately springs to mind is why would they want to do that. One answer could quite possibly be that they might well have realised that it would allow them to achieve the same things that they could already achieve at the normal sites with strong chi. To delve deeper into this, we must revert back to what appears to be possible for humans to do when chi has been accessed by them. It may be that even greater things are possible if a human can tap into the power of earth's chi as well as their own. We know that this is a possibility because the chi is the same and energy relationships exist with chi, not only between humans, but also with the yin yang relationship of chi between the earth and the sun and the moon (not to mention all the other celestial bodies).

Before we look at the implications behind this in a later chapter, we have to ask if there are any other places in the world that might show similar signs of man made mounds, or indeed anything else that achieves the same ends, that might have been put up for similar purposes. We should also look for other areas of relative high ground that would appear to have been used as some assistance to worship or meditate.

12.9 The secrets behind the Ancient Pyramids, the Lost Temples and the mysterious Astronomer Priests

There is plenty of evidence around the world that civilisations and individuals have used high ground from which to carry out their rituals. You only have to cast your mind over the many examples of religious temples and churches that can be found on the tops of high ground all around the world. In the Tibetan mountains, Buddhist priests use shrines high up in the mountains. In Edinburgh the central castle, erected on a volcanic plug of rock that dominates the whole city, has two chapels built on top of it. They were even sited exactly on the high points at the top of the rock. Around 2100 BC in Mesapotamia, part of modern day Iraq, there was a great city called Ur. In the centre of this city King Ur-Nammu built a huge Ziggurat. This was a building that was made up of solid platforms that stepped up higher and higher toward the centre. At the top there was a shrine to the god Nanna. This was considered to be the home of the moon god. It was here that they worshipped and conducted all their rituals and religeous ceremonies. Yet again we find a sacred place connected to our nearest celestial object, the moon, and on top of a man made structure. In this case it is a Ziggurat, but this one is not too dissimilar to the step pyramids found in other areas in the world. In Peru there are many examples of temples and even cities that have been built in a similar fashion. The lost city of Cahuachi, found next to the well-known Nazca lines, was inhabited

2000 years ago. This city, built by the priests and devoted to ritual and ceremony, was full of plazas and terraces all surrounding a 30 metre high pyramid. This step pyramid was erected by modifying a natural high point in the land and it dominated the whole region. The Nazca peoples considered it to be their most sacred place. Alongside this centrepiece there were more than 40 other smaller step pyramids.

There are many other examples of temples that have been built on top of man-made structures and natural high points. One of the better-known examples of temples on top of mountains in Peru is found at the city of Machu Pichu. This city is found on top of a high pinnacle of rock on the bend of a meandering river in the middle of the Andes mountains. The Incas were known to have built and used this place; however there is an even older structure situated within it. In the centre of the city there is a central pyramidal mound made partly from natural rock and partly built by humans. On top of the mound there is a vertical finger of natural rock called the 'Intihuatana' that has been carved purposely to look like it is pointing upwards. Two other older constructions found at Machu Pichu are a cave hewn out of the rock and a megalithic monument called the 'Temple of the three windows'. All of these have been attributed to people who were there before the Inca's and who are known to have followed an ancient astronomical religion. William Sullivan, an archaeoastronomer, in his book 'The Secret of the Incas' suggested that the people who built and used the place had 'some very unusual spiritual perception, with deep insight into the operations of the human mind.' He went on to say that the Incas didn't fully understand all of it and, in trying to follow it, they sunk into the depravity of human sacrifice.

Graham Hancock, in his various books, has suggested that these monuments at Machu Pichu are linked with others around the world. The places he included in these are the Pyramids at Giza in Egypt, the temples of Angkor Wat in Cambodia and the Pyramid of Kulkulkan at Chitchen Itza in Mexico. Along with a few others, he has tried to show that they all have a common denominator in that they appear to have been built in a way that matches the constellations of stars in the sky at around the same time of 10,500 years B.C. Whether this is the case or not, all the larger man-made constructions have one other thing in common and that is that they are all found in areas that are relatively flat. All these monuments were built at different times in the past, however it is possible that the priests at those various times knew very well about the advantages of high ground when it came to being able to tap into the earth's energies. They also knew that these energies could be channelled in the flatter areas by building mounds or pyramids. This early knowledge might easily have been passed on throughout the world over subsequent generations, which is why the general shapes had been kept in mind and reproduced. In many cases this was done repeatedly and on the same site above the ruins of the last. An interesting feature of these early pyramid type structures is that they all seem to have a small flat top instead of an apex. This fact is, however, contested by Egyptologists. They offer as an example the fact that they have found what used to be the apex, or pyramidion, of the great pyramid itself, lying half buried (and intact?) near to its base. Although this might appear as evidence that it was once complete in true pyramid shape, it cannot be ruled as definite proof as it could quite easily have been made up at some later date in the past by some other group of people anxious to complete what looked like an unfinished job. It is also not made of the same Jura Limestone as the rest of the surface blocks, but made from Granite. As this 'pyramidion' also lies next to the remains of a small and later satellite pyramid, it may also be possible that it belonged to that. These satellites functions are acknowledged by the experts to be unknown and they have only guessed at their purposes. It is not entirely impossible that they were built at a later date by people who were ignorant of a true, additional and alternative purpose behind the pyramids. The fact that the many other pyramid shaped constructions found around Egypt and the rest of the world also appear to have flat tops, seems to also 'point' to there being another specific purpose behind their design. It is generally accepted and certainly not disputed here that the original purpose could well have been a burial monument. (One other possibility may be that of a healing chamber.)

One then has to ask why people would go to the trouble of building a pyramid and then purposely fail to complete it at its apex. If this was intentional, as it appears it might be in these cases, then it must have been for a good reason. The most likely one is that it could well have been a stage with which to stand or sit and conduct certain ceremonies. Being situated at the point of the pyramid, with the dense building blocks beneath them, may well have assisted them mentally in their tasks with some sort of artificially enhanced energy. Perhaps the ancient Pharoes and their high priests also knew of the enhanced energies and wished to be buried within their presence. They might have suspected that this might have, in some way, assisted their spirits to travel into their next world.

This is actually quite a common belief amongst ancient races. The Guanche culture in the Canary Islands are thought to hold similar ideas. The Guanche people lived over 3000 years ago and are thought to have at one time come from a race of ancient Berbers that lived in North Africa. The Guanche also built small step pyramids that can be still seen today. They were built as layers of terraces with dry stones, mainly lava stone, and had a flat top. They were also aligned accurately with the sunset at the summer solstice. It was on the tops of these that they were known to have performed their ceremonies and rituals. The connections with the early step pyramids of the Egyptians are more than a coincidence. They used to mummify their dead in almost the exact same way as the Egyptians. Many archeologists now think that these ancient Berber races were the connection between the two cultures and that their beginnings might have had the same origin. An interesting and relevant feature that has been found out about these Berbers was the way they consulted their dead. The dead were contacted for guidance and divination. The living would pray at the graves of their dead and then go to sleep in the same burial chambers called 'sacred dream chambers'. In the morning they would wake up and interpret their dreams in a way that would solve their problems. It was as though the souls of the dead were communicating with them. We know that the main purpose of the pyramids was for burial, but this concept also supports the secondary idea that they might also be used for a variety of forms of psychic communication. Amongst these would have included conversation with those people that had already passed into the next world.

The pyramid of the magician at Uxmal in Mexico (said to have been constructed in one night!) was another such ceremonial place. Orientated to the known planets of the time, scholars believe it to have been used as some sort of mystery school. Being on one of the sacred sites in the area, it was most likely used for enhancing mental powers in the ways mentioned above. At Chitchen Itza, the Kulkulkan pyramid is also found on an ancient sacred site. Built on a limestone plateau on top of a well, it is also documented to be on the Wacah Chan axis. This sacred East-West line is not said to be located in any one earthly place. It can be materialised by certain rituals either at natural high points or on a man made landscape. Mayan scholars also write that these areas were human connections to the Otherworld. This sounds distinctly similar to the stories behind Celtic mounds found the other side of the ocean in Europe. The scholars go on to say that they were said to have been built as a stairway to heaven. This might well be some reference to attaining enlightenment of some sort once at the top of them.

Large ancient mounds have also been found in North America dating back to around the Adena culture of 1000 B.C. The Adena, and later the Hopewell culture, constructed them and used them, amongst many other unknown reasons, for burial mounds. The best known of these is the Great serpent mound in Ohio. The leaders, like their shamans or their chiefs were the types of individuals that they buried there. The Adena used these sites for their religious ceremonies and as a political centre for establishing power over their people. The city of Cahokia, an old Indian settlement that can be found near to modern day city of St. Louis, Missouri, is also known as the city of the earth mounds (There are over 100 in the area). In the centre of them all and built in the 11th Century is the largest man made mound in North America, now called Monk's Mound. This was built in a systematic manner with the selected material of layers of sand and clay and stone. It is four sided and flat topped and had a temple on the top that was dedicated to bringing the sky and the earth together. It is even aligned in direction with the summer solstice. The chiefs that lived there might well have known of the benefits to their rituals because of the shape and nature of the mounds and that might well have been one of the reasons for building them.

Silbury Hill in Wiltshire was another mound that was built with a flat top around 2000 to 1500 years B.C. Its solidly constructed design was packed out centrally with clay and flints and then layered with chalk gravel and stacked turf. Subsequent layers of concentric chalk walls were compacted together to produce an impressive white landmark that has lasted well over the intermediate years.

Sometimes associated with these large mounds were large megaliths. These massive stones have perplexed scientists for ages as to how and why they were erected. Stonehenge is perhaps the best-known example, but there are many others around the world. Often these megaliths would have been chosen from highly dense rock, sometimes having been transported from many miles away. The significance behind this could be similar to the significance of the mounds and pyramids in that they also would provide a sufficient density difference from their surroundings to be felt by the minds of those that erected them. The stones would act possibly in a similar manner and would channel the earth energies in a way that these ancient astronomer priests could benefit personally and in a way that assisted them to carry out their own mental feats.

It has already been shown that there is a link with the sun, the moon and the stars in all of these constructions and from what we have learnt about chi coming both from within the earth, the sun, the moon and the stars, you could quite reasonably expect this to be a sound connection. Even Stonehenge, during its first phase of building, was constructed with the position of the moon uppermost in mind. It was only later, that it was modified to fit in with the positions of the sun. If these ancient priests were aware of the energies from the night sky then it would have been the moon, the closest dense object to us, that would have the most noticeable effect. If they were aware of the power of using the moon in their ceremonies then it is highly probable that they would want to build megalithic monuments to track its position in the night sky. Nearly all antiquarians will agree that henges and stone circles have a connection with the moon, the sun and the night sky in a way that appears to produce some sort of astronomical clock.

Apart from Avebury in Wiltshire, another good example of this connection between sacred hills and stone circles can be found in Aberdeenshire, Scotland. Near to the town of Insch in the Correen Hills you can find three sacred, pyramid-like hills called Dunnideer, Christ's Kirk (Scottish for church) and Flinders. In the surrounding countryside there are twelve stone circles and each of these has a central stone that points toward Dunnideer Hill. This ancient place was well-known to have been associated with high energies and was used frequently by a clairvoyant called the Seer of Dunnideer. Could it be that the stone circles were used to monitor the position of the moon so that these ancient priests knew when to make the most of the combined earth energies and moon's energies. On auspicious occasions they perhaps knew to ascend the hills and tap into these energies in order to perform their amazing mental feats, like foretelling the future.

The power of the moon is readily accepted as having a huge influence on our planet with its effect on the tidal motions. However another less documented, but still known, effect is the moon's influence on our minds.

A prison officer from Armley jail in Leeds, Claire Smith, did a study on behavioural patterns on all 1200 prisoners in the maximum security wing. She found that violent incidents more than doubled in the first and last week of each lunar month. The study, lasting more than three months, showed that although it wasn't exactly on the full moon each time, the violence was definitely related to the lunar cycle.

An American medical student called Arnold Leibner carried out another study. Already having seen the mental effects on people with the normal lunar cycle, he decided to see what results there would be when the moon was going to be closer to the Earth. Normally it is around 240,000 miles away, but on occasions it comes as close as 217,000 miles. It was before one of these occasions, in January 1974, that he approached the Miami police department to gain some statistics. This was not such a strange request to them as they had already witnessed the same lunar cycle increases in violence in their precincts.

Over the period of three weeks when the moon was closest, the murder rate had trebled and arson attacks had gone up by 100%. In several cases there was no motive at all, just mindless violence. When the moon had moved away, it all went back to normal. This would suggest that the position of a body, with as large an influence as the moon, has an affect on the way our minds operate and the way we have a control over our emotions. If a person was aware of this, and was aware of how to harness these influences, then it might be possible to effect an influence and a degree of control over the mind in order to achieve certain things.

If these ancient astronomer priests were able to achieve some of the things that have been suggested in the texts, then we ought to try to find out as much as possible about them as they may have been well aware of the powers that could assist their minds. References to them have been found in the Inca texts as well as the pyramid texts in Egypt. There, they were termed the followers of Horus, observers who followed the path of the sun. They were thought of as mystery teachers of heaven, and although they were skilled astronomers, their work was primarily for spiritual outcome. In Egypt, Peru and Mexico there is reference to these priests travelling out of their bodies using their minds. This was an experience that was facilitated during certain times when the sun or the moon was in an auspicious position, notably the solstices. It was on these occasions that they took their journeys through gateways to the 'Otherworld' or the 'Netherworld'. This could well be a reference to the other sites found around the world and ones that

Graham Hancock has suggested are all connected. It is interesting to note that the ancient Egyptians felt that the site at Giza was a sacred site and, as with many cultures, they only built their most sacred monuments on these sites. They called the Giza site 'Rostau' which roughly translated means 'gateway to the Otherworld'. This site has also been recently dowsed for energies by friends of mine and found to have extreme levels of chi energy deep within its chambers. What remains to be sensed is what energy levels can be detected at the summit.

All this now gives us several sites, both natural and man made, around the world that seem to have been used, albeit at different times in the past, for a similar purpose and all with the common feature that they seem to be associated with strong earth energies.

12.10 The end of the legend of Atlantis?

Evidence is slowly being discovered that these ancient priests may well have also had sufficient knowledge to enable them to travel the oceans of the world. Carvings in Mexico distinctly show Kulkulkan to have Caucasian features, complete with a beard. This hirsute nature is not seen amongst those native to that land. Some skeletons recently unearthed in the USA have also been proved to be Caucasian in origin and over 9000 years old. In both cases it could be correctly assumed that some ancient people might have crossed the Atlantic. In order to have done this, they must have had an advanced knowledge of celestial navigation as well as boats sturdy enough for the voyage. Not much later on the Vikings were known to have reached North America by boat in their thirst for adventure and trade. This fact was unacceptable twenty years ago when everyone still believed that it was Columbus that discovered America. We cannot definitely rule out the possibility that a race as widespread and adventurous as the Celts did not also accomplish this same feat.

If the ancient priests at the time had been able to harness the local energies in ways that assisted their minds, then it's feasible that they could have journeyed mentally along these routes beforehand (as in Remote Viewing) and would have known what to expect. It might also have given them a reason to go physically in the first place! It must also be remembered that the Mediterranean was a sea that, even in these times, was navigated along its entire length with ease. Many seafarers and traders would have undergone passages from the eastern end to the other and out around into the Atlantic and up to the shores of Britain. The distance involved in sailing just the length of the Mediterranean is longer than crossing parts of the Atlantic! It can therefore be safely assumed that it was not the length of the journey that would have been a problem for them. The question that now has to be asked is whether Plato, in his references to 'peoples from Atlantis', was actually just referring to people who lived the other side of the Atlantic. He may or may not have known or been aware of this point of origin, but it would appear to be a far better explanation of where these people came from rather than some lost city on a, now lost, island beneath the seas. Ironically enough those natives from the Americas probably thought the same. Their earliest visitors also came from over the Atlantic sea. The Olmecs (1000-1500 B.C) had huge stones heads carved from Basalt, an extremely hard rock. These all show facial features to be incredibly similar to the negroid features found in African peoples. Thor Heyerdahl showed with his Ra 2 voyage that it might well have been possible for the Egyptians to have crossed the Atlantic. Is it any wonder that there have been rumours that Atlantis was once on an Island in the middle of the Atlantic ocean. With peoples on both sides both talking of a strange race that came from over the sea, they were bound to create the myths.

The Immrama stories of the ancient Celts give many descriptions of the journeys made to the Otherworld. The greatest Celtic hero of them all, Cuchullain, is said to have gone on several journeys to this Otherworld and he features highly in many of the stories. In these, there are clues as to what this world looked like and how people got there. The stories tell of long voyages needed to reach the 'vast islands lying across the oceans to the west of Erin (Ireland)' and of the strange fruits and animals that are seen there. In the voyage of Maildun they tell of large currachs being built for the journey. To the intrepid explorers, arriving at the shores of the Americas from having crossed the Atlantic, everything would have appeared strange and different. They describe seeing shells of nuts the size of helmets that could quite possibly be coconuts. It must be remembered that the early American natives, when first seeing Kulkulkan (Cuchulainn?), told of how he had arrived from over the seas and their prophecies told that after he had left, he would return the same way. Even when the Spanish explorer Cortez arrived at the same shores, he was hailed as the returning figure of Kulkulkan.

The locals had even predicted correctly the date of his arrival!

Further communication between the two worlds could have taken place telepathically or by remote viewing with the ancient priests from both sides finding these mental tasks easier when on top of their mounds and pyramids. From the texts found in Egypt it was found that these were a people that advocated the search for knowledge through direct experience. They taught a form of sky-ground dualism, which is similar to teachings the other side of the Atlantic, and this seems very similar to the yin and yang of chi taught by the Eastern philosophers today. The earliest pyramids at Teotihuacan in Mexico, thought to be Mayan or even pre Mayan, were built with strong references to the Sun and the Moon. These are the two most influential celestial bodies that affect us on planet earth. Were these pyramids of the Sun and the Moon built so that humans could specifically tap into whatever powers that came from them in order to do extraordinary things? It is a question that needs looking into as far as possible.

12.11 'Coming to Know' about Ki

Before we begin to delve deeper into this, we should return to our original quest to find a link between Modern science and Ancient Earth Energies. We must see if the Eastern concept of chi and energy has any counterpart in the West. Fritjof Capra, in his book 'The Tao of Physics' has already made a good comparison between the quantum field theory and this 'energy'. The tiny, indeterminate particles found in the quantum world that exist in all matter and even in space, have been shown by him to have close connections to the way chi is said to behave. He went on to show that science could no longer expect to find stable building blocks of matter the more they searched for the foundations of everything. At this scale there was no longer going to be a definition of parts but that there would be a holistic, collective, interlinked process going on. Science would have to become less objective in its search for a description and realise that the mystic's method of arriving at a 'form of knowing' was going to be more applicable for the quantum world. His parallels have shown many people a new direction to look and to research and he indicated in his book several areas, including that of the mind, that would bring more understanding as time went on.

I believe that we can now take one step further and look into the quantum world and its phenomena to find a more exact connection. I believe we can also do this without being completely objective, without requiring new foundations and without thinking in parts, so it can be deduced that it agrees with all of Capra's new paradigm's. It can be regarded as something that shows an 'interconnectedness' and is at one with the universal. The ability to provide an exact description of what it is would invalidate it under Capra's new paradigm and that is partly why this book has been written in the manner it has. By asking you to undergo a process of searching for a connection, you have allowed a form of 'coming to know' to interact with your mind which in turn will lead to a greater understanding.

We know the mind is the connection between the two sides and we have begun to find out more about the way the mind operates. We have also seen the importance of the inner senses when it comes to achieving the outcome we desire. In our model of time cones and goal setting, we have seen how expectation and visualisation can help 'collapse' the world that we are working towards right into our own reality. These same inner senses also seem to be responsible for directing chi. Accessing that chi also seems to assist in attaining these same goals. We have seen how powerful the mind can be and we have also seen how it may be possible to enhance our own powers through 'tapping' the ki of the universal, or the ki that is around us from the earth, the moon, the sun and the stars. We have even looked at the good possibility that people in our distant past knew of these things and of the power that it can offer the individual. They knew it could achieve great things and possibly left messages for their descendants so that they too could find the key and learn or remember their ways. In the next chapter, we will come to know the connections in more detail before going on to discuss the implications behind all of this and in particular what mankind could achieve from now on.

CHAPTER THIRTEEN

RETURN ON THE EVE OF SAMHAIN

I watched in silence as Domnhuill Dubh and his men disappeared from view into the woods. I could hear them laughing in the distance and I wondered how they could do that after so many of their friends had died just moments ago.

When I was sure they had gone for good, I turned to look down at Lugh. The wolves had vanished and with all danger gone, I knelt beside the old man and put down my sword. I reached out to touch his frail figure and nudged it gently. There was nothing but lifelessness. I nudged it again and still nothing.

"Lugh, come on, they've gone now. It worked, your plan's worked." I whisper as loudly as I dare, shaking him more vigorously. "Come on, get up now." I continue, my voice now showing alarm.

I turn him over onto his side and see that the knife is still embedded deep into his chest. There is blood everywhere. I reach over to touch it whilst looking at his ashen face. "Lugh!" I call out loudly.

His sealed lips begin to curl up at the ends and soon there is a broad smile. I grabbed at the knife in his chest and my hand crashes through the illusion. "You son of a wolf, if you ever trick me like that again I'll tie you up in your cave and leave you for the bats and the bears!" I curse with a grin all over my face.

"You'd have to catch me first laddie." He chuckles leaning up on one elbow. "Are you alright?"

"Aye." I reply, "Though I don't need any more shocks like that. What do we do now?" I ask.

He didn't answer straight away and instead looked pensive as he got to his feet. He picked up his branch and the strange crystal and together we helped each other clamber down off of the Dolmen. I watched him patiently and silently whilst he stood and thought.

"Now we have the advantage," he starts, "we can take some time to prepare our plan. Callum Beg may have the whole of the Crown helm, but he still needs someone to perform the Tarb Feis and that won't be till the end of the year at Samhain. He'll probably try and force Angus into doing it now he thinks I am dead and you're out of the way. My suggestion is that we carry on with your training for a while. We need to find out what your father is planning as much will depend on his actions. If they come over to the mainland, as I suspect they will, we'll meet up with them. Let's go over our priorities."

"We have to rescue the girls first and foremost." I state, looking over in the direction Domnhuill and his men had taken.

"I completely agree with that." He replies, stretching his arms wide, then shaking them to get rid of the last remnants of stiffness that had begun to creep in from lying on the cold slab of stone.

"Then we must somehow discredit Callum Beg and stop him achieving what he wants, which seems to be, to become King of the Northern Highlands." I venture tentatively, wondering if he had any others ideas on the subject. I look sideways at him in anticipation.

"We certainly need to foil his plans, the question is to find out the best way to do that. If I remember you correctly, you said he has a lot of support at the Aes Dana." He pauses and brushes the dust and dirt off of his cloak with his hands. "Well that's a problem, we can't fight them all."

"Aye, I understand that but what do you suggest?" I ask, a note of slight desperation entering my voice.

"I suggest we start back." He strides forward and begins to walk off down the hill. "I'd like to get clean and there's a fine fall around here that's good for just that. Besides," he calls back to me, turning his head over his shoulder, "now we know what we have to find out," he now half-turns and walks backwards while talking, "if we stop thinking about it and do something else, the answer will come in good time." He concludes and spins around to go forwards again.

With nothing else to do or say, I followed on behind him. We left the mauled and bloody bodies behind us, as their friends had also done. Nature would take its course and it was pointless to intervene after death had been and gone.

We headed East back the way we had come almost opposite to Domnhuill Dubh who had gone off to the South West. They would have to cross the Skiehallion pass, then follow down Urquhart glen into the Glencannick forest. Their route would take them past the three women I had stumbled upon some time earlier and then on to the Rougie falls. If they hurried, they'd be back within three days. Letting them get the last piece of the Crown helm and then allowing them to think that they had won was galling. Even thinking about it now, with everything having gone to plan, it was both frustrating and annoying. Lugh sensed my feelings.

"There's no use in giving in to those thoughts Fionn. They'll only hinder your progress. Forget about what's happened both now and before with your friends. Try and think only of the big picture and expect the best that can happen." He pauses, holding his right hand out in front of him. "Trust what you are doing deep down in yourself. Only then can you begin to succeed. If you've planned properly, which I think we have, and you've learnt everything you need to learn, which we are doing, then relax."

He gestures by moving his hand to the side and opening up his palm. "Emotions like anger and worry will only overturn your inner cauldrons." He finishes, imitating this happening by turning over his hand and making it into a fist.

"You're right." I say, marvelling at his ability to not only sense exactly what I was feeling, but in saying and doing the right things as well. "Where's this waterfall then?" I change the subject and force out a lighter tone to my voice.

"Not far. It's downhill all the way." He laughs again in an infectious manner and soon we are both chuckling away whilst striding down through the woods.

In only a short time we got to the edge of a small tree lined loch. Two burns fed it down at the far end. The nearest one burst its waters over a small cliff. With a drop the height of three grown men, it fell with a harsh hissing sound straight down onto a flat ledge just above the level of the loch. The spray bounced up into a fine mist before falling and draining away over the lip of the ledge.

Although the sun had come up earlier and it looked as though it was going to be a warm day, just the thought of the water made me feel cold. Its icy past was not that distant and, in the shadows of the cliff, it sounded about as appealing as badly played pipes to a man with ear ache. Nevertheless, Lugh looked at me with a smiling and mischievous face that seemed to throw away his many years and called out a challenge.

"I may be older than you, but I'll be under there before you and out after you." Without waiting for a reply, he turns and sets off running the last thirty to forty paces, taking his robes off as he goes.

Not to be outdone and not wanting to seem a misery in the face of such exuberance, I called out that I was right behind him and set off in pursuit of him, stripping as I went as well. He got there just in front of me and went straight in. The water splashed off him and deflected onto me. Just those few drops told me all that I already knew. It was extremely cold. I looked over at Lugh who smiled back at me, the force of the water now cascading all over his head and shoulders.

"Remember what I told you." I manage to hear him say over the crashing sound of the water that is reverberating all around us. He points to his middle. I guess what he is talking about.

Thinking with the same state of mind we had practiced so often, I stepped under and stood next to him. The shocking cold was immediately replaced by the power of the falling water and I struggled to keep my balance. With feet now firmly planted on the slippery surface, I centered myself as I had been shown. Soon a sort of warm numbness set in, fuelled by an inner heat. The more I felt and imagined the warmth inside me, the more it spread throughout my body.

A touch on my shoulder awakened me from my trance. Lugh was pointing to the side. Forgetting our bet, we stepped out of the water and went to look for our clothes. In no time we were dressed and dry and feeling completely invigorated. This was soon followed by intense hunger pangs so we lit a fire and boiled up some water. Before long we were eating and drinking a warm meal.

"Have you thought some more about what we should do?" I ask when we had both finished.

"Aye, I have." He replies succinctly, "We need to go back to the cave for a while and continue your training. I think we must make a visit to your father as well to find out his plans and then we must go and see Angus."

"Then what?" I add, hoping there's something more tangible.

"Then, all will become clearer after we've done that." He says in a way that denotes a finality to the subject. He gets up and starts to put out the small fire as if to end further any conversation on the matter.

Back at the cave, I continued my training with Lugh. It all seemed the same day after day as much of what had to be learned was in accessing the same calm frame of mind in all circumstances. This had to be done quickly, wherever I was, and however I was feeling. Control over my emotions at these times was what I found most difficult and needed most of my attention. We spent much of the time in the ancient forest studying the animals and building up pictures of them in our mind so that they could be recalled at will with extreme accuracy. I learnt to send and receive thoughts more precisely by sending visions and feelings at the same time. Eventually we covered the power of suggestion and its visual projection into the minds of others. In all cases it was a question of learning how. After that it was up to me. If I wanted to improve, I would have to keep at it, because even if, after reaching a certain level of proficiency I then relaxed, my newly learnt skills would fade. It was constant effort and one that quickly became a way of life. Once I'd developed a routine, I found it more and more enjoyable.

I learnt to understand how the energies changed in different areas and at different times and how that could be used to my advantage. He told me of the dangers of travelling distances with the mind. There were very great possibilities of never returning to your body if you were interrupted or mentally locked together by connecting with someone who was trying to control your mind. He also taught me how to direct my own energies into deflecting an attacker through a complete extrasensory shout.

Whilst we worked during the day with our minds, at night we studied the stars. Time soon crept around and before we knew it, it was the Eve of Beltain. Beltain marked the beginning of summer and it was now the Time of Brightness. It was an occasion for celebration, the cattle would be driven out into their summer grazing pastures between two huge fires and people would go visiting friends in other clans. Folk exchanged gifts and news and gathered around huge feasts and listened to long stories. It was also a night when the Sidhe opened their doors. In the light of what I had recently learnt, I wondered about the implications of my last thought. It brought home to me the marked transition I had made from a Seannachie to an ovate. Now, due only to the proficiency of my guide, I was almost ready to become an Ollamph, although no ordinary one, as I had been taught powers that others sometimes never got to realise throughout a whole lifetime.

I also remembered my last Beltain back at Donal Broch. It had been our turn to receive guests and we'd had visitors from all over the Island. Dugald had come down a given us all a fantastic story.

Lugh interrupted my recollections. "It'll be soon time to go there." He voices calmly, tapping me on the shoulder from behind.

"What!" I call out at a loss for any other words and wondering again at how easily he could listen in to my thoughts.

"We'll go tomorrow, on Beltain. I've a feeling that it will be then when we'll find everyone together and when they'll make their plans. Besides, even if we are not actually there, we'll at least feel a part of the celebrations and I've not been to a Beltain feast for many a year."

The next day we knelt together as we had done so often before, only this time my hand was free. Lugh had said that I was now ready to make the journey unaided.

Casting aside any fears I might have had, we set off. It was a good clear day and we took our time enjoying the journey. We could have travelled at any speed we chose, the only restriction appeared to be in knowing where you were going and how to return. We levelled out over the surface of the sea at about the height of tall pine tree and followed the coastline South.

We hadn't gone far when I was struck by the thought of checking on my sister and as soon as I had that thought, I found myself heading in that direction. Lugh followed and signalled mentally to me that it seemed a good idea. The Broch was now in view and we entered through the door that was conveniently open and then down the stairs to where I had been kept prisoner. My curiosity turned quickly to joy as I saw both Niamh and Mairi together in the same cell. They seemed well, all things considered, and I wished that I could communicate some way to them.

'You can possibly.' Came the voice in my head. It was Lugh. 'Send your thoughts to them the same way you normally would. They might sense them and hear them, if they are aware enough.'

I tried and then waited to see if there had been any response. There wasn't, they had kept on chatting away to each other as though nothing had happened. I tried again with more intensity, but there was still no sign of recognition. After a few more times, I gave up. I turned to Lugh and he sensed my slight disappointment.

'Don't worry Fionn. They're in good health and seem happy enough. Sometimes people can be too engrossed in the more basic things in life to be keenly aware of a voice in their head, especially if they're not expecting it.'

I nod in understanding and we set off again only this time out over the sea. It was midday and the sun was above us trying its best to lighten the dark sea below. From our height we could see the gulls flying low over the waves beneath us. I guessed that they were playing on the air currents, which was strange as I couldn't feel the wind myself. The gentle swell was blown East by the wind and, as we neared the island of Siegg, we could see and hear the noise of the breakers on the beach. Moored just off shore of Donal Broch was a small empty currach. It was Ruadh's and I immediately wondered what had brought him to anchor on these shores.

I found the answer with my next thought. Conal Brus was standing next to my father amidst a crowd of familiar faces just up from the beach above the high tide line of the seaweed. Seeing them all again filled me with joy and that very feeling led to a surge in my levels of energy. At that moment I felt I could have achieved anything. Both Lugh and I moved closer, curious to hear what was being said.

"Conal, my old and dear friend." Begins Donal in his deep and burly voice, clasping his arms around the bigger man in a tight embrace. "It's been too long since we last met. It makes me happy to set eyes upon you again, yet I feel sad that it's under such circumstances. Nevertheless my home is your home and today we shall feast and enjoy the delights of Beltain."

"Donal." Replies Conal Brus in slowly, "I have no fill for feasting on such a sorrowful time as this. But for the sake of your good friendship and sense of occasion, I'd be happy to join you all in celebration. There's much seriousness to talk about my old friend. But first how are you mending? And how is your good wife?"

"She's fine and longing to see you again. No doubt she's up there combing herself for you right now. Don't think I haven't forgotten that we both had eyes for her when we first saw her." Jests Donal with the beginnings of a small impish grin appearing on his face. He turns to lead Conal up along the path to the Broch and places a friendly arm on his shoulder.

"Aye, I remember the time well and if it wasn't for your trickery at the time, you'd have never had got a head start in the race to win her heart." Grins Conal, also now putting his arm over his old friends shoulder. "Tell me fair now, I bet you she's regretted her choice a few times."

"Away with your rubbish. It was fair and square. Besides, if my memory serves me well, was your heart not really set on the fair and lovely Aine?" Rebukes Donal as he begins to limp forward, favouring his good leg.

"You're right of course," sighs Conal, noticing his friends awkwardness, "but what's more to the point is how's your leg?"

"It's mending well, thanks. I'm lucky Etain's a good healer, if wasn't for her I'd probably have lost it."

We watched as my father introduced Conal to the others and then followed them up to the Broch. It was there that Etain stood watching my brother Cethan at work. He was busy turning a large spit that stood above one of the two huge open fires in the central area between all the crofts and the Broch. It was the only time of the year that two were built side by side. By driving the cattle through the two fires it was said to drive away the evil spirits and kill any diseases and pests they might have picked up over the winter. Having already put out the animals, the many helpers were seated about the fires in a large circle waiting for the food to be fully cooked. Children were playing games of dare running between the fires and pretending to be bulls and the womenfolk were taking round pitchers of ale and filling up any empty tankards that were held up to them.

As I watched my brother working, in a way I had never been able to before, I noticed how similar he was to my father. Not only did he have the same stocky, sturdy body and long dark brown hair, but he also carried a lot of the same habits. The way he turned the handle and wiped the sweat from his forehead with his heavily tattooed forearms reminded me exactly of Donal. He even swore the same way. Etain began to throw some herbs and scented woods onto the flames. She looked dazzling in a long, dark, woad blue robe that fell just above her ankles and her long light brown hair that flowed down her back.

"Etain, Cethan. Come over here. Conal's arrived." Calls Donal, in a way that invited no discussion.

They both look up and feign surprise and delight. They both knew full well of his arrival, but had had to carry on with their work rather than wait on the beach. Cethan now bounded over to the small group and wrapped his arms around the tall man in just the same way my father had done previously.

"My, you're a fine image of your father Cethan." Booms Conal. "You remind me of him when we set off on our adventures many years ago. It's good to meet you." He clasps him firmly in a warm embrace.

"And you too." Replies Cethan in his strong heavily accented voice.

"My father's nay stopped talking of the two of you since we heard you were coming. I can't wait to hear your side of the stories he tells as I can hardly believe his versions." He smiles at his father and turns to walk alongside the big man.

"They're all true, I'll be bound." Replies Conal mischievously, smiling first down to Cethan and then back at Donal. In a few moments they reach Etain. "Etain." Calls Conal warmly, holding out his arms to her, "You look as well as the fond memories I have of you." They hug and because of his huge frame of a body, it lifts her up onto her toes. As they part, he lowers her delicately down and stands back.

"Away with your lies Conal Brus." She rebuffs him playfully, "You and I both know the number of years that have passed since. Still it's lovely to see you again." She holds her arms wide and they embrace again like old friends with shared secrets and I notice a twinkle in my mother's eye. Both Donal and Cethan glance awkwardly at each other then back to the two of them, now pulling away from each other for the second time.

"Conal. I seem to have so many questions. How is Aine? And tell me about your children." Asks Etain, diffusing neatly the new concerns of the men in her life.

"They are all well thank you. Aine sends her love and wishes that she could see you soon. She asked me to give you this and to apologise that she was unable to accompany me here." Conal takes out a small carefully wrapped bundle and hands it to her. Slowly and with mounting curiosity she unfolds the cloth to reveal a beautiful comb. Made from a whale bone, it had been carefully inlaid with mother of pearl. Its fine teeth were as thin as I'd ever seen.

"It's beautiful, such fine craftwork." Cries Etain excitedly, "How can I ever thank you enough, I am forever breaking the teeth off of my combs. Thank you both very much." She reaches up to the tall man and kisses him hard on the cheek and then turns to Donal who seems to be lost for words. "Look Donal, look at the work that has gone into this. Isn't it wonderful."

"Aye, it's work at its best alright. Conal thank Aine for me and tell her we shall visit soon." Says Donal, a little off balance with everything. "Come let's get a drink Conal, we can sit and talk."

"Well I've a gift of my own for you, my old friend." He turns and calls for the skipper of the currach who is just behind them. "Ruadh. Have you got that barrel?"

"Aye, it's here." Comes the response from Ruadh. He moves up through the others with a wooden cask on his shoulder.

"What's this?" Calls Donal, his joyous and playful mood immediately returning.

"Just a little nectar from the gods, the water of life I make myself. To me it's Uisgebeathe at its finest and it sells well too. Here," he says lifting the cask off of Ruadh and handing it to Donal, "perhaps, you'd like to start by trying some of it."

"That we will and it's kind of you to consider my very needs at this moment. Come let's sit, my leg wearies me." Donal shakes his leg and smacks it with his hand trying to get the stiffness out of it.

Lugh and I watch as they move over to the fire and sit down on a carefully placed log.

The two of them sat next to each other whilst Cethan and my mother returned to preparing the meal. I listened as Conal talked of my journey and of my exploits at Invercarrie. Pride surged through me as I heard my father applauding my success at becoming an Anruth and in confronting Domnhuill Dubh and his men. It was soon followed by embarrassment and discomfort as Conal mentioned how Niamh had explained to her father how much she had enjoyed my company. Being a third party to a conversation like this was a weird experience and I could sense Lugh's harmless amusement.

Before long, the food was ready and everyone gathered round as my brother began to deal out slices of meat from the wild boar. Its flattened carcass, now dripping and ouzing its last pockets of fat, was lifted off from the spit over the fire and onto a piece of flat wood. He hacked expertly at the ruddy brown and black tinged flesh and soon there were slices enough for everyone. A rear leg bone was torn out of its socket and given to Conal, the rest of it was then put back onto the spit.

Everyone now sat around the fire, yet my father, Cethan, Conal and Etain sat closer together and in more of a half circle with each other. The children had settled down and were ravenously devouring their helpings over to one side. Behind them the work dogs barked for attention knowing that at any moment they would be offered some of the remaining scraps.

Lugh and I hovered just behind them. It was then that I spotted my old friend Dugald, the Seannachie. He appeared from the direction of the mountain, walking with the help of his long staff. He too was greeted like a lost friend and was invited to sit next to Conal. It was clear from the conversation that they had been waiting for him. Once they were all seated with wooden plates of food on their laps, they began to eat. At first there was silence as they tucked speedily into the meat, just watching the scene made my belly ache with pangs of hunger. Later, as their pace slowed, they found time to look up and around.

"Music!" Cries Donal. "Urien, fetch your whistle! Owain get the drums! By all the gods let's have some fun. Beltain with no celebration, no matter what has happened, would never bode well for the coming season."

A passionate shout of good cheer went up from everyone around the fire and a few of them rose to their feet. Before long there is music and clapping to the beat of the drum. In next to no time a group of friends the other side of the fire had started to link their arms together and had begun to dance an Island fling. Hoots of laughter burst above the joyous sounds of music as some of the more adventurous revellers soon fell down exhausted. Along with their earlier over indulgence of ale, their imaginative leaping and prancing had finally overwhelmed them.

Donal looked around about him and smiled, liking what he saw. He now seemed happy that the rest of his clan could to continue the celebrations without him. I watched as his smile now faded and his face turned serious. He turned to Conal.

"It was good of you to send word of what Fionn had found out Conal. As I understand it then, Mairi is being held at Domnhuill Dubh's broch just North of Invercarrie. You say Fionn's gone off to find Lugh. Who's this Lugh and how can he help? Also do you know for sure where Niamh's being kept?"

"I'm not sure about that, possibly at his broch, possibly at the Aes Dana," starts Conal, now fully aware it was the time to talk of such grave things, "as for Lugh, all I know is that Angus tells me people know him as the Samildanach, the many gifted one. Apparently he may be able to teach young Fionn something about how to handle Callum Beg."

"What's that!" Dugald interrupts, holding up the bone he had been gnawing. Are you telling me that Angus says Lugh is real!" He asks having caught up with the last few comments of conversation. Conal nods slowly in reply, unsure of what Dougal is meaning. "Well I can certainly tell you about Lugh." He states. "Although it's a bit of a surprise to me to hear that he actually exists."

"Angus seems quite sure of it." Conal reinforces his earlier nod, still looking round at Dugald.

"Ah, Angus!" Mutters Dougal, distracted by the memories of his friend. "By the way how is my old friend and what do you know of the part he's playing in all this?" Asks the old Seannachie, now munching merrily again on his chunk of meat.

"He told me how he met Fionn at your cave and that he went with him to Invercarrie. As I understand it, he has now infiltrated the Aes Dana having got back in favour with some old friends. He is trying currently to find out what Callum Beg's plans are." Answers Conal, choosing also to now return to his food, instead of waiting for Dougal to say more about Lugh.

"Do we know what these plans are exactly?" Inquires Donal from the other side and looking directly at Conal.

"It's not good. I couldn't tell you in the message, it was too dangerous." He pauses, aware of the gravity of his next few words. "His ambition is to be King himself..."

"A Bolg's chance he has of that if I have anything to do with it!" Swears Donal, interrupting Conal's answer and slamming his fist into his wooden seat underneath him.

"...he has no intention of declaring Queen Irnan's son Bran to be king after the Tarb Feis on Samhain." Continues Conal.

"By the wrath of Fraoch! There is no way I'll let that cur get away with that." Donal struggles to his feet and hobbles over to the fire, his fury not allowing him to remain still any longer. "I've fought for the king for too many years to see such treachery go by unattended. By Demne, I wish my leg were better right now." He kicks at the nearest object with his bad leg and a branch half out of the fire moves further into the middle of it. A shower of sparks fills the air and rises above the flames.

"How was he going to get away with that anyway?" Stifles out Cethan with his mouth full but too genuinely curious about it all to swallow first.

"We're not sure. It was our guess that he was going to coerce Lugh into performing the ceremony and to declare him king afterwards. The trouble is we can't work out how he's going to do that." Replies Conal, watching the grey specks of ash now falling through the air caught on the light wind.

"What do you think Lugh can do?" Asks Donal now standing with his back to the fire looking over at Dugald who is busy licking his fingers.

"If the stories are to be believed, he could have the power to influence a large number of people, so that there would be little resistance afterwards." He suggests tentatively. "However, I couldn't really say. So much is legend and it's difficult to know what might be true."

"But where does the crown helm fit in and why take Mairi and Niamh?" asks Cethan, still feeling lost without reason to it all.

"Have any of you heard of the Cult of the Dead?" Asks Conal, looking at every one of them in turn.

"Urgh!" groans Dugald, putting his hand to his forehead then looking around him. He sees that Donal also understands.

"I'm afraid so." Says Conal, nodding.

"What! What is it?" Demands Cethan, with increasing anxiety. Having now forgotten about his food and placed his wooden plate by his side on the ground, he now sits forward in a far more attentive manner.

"The cult requires human sacrifices in order to influence the outcomes of events in the future. It used to be common around these parts many years ago and it now seems, from what Conal is implying, that Callum Beg is resurrecting it for his own purposes." States Dugald, looking to Conal for confirmation.

"That's what Angus thought as well." Adds Conal.

"If you mean what I think you mean, then when is this likely to happen?" Asks Donal, pacing in front of the fire in small circles twisting around on his good leg.

"There's only one possible time that makes most sense and that's on the eve of Samhain." Replies Dugald.

"Then we need to rescue the girls before that. At least it gives us time to plan and a chance for my leg to heal. I just hope you're completely right about that." Says Donal, looking for some back up from Dugald. He nods in reply.

"What about Fionn and Lugh then? What do you think they are up to?" Donal goes on, taking to no one in particular.

"Well Fionn has to find Lugh first. No one's seen him for years. What we do know is that he has the last part of the Crown Helm, which is why Callum Beg is also looking for him." Conal replies, "This helm seems to be very important to Beg. Why is that Dugald do you think?"

"With that complete, there'll be very little that could stop him. The symbolism that it can represent, will give a tremendous power of influence to the wearer. If anyone doubts that he should be King, then the crown on his head will certainly change even the most stubborn of minds." Answers Dugald, shaking his head.

"We know he has three parts already. Angus has seen them." Says Conal holding up three fingers. He looks at them then licks them in turn.

"I don't understand what all the fuss seems to be about this crown helm." Cethan butts in, obviously frustrated. "Why can't we just go straight in and get the girls and leave?"

"It's not that simple now, Cethan," Conal goes on, "Though I understand and hear what you are saying. Unfortunately Callum Beg has a lot of power and support and if we go charging in there, we are likely to find trouble. No, we need to not only rescue the girls but to also start to undermine Beg's authority. I think we need to start by helping Queen Irnan. You know her better than I do Donal, what do you think?"

"You're right Conal. I need to meet with her before we do anything. What about Fionn? Did he leave word as to what he was going to do?"

There was silence as Conal tried to remember. I willed him mentally to listen to me, trying to make him hear my thoughts. 'I will meet you.' but nothing happened. Donal moved back over to his seat and sat back down between them all.

"No, not that I recall." Replies Conal eventually.

"Then we shall have to act without him and Lugh." States Donal, "I suggest we make a plan now. Firstly, Cethan and I will come to Drummorchy just before Samhain. All three of us will then go North by land to Invercarrie. Any more than three and we'll be unable to disguise our presence."

"I think it best that I come too." Interrupts Dugald, "I may be older by a few years, but I know a few things about Callum Beg that could help. I also have friends in the Aes Dana that may help us. Besides I've been in exile too long."

"As you wish. It would be good to have your company." Consents Donal. "I shall speak with the Queen, whilst Cethan can search out the area around the Broch. There must be a good place we can make an ambush. Conal, we'll need to make arrangements to make our escape. I suggest two options, firstly having a currach standing by and secondly having some horses ready just outside of Invercarrie. What do you think?" The speed of his voice increases as his anticipation builds.

"It's good, it takes care of rescuing the girls, if they're both held together, but what about Callum Beg?" Adds Cethan, at a similar pace.

"That's something we'll have to consider nearer the time." Ponders Donal, sitting forward and placing his chin on his right fist with his elbow on his knee. "It'll depend largely on what else we find out along the way."

They sit in silence looking into the flames chewing over the last few words in a similar fashion to the meat that they held in their hands. I sensed Dugald was in more of a mode of awareness and again tried to send him a thought. I watched as he sat up a little and looked about. I spoke again, 'Dugald, it's me, Fionn. I'm here. I can see you all. I'm with Lugh. We'll meet you at the ambush. Listen carefully to me, the girls are both alive and well in the Domnhuill Dubh's Broch and Callum Beg has all four pieces of the helmet now. Tell my mother I'm fine and not to worry about me and that her new comb looks lovely.' I repeated it several times and still there was silence. Then I heard him think a question my way. 'If you are Fionn, how did your presentation go at the Aes Dana?' He asked. 'It went well thanks to you. I am now an Anruth.'

With that reply, he stands up and looks around and calls out, "Fionn, is that really you, did you really pass. That's great, well done."

The others look at him in complete amazement. He turns to them and sees them watching him with strange expressions all over their faces. "I've just heard from Fionn, he's with Lugh now and they're here."

There was a still silence and looks of incredulity, especially from Cethan. Some of the others that had been dancing nearby to the music now stopped to look at the spectacle of their Seannachie talking to himself.

"He's just told me he passed at the Aes Dana. He's now an Anruth." He calls out to the others, looking at each of them in turn.

"Well I'm not sure that's not going to be much help." Interrupts Cethan with an edge of sarcasm, showing he is still dubious at Dugald's outburst.

"No wait." Shouts Conal. "I told you all about Fionn passing before Dugald arrived, there's no way that Dugald could know." He declares.

"That's an interesting point indeed Conal," decides Donal, "and these are strange times. If you really believe it was Fionn. Did he say anything in particular? Something that might be of use to us?"

"Yes. He said the girls were both alive and well at the Broch and that Callum Beg now has all four parts of the helmet. He says that he and Lugh will meet us at the ambush site." Dugald goes on. "Etaine. He tells me to tell you not to worry and something about a new comb looking lovely."

I could sense shivers going down all their backs at the sudden realisation that I must have been there recently as they had only just decided upon the idea of an ambush and Dougal didn't even know about Conal's gift to Etain.

Donal looked up, away from where Lugh and I were and steadily gets to his feet. "Fionn, if you're still here son," he starts nervously as all the others around the fire were now looking at him, "you're doing well. We'll all be over before Samhain, five moons from now. We'll meet you where Cethan decides it best to ambush Domnhuill Dubh, use your wits and you'll find him. If there's anything else we need to know, just do whatever you've just done again." He finishes, still unsure of which way to look.

With that he sits down. I had never before seen him as humbled as much as I did now, knowing how far out of his depth he was with these mystical things that were inexplicable to him. It was more than obvious that these strange and unknown things unsettled him, as they did most folk. Etain now appeared behind him and put her arms around his shoulders. Together they rocked a little from side to side in contemplation, mindful of the comfort they gave each other.

Lugh sent me a thought that we should now leave. Apparently I'd been away from my body for long enough. We'd achieved what we'd set out to achieve and that was good. Leaving for the second time though, even in such a way, left me feeling slightly gloomy and reminiscent. It was hard because I could see all my friends and family together. As these thoughts began to build, Lugh immediately came closer to me and sent me some energy.

'Fionn, remember to fill your heart with joy or you'll not make the journey back.' He warns.

He sent a thought to Dugald to say that we had to leave and we rose up into the air. I looked down at the assembled circle of friends and family and made a mental note to remember the picture in my mind. It would help to recall it all at some time in the future. In next to no time, we were back in the cave. Its cold and dark atmosphere hit me hard being quite the opposite to having just felt very much part of the Beltain celebrations on Siegg.

We continued to work together as we'd done before. There seemed plenty of time as we had the whole summer ahead of us. Lugh explained to me that there was a never-ending list of what could be achieved mentally all stemming from the same initial state. If the energies were good, maybe due to the earth's environment or good conjunctions in the skies, then these feats became easier. He showed me that all it needed was constant practice in order to create an improvement. If I stopped working with the flow of energy, then my abilities would fade. He also demonstrated to me the many seemingly amazing feats that were possible if I only persevered. I witnessed him lift heavy objects effortlessly and even raise his body up into the air. He explained that trips could even be made to distant stars and planets and across the oceans to far off lands. We talked over all the possible dangers involved in these mental flights and how to overcome them. Until at last our time was up and we had to begin our travels back down to the South.

It was an enjoyable time of year to cross the mountains. The heather was in full bloom, with whole glens covered in white and purple flowers. Only the incessant attention from the midgies detracted from the overall beauty of the place. Their bites left us blotchy faced from the slaps we had given ourselves in our feeble attempts to combat them. As we descended lower and followed the burns down, they got worse. Only once we'd lit the evening fire did we usually get some respite and have a chance to relax. Lugh had suggested we head for Rougie Falls, the same way Domnhuill Dubh had returned. Detouring back through the Achentoul forest was something he had wanted to avoid for reasons he wouldn't go into.

We soon arrived at familiar territory to me and that was when I found myself outside the log cabin where I had met the three women. Lugh had said that he wished to stop there as he had things he needed to discuss with them. As we approached their door I remembered my last encounter and wondered now what was in store for us. The door opened as we'd just got to it.

"How wonderful to see all you good ladies again." Cries out Lugh smiling cordially, "It's been far too long since we last met and I apologise wholeheartedly as it's entirely my fault. How are you all?" He holds out his arms wide open and leans back a little to embrace them all.

"Lugh! Lugh!" They all cry out, flinging their arms around him.

I watched them from behind and found that it lifted my heart to see such genuine affection. Their long dark brown robes, made from a fine tweed and covered in strange black dye designs, swirled all around him as they hugged and kissed him all over. Before I knew it, their attention spilt over onto me as well and I was pulled into their midst. Not long afterwards, they stood back to look at us properly.

"Expecting, friends of the land eating and drinking together now." Remarks the older lady. "Speech getting used change, sorry." She continues, looking at me.

Lugh turns to me and says, "Fionn. Mathalewch is apologising that she is not able to talk our language just yet and needs time to adapt. They talk the language of dreams and thoughts and live much of their time in that world."

"Who are they exactly?" I ask without thinking. They all smile at me and I realise they understand me perfectly.

"This is Mathalewch and her sisters Maeve and Nemain. I thought you had said you had met before." Says Lugh slightly perplexed and raising his customary eyebrow.

"Oh. We have," I reply, "just not introduced properly."

"Ah! I understand." He nods. "They don't say much, but they're friendly and helpful if you are to them."

"Well they helped me tremendously." I turn to them, "Thank you all very much. If I can return a favour, please ask."

"Your way is help indeed." Replies Mathalewch, leaving me feeling curious as to what she meant. "Must rest beforehand. Come eating and drinking are good today." She guides us over to sit before a large table that has five places set.

"There is still much to learn about the world Fionn." Laughs Lugh, as he sees my bewilderment. "Just relax and take everything in with a light heart. I have things to discuss with Mathalewch after dinner, I'm sure her sisters will do their best to attend to your needs." He smiles at me, having sat down across the other side of the table.

"Lugh. Do you mind if I ask you something that's been on my mind?" I start, after hearing his words.

"Not at all, go on." He replies beginning to reach for some of the food.

"Well, ever since we met you have been good enough to help me in every way you can. I know you have your reasons, especially with regard to your earlier meeting with Callum Beg, but what are your plans? You seem to have something on your mind. Now is the first time I have ever heard you talk of something else. If there is something, I really feel that I would like to help some way, just to return all your kindness and assistance."

"Fionn." He starts, sitting down at the table, "We all have a role in life. Some people find it; others never do. You and I are two of the fortunate ones that have discovered and are following that role. As you have already found, it has a pace and direction of its own. We don't always know the outcome but we can sense when we are near. My time is now near. I have done much in my life and there is only a little left to do. We will soon be parting, for how long I have no idea."

"But when?" I exclaim, putting down a piece of bread that I had just picked up.

"I am unsure exactly when. I only know that it has been important to pass on some knowledge to you at this point of my life. Soon I have another journey to make. It may be my last."

"It sounds dangerous, are you sure I can't help in some way." I offer, picking up the bread again.

"It will be nothing like as dangerous as the journey we now face Fionn. No. I am afraid there is nothing you can do to help me afterwards. However, I would be eternally grateful if you remember all that I have taught you. That in its own small way is repayment enough. Now. Enough of that. Let's eat." He concludes, leaving me slightly deflated and confused.

Maeve, the girl with the blond hair senses this and passes me a plate of fruit. "Be eating this." She calls lightly, her voice almost singing the words," Picked by me at sunrising."

In front of me she had put a bowl with a selection of many fruits of the summer. There were loganberries, blaeberries, mountain strawberries, blackberries and wild damsons. On the rest of the table, there were loaves of several different breads, cheese and honey and on the side there was a large bowl filled with the greens of the forest. This herbal salad contained a mixture of many leaves, some of which were new to me and probably only found on the mainland. I reached forward to them eager to yet again try something new.

We ate well and afterwards Lugh and Mathalewch disappeared outside for a long walk. Nemain and Maeve invited me outside as well and took me down to the pool. It was a warm and sunny afternoon and I was soon persuaded to join them in the water. Nakedness and embarrassment were eventually forgotten on my part and we were soon playing games of catch and tag.

The day passed quickly and even though communication was limited, we became close friends in a way that can only come about after having had a strange kind of complete openness between people. I slept well that night and woke up having had the feeling that I had experienced another part of my recurring dream. I had been travelling in my mind high over a massive expanse of water with no land in sight at all. I asked Lugh about it, but got no answer other than all would be revealed to me at the right time.

We said goodbye to the women after a large oatmeal breakfast and then set off towards the South. This time we travelled openly along the coastal road. It was only four days from Samhain and we were still two days away from Invercarrie.

I looked everywhere, all the around the area Angus had said, but there was still no sign of any message. I checked thoroughly each one of the animal pens and also found nothing. I tried to work out what this meant. Maybe there was nothing to say. Maybe he had been followed and the message taken. There were too many possibilities. After checking the area again, I resigned myself to the fact that I wasn't going to find anything. I thought about speaking to the crofter whose animal pens they were, but decided against it. In the end we decided to press on to find out where Cethan might have decided to set the ambush.

It was a fairly barren landscape that led from Invercarrie up to Domnhuill Dubh's Broch, there were the few odd yew trees and small bushes, nothing to hide five armed men. We walked the route as nonchalantly as we could so as not to arouse suspicion, but we needn't have bothered, as we saw no one. We were only a few hundred paces away from the broch when I heard the call. I'd heard it a thousand times before as a kid when I used to play with my brother along the cliffs of the Siegg. An expert at all animal calls, he had made the low grunting and repeating noise of a northern fulmar. An instantly recognisable bird call. I turned toward where the sound was coming from, but saw nothing.

"Stop gawking," hisses Cethan, "and get over here and out of sight quickly." I look more carefully and notice that there is a slight drop in ground level ten to fifteen paces away from the path. The area had slipped down and away and left enough room for several people to lie flat and out of sight. His head appears from over the top of the miniature cliff.

"Over here." He calls again, now smiling. "It's good to see you again Fionn,"

"And you too Brother." I reply jumping down over the edge and clasping him by the shoulders. "This is Lugh. He has been a good friend to me."

"Any friend of my brother is a friend of mine." He holds an arm out and gently holds Lugh's shoulder. "Come let's get down out of sight."

Cethan had hollowed out a small area of the cliff making it an over-hang. It would give little shelter but that didn't matter, it was still summer and at least we were completely unable to be seen down there.

"Is this really the best you could do?" I ask, half smiling and half mocking my elder brother.

"It fooled you brother," he rebukes, "and several other people who've passed today and yesterday."

"Where are Donal and the others?" I ask, as Lugh and I settle in to squat beside him.

"Still in Invercarrie, I'm expecting them just after midday though." He replies. "Well how are you brother? Good on you for becoming to be an Anruth as well. I suppose we're all going to be bored by your stories for ever and ever now." He goads, grinning at me whilst offering me one of several apples in his bag. "Freshly picked today, do you want one?"

I took it and offered it to Lugh who accepted it as I took another. It was typical of Cethan. He spoke and changed subjects as fast as he did everything. He was never one to sit still for long periods of time, or one to concentrate for any length of time, unless it was part of a hunt. Then there was no one better. We ate and talked about what we had been doing since we had last seen each other and finally I asked about Domhuill Dubh and whether Cethan had seen him pass by. From his descriptions of the people he had seen, none fitted that of the Dubh. Gruach on the other hand was definitely in the Broch and so, we could only presume, were Mairi and Niamh. Things were not going to plan. The longer we waited here, the less time we would have to get to the Aes Dana in time to stop Beg's ceremony. They were however bound to leave it to the last moment to bring the girls into Invercarrie. Any earlier could have raised suspicions.

Things were certainly not looking good though. Lugh had said that the area we were in was lacking in energy and because of that we were unlikely to be of as much assistance as we would like to have been. I tried feeling for some and had no luck. It was a nuisance because we wanted to check to see if the girls were still locked up in the cells of the

Broch and it was too late to go somewhere else and try.

By mid afternoon, Donal and Conal Brus appeared. I was pleased that they too didn't spot us. I was also happy to see him walking well, albeit with a slight limp.

"Father. It's good to see you again." I call out standing up, shoulders above the level of ground and surprising him. His hand instinctively reaches for the sword hanging from his belt, but as soon as he sees it's me, he rushes over.

"Fionn, Son. By Belenos it's good to see a familiar face in this land of iniquity. How are you?" He asks briskly, jumping down next to me.

"Very well thanks father." We clasp each other firmly about the shoulders and after a short moment he pulls back to get a good look at me. "Father this is Lugh," I turn to introduce him. "He has been helping me these last few moons."

"It's a pleasure to meet you." Beams Donal reaching over to Lugh and, as he does so, his eyes screw up slightly as if trying to remember something. "Have we met before?" He asks in an unsure way.

"That's entirely possible, but now's not the time to talk of the past." Smiles Lugh enigmatically.

"You're right. Come let's talk about what we have to do." Replies Donal, touching Lugh's shoulder gently. "Ah Cethan." He continues. "I knew I could rely on you to find us a good place. I was beginning to wonder on the way here though." Donal reaches over and greets him with a quick one-armed hug.

"Donal, Conal. It's good to see the two of you together. Have you any news?" I ask, musing upon the similarity of their names and how they had been inseparable in their youth.

"Aye lad. Plenty. And none too good, sad to say." Replies Conal, shaking his head.

"What's up then?" Cethan asks, turning to face Conal.

"Let's get out of sight first." Suggests Conal, "I think there was someone behind us." We all squat down in a circle close to the cliff wall. Lugh kneels down a pace away.

"Firstly," starts the big man, "I've arranged a currach that'll sail when we want, wind and tide permitting. I've also got horses ready at a croft just to the South of Invercarrie. I didn't know anyone this side that I could rely upon, so South will have to do."

"It'll do." says Cethan, "We can skirt round Invercarrie if we need to, I found a place we can cross some way upstream."

"Good," continues Conal, in a definite tone. "But the rest is nay so good. There's no sign of Angus. Dugald has tried to find him but has nay had any luck. He'll be along later. Apparently he's not even been able to get into the Aes Dana, though that might be because he did n'y wish to say who he was."

"What about Callum Beg?" Interrupts Lugh from just outside our small group. "Is there any news on where he is or what he's up to?" I look round to where he is kneeling and see that he is still kneeling and contemplating things with his head bowed down.

"I saw Queen Irnan." Answers Donal. "She has been having a daily audience with Beg and her son. So we know he's around. As to what else he's been up to, you're guess is as good as mine. She was none too happy to hear my news though. If it hadn't been for the fact that I'd been so close to her husband, I doubt she'd have believed me at all. As it is, she's offered us shelter if we should need it but only in return for openly supporting Bran immediately before and after the ceremony."

"That might make things difficult." I add quickly.

"True, but we may not need to call on her for a favour in the first place." Donal replies.

"It appears that I now need to be making for that place I mentioned Fionn." Breaks in Lugh, changing the subject. "All of you seem quite capable of handling events here without an old man like me. It's time I was now off to deal with Callum Beg in my own way. Fionn. Walk with me for a moment will you?"

"Certainly." I reply. The others look at each other and visibly show understanding and respect at what Lugh was about to try to do.

We get up together and set off away from the path so as not to be seen. As soon as we were out of earshot, he began.

"Listen Fionn. There's little either of us can do here. My feeling is that there's nothing happening here and everything is now centred on the Aes Dana."

"What do you mean?" I state, amazed at his comments. I stop walking and look at him.

"Just as I said." He turns to me. "I don't think that the girls are here still. They must have already been taken to Invercarrie some time ago. There's been no sight of Domnhuill Dubh and I suspect that much of what we are looking for is back at the Aes Dana. That's where our contingency plans now lie."

"Is that a guess or a gut feeling?" I ask knowing of his abilities.

"You could call it a very real sense of knowing." He replies, honestly.

"Shouldn't we tell the others." I say pointing back in their direction.

"Do you think they would listen?" He aims his question to me rather than them.

"Yes." I say, getting slightly exasperated and placing my hand on my hips.

"Eventually, but then it might be too late. No I must go now. Whatever happens here, leave in enough time to get to the Aes Dana tonight and bring Dugald if you can."

"What are you going to do?" I ask wondering how he thought he could cope on his own, no matter how much I believed in him.

"We won't be on our own." He smiles, reaching out and touching my upper arm. "Just remember our plan. I will be distracting Beg from his rites while you get in and rescue the girls."

"You worry me." I say, shaking my head but returning his smile.

"That's quite needless. You look after yourself here and remember it's not a good area for energy and I'll see you later." He reaches out and takes hold of my shoulder with one of his frail hands and I reciprocate with my arm slightly overlying his arm and grabbing his shoulder.

With that he set off in the direction of the Glencannick forest, the opposite way from Invercarrie, our arms are left to fall to our sides as we part. Perplexing as always, I thought, turning to head back. As I walked across the low undulating grassy ground, I remembered back to when it had been covered in snow and when I had made my hasty exit from the broch. Looking back on it now, the escape had seemed easier than I expected, which was no wonder if that had been their intention. All along I had played into their hands. I determined from now on to change things and to regain control over my destiny. I had finally discovered that it was only then that the really great things started to happen.

It was as I neared the path that I noticed the small dark figure approaching. If I crossed over now to meet with my friends it would give away their position. Had the man seen me? If he had and I tried to hide, he would be suspicious and immediately on his guard. There was no alternative. I would have to alter my course to confront him at exactly the right spot on the path. If he didn't know who I was, I could make some excuse and pass, if he did, it would take some quick thinking.

The two of us got closer and closer. We'd both spotted each other now and both of us knew we were on a collision course. Coming from the direction I was though, would certainly draw the attention away from the others.

It was Domnhuill Dubh. If he was heading for the broch, it could mean only one thing, he was about to get the girls and take them to Beg. The thought stirred me inside and I readied myself for action. Now he was nearer, his costume and gait were unmistakable. He looked hard at me and then reached for his sword. I could make out the grin appearing on his face. I instinctively centred myself and began to send into him thoughts of fear and distraction. Nothing happened and I remembered the area. Instead of energy, doubt now entered my mind and I reached for my sword. He and I were now only ten paces apart. The broch was behind me and he'd now passed the others so I stood and waited in the middle of the path. I had to carry on this charade to give the others time to come out from behind him.

"Well if it isn't the young lad we left in the hills not half a year ago." He began speaking slowly, "To say that I'd missed you would be a lie, but I am happy to say I'm glad we've bumped into each other now."

"Oh. And why is that? Why would someone with a brain the size of bee want to bump into a beekeeper such as myself, if it wasn't to do exactly what I wanted." I challenge.

"Beekeeper is it," his voice rising and his sword now swinging backwards and forward low down in front of him. Distracted, as he now fully was, the others crept out and now fanned out behind him. "I see no bees around here for you to keep. That must mean this is no place for a beekeeper. Not now, not here and not in this world." Shouting his last words as he raises his weapon to strike downwards.

"And not for you." Comes the voice of my father, now standing directly behind Domnhuill Dubh. The Dubh spins around to see Cethan, Donal and Conal Brus now circling him. "There's no place here for the scum who need to trade women for a living. No place for the half-men that need to steal the women folk from others. Your journey to the Otherworld begins and ends here and now." Donal growls out slowly and deliberately.

"What's this? Four against one. I'm pleased to see you behold me with such fear. Well I've some sad news for you. You should have chosen odds of ten to one, just to have lost a good fight. Instead you're all going to be feed for the birds, one by one." Domnhuill sneers back at them.

"Don't be too sure of those odds, you lame excuse for a piece of rotten black pudding. It's only I that intends to send you on your way."

Retorts Donal now limbering up his shoulders by swinging his sword arm up and around in a large circle.

"An old man like yourself, have you forgotten the last time I bested you. Didn't you ever stop to wonder why I didn't finish you off then? Well it's of no matter because it'll be my pleasure to give you your last lesson." He calls out, launching into a fierce attack.

The two struck and parried each other, then struck again, each adjusting to the others style of fight. Blows and half blows were all sent in toward one another in an attempt to learn of weaknesses. The rest of us cheered and jeered with every clash and I began to wonder whether my father, with his age and recent injury, was good enough to overcome such an expert adversary. One moment they were locked together in deadly embrace; the next they were apart. Curses and threats flew from each of them, amidst much puffing and panting.

A noise interrupted my thoughts from behind and I turned to see the large shape of Gruach charging towards us waving two axes in the air above his head. Behind him I recognised two of the guards I'd seen before. It looked like we were all going to see some action. Soon after I'd turned, my brother and Conal passed either side of me in full pelt. Cethan was letting out a scream that sounded like a wounded bear. I followed only marginally more cautiously.

Conal just beat Cethan to take on Gruach. In a neat side step, twist and a turn, he slipped immediately inside the big thug's reach and sliced his sword across his chest. The cry that came from Gruach was one of excruciating pain and disbelief. He looked down at his chest in time to see his thick leathers split asunder and his innards beginning to fall out. It was his last sight, for Conal, now behind him, finally disposed of him with a thrust through his back that came out through his guts.

If the yell hadn't checked the guards, the sight of him felled so quickly certainly did. Unfortunately for them, their momentum carried them into the path of Cethan and myself. Unprepared for such a fierce onslaught and the new role of fighting for their lives, they began to back away under a fury of strikes and blows. Conal joined in the attack and it was soon over. They died bravely, never once calling for mercy.

I turned and ran back to my father. Their duelling continued and each was tiring rapidly. Domnhuill Dubh had seen the demise of his men and was now backing off. With no route forward to his broch or back along the path to Invercarrie, he backed toward the cliffs. First they fought over the short drop that we had hidden behind, then between the massive boulders nearer to the edge.

It was only my father's superior skill that was keeping him alive now. We followed behind the two of them circling and cutting off any paths of further retreat. The only ending now was whether the one or the two would die and we all knew what that meant. In desperation Domnhuill searched for some escape along the cliff's edge. Fending off ever weaker blows with weaker parries, he jumped backwards from rock to ledge. Then, through tiredness and exhaustion, the Dubh slipped. Down on one knee and off balance, Donal lunged at him piercing his cloak just below his shoulder. The pain and the force threw him backwards. He reached behind him with his free arm in an attempt to steady himself. What looked like firm ground turned out to be a grassy overhang. With a struggle and a last defiant look, he fell silently over the cliff still clutching his sword.

Hearing only thuds and bumps, we waited until the only sound was from the waves crashing on to the rocks below. There was no way down and there was no way back up. The drop was all of thirty paces high and nothing would have survived such a fall.

The three of us stepped back from the edge, only to see Donal collapsed in a heap. His breathing was heavy and laboured and words were failing him. Desperate to talk, yet unable, we could see visibly how much the fight had taken out of him. Cethan and I helped him up and between us carried him with his arms flung over our shoulders. Conal went on ahead.

By the time we reached the steps to the Broch, Donal was able to walk and talk like old times.

"By Cuchulainn's mighty sword, did you see the way I destroyed that beast 'Dubh' in fair combat. Was it not pure skill that won the day, that finally pushed him to his fate and finished him for ever." Beams out Donal.

"Conal my old friend, I see yours was an easy victory too. Does it not remind you of the days gone by, when we fought side by side?"

"Aye, it does and I remember it was always me that seemed to have the easier foes then as well." He rebuffs trying badly to hide a wry smile. Donal in his exalted state misses the expression and continues.

"Cethan. Fionn. By the gods it's good to fight alongside one's sons. Well done lads."

"It feels great indeed." Cries out Cethan, now releasing Donal from his support.

"Especially when the gods have looked upon us so favourably." I add, also now letting my father stand up by himself. The sudden weight on his legs, so soon after the fight, makes them buckle slightly and I wondered whether it was just his pride that kept him upright.

"Let's go up and get the girls." Suggests Conal, eager to press on. "I'll be much happier to talk once this is all over and we found them safe and unharmed."

We ascend the steps and push on the door. It is shut and locked.

"Open it, or we'll burn the place down!" Calls out Cethan, ever the impetuous one. He bangs the door with the palm of his hand and then kicks it.

"Who is it? What's happened to Gruagh and the others?" Comes a fearful voice.

"They're all dead, now open up and we might spare you." Barks Cethan again, this time a little more sombrely.

Crying starts instantly, joined moments later by several other female tears.

"Open up!" Growls Donal, finally losing his patience. The door opens and we find a group of women in a circle consoling themselves. I recognise Igrainne.

"Igrainne!" I call over to her, "Where's Mairi and Niamh? Are they downstairs?"

The crying increases and Cethan pulls up the door in the wooden floor that leads to the cells and rushes down the steps. I go over to the women who have now backed away over to the fireplace.

"Mairi, Niamh!" Calls out Donal. Still no answer.

"Igrainne, where are they?" I ask using all the techniques of persuasion that I had learnt to get her to answer more quickly.

"Domnhuill took them away four days ago." She replies slowly, having now stopped crying.

"There's no one down there." Calls Cethan rushing back up into the room.

"Where did he take them Igrainne?" I ask again, cursing my bad luck at Cethan's interruption. But my control was broken and I could see hatred build up in her eyes.

"You're too late!" She spits out. "By now they'll be dead at the hands of Beg. Curse you to the Underworld for ever, all of you!" She screams and reaches out with fingernails the size of talons to scratch me. I grab her wrists in time to save my skin some severe laceration.

This incenses her and her head shakes wildly as she tries to bite her way free. Cethan reaches across and smacks her harshly on the face. Fear replaces her brief attempts to be brave.

"Answer, or my brother will turn you into a toad, forever to taste the delights of festering flies!" He swears at her, grabbing her upper arms from behind with his large hands.

I am momentarily caught off guard at my brothers new found, if not misguided, belief in me. However, the threat appears to work.

"They're being held in a secret cell at the Aes Dana. They're going to be sacrificed tonight in one of Beg's death rituals. You're too late." She shouts, "There is no way you can get there in time. Even if you could get in." She gasps out, as Cethan holds her more tightly, his hands now around her throat. She was now fearful of death herself, possibly for the first time in her life.

Cethan lets her go and she falls to her knees in front of me and starts to whimper.

"We've got to go now." Calls out Conal, "I know we can make it in time if we run."

"Conal you'll have to help father get there, he'll not be able to keep up with all of us." Commands Cethan, already pulling me towards the door. "Fionn and I can get there faster if we go together and you two follow on."

"I agree. If we split up, the two of us will have enough time." I say. "It's not dark yet and I'm sure Beg will wait for the full moon later tonight. That gives us a good chance to get there first and to stop him. Besides Lugh will be there to help, I am sure of it."

"Well don't just stand there, get going!" Shouts Donal.

CHAPTER FOURTEEN

CONNECTIONS

In this chapter we will be summarising all that has been learnt from the previous ones in a way that combines all the relevant information in order to conclude our quest. If you have not already reached a conclusion about the link between modern science and ancient earth and human energies and seen what the Key is, then you will be able to find the answers to it within the next few pages. The incredible implications behind this link will then be encountered briefly in the epilogue.

One of the first things we looked at was the model of a light cone. This provided the framework with which we could conceptualise our journey through life. The journey we make is, effectively, through space and time. We can imagine ourselves, as a mass in our own right, at the points of the cones in the present position in time. In front of us lies our future cone with all its possible paths open to us. All these paths exist within the quantum world and it is the process of observation in the present, by our external senses, that collapses (or reduces) the quantum world to the classical world. The classical world is only represented in the now of the present.

Our future journey is dictated to us partly by our genes and partly by our experiences. This occurs when we are externally led, by circumstances about us, and by the internal use of our senses, which we term being internally driven. The outcome of a goal that we wish to work towards is thus determined, in part, by the use of our inner senses, which is a form of inner observation. If we use all of these senses with sufficient intensity, as we have seen from the examples of all successful men and women, then we can create the outcome we want and find the path through the future time cone to our aspirations. The only other proviso is in the making of the right preparations and correct planning in order to improve the probabilities. If you are not successful at something, question what it is of these things that you are not fully doing.

Many people have likened the quantum world to the collective unconscious. It is a world where all things appear interconnected and where there are answers to all things. We have even seen the possibility that this quantum world might exist inside our brains. A reductionist approach to consciousness shows us that we can look from the top down and the bottom up to begin to understand the role that our mind plays in creating a specific outcome.

Looking at things from the top down, we can see evidence that communication, both verbal and non-verbal, plays a crucial role in the way we are programmed. Using language in our thoughts we allow belief systems to develop that can ultimately lead to changes in reality. This self-suggestion is taken to even greater extremes with the use of deep level hypnosis. Successful people talk to themselves in a similar way that hypnotist's use all the inner senses at their disposal to confuse and change a mind to the reality they want us to witness. Reality of choice can come about either through individual self-suggestion or through the control of another through this type of hypnosis.

We know that our external senses create our own personal reality and we also know that our internal senses cannot distinguish between what is real and what is not real. However we also know that these inner senses can become our steering mechanism within the quantum world in a way that leads us to the reality of our choice. We have also looked at the possibility that if these inner senses are used with sufficient intensity, then they too can replicate the conditions in the brain that bring about reality.

We have read that a bottom-up approach to consciousness has suggested that this quantum world could exist within the microtubules inside the matrix of our brain. The way these microtubules work suggests that a disturbance of their inner environment causes a collapse to occur. This collapse or reduction would appear to have several possible modes of operation, depending on levels of consciousness. Sufficient disturbance on a large enough scale causes widespread collapse and a full reduction from the quantum to the classical real world. This real world, however, is only real to the observer. We also know that each and every observer creates their own reality (as witnessed by Wigner's friend inside Shroedinger's box). We also know that the way we make our observations also determines the reality we discover. This is seen in the strange phenomena of wave/particle duality and the double slit experiment.

It would therefore appear that we create a very individual path through our journey in space-time. However, using our inner senses to create our own reality could well require an extra model of microtubule action. This has been suggested as self-induced reduction. In all the cases of reduction that have been offered by the scientists, quantum gravity plays a major role in bringing about sufficient disturbance. This is the first stage, and a not unknown stage, of the overall connection and it makes the first part of our link with the mind and modern science.

If quantum gravity is part of one end of the link, then we must remind ourselves just what we know about it that is also relevant. Gravity has been described as the distortion of space-time by mass. Examples of intense cases of distortion are black holes. However, every particle or entity with a mass has its own gravitational field and creates its own field of distortion. The greater the density of the mass; the greater the distortion and the greater the gravity. As we ourselves have a body of mass, we each also have a gravitational field, to a small degree, about us. Considering ourselves at the centre of our time cone model, we would distort our way through the space-time of our journey through life.

Yet we must also remember that very little is known about gravity. It has still yet to be measured. All we can currently measure are the effects of gravity. As one of the four accepted forces in the universe, and one that doesn't seem to fit in with the other three in a way that can yet be agreed upon, it must have a mass that is accelerated. The mass in question is the theoretical graviton particle. Too small to have been measured by any experimental means, it makes quantum gravity highly controversial. Even though however, it is considered by most to exist at the smallest of possible scales (Planck's scale), its existence has yet to be proved beyond any doubt.

If we allow ourselves to consider it plausible to exist as a particle, we can also consider it to behave like a wave. However gravitational wave detectors have also yet to measure a gravity wave. Even scientists searching to put a uniform value on earth's gravity have failed, as there always seem to be discrepancies and variations.

We know gravity is responsible for the movement of celestial objects in a way that is relative to one another and that it provides the framework for the understanding of our classical world. However, we don't know how it interacts with the quantum world. The assumption here is that because we are here and witnessing both, it does and quantum gravity must therefore have some role to play. Quantum field theory has shown us that virtual particles and antiparticles can be created out of the fabric of the vacuum of space itself. Quantum gravity would therefore also exhibit these space time fluctuations and would appear and disappear at rapid speeds as forms of virtual particle/antiparticle pairs. It is these tiny separations of states, down at Planck's scale that has been suggested to be sufficient to induce reduction from the quantum to the classical world. It is this presumed action that creates the disturbance, by reaching a specific threshold related to gravity within the length of the microtubules, that shows us that there is really a strong link between gravity and the way the mind works.

So although we know quantum gravity has an effect, we still know very little about it. It seems to exist within the fabric of space and throughout the whole universe. One thing we do know about gravity, from the evidence surrounding the theories of black holes, is that changes in the density of a mass clearly alter its field position and strength.

In an analysis of the use of our inner senses, with top-down (hypnosis etc.) and bottom-up (microtubule action) explanations, it has been shown that there is a link with the creation of reality. Therefore the inner senses must also, by association, have a link with gravity. Density variations occurring inside the brain, due to changes in blood flow from one region to another when the inner senses are used, could be just sufficient to change gravitational fields and particle directions, spins and positions. Although extremely small, these changes could be sufficient to alter microtubule activity. If microtubule activity is affected then reduction from the quantum world to the classical world would also be affected. Gravity would then appear to have a direct relationship with creating the reality, or the outcome, that we want.

If our inner senses are connected with this unmeasured and relatively unknown force called quantum gravity, then there are similarities that also exist in the way that we use our inner senses, specifically visualising, feeling and thinking, when we wish to interact with the universal energy called ki (chi).

The intensity of using these inner senses has been shown to produce greater and greater effects. In the case of chi gung, amazing feats of healing, inner strength and many other strange realities have been witnessed. In all cases it has been done by individuals who have simply been in touch with what they refer to as the universal energy force and who have focused their inner senses on establishing a new outcome. Of all the possible future paths, they have chosen a particular one in their minds and concentrated on that. When they are successful it is that outcome that occurs.

Students of aikido and the other aforementioned arts use their inner senses to access ki in order to achieve a harmonious interaction with their opponent. They do this as they seek to influence the positive outcome of a conflict in a favourable way for both parties. The more intensely they learn to use their senses, the more able they are to access the universal energy and the easier it is to influence the outcome of their choice because they seem to become more powerful.

In each case ki has a definite link with the use of the inner senses and in a manner that is similar to that of quantum gravity. It seems to me that this makes it reasonable to deduce that they are one and the same.

This last statement requires further exploration. If the two are indeed the same, the first thing that must be said, in the light of all the false connotations that exist in society today, is that the statement that is being made is done so with no intention to denigrate or diminish the complexity, the importance, the reverence or the beauty of the subject. I have tried to point out that from both angles very little is known factually about the subject. Calling it by either one or the other of its names simply provides too many connotations for the mind to cope with initially. It is best thought of as a completely knew name, possibly gi (pronounced jee). That way the subject can be approached from all directions with an open mind.

In all martial arts and many other eastern disciplines gi (G, ki, chi, etc.) is said to stem from a point in the hara. This point is often referred to as the body's centre of gravity. All energy is said to stem from this one point and then, with the use of the inner senses, it is directed or utilised accordingly. The centre of a celestial body, like the earth or the moon, also has a centre of gravity. It is from this point that gravitational waves or gi particles first start to emanate. A mass the size of the sun is sufficient to have a measurable effect, called gravitational lensing, on light. Its gravitational field distorts the space-time surrounding it. We, as human beings, have a body mass that also has a gravitational field. With the air all about us, there is a sufficient density difference between us and the surrounding space to cause a small distortion of space-time.

If you imagine all of us each walking around with tiny distortion fields about us, then every time we interact with other people there is an interaction of these fields of distortion. This is similar to the interaction that is talked about when human auras are supposedly interacting It is quite possible that human gravitational fields cause the auras, or more specifically are the fields themselves. In our time cone model, the mass of the human body causes its own interaction within the space-time matrix in a way that collapses the quantum worlds, of past and future, down into the real classical world of external observations. Our journey being dictated by the way we use our internal senses and/or how we are affected by the experiences around us.

Just as we are at the centre of our own time cone, we also appear to be at the centre of our own universe. Space has been found to continually expand in all directions. In fact wherever we choose to be to make our observations of the universe, it is found that space is expanding out from the position we are in. We always appear to be at the centre. This is just the same as the sayings we find in Eastern philosophies. To access the gi of the universal, as opposed to just the gi from the human body, we are asked to picture ourselves at the centre of the Universe and to reduce it all into one point in the middle of our own centre of gi.

We know now that the universe is forever expanding and this is explained by the concept that there is also an antigravity force as well as the force of gravity. This two-way nature of the same force exists between celestial objects like planets as well as between any particles of mass. The force between the earth and the moon is both attracting and repelling with a continual exchange of virtual graviton particles and anti particles within the space between them. This interaction also has its mirror in Eastern philosophy and is described as the yin and yang of gi. Disciples talk of earth's gi and the heaven's gi as though they continually interact with each other. Human gi, as we walk and move around and just exist, is a further interaction still. Gi is considered the one and the same thing, just differing by its point of origin and how it is utilised.

Dowser and Feng shui priests have sensed the Earth's gi and it exhibits all the expected characteristics of waves and particles that have been emitted from the centre of the Earth. We have seen a close correlation between areas of high ground and these areas of energy. Sometimes they have even appeared to exhibit linear features, but on all occasions they are connected to variations of density. These variations can be due to a variety of reasons like changes in underlying rock type, or geological process, or due to the topography of the land. We know that the density of a mass plays an important role in the amount of the gravitational field that exists around that mass. If we increase the density, or density variation, then we get a stronger field. With this in mind, we can measure density variations over large areas in order to determine the regions where there are low and high gi readings.

This is something Geologists have known about for many years and they conduct gravimetric surveys to determine just these differences. However anyone looking at a gi anomaly map with regards to seeing if it had any positive connection to the position of energy lines would have be extremely disappointed. Geologists use a tool, the gravimeter, principally for assisting in the understanding of the geology beneath the surface. In order to do this they take the raw gi readings and then make adjustments to these readings to enable them to interpret the data for their own benefit. This is commonly known in the trade as using fudge factors! The resulting gi anomaly map shows no similarity to the original actual gi readings.

Gravimeters measure density changes. They are essentially very accurate springs calibrated to measure gi differences rather than field strengths. The readings that are taken are affected by several factors. The position of the moon needs to be taken into consideration, so a time correction is made. A free air correction is made due to the low density of air. A Bouger correction is made to take into consideration average rock densities. A terrain correction is also made. It is only when you look at the raw gi readings, with adjustments made for the position of the moon, that you begin to see how gi variations show a correlation with earth energies. The graph in diagram 8 shows these gi readings in relation to their elevation and over the same area in the south-west of England that we looked at in chapter 12 which was found to have the dowsed energy lines. (Figures were provided courtesy of the British Geological Survey). There is obviously a definite correlation between the two. The higher the elevation; the lower the readings.

This might at first glance give the impression that there is low gi at mountain tops and therefore mean that earth energies really should be found at a low elevation where there are higher readings. However, it must be remembered that gravimeters just measure density variations, in just the same way a dowser would be more sensitive to large variations rather than subtle differences. At mountain tops there is a massive low density region right next to any measuring point and that is due to the vast amount of air on the one side where a valley is. This produces a huge variation of density. The only dense area would be the mountain (or mound, or pyramid) itself. This is where any gi waves or particles would naturally travel and come from. It could be that the shape of the earth's surface assists in producing some areas that emanate streams of

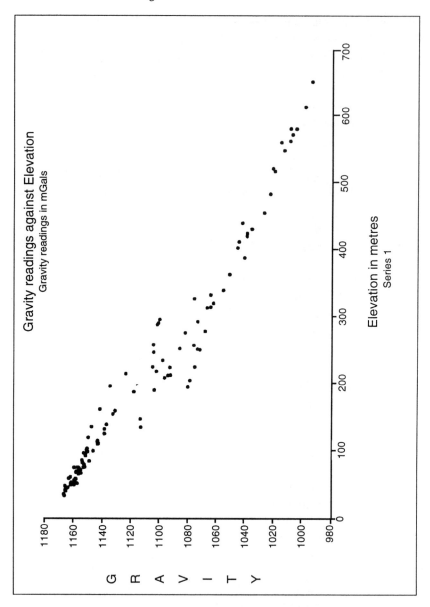

Diagram 8

Data supplied courtesy of the British Geological Survey

directed gi particles and others that emanate a more wave like field (especially if we set out to internally measure/observe one or other of them). Human intervention at these points might allow for a form of inner focusing to tap into particle streams or by harmonising and attuning tap into an awareness of gi's more wave like qualities. Both exercises could therefore produce different benefits and outcomes. The inner focusing and mental projection would be a proactive method of achieving a required reality. The harmonising and tuning into the earth energies, and the collective unconscious of the quantum world, would be a more reactive method and could allow for a form of understanding to enter into the mind. Both mental processes would appear to be integral to achieving a fulfilling life and appear to have their similarities with all the paths that were discussed in chapter two.

In the low elevation areas, where the ground is flat and where you get no great contrast in density variation, you get gi readings that are high. The principle reason is that being nearer to the centre of the earth you get a stronger gi field. However, it is perhaps, not picked up by dowsers as well, because the density variation is not as noticeable there. One other important factor is that the gi waves are emitted from all over the ground area and are only concentrated by density. It is only when a mountain or a man made, high density, object is erected, that the gi waves and particles can become channelled up and out through the mass and enter into a person in a far more directed and particle-like manner. It must also be remembered that at the higher altitudes a person would also be closer to the gi field of passing celestial objects. As the gi between them is essentially one and the same, an enhanced affect could be created.

Diagram 9 shows three situations of ground relief. A particle with a mass will theoretically give out gi in all directions. On flat ground, the predominant gi direction will be upwards away from the earth's centre of gi. Gi will also, to a lesser extent, be emitted in other directions. The result for a person is that they receive gi from several directions at once. This is even more extreme when they are standing in a valley, as in the second example. Here gi will seem to come from more angles and could be described as confused or muddled. On the top of a mound or pyramid a person will only be subjected to gi from one direction. Due to the nature of the topography, other directions of gi particles, if one attunes one's mind to be aware of them, will be away from the body. This results in a pure, directed form of gi, straight from the centre of the earth, entering into a persons mind in an unconfused manner.

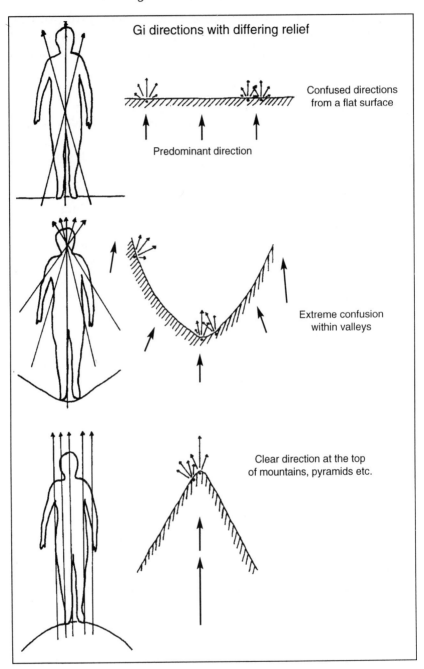

Gi directions with differing relief

Confused directions from a flat surface

Predominant direction

Extreme confusion within valleys

Clear direction at the top of mountains, pyramids etc.

Diagram 9

This could seem to explain why gi appears to be channelled by this type of relief and why it appears to be of such potential use to people wishing to tap into this energy. Gi will also emanate from the earth as waves, but it may well be possible that, by some form of internal observation in our minds, we can detect a stream of gi particles more easily in certain places. These particles might well add some assistance to the way we create our own reality as seen in the models of microtubule action. This altogether enhanced effect could well lead to some interesting consequences! This could increase the chances of some of the more improbable outcomes occurring. By allowing our own Gi energy to become enhanced by the Gi energy from the earth, it may be that own powers of determining which future path we take become more successful.

In other words if we would wish to heal a wound or cure a disease quickly, all that we would have to do is to use all our inner senses, with sufficient intensity and Gi energy, to imagine being healed and cured. Of all the possible future paths in our future time cone, the majority would most probably lead to continued disease and a lasting wound. There would only be a few of the more improbable paths that would lead to a cure. In order to 'collapse' one of the more improbable paths, a greater amount of Gi energy would be required to be directed in that specific direction. Tapping into this greater amount of energy would then be sufficient to disturb the microtubules that were at that time holding that particular quantum future path. With enough directed Gi energy, these microtubules would 'collapse' and bring about the reality that we wanted.

Natural healers are almost certainly doing just that when they cure people of major diseases. I have been fortunate to have worked with Carol Everett, the world's one and only scientifically tested healer. At her clinic in Devon, I was able to interview her and to find and model the strategies she uses to get into the right frame of mind when she heals her clients. Carol was fully tested at Denki University in Tokyo by Professor Yoshio Machi. Under live filming by Fuji T.V. she was wired up to an E.E.G. machine whilst the patient was scanned by thermal imagery. Having never met the patient before (who had just been diagnosed that morning as having a tumour in her ovary) she proceeded to do a blind diagnosis and correctly told the doctors about the tumour. This was done in under three minutes. In the next five minutes she went on to heal the woman. The tumour, visible on the thermal imagery as a red heated area, disappeared. The red area on the scan had returned to a normal blue colour. This occurred back in 1995 and the woman has been fine ever since.

To do this Carol says she first raised her own inner energy levels and then began to tap into the surrounding energies from the environment. Having done that, she then shut off the left hand side of her brain and solely used her right brain to create new images of how she wanted to see her patient. The E.E.G. machine actually showed this occurring with all electrical activity in the right brain hemisphere). This involved creating images of a disease gradually disappearing. Sometimes, Carol talks about 'zapping' problem areas, like tumours, with an imaginary laser gun. For more detailed information the reader ought to visit Carol Everett's Web site.

www.everetthealthcare.com

(There they can also find details on how to order C.D.'s on how to meditate with these higher energies. Having uncovered the strategies that she uses, we were able to produce clear easy instructions that everyone will be able to understand and follow.)

This projection of a healer's inner senses onto the patient (imagining the conditions/reality that are wanted) along with the power of the energies that have been tapped into, must recreate the right microtubule conditions in the brain (the ones with the particular quantum world future path) for the 'collapse' of the one future reality that is desired. This would undoubtedly be a future where the patient had a fully healthy body. The use of the inner senses alone without tapping into the energies to any conscious extent has also been shown to have results.

A young lad in the U.S.A called Garett Porter was only 9 years old when he was diagnosed as having a brain tumour and was given only a few weeks to live. Having been sent home by the doctors, it was reckoned to be futile to continue on his medication. On the advice of a councillor called Pat Norris, Garett was told to try some visualization. At that time the new Star Wars movie had just come out and Garett was a big fan. Using the analogy, he set about his own nightly battles in his mind. He strongly associated his tumour with the enemy and set about with every imaginary mission to shoot down all the enemy spaceships. Every night he won his battle and after a few weeks he imagined bringing out his forces for his usual battle only to find that he couldn't find the enemy anywhere. A hospital check the next day found no trace of the tumour except some small calcification. Over thirty years old today he has had no more tumours. His internalization of his problem followed by intense visualization led to creating a new reality for himself. This visual process is very similar to that which healers undertake with their patients. It can take them far less time to get the results that they want presumably because they can tap into the universal gi energy and collapse the right groups of microtubules more quickly.

To get really powerful results, known healers could work at energy high points at times of planetary conjunctions. These extra energies might well ensure a greater level of success at collapsing the desired future quantum world path. One of Carol Everett's strength's is that she seems to be able to tap into this gi energy far more effectively than most other people. Although she can heal people wherever she goes, one interesting factor is that she lives right on top of the St.Mary Energy line. There have been many incidences of her healing people over in the U.S.A whilst still being at home. Distance is not an obstruction, but then the concept of non-locality, an important part of the process, also does not find distance a problem.

We know that quantum gravity has a strong link with the mind and the use of the inner senses. We have also discovered that the inner senses have a strong connection when it comes to tapping into and utilizing these 'Energies'. It would also appear then, that there is now strong evidence of a more direct connection between gravity and earth energies in that they both have a good correlation with relative high ground. Other researchers in the past have observed similar phenomenon. However due to the vast amount of data procured from a variety of sources, the majority of people have probably overlooked this point. Pierre Mereaux-Targuy, a Belgium researcher, looked at gravity readings at Carnac in North-West France. Carnac is known to for its many standing stones all of which are roughly aligned in a South-West to North-East direction. What fewer people know is that it is also situated on granite, the same type of dense rock found in the South West of England. Whilst taking Gi reading's across the area, he found that along the alignments there was a 'precise frontier' where there was a slight negative gi variation from a positive one.

Even with this and all the other clues that have been shown in order to show this link, we are still unable to provide tangible scientific proof. However, the theory of quantum gravity itself also still has some way to go before it is widely accepted and substantiated. Due to the supposed size of graviton particles, it is only likely that they could ever be proved theoretically not to exist and, as such, this link could be considered in a similar manner. In the meantime there are many tests that could be done that will help add extra evidence to show that the link is likely to be correct. These would include tests in near zero gi environments as well as comparative tests on mountaintops at times of planetary conjunctions. More will be suggested in the last chapter, which goes on to discuss the implications behind the concept of gi, both for the individual and for large groups of people.

At this stage some people might well be asking what about all the related electromagnetic phenomena that have been sometimes witnessed to be in association with these energies. An explanation for this potential misunderstanding needs to be put forward. Firstly science knows a great deal more about measuring electromagnetism and has developed many devices that can record it in all its variations on an extremely accurate basis. The fact is that there are many occasions when scientific analysis fails to measure the phenomena associated with these energies. To be conclusively connected to electromagnetism, one of the four known forces in the universe, it would need to be able to be measured on all occasions. It is for this reason that I believe that this gi energy is not related to the electromagnetic force in a direct way. However, I believe that there could be an indirect connection that results in occasionally showing electromagnetic movement. It may be that the wavelengths that the gi particles/waves operate on could occasionally, operate on some sort of similar basal beat frequency, and therefore have an influence over the larger photon particles/waves. An example would be the measurable electromagnetic field found around the human body. Many people have gone on to say that this is the beginning of the human aura. However it is not entirely impossible to envisage that measurable effect being due to the gi field that the body emits due to its mass. The gi particles/waves might, in some way, vibrate on a similar underlying resonant frequency and cause measurable disturbances on an electromagnetic level. This is what is then detectable.

The epilogue at the end of the book goes on to look at some of the amazing possibilities that could arise, and probably have already risen, for individuals and groups of individuals that have learnt to tap into these energies.

CHAPTER FIFTEEN

A SUCCESSFUL SACRIFICE

We set off at a steady pace running side by side. To walk this same distance to Invercarrie would take a quarterday, at the rate we were going we'd be there in a third of the time. Sunlight would be gone by the time we arrived, but the full moon, now already fully visible in the sky, would be more than enough to guide us. The question on my mind though, was when it would be high enough in the night sky for Callum Beg. As soon as it came into view from inside the Aes Dana, he would begin his sacrificial slaughters. My stride lengthened.

"Easy brother." Calls Cethan, "We'll not make it at all if we go too fast."

"You're right," I reply breathing easily still, yet easing back a little.

Neither of us wanted to continue talking, our minds on things to come as well as times gone by. Running next to Cethan like this, reminded me of when we were boys. We often used to go on long runs together, generally over to Lairg where there were more friends our age. He had always been faster than me, being the eldest, but on the longer runs it was more equal. We hardly ever talked then. We just seemed to sense each other's needs and thoughts. We ran with deep easy breathing, our minds often somewhere else and oblivious to our surroundings.

It was like that now and I settled into an easy rhythm and soon found a similar state of mind to one I had so often practiced attaining with Lugh. Resisting the urge to leave my body out of curiosity, I concentrated on calming my mind in anticipation of events to come.

Half way there, and not yet feeling tired, a voice came into my head. It was Lugh. 'Fionn.' He began, 'I am listening,' I reply at the same time, 'There's little time left', 'I know, where are you?', 'At a sacred mound in an ancient part of the Glencannick forest. Listen carefully to what I am about to say', 'Go on', 'I have found out exactly what Beg is up to. It goes far beyond just being king. His powers tonight will be forever increased if he is allowed to succeed', 'How?', 'The answer to that will take too long and must be for another time, all I can say now is that as the moon gets higher in the sky tonight, so you will find his powers increase. I will stall things for as long as I can from where I am, but I am limited to what I can do from here. You must reach him and interrupt his ceremonies for long enough for the moon to pass', 'When do they start?', 'They're beginning now. When you get there, contact me, you'll need my help getting in. Good luck and hurry.'

He was gone as abruptly as he had first entered my head. I ran on carefully thinking about his words and then how to tell Cethan I had just had a long distance conversation with Lugh in my mind.

A few hundred paces further on, I told him. I could sense it was hard for him to take it all in, especially me being his younger brother. However, he also knew I had no reason to lie. It gradually dawned on me that his previous words to Igrainne, about me turning her into a toad, was something he believed I might actually be able to do. I let the thought go. Explanations at time like these, to people who have yet to experience different ways in life, are of little help and generally add to the confusion and create rifts. It was far better not to tell people about new things, but rather let them find out for themselves in their own way and in their own time and as a result of careful questioning. I resolved to take time to talk to him after this was over. It was a long time since we had last chatted and I let my mind wander back to then as I continued to run.

The sun was just going down over the horizon as we reached the earthen embankment that surrounded Invercarrie. As we neared the North gate, we could see the lonely figure of Dugald huddled next to the doorway of a nearby croft.

"Dugald," I cry out, still not out of breath and continuing to inhale deeply through my nose. "How come you're out here?" We run up to him and greet him by shaking our forearms.

"Fionn. Cethan. It's good to see you again, and all in one piece. How did you all fare back there?" He looks at us anxiously, rubbing his hands together to keep them warm.

"Good and not good." Answers Cethan firmly, "We're all fine, my father is avenged but there was no sign of the women. How are things in there?" He nods his head toward the gates.

"Not good. I still haven't found Angus. I can't even get into the Aes Dana, it's locked and barred from the inside, I couldn't even get to speak to anyone inside." Dougal answers looking down at his feet and shows his frustration by kicking the dirt under him. As if it was a sign, we all start ambling over toward the gates whilst continuing to talk.

"There's little time left," I state urgently, "Beg's started his ceremony, we've got to get in somehow. What else can you tell us?"

"The only other thing that's strange is that there is no gate watch tonight. There are no guards visible anywhere and the word is out to stay inside and ignore any strange sounds."

"That's fine by me," calls out Cethan now striding ahead, "it makes our task easier without any bystanders getting in the way."

We walked faster to catch up with him and soon we were all running again. The North gate was open and the muddy track through to the centre was eerily quiet. Our feet squelched in the mud from old puddles as we ran past the Selkie inn. At least there were some familiar sounds coming from within there. Moments later we were in front of the main doors of the Aes Dana where we could hear a muffled drum beat coming from within. Flashes of the past again rushed into my head with the many experiences of standing there. My recollections instantly ceased when Cethan began banging on the door with his fists.

"That won't do any good." Exclaims Dugald calmly, reaching up and touching Cethan's shoulder as he spoke.

"The roof." Cries out Cethan, looking up. "Quick. Give me a leg up Fionn."

I cupped my hands and he stepped up and on to my shoulders. At that height, he was just able to grab onto the wood and reed roof. Climbing up, he turned and beckoned to me to follow. I looked round at Dugald, who nodded and cupped his hands as well. In next to no time I was up on the roof with him and now crawling up the slight incline and over to the large gap in the centre. Looking up we saw that the moon was already half way up the night sky, but not yet shining straight down through into the open area below. We still had some time.

Lying flat against the roof, we strained our necks to look down over the edge. Even before we could see anything, we could hear the steady beat of a drum and the sound of a resonant human chant. The musky smell of animals mixed with the burning of incense greeted us just before we caught sight of them. Below us, with a drop a little more than the height of three men, Callum Beg was presiding over a ceremony of gigantic proportions. A circle of fires in small, low braziers surrounded the central altar stone. In full costume, nine Ollamphs stood around the fires, each one in a trance-like state and deep in meditative word-song. Opposite and further inside in a hastily erected wooden animal pen were three bulls covered in red and blue paint. Each one had obviously been carefully prepared for ritual sacrifice. In amidst of all of it, and what caught our immediate attention, was the sight of Mairi and Niamh. They had both been tied face down onto the slanting stone slab with their heads hanging over the lower end. Beg had stripped them naked and had blood-marked a strange round symbol on their backs. He was standing with arms aloft, to the side of the altar with his back to us. In one of his red-stained hands there was a jewelled dirk that sparkled from the light of the fires.

A scream from one of the girls quickly brought us round from our numbed senses. Transfixed as we had been by the scene we had witnessed, we pulled back and I whispered to Cethan.

"I have to get in." I start, "I'm going to contact Lugh. He said he could unlock the doors for us. I'll call you when they are open, in the meantime stay here. You may need to distract Beg at the last minute."

"What do you suggest my good brother, a quick lorica?" He whispers in a husky voice not short of a little sarcasm.

"You'll think of something." I smile back at him, "Just be careful and don't do anything foolish like jumping down from this height."

I crept back to the edge of the roof and lowered myself down. Standing away from the door and in some shadows, I tried to speak with Lugh. Dugald stood guard. I called several times using all the force I could muster from within me. Strangely, I could get no direct response from him, but I suddenly had the sensation that he had done something to help and that it was now possible for us to enter.

"It's open." Dugald calls, arousing me from my thoughts. "Quick, let's go!" He continues more urgently as I get to my feet.

At that same moment a monumental scream cut through the air, followed by several others quite obviously from different sources.

"What's happening?" I shout up at Cethan. There was no answer until, moments later, I see his stocky form appear from above and jump down next to me. I look at him expectantly.

"It was Beg." He gasps out, beginning to run inside behind Dugald. "He was about to cut Mairi open. I threw my Ochie Dhu at him and at the same time all hell was let loose, everything went mad."

"What? What do you mean?" I call out, now right next to him.

"See for you'self brother." He replies barging with the full force of his shoulder at the door in front of him.

He bounces off back towards us, winded from the unforgiving solidness of the ash doors. Dugald reaches forward and takes hold of the handle.

"They open towards us." He says with half smile, half grimace, "They're the only ones here that do." His words were then drowned by further screams mixed with the bellowing of agitated cattle, all coming from the inside.

Cethan and I draw our swords and with a brief glance at each other followed by a nod, we charge in as Dugald opens the door.

Inside was mayhem. Our sudden entrance caused no impact whatsoever. The circle-of-nine were gripping each other's hands in an attempt not to break their ring. About them and in and out of the massive megaliths flew three wailing phantasms, ghost-like apparitions screaming in an excruciatingly painful high pitch. Beg stood struggling in the middle with some unknown force that seemed to be trying to take possession of his body. The two women, who could now see us, cried out for help. The three bulls strained at their leashes in the pens, kicking and bucking in an effort to escape. The fires now raged high and out of control, their flames licking out in all directions by a swirling wind that swept all around the room. In the midst of all this, I could just begin to see the top of the full moon beginning to appear from over the top of the roof. There was no time left and nothing else to do but to charge forward in attack.

One of the phantasms immediately spied us and darted our way. What at first appeared to be a face filled with horror, turned into something that stirred deep in my memory. An unrecalled, yet strangely familiar, smile appeared briefly as it flew towards us then swung around and away back to the Ollamphs. Startled and a little confused I continued my run, but now some two strides behind Cethan.

The force of our attack crashed through the circle of hands, assisted by the severing of an arm caused by Cethan's initial downward slicing blade. As soon as their circle broke, so was their trance and whatever power they had been able to harness. In complete disarray and fear filling them fast due to their sudden change of fortunes, they fled. Cethan charged after them shouting and cahouting and waving his sword above his head. Like sheep harried by a wolf, they scattered and ran towards the rooms that led off to the side. I watched them begin to disappear inside along with Cethan striking at them from behind. It was then that I noticed Dugald pull one of them away from the others. It looked like Angus.

Putting aside my shock for the moment, I ran up to the altar stone. Beg was still locked in a devilish combat that seemed to hold his total concentration, so I began to hack away at the ropes that bound the women. But before I had managed to undo any, I was distracted by a mighty crash. The bulls had broken out of their pens. Freed at last to make their escape they stampeded off in all directions. The phantasms, now having lost their human quarry, turned their attentions onto Beg. One of the bulls then careered past the fires towards me and I jumped and clambered over the altar stone to avoid a goring. In doing so I tumbled over the women and fell head first down the other side. Drawing myself up into a crouched position, I glanced around to find I was right next to Beg. A faint shimmer of light outlined a body next to him. Peering more carefully at the wrestling form, I found that I could just make out a face. It was Lugh. Somehow, it was him fighting with Beg. A movement out of the corner of my eye distracted me and I turned my attention back to the women.

As soon as I did, my heart and hand froze. Opposite me was the uncowled figure of Fiacal. His hideous features, now fully visible in the flickering light of the fires, wrinkled into a malicious grin as he pressed the point of a long dirk into Niamh's neck. I raised my outstretched arm from behind me into his view. In it was the sword I'd dug up from under the Dolmen and it was ready to swing.

"Touch that woman further and you'll lose your head." I warn menacingly. He answers with a smile and slight extra pressure that causes Niamh to cry out in pain. "Why take the chance?" I call out louder, "Surely a man of your supposed skills could take me first, then go back to them." I challenge, rising up to my full height and counting heavily on his pride not to back down from my offer.

"It would be my pleasure to oblige you." He spits back and as swiftly as he draws his blade back from Niamh another appears in his left hand. He steps away from the altar stone allowing me the space to come round in front of him. Slowly we circle each other with my sword out in front and only half a pace from his face. Showing no fear, he casually plays with his weapons, proficiently spinning them between his fingers. I back away between the fires into the larger space behind, remembering Conal Brus's earlier warnings about this man and his skills with knives.

"Why are you even here?" I growl out teeth clenched and admitting my curiosity.

"You haven't found that out yet?" He seems surprised, "Did it ne'er strike you as strange that I was on the boat the first time we met?" He jeers condescendingly. "Why would I have put myself through such torment had it not been for some higher purpose?"

"I thought it was the late 'Dubh' who was in liege with Beg, what benefit do you get by being second to that hell spawn?" I taunt.

"So you managed to kill Domnhuill, did you? He was getting careless anyway." He shrugs, "It appears I have something to thank you for after all. I offer my sincere gratitude to you for carrying out that act of mercy, it will save me much time and trouble and will make our plans even easier." He mocks, going down into a half bow.

"Our plans?" I repeat, still slowly circling and backing towards the nearest open door, which happens to be Callum Beg's antechamber. "What makes you think Beg considers you important enough to be included in his plans?" I utter as convincingly as possible, now beginning to calm my mind.

"That you'll ne'er know." He lunges at me, testing my reactions. I nimbly sidestep his thrust without making the mistake of attacking him straight back with my sword.

"Oblige me." I go on, "What matter is it now if you're so sure you'll kill me?" He lunges again, but this time feints and drops his shoulder waiting for me to make a move. I feign surprise and shock and begin to back off, this time starting purposely to circle him again. His confidence rising, he answers, now with his back to the open door.

"It was in the 'roll of the woods' that someone would come to the mainland after the attack on your Broch. We had to know who and what threat you posed. You see Callum and I are..." He attacks again, cutting himself off mid speech.

With the empty antechamber behind him, I was now prepared and ready for his attack. As he came forward, I mentally drew him fully into me and at the last moment let out an inner shout. With the full force of the power of the universe, combined with the force of his attack, his whole body flew backwards in the face of such a verbal and physical onslaught. Five paces away, he landed dazed and in a heap on the stone floor. Moving quickly, I slammed the door shut and slid the wooden bar across the slots. There was no way out except through Beg's own private chamber. I ran over to check the door. It was bolted. I wondered briefly what he was going to say and found myself wishing I had waited a little longer, but perhaps that was what he wanted.

My heart now pounding rapidly, I turned towards the women still tied down. At the same moment an urgent voice entered my head, 'Fionn, I have done all I can. I can go on no longer. Remember well. Goodbye.' and with those final thoughts came a warm flood of kind emotions and then nothing.

Feeling warmed but suddenly alone, I wondered where Cethan had got to but was interrupted by another scream and the sight of Beg raising his dirk again high in the air above the naked women. The full moon now shone fully through the large open roof and its rays glinted off his long metal blade. I could see the three phantasms spiralling around his body and arms in a vain attempt to arrest his downward thrust, but they were no match for the man as he now stood glazed in moonlight.

I ran forward having to leap through the flames of one fire in order to dodge a rampant bull, reaching Beg just in time for me to witness him dismiss the wailing trio like they were just a minor irritant. In less than a cow's flick of a tail, I was up and next to him, my sword raised and ready to pierce his neck. Armed with only a sacrificial dirk and with me now being in between him and his prey, he backed off. His first look of pure hatred on seeing me, soon turned to one of intense concentration. A burning sensation began to grow in the back of my head and the fires around me seemed to grow in size. Realising his game, I stopped fighting him in my mind and welcomed his power into my inner self. This, along with a few tricks that Lugh had taught me, soon took all the power out of his attack on my mind.

The burning ceased but was instantly replaced with the flickering illusion of three images of Beg, each identical and doing the same thing.

I sliced across each image in turn with my sword, advancing all the way in the face of my now three retreating foes. Out of the corner of my eye, I could see Dugald deep in conversation with Angus and holding him firmly by the shoulders. I shouted at them to help and I was relieved to see them both turn their heads towards me.

Beg continued to back away from me, heading for his chamber. With every step I came nearer to him, I felt his awesome power exude outwards from all over his body. His black robes swirled about him in a way that added to the visual confusion he was trying to plant in my head. The three images merged and parted with every twist and turn of his body as he sought to avoid my blade and escape me.

His shoulders were now against his door and he fumbled behind himself to undo the bolt. Sensing victory, I thrust forward only to miss as we both fell into his room. We rolled away from each other, both knowing the dangers of close hand-to-hand fighting on a floor, especially as he still had his dirk. As I stood up and faced him, I began to recognise the room. Unwanted memories flashed up before me and focusing on anything began to be an impossible effort.

"Do you remember when we were last here together?" He asks, with a vocal manner that was now growing in confidence. My mind began to swirl as it had done once before. I fought to regain control. There was nothing I could do, some deep rooted, implanted command held me transfixed and under his control.

"You will feel better if you get up on the bench." He orders. I comply unwillingly but powerless to resist. "Lie down and put down your weapon." Again I fight it, "The more you fight me; the harder it is for you to resist." He adds sensing my rising inner turmoil and turning it to his own benefit. He comes round to one side and the dirk appears from out of his sleeve as if by magic.

I try to relax, the opposite of what he would expect. Maybe that would allow me time to break his hold on me. A loud noise followed by several shouts came from out in the main hall. Thankfully it halts Callum Beg. I can hear Conal Brus arrive and with him Cethan. Now Dugald and Angus are talking with them.

Beg looks down at me and then out through the door. He then looks back at me. "You may think you've won this time, but I've not lost." He hisses, walking over to the connecting door, "By the time I've finished, you won't be able to walk the land in safety and I'll have what I want by then. There are many other times. Goodbye for now young Fionn. Believe me when I say our paths will cross again... and soon I hope." With that he disappears and shuts the door behind him.

I struggle to get up but something was not yet fully functioning and all I can do is lift my head. I shout out and within moments Cethan, Angus and Dugald are standing next to me.

"Through there!" I shout again in desperation, still unable to regain fully all my movement. "Quickly follow him."

They turn away and Cethan heads as fast as he can for the door. "It's locked!" He calls out, "Are you sure he went this way?"

"There's no other way out." I reply with rising urgency, "He must have locked it from the other side. You can get in from the main hall. He has to be stopped Cethan, Get him!"

At that Cethan took off and went round to the other entrance, where I had shut Fiacal in. I called after him to watch out but I doubted that he heard. That sudden emotional outburst broke me free from my invisible bonds and I managed to sit up. Together, with a hand under each of my shoulders, Dugald and Angus helped me off the bench. I take a moment to stretch some life back into my body concentrating on each limb in turn. Once I knew I was fine, I looked at them both and smiled.

"Are you with us again Angus?" I ask, slightly cheekily, and now heading for the door. "For a moment there you had me worried." I finish with a big grin as I pass him eager to follow after Cethan.

"Aye, I am lad. Just like you were a while ago, I too was under Beg's spell." He responds in a quick-witted way.

I stepped out into the main hall to see both Niamh and Mairi hugging Conal Brus. As soon as they saw me, they came running over as best they could without tripping up over the drapes that they had found and thrown hastily about themselves.

"Fionn." They both say together throwing their arms around me and holding me tightly. "By the Dagda you are alright." Continues Mairi, who then pulls back to look at me leaving me with Niamh. Tears start to flow freely down both their faces and I reach down and wipe Niamh's cheeks with the back of my finger. I stop and pull back aware of Conal's presence and his gaze.

"Come we must be off," interrupts Conal, releasing a brief smile at me before looking about the room in continued state of awareness.

"There's no one in there," calls out Cethan, having run back out of the ante chamber, "and there is no other way out." He continues, now looking to me for any more information.

"Are you sure?" I question, disregarding his inquiring gaze.

"Of course I'm sure Fionn." He answers brusquely. "I've searched everywhere and I'm telling you there's no one there. If anyone did go in, they must have used magic to escape!" I move quickly over to the door and look in, only to discover the place empty as well.

"We have to go now before they regroup and come back with help." Urges Conal again. "Dugald. Angus where are you?" He calls.

"We're searching Beg's room." Dugald answers, appearing in the doorway. "There must be some clue as to what he's up to in here."

"You'll have to leave it. We've got to get the girls out and to safety." Conal shouts now more forcibly and taking hold of my shoulder to gain my co-operation.

"He's right," I add loudly, "We'd best get out. We've done what we set out to do, so let's get out while we're still ahead. Besides I don't trust Beg a bit, he could even still be here planning his own return attack."

"Right let's go." Agrees Cethan, turning toward the main entrance.

The seven of us began to leave, stopping only to pick up our personal belongings lest they be used as some sort of evidence against us. We didn't want to leave anything behind that might connect us to this night. The ceremony tomorrow had to go ahead as though nothing had happened.

With all the noises we felt that it wouldn't be long before the guards came looking. Our best course of action was to hide. Escaping the town now could attract attention, so we decided to risk our chances in the morning after staying a night at the palace.

As we got back to the main outer doors we ran into a very tired looking Donal. After a few hurried embraces, and refusing to be assisted, he led us all across the bridge toward the small, stone built central dun that was Queen Irnan's palace. Using a pre-agreed password we were all allowed in.

We were ushered in by a thin little man and led into a small paved stone courtyard that was surrounded by white wattle walls. There was a large, deep central pond in the middle and each wall had a slatted door in the middle except the one ahead of us where three steps led up to a large open entrance. In front of that there were several carved, upright tree trunks supporting an ornate wooden balcony. The thatched roof glowed a blue-grey colour under the rising moon that was also throwing long moonshadows behind the pillars. It felt like a strange eerie calm had descended amongst us.

We were led up the steps in silence and in a slow deliberate manner as though we had been expected. Inside the main chamber there were hundreds of other vertical timbers, many only an arm span away from each other. The lone courtier that had bidden us follow him, weaved his way about them with the help of a single flickering candle. At the far end of the room was a shrine to Danu, the mother of all the gods. A large stone was carved with a figure of her with her followers all around making offerings. Two large incense candles were burning at either end of the stone. Flickering shadows darted amongst the nearer pillars adding to the solemn mood of the temple.

"It is too late for an audience." He says turning to us, his face illuminated from below in a way that accentuated some unfortunate facial features. "Queen Irnan has retired already but she bade me welcome you and offer you these secret quarters for the night. You'll understand that she wishes to be seen to be impartial until her son becomes King. That is why you are not being offered more gracious accommodation. However, you will be warm and dry in here." He points to a small door in the wall in the corner of the room.

"I am also to tell you that she would prefer it if you were to leave as secretly as possible as soon as you rise in the morning. She apologises for this but requests your attendance at the private celebrations here tomorrow afternoon when there will be a large feast to celebrate Samhain and the coronation. She says she will be delighted to entertain you all then." He finishes his instructions in the same monotonous voice that he began them and then turns and walks off.

"Well I am impressed with all this Donal." Jokes Conal, "You must have made an amazing impression on the Queen to warrant quarters like this." He laughs.

"Enough of your rubbish Conal." Replies Donal, half shoving Conal in the shoulder in the direction of the door. "It's a safe place to lie down for the night and right now I doubt there are many of those around these parts for the likes of us right now."

We duck our heads and enter. The place is tiny and room only for six people at the most. However, the floor is covered with woollen palliasses and furs and there is a lit candle on a small corner shelf.

"How by Demne's name can we all fit in here?" Cries out Donal, as soon as he sees it. We all look at him and then burst into laughter. Sheer elation at our success and survival rushes out of us and uses up all our final reserves of energy. Shattered, we take off our boots and sit down leaning against the walls.

After several moments of silence, I suggested we discuss our plans for tomorrow. The Samhain celebrations would start first thing and the streets would be busy. Moving around without being seen with all the people in the market square would be no problem. The trouble was when to stay and when to go. Dugald and Angus had decided to stay for the time being. Donal felt honour bound to repay the Queen's hospitality by staying until her son Bran was crowned. Conal, Niamh and Mairi quite understandably wanted to leave straightaway. That left me. Now everything seemed to be over, or at least resolved for the moment in our favour, I was left wondering again where my own future lay.

I had become an Anruth and with the training I'd received from Lugh... Lugh, I'd forgotten about him in all that had been going on. I immediately set about contacting him with my mind. There were enough energies around me so I mentally called out for him. There was no answer. I began to worry. Even though not being able to contact someone wasn't necessarily bad, as they might well be just asleep, I was concerned with the memory of his last words. Remembering them now, they seemed to have a tone of finality to them. I decided to try to find the mound in the forest where he had said he was going and to do that as soon as the others were asleep.

After much discussion, we agreed to split up, but only after we'd had an early meal at Leag's inn. Dugald and Angus would then stay behind and join the parade with the other Ollamphs and Donal and I would stay long enough to hear Bran announced as the King. We would then take the currach, all being well, and join up with the party down the coast at Comrie. The others would leave straight after they had eaten and go south to take the waiting horses. There was still much we wanted to talk to about to each other, but it was getting late and some of us were more tired than others.

All of us lying down made it a tight fit and in doing so all our shoulders were touching. Niamh had cunningly manoeuvered herself next to me. It had gone unnoticed by everyone except Mairi who gave her a impish glance followed by a mischievous grin that was directed at me. I was obviously more than glad and a little flattered, but it was tinged with a degree of embarrassment due to the proximity of Donal, Conal Brus and Cethan, all of whom would have been quite open to a bit of teasing if they had been more aware.

With the candle left burning, we settled down to a cramped night under the furs. I lay flat on my back looking straight up, fully aware that my favourite initial sleeping position was on my left side. Niamh lay on her right, facing me. We were all silent and still until someone at the end of the line stirred and turned, this left the person next to them more uncomfortable. They then turned and soon, I too, found I had to turn. I resisted the temptation but in the end it became too great and I found myself face to face with Niamh. She immediately smiled. Our faces were so close that our noses nearly touched and her smile was so instantly infectious and warming that I couldn't resist smiling back at her.

A snore from Donal interrupted our moment of joy and our smiles grew to near laughter. She slid a bare arm out from under her furs and touched me tenderly on my cheek, sliding the backs of her fingers down and around the stubble on my chin. Without thought, I opened my mouth and lightly bit them as they passed. Her warmth inside me was intoxicating. She half sighed and half moaned as the tip of my tongue tickled the end of her longest finger. My heart pounded so loud I thought it would keep the others awake.

I raised up my free arm quietly and slowly and touched her on her face as well. It was wonderfully smooth, more so than anything I could remember. As she kissed my finger and sucked it inside her mouth, I drew my knees instinctively up to my chest. Thoughts of seeing her naked upon the altar only a short time ago flashed through my head and I was shocked at the feelings that welled up within me.

We lay like that for what seemed like ages. I tried to sense what thoughts she was having but it was to no avail and after sleep began to show in her eyes, I raised my fingers and closed her eyelids gently.

Sleep would have come easily then with our hands held together out of sight under the furs, but I had other things on my mind as well. After a good while, I steeled my way out from under my covers and crept barefoot out of the room.

I made my way through the temple back to the courtyard and was happy to find that the moon was still visible. Only the sounds of the night disturbed the tranquility. I knelt under the balcony opposite the pond and began to seek my now familiar state for travels in my mind. I soon found myself able to drift up and out over Invercarrie. For a place where a large number of people dwelt, it was strange to hear it so silent. Nevertheless, I continued North, resisting the temptation to look inside the Aes Dana. It wasn't long before I found the sacred mound hidden in the Glencannick Forest. I searched everywhere, calling as well, but found and heard nothing. There was some small evidence that he had been there, but that was all. I had no idea what to expect and began to feel a little despair. As soon as I did, my form began to fade and wander away from my control. Knowing of the dangers, I changed my thoughts to ones that were more positive. If there was no sign of Lugh, then that would be good news. He had obviously returned to his body and then left to go on to other things. I wished him well in my mind and left myself with the expectation that I would see him again.

I returned faster than I had intended and realised why when I saw someone talking to me.

"I'm sorry, I didn't mean to disturb you." Says a young voice to my side.

"That's nay a problem lad." I reply, "I'm Fionn." I start getting to my feet and hold out my arm in friendship.

"You looked so peaceful just kneeling there." He takes my arm with his in a firm clasp of greeting, "I was only watching for a short while. What were you doing?" He asks.

"It was just a form of deep thinking." I reply again, a little lost for words as I didn't yet know whom I was addressing. All I could see was a medium sized, slightly lanky individual with neatly tied back dark hair.

"I'm sorry, my name is Bran." He says seeing my disquiet, "I forget that some people might not know who I am."

"Bran. Please excuse me. " I dip my head in quick deference, "I didn't know. I'm from the Islands." I reply rather feebly.

"Yes I know. My mother's told me all about you." He smiles warmly back at me.

"Really." I reply slightly startled that I'd been talked about by the queen.

"I couldn't sleep because of tomorrow," he goes on, "that's when I came out for a walk and found you. Mother says you've all come here to find your sister and her friend."

"That's right." I say unsure yet how much to expand on the answer.

"How did you fare?" He asks, turning from looking up at the stars.

I look down at the pool, wondering how much to tell him and slowly walk down the steps to be closer to its still waters. He follows and for a while we walk around in silence.

"We found them at the Aes Dana." I pause, "They were about to be sacrificed along with the bulls by Callum Beg." I end accusingly.

"What? Why would he do that?" He remarks, sounding honestly shocked. He stops and faces me squarely.

"So you've not heard the real story about Beg?" I state, and not expecting a reply I continue, "He may appear kind and helpful on the outside, however he's quite the opposite on the inside. Have you never sensed that yourself?" I ask, more than slightly interested in how he would reply.

He ponders my question for a while and then answers, "Sometimes, I've heard him shouting when I've been over there and there was one time recently when he was in such a rage he didn't even come out to see me."

"Well. My advice to you is to watch yourself when he's around. There was a time not long ago when he wanted to be King himself."

"I can't believe that, not old Callum. He's always hated being in charge when I was young." He refutes in a falteringly assured way.

"Listen Bran. Tomorrow, you're going to be crowned King, by virtue of your father. Just be mindful of my words and of Beg's power. He controls all the Ollamphs at the Aes Dana and has objectives of his own that are too evil to even consider. If you find you need to talk to someone you can trust, find my friends Angus or Dugald. They might be able to help you." I advise.

"What about you. Couldn't you help?" He suggests tentatively.

"Aye, I might be able to but my work here is done and tomorrow I'll be going away for a while. I need to get away and start my new life as a Seannachie." I reply.

"I'm sorry to hear that Fionn. I would have liked to get to know you better and to hear some of your stories as well." His lips tighten together.

"I'd be happy to another time, if you still remember me when you're King." I grin at him. "You'd better get some sleep though if you're going to get through all the festivities tomorrow." I add.

"You're right," he replies, "and thanks, thanks for the warning. You seem like someone I could trust, and I'm sorry there's no more time before you go." He turns and heads back inside.

"There is plenty of time in the future." I say, turning and walking with him for a short way with my hand on his back below his neck. I then let him continue on his own as I needed time to reflect on things.

As he disappeared off into the darkness, I wondered what the years would bring for him. He looked very young for someone who was just about to shoulder a vast amount of responsibility. However, I thought, we all had to start somewhere and we all make mistakes along the way. I imagined though, that he'd be someone who could learn from them.

I returned to my knees to continue my meditation. I still wanted to review the day's events over again in my mind and to rehearse mentally the plans for tomorrow before I went back to my own sleep.

It was not to be. Just after I had knelt down again, Dugald and Angus came out and tapped me on the shoulder.

"Dugald, Angus. You should be asleep. Tomorrow's a big day for the two of you." I scold lightly.

"You're right." Replies Dugald. "But we need to talk if you're leaving and there won't be time or any secrecy tomorrow." They both kneel down next to me.

"What we need to do first is to pool all our knowledge about Beg." Starts Angus, in a hushed voice.

"He's going to be even more dangerous now he knows some of us are on to him and we need to develop some way of handling him."

We went over all the things that had happened to each of us. I spoke of my time with Lugh and what we had learnt and seen together and Angus retold what he could remember of his time with the other Ollamphs leading up to the sacrifice. Afterwards I detected an awe about them in the way that they looked at me.

"Why are you both looking at me in a strange way like that?" I ask eventually.

"We're sorry," replies Angus, "it's just that you talk about your time with Lugh as though it was all so normal. I don't think you quite realise how special it really was. Lugh has for years and years been some kind of mystical, all knowing person in many people's minds. He's now become a man of legends. If I hadn't met him myself, I'd even have trouble believing he existed."

"I'm sorry," I apologise, "I didn't mean to make it sound so matter of fact. It's just that I'm telling you all of this as quickly as possible. You're right it was an amazing experience and I feel very lucky to have had him help me."

"What's also amazing is your account of the Otherworld being a real place," interrupts Dugald, "and that Callum Beg first met Lugh over there. It's all a little much for me." He shakes his head, whilst twiddling his fingers through his beard.

"If Beg has been over there, then we need to find out what it was he learned and what it is that he is working towards now." Ponders Angus talking his thoughts out loud.

We continue talking until well after the moon had gone down over the horizon, only then had we decided what our next moves would be. The first thing was to teach them a trick that Lugh had taught me. It would possibly help them to stop falling under Beg's control, as Angus had done before, and hopefully give them sufficient protection. The lorica that Lugh had taught Angus, was only a small part of the precaution. I added a little more, which gave it more power as long as they practiced it regularly. This included the use of the imagination and working towards an inner seeing and feeling at the same time. Lugh had told me that not everyone was able to achieve high levels of power, some people were naturally more able with these mental feats than others. Everyone could achieve something, but some people would have to work harder than others. After some quick work on it together, we went back for a short nap with the others.

It hardly seemed as if I had fallen asleep before Cethan was nudging me awake. I awoke to find Niamh's arm across my waist and my brother's face grinning down at me.

"Did you sleep well, little brother?" He whispers with a hint of a tease. "It's time we disappeared out of this place."

"What's that?" Calls out Donal in a loud croaky voice. It has the effect of waking everyone immediately.

"Time to get up." Answers Cethan gruffly, "Come on ladies, there's no time for any lazing this morning." He concludes by looking specifically at Niamh who quickly takes her arm off of me.

Within moments we were all outside standing by the pond shivering in the cold morning air. The sun was beginning to rise and there were already sounds of activity outside the walls. The door was opened a short way first to check if it was all clear. We didn't wish to be seen leaving, so when the timing was right, we quickly nipped out into the square and half ran, half walked across to the inn.

Leag was up already and again I found myself wondering if he ever slept. He greeted us all like naughty children.

"Are you all mad to show your faces here today of all days. You should have left by now." He chides us.

"Is that any way to treat your closest friends, especially now they've decided to stay here for good and put up with your cooking." Calls back Dugald from behind the rest of us.

"Is that true or are you just jesting with me?" Replies Leag keenly.

"It's true Leag," adds Angus, "we do put up with your cooking." He says, laughing generously and in a way that brings smiles to all of us.

We were soon seated around a large fire with heated bowls of oatmeal, milk, honey and wild fruits. There was silence as we all ate as fast as was polite. It had been a while since our last big meal and our appetites were excessive with all the past action.

We had all decided that it should be Conal and Cethan that should take Niamh and Mairi away to the South straight after the meal. There was no need to keep them here any longer than necessary. Leaving last night had been ruled out as being too risky, not least because of how tired we had all been. Now, however, Donal had given his word to Queen Irnan to stay and assist Bran in any way that was necessary in order for him to become King and I had decided to stay with him. We had also wanted to split up into two groups to reduce our numbers and to become more inconspicuous.

We said our goodbyes and arranged to meet later in Comrie where the currach would then take us back to Siegg the following morning. Donal and I would follow on, one way or another, later in the day.

There was still very little activity outside in the square, only a few morning traders making their way down to the docks. Most people would be out in the fields right now bringing their cattle back down from the highland pastures for the coming winter. Donal and I watched from a distance to see if there was any trouble at the South gate with the guards. Luckily for us, they still hadn't returned from being away all night and all four of them passed unnoticed. Niamh turned and waved and I felt a momentary twinge deep in my stomach.

We returned to the inn to discuss our next moves with Dugald and Angus. After the fighting at the Aes Dana we were all unsure of what would exactly happen and how Callum Beg would react to having his plans foiled. As the Ard Ollamph, it was to him that the others would turn naturally for advice on how the ceremonies would be conducted. The Tarb Feis, if it was to be done correctly, would have to have been carried out the night before and a seer would have had to have slept with the hide around themselves and wake, hopefully, with the new king's name first and foremost in their mind. They would then be paraded into the central square where they would announce who will be the next king.

"Let's have a drink over here Leag." Calls out Donal, now seated at a table in the corner. "We need to celebrate our success a little. I think."

"It's not over yet Father." I say, preferring to err on the side of caution and still feeling a little uncomfortable.

"Rubbish lad. We've all but done what we set out to do. The girls are safe and there not much that's going to stop Bran being acclaimed the next king later today."

Leag comes over with four large tankards, two in each hand and ale spilling liberally over the sides.

"It's too early in the day for me," refuses Dugald holding his hands up for a moment, "but today is a day for celebrating." He smiles and reaches with his two outstretched hands for the nearest tankard.

"To long life and good health..." He toasts.

"... and to a fair wife and great wealth." Adds Donal, with hearty cheer. We all take large swigs of the warm, dark brown, liquid and smiles slowly appear across each of our faces, our lips white from the frothy top.

"I've left a little gift in your bag Fionn." Mentions Angus. "It's just my way of saying thanks for last night."

"That's very kind of you, but you didn't have to." I reply.

"I know," he waves his hand up at me, "but I wanted to, just don't embarrass me by opening it here. Open it in a couple of days time when you're well away from here."

"That's very kind of you. Just look after yourself here so I can repay you sometime. Will you really be safe now with Beg still around?" I ask as an afterthought.

"We've thought about that a lot." Replies Dugald, looking at his friend. "Beg still has no idea that Angus has any connection with last night, so it will be safe for him to return. As for me, I will turn up for the parade and the ceremony as my rank allows me. Afterwards, I thought that it would be the right time for me to go west to Port Athel. I've some colleagues over there I would like to talk with. They may also be able to help us to understand what Beg is up to. It's a nice walk and I'm feeling restless after staying in one place these last seven years."

We chatted and finished our drinks then said goodbye to Angus and Dugald who made their way over to the great hall.

"I've got a strange feeling inside me." I say to Donal, when they had gone.

"Nonsense lad, have another ale." He bellows out loud, already having drunk a whole tankard ahead of me.

"No, it's not from them leaving." I reply to his guess, "It's something else. I can't tell yet what, but something is not quite right."

"You've been around too many strange things lately son. It's got you jumpy." He gestures to Leag to bring over some more ale.

He had a point, so I dismissed my inner sense and returned to talking and listening to tales of his past fights. I'd heard them many times, only this time, having seen him fight in earnest, they seemed to become even more fascinating and almost totally believable. It was not that they weren't basically true, it was just that everything my father did was subject to a healthy amount of exaggeration. He even admitted it himself but continued to do so on the grounds that all stories needed a little colour to make them more memorable. Who was I to disagree with him.

"Father." I begin, after my second ale, "Are you sure we were right to stay?" My gut feeling of impending doom seems to rise within me again.

"I gave my word Fionn. Staying around these parts last night was not something we would have been expected to do. Even if it was, no one would have thought to look for us there. Besides, we have to stay until we hear that Bran is announced as the next king."

"What if he's not?" I venture.

"If Beg really is foolish enough to try and do anything else, then we will have to act. He will die before he finishes his speech and I, with the support of Bran's own men, will take over and finish the ceremony." He clenches his free hand and taps at the tabletop at the thought of yet more action.

I looked at him in slight awe. It seemed that he already had plans he had discussed with Bran and his mother just in case of that eventuality. I also felt a little distanced from him due to this omission when we were talking things over. I decided not to pass comment and stayed silent. I supposed he had his reasons for not telling me.

The sounds of the drums and horns started outside and we went out to find the place now packed with people. It was nearly midday and the stalls were doing good trade offering cooked meat and drink around the outside of the square. In the centre, four guards surrounded a sturdy wooden platform. Shoulder high, it was large enough for ten people to stand upon. However, all that stood on it now was the Throne of the North. Beechwood with gold and silver inlaid around its edges, it glinted in the sun. Its thick legs supported a large grey stone that acted as the seat. This stone of destiny was said to be older than time itself. I stood transfixed looking at a piece of history, well aware of the fact that few ever lived to see such a sight.

My attention was interrupted by Donal tugging at my sleeve. His intentions were that I was to follow him. The noise was getting more intense so we moved down towards the docks.

"We need to check on a couple of things here." He whispers to me. I nod and we make our way toward one of five currachs that are moored up. On the one at the end, eating a leg of roasted chicken, is Ruadh.

"It's good to see you two again." He starts, after swallowing his mouthful. "I was wondering whether I would or not after yesterday."

"Yesterday was nothing." Donal brags, climbing on board to talk more quietly.

"That's not what I've heard." He replies, sucking at a finger.

"Oh and what was that?" Donal smiles back at him and squatting down by his side.

"Talk around here is that Domnhuill Dubh is dead. Some say it was the demons that Callum Beg commanded appear at the Aes Dana last night." Replies Ruadh, twisting the bone around and looking for the next best bite.

"Aye, Demons it may have been, but not of Beg's liking." Chuckles Donal.

"Ruadh." I break in, eagerly. "Did Conal Brus mention we have need of your services?"

"Aye, that he did." He stares up at me. "What would you want from me now?" He muses.

"How soon can you be ready to go?" I ask, in the same quieter tone.

"Well." He ponders, looking upwards as all sailors seem to do, "With these winds, it could be anything from a few moments to quite a while."

"What do you mean?" I go on.

"There're light winds today, and all over the place. Added to that, there is the tide. If you wish to leave soon we'll be going out with the tide. Leave it too late and there won't be enough water. That'll make it even longer to get away. So the answers really up to you." He sits back and waits for us to talk.

"I think we should be ready to leave anytime." I say, "Whenever the ceremony finishes."

"That's fine by me. I'll be ready." Replies Ruadh. "So long as we still can." He returns to chewing at the flesh on the chicken bone.

We talked some more, then left to go back up to the square. It was just as crowded only this time there was a heavy presence of town guard. Donal and I blended in as best we could with our dark cloaks thrown about ourselves to hide our weapons. We chose our vantage point behind a vendor's stand. The roasted chickens that the man was selling smelt delicious and after having just seen Ruadh munching on one, we were drawn to purchasing some ourselves. Soon we were busy chewing on them, whilst also casting around a wary eye.

The fanfare of sound continued to build until a shout went up and, from over the bridge, the parade appeared. The Ollamphs, including Angus and Dugald, marched in pairs out, into and around the square. Following them was a figure covered completely in the bloody hide of a freshly slaughtered bull. My immediate suspicion was that Callum Beg was underneath and that seemed to be confirmed by the fact that behind him was Fiacal and a couple of large guards. I wondered how they could possibly have escaped us last night.

When the procession had stopped and the hide wearer was the only one on the central stand, the drumbeat ceased. In what seemed like an age of silence, we waited and watched. Slowly and deliberately the illusion of a bull rearing up on its hind legs began to unfold before us. What appeared at first to be front legs became arms outstretched and held high. A drum roll began and started to beat faster and louder and with a final deafening thud, the animal hide slid off behind the man. Beg with his near naked, bloody body stood before us all. It was an imposing sight, guaranteed to strike fear into the hearts of normal men. The crowd visibly backed off away from the platform, fully aware of the man's power.

"In a wood, in a land far away across the seas to the East, there was a young bear cub." He begins and a rustle of applause rippled around the gathered throng for everyone love a tale. *"In my dream, this bear was lost and couldn't find his way out of the wood. In desperation, he sat down against an old oak tree and saw, lying next to him, a magic acorn seed. Thanking his luck and feeling now blessed by the gods, he picked the seed up and held it between his teeth. Setting off he found that every way he turned seemed to lead him towards the edge of the wood. Soon he was back out and into an area he knew. However the magic seed now held him in a powerful spell and he continued onwards right to the islands edge and into the water.*

Although the seas were rough and waves broke over him, he continued to wade deep into the water and was forced to start to swim. After a while he became tired and he started to swallow the salty water and with it the seed. As the seed entered his stomach it wove its final spell and changed the bear into a large fish.

Now the fish swam and swam without knowing why until it ran out of water and lay in a rock pool on a beach the other side of the ocean. Nearly dying through exhaustion and starvation, it saw a pile of seaweed and under that a Sylph, a tiny water nymph that offered it another magic seed. It gulped the seed down and immediately changed into a seal.

Squealing with delight at being free again, it leapt off towards a dark cave where it met a Korrigan, an evil cave dwelling sprite who offered it another magic seed in return for the directions back to the land in the East. This exchange was duly agreed upon and carried out and both of them now left the cave. The seal now lay happily basking in the sun thinking how lucky it was. However, it was woken by the noise of hunters looking for seals. In terror and now with no way back out to the sea, it turned and hid back in the cave. The hunters, who knew where to look, came straight in and began to creep up to club the tiny seal to death. At the last moment, remembering the seed, the seal popped it into its mouth. In a blinding flash, which dazzled the hunters, the seal turned into a cormorant. The cormorant seeing its chance for freedom flew high up into the cave and straight over the heads of the hunters. It flew out into the waves and dived down into them and swam out of sight. The hunters gave chase, annoyed at losing their prey and searched for the bird all along the shores. Nearly exhausted and out of breath the cormorant surfaced out of sight behind a rock.

Not knowing why, the cormorant was compelled to get away from the safety of the sea and flew inland to avoid his troubles. It wasn't long before he was completely lost and tired out so he rested on top of a tall pine tree. A falcon, on seeing the cormorant so far from the sea, and looking a little lost, flew over to talk to the cormorant. The cormorant explained to the falcon that it was once a bear from a far off land and that it had changed into a fish and then a seal and then into a bird, and each time because of a magic seed. The falcon replied that he could give the cormorant another seed and that would take him all the way back home and change him back into a bear in return for some help at a nearby sacred grove. This was duly agreed and off they both flew to the grove.

In the centre of the grove amidst lush green grass, there was a young man. This man was due to be king of all the lands from far and wide. However first he had wanted to recover a magical crown that would forever seal his right to be king and no man on earth could then say otherwise."

The crowd were spellbound. They loved a good story and at the mention of the young man there were a few cheers of anticipation. I, on the other hand, was feeling distinctly uneasy. I had half hoped Callum Beg wasn't going to show himself today after the events of last night. Now the story, especially with the mention of the crown, was beginning to add weight to my previous worries.

"In the middle of the grove lay a fourth magic seed. The falcon flew over to it but in a moment of greed the cormorant swooped down in front of the falcon and ate up the seed. In an instant, the cormorant turned into a bird man with the magical crown helm on his head. This was the same mythical helmet that was made for the high king Diarmaid mac Cerball, made by the hand of the sidhe. This was the very helmet that had been made with four parts to represent the four kingdoms and which had been lost to the world for many generations. This helmet was however the rightful property of the young man, who was really a prince in his own right, and he had been searching throughout the land for it for the last ten years. The falcon flew down to talk to the bird man who now had envy in his heart. Knowing what he now had to do to become the rightful king, the bird man drew his sword to attack the young prince. The falcon seeing his master in trouble tried to distract the bird man and flew in front of the striking blade. The blade cut deep and tore at the heart of the bird. Saving the prince by its actions, the falcon fell dead and as soon as its body hit the magical grass of the sacred grove it turned into the shape of a human. Before the two of them lay the dead body of Domnhuill Dubh."

Gasps, without exception, came from everyone that heard those words. Message had already reached the ears of many that the Dubh had been slain, but few dared to believe it just yet. This was confirmation of the news and it left them rooted to their spots eager to hear more. I stared at my father, who looked back at me. We didn't need to exchange words, things were suddenly not looking good.

"The prince and the evil bird man now circled each other, each wanting the death of the other. Only the winner could now be recognised as the future king. They grappled and wrestled each other until it was dark and the stars lit the sky. At the final moment, just as the bird man was about to kill the prince, the moon came from out behind a cloud and a voice appeared from the middle of the grove. Turning to see who had spoke, the bird man saw a ghost of a spirit from the Otherworld come towards him. With a touch as cold as ice, it took the

415

bird man by the arm and led him off away from the prince. Together they disappeared never to be seen again. The young heir to the throne was left tired and all alone and sad that he still didn't have the crown of his forefathers. However as he left the clearing and walked back through his kingdom, he grew into a man. The next day he was crowned King without a crown and he vowed vengeance against the man that stole his rightful heritage and declared him outlawed from the land for all time."

His story nearly complete, all the crowd was now waiting for was the revelation of the naming of the king. Who it was, was beyond doubt, what was in doubt was what else Beg would say. Whatever power he had over them before, it now seemed to be fully restored, as well as in the eyes of the future king.

"I sense the evil murderer of Domnhuill Dubh is with us now." He began again, this time with menacing and accusing tone. *"This murderer is a threat to the rightful king and all here need be aware of this and to seek him out and bring him to justice. But now I call upon all of you here now to give cheer to the new king. To King Bran."* He calls out drowned by the cheers of the people below him.

"Time to go." Whispers Donal, and turning silently slips behind the backs of those nearest in the crowd.

We slipped slowly in between all the bystanders and then moved along the side of the inn with our backs to the wall. Nearing the edge of the square, we were just able to see Bran climb up onto the platform and onto the throne. On his lap was the great mace of state his father had once held. We didn't wait any longer. Guards were circling around about, more intent seemingly on looking into the crowd rather than up on the central stand. It was a bad sign. The cheers went up as Bran stood arms aloft holding the mace high in the air. His father had been held in high esteem and many expected great things from his son. In the extra commotion, we nipped down to the docks and as soon as we were out of sight we broke into a run.

We caught up with Ruadh at the end of the pier. He had been watching from a distance and noticed us running toward him. Quickly and quietly we slipped the ropes and jumped aboard. The sail unfurled and set straightaway in the gentle breeze. As soon as the lines snapped taught we saw four guards rushing down the slipway waving and shouting at us to stop. Donal immediately drew his dirk and held it to Ruadh's throat.

"It's for your own safety when you return, old friend." He breathes quietly to Ruadh.

The shouting from the shore continued and two more guards ran down to join them. We continued onwards out to sea ignoring the calls. Even with the tide our pace was excruciatingly slow. However, it wasn't until we were out of their sight and then out of hearing, than we began to settle our nerves. With only the three of us, the currach made good progress. The cold North wind freshened further out at sea and as soon as we rounded the headland of the Cae Carn Beag, we settled into a rhythm of bobbing up and down on the rolling waves, surging forth after reaching one crest and then slowing down as we climbed the next. The constant sight of land was reassuring but we kept one eye on it at all times, half expecting to see a group of people trying to follow us on horses.

"I don't think we'll be going back there for a while." Remarks Donal, "Things just seemed to take a turn for the worse against us. That Beg's a cunning one alright. By the Dagda I'd like to have been able to catch up with him last night."

"That story of his has certainly made it difficult for me to ever return. It won't be long before word gets out that it was us that killed Domnhuill Dubh and then everyone, including Bran, will think we are after his throne." I add.

"It's not our problem any more Fionn." Sighs Donal, leaning back at the stern alongside Ruadh. "We've done what we set out to do."

"We've not got your piece of the crown helm back." I state. "I wonder why Beg didn't use it at the ceremony."

"I've no idea. Probably more deviousness on his part I expect. Leastways, we did stop Beg taking over and becoming King himself. From what I saw, Bran has the support of the people, even if he does have Beg by his side."

"I can't let it rest at that." I say keeping one eye on the shore. "All my time with Lugh, everything I've learnt. There must be something more I can do, than leave it like this." The note of exasperation is clear in my voice.

"Fionn." Says Donal after a moment's contemplation. "There certainly is more. It's just that you have to recognise that life should be taken one stage at a time. In every stage there is a beginning, a middle and an end. The end of one battle doesn't necessarily mean it's the end of the war. In your case it could just be thought of as the end of the beginning. Your time will come again, in the meantime it's important to learn to rest and enjoy life. It's in those times that you can begin to reflect and learn. Just as I used to teach you how to fight when you were younger, you need to assess your opponent. Take time to learn of his skills before rushing in." He pauses to see if I have been following his words. After a moments silence I answer.

"You're right of course," I say, "and if I forgot to mention it before, you were terrific yesterday. When you fought I saw everything that you taught me and then some."

His face came alive at the memory, his eyes grew wide and were matched only by his beaming smile. He was back in his favourite pastime.

"Ha! That was only a few of the tricks I've learnt over the years." He boasts gleefully. "I could have bested him far sooner, but I wanted him to make me look good for all of you lot." He turns to Ruadh eager to retell his story to new ears.

"Well you did that, but not without giving us a few scares as well." I encourage him.

In no time I began to hear his version of events again. With each telling, his escapades became more and more fantastic and amusing. Ruadh and I were soon laughing till the tears ran down our cheeks.

Darkness crept upon us and at a time when most boats were held fast on their moorings, we were still sailing South. Luckily for us the stars were out, but I guessed that even if they weren't Ruadh would have had no problem with directions. We'd kept near to the coast and would be at Comrie before midnight. If all things were well, we'd meet up with the others at Jamie mac Lean's house.

As we approached the rocky shore, I threw out the rope that was attached to the stone with the hole through the middle and the boat swung around against the strain. A short, half swim, half wet walk later and we were among the crowd waiting for us on the beach. All the others had arrived safely late in the afternoon, having not seen any of Beg's men following. After much hugging and shaking, we all crammed into Jamie's roundhouse and ate and drank till early in the morning. It was only aching tiredness that forced us to sleep and most of us woke in the morning in the same seats we'd been in the night before.

I hadn't slept well. My mind was again filled with all the options that were open to me. However, in the morning my mind was made up.

I was not going back to the Islands, I wanted to travel South. Bearing in mind the fact that Beg might still be following, we made our goodbyes hastily with Mairi, Cethan and Donal setting off on the currach back to Donan Broch. My decision not to go with them was considered differently by everyone. Of most concern to me was Niamh, who had seemed at first more than excited by the news. It was going to be difficult to tell her I didn't mean to stay at Drummorchy. Conal seemed happy with the company on the journey and as a father was possibly aware of the dilemma I faced, but was also anxious that his daughter wasn't going to be upset. With all those mixed feelings and assumptions, it wasn't the relaxed and carefree journey that I had hoped for. Things got better though when we reached the well of Leght. Memories of our previous time together brought easier conversation and by that time I think she had guessed that I was not going to stay.

But I did stay for a couple of days as I remembered that I had promised Conal's family a story. Having told them several and then answered their many questions on my recent travels, I was in need of a break. Also, Niamh and I hadn't even shared a private moment together in all the time I had reached Drummorchy and I really wanted a chance to explain my decision.

On the morning of the third day, I packed my things and said goodbye. Niamh took her horse and walked with me. I had decided to head South to Cambelltown for no particular reason other than it seemed a good idea and somewhere to start my next journey in life. I was glad she had decided to come with me for the morning at least. We walked in silence until we were well away from the coastal settlement. Before long it was like the first time we had set off together and our spirits began to lift. Conversation ranged across many subjects and we talked of our likes and dislikes. In all cases we found a deep similarity and understanding.

At midday we stopped at a small copse beside the river we had been following. Niamh had packed a light lunch and we sat shoulder to shoulder on a large plaid rug looking over the wide and shallow waters. We chewed on the food in silence, both recognising that the time for goodbye was getting nearer and neither of us really wanted to think about it.

It was only then that I remembered Angus's gift. I took out the bundle and carefully unwrapped it. What lay before us took both our breaths away. Shining in the warm sunlight were the four pieces of the crown helm. Feelings of guilt rose up within me and I quickly covered them up again and put them away. It was a while before either of us could say anything.

"Angus had his reasons for giving them to you to look after." She mentions. "Don't feel bad about it."

"It's best you forget what you saw Niamh. Whatever his reasons this is dangerous knowledge." I state guardedly.

"I understand." She replies sounding almost happy with the shared secret.

We fall back into an uneasy silence as my mind races with this new and unexpected situation. But it soon comes round to my more immediate problem.

"Niamh," I say at last, "I really would like to stay and I would also really like you to come with me."

"I know." She sighs, trying to hide a tear by turning her face away from me. "I'd be happy with either choice as well."

"I just have this strong inner feeling that I have to go on right now. Just as I'm as sure of that, I am sure in the knowledge that some day I'll be back this way. It's just that I don't know when. I have some questions that need answers and something that Lugh said to me about a dream I keep getting, but not fully remembering, suggests that I have a long sea journey to make. There is a small port to the South West that he once mentioned. I believe that by going there, trusting my intuition and exploring some sort of coincidence, it might give me an indication as to my next move."

"Fionn." She says in a slightly more forceful tone, "You do what you have to do and don't go worrying about me. I'll be fine here in Drummorchy. If you do come back, it will be good to see you again."

The change in her voice and the strength of her words takes me aback a little and my desire to change my mind and stay increases.

"Niamh..." but words for the first time fail me. Instead I put my arm around her shoulders and hold her close. Her silent tears begin to stream down her face and her body starts to convulse with every sob.

"Niamh," I begin again, "I will come back here, as soon as I can. Quite possibly within the year. I will miss you all the time I am away and not a day will go by without me thinking of you. And when I do come back, I am going to surprise you with the nicest gift anyone ever saw."

"Seeing you return safely will be the nicest gift of all." She turns her head toward me and our noses nearly touch. The sweet scent of her breath fills my mind and I feel myself leaning in towards her. Our lips meet and tickle us with their dryness. Instinctively we press harder together, searching and enjoying the passion.

Time seemed to stand still for us in that moment as if offering us some brief respite to the coming parting.

Cheek to cheek we sat staring out over the waters. A flicker of movement caught our attention to the left. A kingfisher had just landed on a nearby branch. It looked at us both, then stared down into the waters. I looked about, grateful for the absence of any boulders, then returned to watching the skilful creature. After only a short moment, he took off and dived down into the swirling depths, only to reappear in one breathtaking instant with a small fish in its beak. Then he was gone, preferring to fly on rather than return to the branch.

EPILOGUE

Now that we have seen that there appears to be a strong link between ancient earth and human energies and modern science, we must really ask ourselves how we can use this knowledge to progress, in a positive manner, towards a better future. What implications it has and how can we learn from these are questions that also need to be addressed.

In order to provide a brief insight into the potential of all of this, I wish to look more closely at four specific areas. In doing this, I hope to provoke the reader into considering what the future might bring and to inspire some of you to go on to further research. These areas are:– The impact of scientific credibility on 'alternative' subjects; finding one's vocational path in life; enhancing one's psychic abilities, and the potential that can come from groups of people working together using gi.

Knowledge of this scientific connection should allow more people to accept several of the 'alternative' therapies and practices that currently exist. It should also allow others to increase their existing beliefs and, knowing what we now know about the power of that subject, one must ask the following question. How is this going to impact on individuals in the future? Will more people have their problems solved? How much more positively will this extra belief and confidence, in subjects like acupuncture, homeopathy, shiatsu and reflexology affect the numbers of unhealthy people around the world? Will it mean that more and more people turn to these areas in order to attain the results they cannot get elsewhere within conventional medicine? How will western medicine react to the changing demand? Will they now accept, due to the nature of this scientific connection, that these arts can never be truly tested in the way medical associations currently require and will that lead them to relax their restrictions and allow further integration? Will larger amounts of money now become available for further research? Just how could this then impact on the health of the nations around the world?

This extra scientific credibility ought to impact on other areas like feng shui. Now that we can understand just how important the landscape is to us, the question to ask is how will we let it it affect our lives. What will other peoples reactions now be to that? Will they consult experts more before relocating as they do in the East? If more and more people now recognise the consequences this whole subject can have on their lives, what actions will they take? With certain areas now deemed to be more advantageous than others how will people congregate in the future, both in their business and their social lives and even for healing purposes? Will some people start building pyramids and mounds of their own!?

What is the impact going to be on a subject like astrology? As a tool for guidance through the future, how does it now fit in with what we know of the quantum world and our future time cones. We know what a direct impact gi can have on our minds and of the relationships that can exist with gi and the world around us, but where does that leave us when it comes to the interpretation? Evidence has all ready begun to accumulate that astrology may be more linked to the sun and not the stars. Cyclical sunspot activity has been analysed by Maurice Cotterell and written about in his work on Astrogenetics. Cycles of activity in the sun have been shown to have some correlation with the different astrological star signs. Whether this is true or not, it provides for the possibility of a further link between the Sun and its changes over time (and therefore over changing astronomical skies) with human activity.

Astrology would appear to be an art that may now have scientific relevance, which many will rejoice in hearing, but it is still subject to human intervention on account of the translations and interpretations that are needed from all the observations. This one feature could well separate those that offer plausible and useful advice from those that are solely in it for themselves. One can only guess at what the implications there are for all this. It would appear to be clear that some change is inevitable, just how beneficial though will still remain largely in the hands of the individuals concerned.

Also very much at the hands of the individual, is the ability to find one's own path in life. Whether this is an aspired path or a vocational path, there is now a model from which we can understand how we pass/distort our way through space-time. By asking how we can improve our lives and the lives of those around us, we can perhaps look with confidence into new areas for answers. Questions like 'How can I become more successful?' ought to lead more of us to search out the effective ways of personal development, utilising subjects like self-hypnosis and N.L.P.™· As we seek to program and reprogram our minds and to intensify all of our inner senses in a goal directed manner, will that not lead to the creation of many new positive realities? And these realities will be ones that we, as internal and external observers, have played a major role in bringing about. If many more people in the world became aware that we can personally bring into effect these future outcomes, by the actions we take in the present, one can only imagine the enormous implications and consequences that would result. How would society differ if there were far more successful people? With everyone now having far greater levels of self-esteem, how would that affect future generations of children and their upbringing? Now that we have an indication of how to find our vocational path, have an idea of how to become aware of our strengths and how to build up our weaknesses, we can learn to live more closely with gi. In doing this, along with trusting our intuitions, exploring coincidences, increasing our communication skills, we will begin to find that life is sweeping us up in its current and taking us on a very special journey. Our lives will become more and more inter-dependent with those around us in ways that still allow complete freedom of thought and action. If it became the one main goal for every educational establishment to assist pupils in finding their vocational path in life, what affect would that then have on young people today? One can only guess at the social improvements that it could bring if they were even partially successful in their task.

If individuals become adept at using their inner senses and programming their minds (quite possibly like the Ancients of the past), one must next ask what else might be possible. What might people achieve if they learnt to harness their own, and the earth's, gi in order to 'collapse' the outcomes that they wanted. Each of us is born with talents in a variety of occupations. Not all of us are proficient at the same ones and our abilities all vary from one level to another. We know that if we neglect to nurture our talents, they will dwindle away and die. Likewise we know that if we work hard at improving them, we can achieve great things. Psychic ability is one such talent that each of us has to a greater or lesser extent. Knowing what we now know about gi, it ought to be possible to suggest a mechanism by which some of these abilities may work. If we can accept a possible method behind them, then it might be easier to accept them as a talent that can be improved. I would therefore like to propose a possible model for telepathy in the hope that it sparks further conversation and debate. It is not expected to be definitive, but just sufficient to open peoples minds toward finding a scientific basis that fully substantiates it.

We know now that our bodies emit gi particles and/or gi waves and that these interact with the world around us. We have also seen that energy relationships exist between humans presumably, again an interaction of these particles/waves. We know that these particles have a spin (ch.6.3) and also that they can have a left or right-handedness when it comes to spin direction. We also have an understanding of non-locality (ch.6.10) in that a particle, once measured, becomes part of a total system. If we choose to observe one spin direction, we know that its counterpart must have an opposite spin and that this information travels instantaneously from one particle to the other. It is then possible to suggest that telepathy may work with a similar mechanism using the gi particle. Our thoughts might well, by some process of internal observation, determine the initial spin direction of the particles and these would then be emitted though a 'projection' of gi to another person. This other 'attuned' person would be instantaneously aware of these thoughts in the same 'non local' manner as they would have become, through the way projection occurs, part of the same system. A combination of different spin directions could, like some sort of Morse code, be a method for transmitting information. The recipient would then receive the incoming spin directions and, using their internal observations when in a state of intense awareness, they could decipher the message.

Information that also might be sent in this way could be feelings and emotions. They need not necessarily just be sent to other human minds in a direct manner. As part of an overall holographic system, these tiny, spinning gi particles could affect all types of matter and leave their spin imprint within the matter particles. Another human passing at a later time might, if attuned or in some way aware mentally, access these spinning gi particles and receive the emotional message in an indirect manner. Could this be a method by which we appear to sense ghosts? Can strong emotions be stored in matter like walls in this way, only later to be detected by passing humans that happen to attune themselves to the necessary frequencies? How often do we walk into some places and detect 'vibrations' whether good or bad? (Haunted houses or churches?) Is it possible that greater concentrations of gi energy have a greater affect on the workings of the mind?

Are dowsers of Earth Energies, psychics etc., more susceptible to this and along with their increased levels of sensitivity are they also more susceptible to suggestion, belief and a whole host of other feelings and visions? Could it be that things like good luck charms, talismans, amulets, (throwbacks from ancient times) and modern day power discs can now become more believable and work with some basis of fact and truth? If the right thoughts and feelings and energies can be stored in them in some correct way, perhaps, now that they too can be understood as to how they actually work. With rising levels of belief, might it not have more effect on the wearer and the people that come into contact with them. Even if the wearer has low levels of belief, might it be that the power of belief from within the person creating these items is sufficient to bring about new and favourable outcomes.

If a model can be proposed for telepathy using gi particles, then it may be able to explain further psychic phenomena. Levitation has long been thought of as just an illusory trick. Some present day magicians even successfully replicate this illusion, however there have been reported incidences of actual levitation occurring and this is often associated with those people being in specific states of mind. The famous medium Daniel Home (1833-1886) was seen by notable members of London society in 1868, to rise into the air and float out of the window (which was over 40 feet off the ground) and back in through another one. A Franciscan monk called St Joseph of Copertino (1603-1663), was witnessed by many people, including outside observers, to fly into the air on over a hundred occasions. He was known during his life as the 'flying friar'. These occasions were seen to have lasted several minutes and occurred both inside and outside. Pope Urban the third witnessed a levitation when St Joseph came to visit him in Rome. As he knelt to kiss the Pope's feet he immediately rose into the air. St Theresa of Avila, Spain (1515-1582) was known to be a devoutly religious nun. On many occasions she was witnessed to rise up into the air. She herself wrote that this was something that annoyed her and embarrassed her. When she could, she would hold onto something to stop herself moving. In many of these instances it was reported that it came about as a result of a particular state of mind. In St Theresa's case she was said to have been in a calm state of intense inner joy. The prayers she said, along with her overall feelings could well have brought about the right mental conditions to counteract the natural gi forces. Many observers also witnessed her body to be surrounded by a glow of white light. St

Theresa herself said that it was as though the spiritual force was drawing her upwards.

If we allow ourselves open minds and are prepared to believe that it is possible, although not yet proved scientifically, we may be able to accept a mechanism for this happening. This should provide us with a reasonable theory and as Karl Popper, scientist and philosopher, once said, "Theories can only ever be disproved, not proved."

In this state of open-mindedness and our greater understanding of gi, we may well believe that with sufficient mental training a person may eventually be able to levitate. A faster method of attaining this ability might well be through deep level hypnosis and current accelerated learning techniques. We know from basic physics that when two equal and similar forces meet in opposition, they will balance each other out. If one applies that to the gi force, it doesn't take much of a stretch of imagination to accept that it might be possible to overcome the force from one direction with a little extra effort from the other. By attaining the right state of mind and projecting gi upwards from out of the top of one's head, one might be able to counter the effect of the gi force holding one's body down on the ground. If done with sufficient intensity and ability then levitation might possibly be able to occur.

I would ask the reader to consider again some of the ki tests mentioned in chapter 10.1. 'Unraisable body' shows an interesting comparison to this possible phenomenon. Having written this, I would like to add a disclaimer by mentioning that I do not expect anyone to try to levitate, without first making sure that all dangers are eliminated beforehand. Stepping off a cliff is not a sensible way to test your abilities.

A scientific model for other subjects like remote viewing could also be suggested and I would invite the reader to look further into all of them both in a practical and analytical way. In doing this, it is suggested that you try experimenting in areas where there are enhanced levels of directed gi and also on normal ground. If you were to carry out basic psychic tests, (like using Zener cards and guessing what symbol was on the reverse side of them) what results would you get in both areas? How much of an improvement in results is seen in the high gi directed areas? How much does it depend on your state of awareness and does that differ from area to area?

Building from early successes in these experiments and with growing belief and confidence, one has to ask what else can be achieved?

How can we program ourselves for even greater abilities? What would happen if more and more people achieved high levels of psychic aptitude? With telepathy and remote viewing becoming common, how would that impact on those in the world who wished to keep things secret? What would the world be like if there were no secrets from a few talented psychics? If certain places in the world assisted in these mental feats, might they not become sacred again or even restricted areas? Would this be a good thing? What other impact does this understanding of gi have on our current future course? As a species, our mental functioning has been developed within a gi environment. Our evolved microtubules act taking this into account. If we were to sustain a prolonged period of absence from our gi field what affect would that have on our behaviourable ability? Would this rule out long distance interplanetary space flight in the future?

With only these changes, one has to consider the ways in which increasing numbers of 'gi aware' and 'psychic' individuals would alter societies around the world. They could quite easily bring about large-scale changes, many quite possibly not for the better. One reason for this is the current desire for individuality, independence and the current lack of two-way communication. If left to run its own course, as it has done in the past, it invariably leads to conflict and strife. One has to ask how one evolves from this state to one that is more harmonious, yet not restrictive. Freedom to think and act are the cornerstones of true progress and must not be lost along the way. Can a move to interdependence, a healthy win/ win mixture of dependence and independence, be brought about by a greater understanding of what is needed in communication?

If so, what communication is necessary in order to achieve this? How could groups of these adept individuals influence future outcomes by their actions and what form of communication is it that might achieve all these aims?

We have seen what can be accomplished by individuals with a view to bringing about their reality of choice. We must now look at what might be possible if groups of people all get together and access the universal gi to bring about a reality of communal choice. We know that as an individual a person has a control over what happens to themselves by collapsing their aspired goal from out of the all the possible quantum worlds. As long as this goal is personal to them and provided they follow the right planning procedures, they will get what they desire. The same principle must also work for groups of people all wanting the same thing and working towards it in the same way, but this time with the combined use of all their senses. This in itself is not that strange as many people get together on new projects and work collectively together to produced a desired result. Powerful individuals often have visions of something that they want to do and then proceed to get many people together to work for them in order to achieve these things. They do this by effectively selling their vision to their employees in such a strong way that they all see the dream too. Many employers require their workers to eat, sleep, think and feel their work 100% of the time. They know that this is an immensely powerful way for them to reach their goals. Instead of just bringing to bear all the intensity of their own inner senses, they encourage many others to build on this by using their inner senses as well.

As with the individual, and self-suggestion, this is only a short step away from a powerful form of mass hypnosis. Large numbers of individuals who are all listening to a hypnotist making suggestions to them will result in the creation of similar perceptions and images in all of their minds. Instead of individuals collapsing their personal reality from out of the quantum world, groups of people are all 'collapsing' the same reality and that reality is decided upon by the hypnotist. With its many possible futures, the quantum world is suddenly and dramatically affected by this. The numbers of optional paths that are open to everyone will drop. If this was taken to the extreme and everyone in the whole world visualised, thought and felt the same thing at the same time, then there could only be one reality and one outcome and for that moment there would be no randomness left in the quantum world.

This may seem a little far-fetched but there is all ready possible evidence that this might be the case. Random number generators that are driven by electrons randomly emitted by radioactively decaying atoms, can produce a series of numbers and have been used to detect degrees of randomness. Dean Radin from the University of Navada did some work using five generators in his studies on psychokinesis. Whilst the machines were running, he discovered two periods of time when all five of his machines started to produce a series of sequential (non random) numbers. It was as though there was suddenly no randomness around, even on the sub atomic quantum level. What was remarkable was that these two periods corresponded with the exact two moments in the trial of O.J.Simpson (the American football star accused of murdering his wife). These two moments just happened to be when nearly everyone in America and millions of people around the world tuned into the television and radio to listen to the verdict. Such was the media interest in the trial, it generated millions of people to all wonder about the verdict of 'guilty' or 'not guilty' at the same time, along with an incredible intensity of interest. With no other thoughts or visions or feelings in peoples minds, the question has to be asked whether that 'incident' might quite possibly have reduced (by large scale collapse of the wave function) the number of options open in the quantum world, hence giving rise to the 'effect' of only sequential numbers being generated by the number machines. The coincidence of all the generators all producing sequential numbers and along with millions of people all tuning in are probably too great to work out. It does however provide us with an inkling of the power that might be open to us if we get together in groups to produce a collectively desired outcome.

Some people at this stage might say that it would be almost impossible to recreate some phenomena like this because of the numbers of people that are required to be involved. However there have been several groups of far smaller numbers of people around the world that have achieved collectively desired results. Shirley Maclaine, the American actress, in her book 'Going Within' described one such collective experience that she herself was actively involved in. Whilst giving a seminar in Dallas, the water supply, in the hotel she was working in, was suddenly cut off due to a breakage somewhere in the pipes. She suggested to her audience (a group of people all seeking inner enlightenment) that they collectively visualised the water backing up so that the workers could find the break. This they did and to the workers astonishment (as they weren't party to this experiment), the water stopped flowing and backed up and redirected itself into the basement. Many of you might well say that there was a sound scientific reason for this, but Shirley Maclaine found many strange happenings throughout her tours when she did this sort of group exercise. Although this is not offered as proof, it does suggest that smaller numbers of people might be able to have some group effect over the reality we choose to collapse from out of our future. Further evidence exists for smaller numbers of people being able to influence larger numbers.

Rupert Sheldrake, a Biologist, postulated the existence of a morphogenetic field to explain the transmission of information within a species. He described the reaching of a critical mass before any information got conveyed from one animal to another. In a study on rats that went on for 34 years, William McDougall found that when he taught a sufficient number in one group some new tricks, then others, even from different rat species, had at the same time all learnt them as well. It was as though the trick information had suddenly become universally available. In another observation, monkeys on an island called Koshima were given sweet potatoes by researchers. Unused to these vegetables and because they were covered with sand from the beach, they learnt to wash them in the sea before eating them. As soon as a critical number of monkeys had learnt to do this, researchers on other islands nearby witnessed all their monkeys suddenly taking the sweet potatoes that they had been given, down to be washed in the sea as well. They even used the same washing techniques to clean the potatoes. Sheldrake suggested that this morphogenetic field existed on a subatomic scale and that it allowed for information to be sent and received across space and time. This is not dissimilar to the quantum field which is said to contain the collective unconsciousness and which has been called holistic in its nature. This relaying of information is also similar to the non-local effect that could be attained by using quantum gravity. We can now take a positive viewpoint from all of this by realising that it only takes a few like-minded individuals on the planet to make beneficial changes for everyone. Everyone else would then suddenly also become aware of these changes and find that they too have acquired new skills. This is also like the concept of millions of microtubules working together in harmony to bring about orchestrated reduction. Its non-local method of operation could well be extended to include the brains and minds of other animals or humans.

All this also raises an intriguing possibility as to the origins of prayer. As something that has lasted through the ages, it must have had an above average number of positive results for it to retain its status and popularity. With far fewer numbers of people in the world and groups of them all coming together for mutual benefit to aid their survival, did their communal actions whilst praying simulate the necessary conditions required to attain what they all wanted? Did enough of them get together in the correct way such that it was sufficient to collapse all the possible future paths in the world into just one group reality? Are not modern day evangelists attempting to do just the same thing? Their methods employ large amounts of mild mass hypnosis as they endeavour to manipulate the inner senses of their audiences into thinking along the same lines. In our model of future time cones, it is as if they are all being externally led down the path of the same future cone. This would begin to reduce all the other possibilities and make the one path all the more probable. Whether you agree or disagree with their methods or these explanations, the comments are not made as a statement against them as much good can come from these organisations. It is mentioned purely as an example of large numbers of people being influenced by a form of hypnosis.

The marketing industry provides us with another example. We are bombarded daily with advertisements in an attempt to change our perceptions and create new associations in our minds with specific products and services. We know how much our brains can be programmed by these people and we have seen that this form of hypnosis is highly effective. From what we now know about how gi is directed by our minds and how deep hypnosis can actually bring about new realities personal to ourselves, we can begin to get an idea of how powerful and how potentially useful large groups of people could be. Now that we understand the principles at work here, in a better way than ever before, it might be possible to construct a large program in order to create a new and better future whereby the group can get together to obtain a collective outcome of global benefit.

Just as we can acknowledge that there is a collective unconsciousness at work within the quantum world, we can also find signs of consciousness working collectively in our everyday classical world. We can seek to understand these events to learn more about how we can progress as a group. The most obvious examples of animals that move collectively in harmony are shoals of fish and flocks of birds. Each member of the group moves exactly in time with the other. Whether they are linked mentally in a non-local manner or are just able to adjust individually, by means of a greater reaction time/ brain speed ratio, is not really the point here. Each member of the group must want to work in harmony with the others for the benefit of the whole. This requires being led by the group and attuning their minds for that purpose. However, each and every member must also be able to individually sense for a sound reason to take decisions for the benefit of the whole. When the whole shoal or flock suddenly changes direction, it will have been initially the result of one of them taking the decision to turn, turning and then all the others following suit.

The basic need for all of us is to know when to be aware and attuned for the benefit of the whole and when to take decisions and act to take a new path to a different and better future. We must be both proactive and reactive, and not just one or the other, if we are to survive and evolve toward a beneficial group outcome. If we adhere to these principles and apply what we have learnt from enhancing our mental faculties then we can go on to produce almost any reality we want.

Crucial to creating this group outcome, and not a concern when it comes to individuals, is that of timing. Just as was seen with the random number generators, everyone must be thinking of the same thing at exactly the same time. One possible method is to use the internet. Just imagine what might be achieved if we all regularly tuned in to the same site and fulfilled all the conditions needed to create new realities. How many good causes could then be initiated and fulfilled? How much change for the better would r...ult? Would regular action like this, with individuals now seeing that they can really make a difference, eventually lead to a true new age of consciousness? There are an ever-increasing number of doom and gloom merchants telling us the world is going to end in mass disaster. Now we should be able to understand that, by joining that sad band of people, we are actually assisting that outcome to happen. By thinking collectively about their doomsday reality scenario, we would be helping to slowly bring it about. Knowledge of that should be enough for people to now realise that their energies are better placed elsewhere.

Group work needs to concentrate on a positive healthy future for humankind and our planet. Our 'evolution day' could then arrive and with it can come a time of positive change.

All this however might give you the impression that we have discovered something new with this link. I believe that our ancient ancestors knew instinctively of these things and worked regularly with these energies, and all that has really been uncovered is the key to their secrets with the modern understanding of how they appear to work.

By leaving you with all these thoughts and questions, I would wish to inspire you on to even greater things. As an individual you have the power of choice and the free will to decide. I hope that this book will assist you with your choices and give you the power to recognise the importance and effect you can have with your future decisions. Thank you for your time.

THE BEGINNING

BIBLIOGRAPHY AND SUGGESTED FURTHER READING

Chapters 1,3,5,7,9,11,13,15

Mathews, Caitlin & John **Encyclopedia of Celtic Wisdom** Element 1994
Mathews, Caitlin **The Celtic Tradition** Element 1989
Mathews, John **Tales of the Celtic Otherworld** Blandford 1998
Cotterell, Arthur **Celtic Mythology** Anness 1997
Spence, Lewis **Celtic Britain** Parragon 1998
Cunliffe, Barry **The Ancient Celts** Oxford Iniv. Press 1997
Baggott, Andy **Celtic Wisdom** Piatkus '99
Armit, Ian **Celtic Scotland** BT Batsford Ltd 1997

Chapter 2

Fergusson, Marilyn **The Aquarian Conspiracy** G.P.Putnam's Sons 1980
Plomin, Robert & DeFries, John. C et al. **Behavioural Genetics** Freeman 1997
Hawking, Stephen W. **A Brief History of Time** Bantam 1988
Wilson, R.S. Twins & Siblings: **Concordance for school age development**
    Child Development 38 pp211-16 1986
Vandenberg, S.G. **Contributions to twin research to psychology** Pyschological
    Bulletin 66 pp327-352 1984
Burt, C. **The genetic determination of differences in intelligence** British Journal of
    Psychology 57 pp137-153 1966
Bouchard, T.J. & McGue, M. **Familial studies of Intelligence : On review** Science
    212 pp1055-8 1981
Jung, Carl.G. **Syncronicity** Routledge Kegan Paul & associated book publishers
    (UK)Ltd. 1972

Chapter 4

Tracy, Brian **The Psychology of Achievement** Phoenix Seminar & Tape Program
Schwartz, David J. **The Magic of thinking BIG** Thorsens 1984
Robbins, Anthony **Awaken the Giant Within** Simon & Schuster 1992
Covey, Stephen R. **The Seven habits of Highly Effective People** Simon & Schuster
    1992
Heller, R & Carling, W. **The Way to Win** Little Brown & Co 1995

McCormack, Mark H. **What they don't teach you at Harvard Business School**
Fontana 1986
Hill, Napolean **Think and grow Rich** Carnegie 1928

Chapter 6
Hawking, Stephen W. **A Brief History of Time** Bantam 1988
Davies, Paul **Other Worlds** Penguin 1980
Peat, F. David **Superstrings and the search for the theory of Everything** Abacus 1992
Coveney, Peter & Highfield, Roger **The Arrow of Time** Flamingo 1991
Capra, Fritjof **The Tao of Physics** Fontana/Collins 1976, Flamingo 1983
Schultz, Bernard F. **A first course in General Relativity** Cambridge University Press 1990
Bohm, David **The Special Theory of Relativity** Routledge 1996
Bohm, David & Peat, F.David **Science, Order and Creativity** Bantam 1987
Silver, Brian **The Ascent of Science** Oxford Univ. Press 1998
McEvoy, J.P. & Zarate, Oscar **Quantum Theory for beginners** Icon 1996
Barrow, J.D. **The World within the World** Oxford Univ.Press 1988
Barrow, J.D. & Tipler, F.J. **The Anthropic Cosmological Principle** Oxford University Press 1986
Prigogine, Ilya **From Being to Becoming** W.H.Freeman 1980
Popper, Karl **Quantum Theory and the Schism in Physics** Hutchinson 1982
Dawkins, Richard **The Blind Watchmaker** Longman 1986
Redfern, Martin **Journey to the centre of the Earth** BBC World Service 1991
Feynman, Richard P. **The meaning of it all** Allen Lane 1998
Kestenbaum, David **The Legend of Big G** New Scientist Jan 1998 No 2117
Linde, Andre **Particle Physics and Inflationary Cosmology** Harwood Acedemic Publishers 1990
Chown, Marcus **Afterglow of Creation** Arrow 1993
Appleyard, Bryan **Understanding the Present: Science and the soul of the modern man** BCA 1992
Durr, S & Nonn, T & Rempe, G **Origin of quantum mechanical complimentarity probed by a 'which way' experiment in atom interferometer** Nature vol. 395 pp33
Buchanan, Mark **An end to uncertainty** New Scientist article No2176 pp25-28

Chapter 8
Chalmers, David J. **The Conscious Mind** Oxford Univ. Press 1996
Dennett, Daniel C. **Consciousness Explained** Penguin 1993
Dennett, Daniel C. **Kinds of Minds towards an understanding of consciousness** Phoenix 1997
Penrose, Roger **The Emporer's New Mind** Oxford Univ.Press 1989
Carter, Rita **Mapping the Mind** Widenfeld & Nicholson 1998
O'Connor Joseph & Tortora, Gerard J. & Grabowski, Sandra Reynolds **Principles of Anatomy and Physiology** Harper Collins 1993
Bandler, Richard & Grindler, John **The Structure of Magic 1** Science and Behaviour

Books 1975
Bandler, Richard &Grindler, John **The Structure of Magic 11** Science and Behaviour Books 1975
Greenfield, Susan **The Human Brain, a guided tour** Weidenfeld & Nicholson 1997
Calvin, William H.**How Brains Think** Weidenfeld & Nicholson 1996
Pinker, Stephen **How the Mind works** Allen Lane 1998
Gardener, Howard **Extraordinary Minds** Weidenfeld & Nicholson
Ostrander, Sheila & Schroeder, Lynn **Superlearning 2000** Souvenir Press 1994
Pribram, Karl **The Language of the Brain** Brandon House 1983
Bandler, Richard &
Grindler, John **Patterns of the Hypnotic Techniques of Milton H.Erickson, M.D.** Volume 1 Meta Publications 1975
Bailey, Rodger **Hiring, Managing and Selling for Peak Performance**
Charvet, Shelle R. **Words that change Minds** Kendall/Hunt Publishing.
Peat, F. David **Blackfoot Physics** Forth Estate 1995
Douillard, John **Body, Mind & Sport** Bantam 1994
White, John Manchip **Everyday Life of the North American** Indian Bookclub Associates.
Kirsch, Irving **Suggestibility or Hypnosis** The International Journal of clinical and experimental Hypnosis, vol 45 p212 1997
Gruzelier, John **A Working model of the Neurophysiology of Hypnosis –A review of the evidence** Contemporary Hypnosis vol. 15 p 5 1998
Benor, Daniel & Furlong,David **Your healing Power: Awaken and develop your ability to heal yourself** Citadel Furlong,David97
Carskadon, Mary A. **The Encyclopedia of Sleep and Dreaming** Macmillan 1993
Jung, C.G.**Memories, Dreams, Reflections** Routledge & Kegan Paul 1963
LaBerge, Stephen **Lucid Dreaming** Ballantine 1985
Hearne, Kieth Dr **Visions of the Future**
Neate, Tony **Channelling for everyone** Piatkus 1997

Chapter 10
Penrose, Roger **Shadows of the Mind** Vintage 1995
Tuszynski, J.A. & Sept, D & Brown, J.A. **Polymerization, Energy transfer and dielectric polarization of Microtubules** Physics in Canada Oct. 1997
Jozsa, Richard **Entanglement and Quantum computation in Geometric Issues in the Foundations of Science** Oxford Univ. Press 1997
Hameroff, Stuart & Penrose, Roger **Conscious events as orchestrated space time selections** Journal of Consciousness Studies, 3,No1 1996 pp 36-53
Tuszynski, J.A. & Trpisova, B & Sept, D & Brown, J.A. **Selected physical issues in the structure and function of Microtubules** Journal of Structural Biology 118, pp 94-106 1997
Hameroff, Stuart & Penrose, Roger **Orchestrated reduction of quantum coherence in brain microtubule: A model for consciousness** Mathematics and computers in simulation 40 1996 pp 453-480
Hameroff, Stuart **Quantum computing in microtubules- an intra-neural correlate of consciousness?** Cognitive Studies: Bulletin of the Japanese Cognitive

Science Society Vol.4, No3, pp 67- 92 1997
Peat, F.David **Blackfoot Physics** Forth Estate 1995
Mitchell, Edgar with Williams, Dwight **The Way of the Explorer** New York
  G.P.Putnam's & Sons 1996
Leary, Dr.Timothy **Info-Psychology – A revision of Exo-Psychology** New Falcon
  Publications
Wilson, Robert Anton **Prometheus Rising** New Falcon Publications 1983

Chapter 12 to Epilogue
Tohei, Koichi **Ki in daily life** Ki No Kenkyukai HQ Tokyo 1978
Page, Michael **The Power of Ch'i** The Aquarian Press 1988
Kit, Wong Kiew **The Art of Chi Kung** Element 1993
Palos, Stephen **The Chinese art of Healing** Bantam, New York 1972
Huard, Pierre and Ming Wong **Chinese Medicine** Weidenfield & Nicholson London
  1968 Translation by Bernard Fielding
Chuen, Master Lam Kam **The Way of Energy** Gaia Books Ltd. 1991
Miller, Hamish & Broadhurst, Paul **The Sun and the Serpent** Pendragon Press 1989
Millar, Hamish **It's Not Too Late** Penwith Press 1998
Devereux, Paul **Shamanism and the Mystery Lines** Quantum 1992
Devereux, Paul **Earth Memory** Quantum 1991
Devereux, Paul **Places of Power** Blandford 1999
Rossbach, Sarah **Feng Shui** Rider Books 1984
Chuen, Master Lam Kam **Step by step Tai Chi** Gaia Books 1994
Siliotti, Alberto **The Pyramids** Weidenfeld & Nicholson 1997
Hancock, Graham & Faiia, Santha, **Heaven's Mirror. Quest for the lost civilisation**
  Penguin 1998
Sugden, Kieth **The prehistoric temples of Stonehenge & Avebury** Pitkin 1994
Fidler, Dr J.H **Earth Energy** Aquarian Press 1988
Graves, T. **Needles of stone revisited** Gothic Image 1988
Capra, Fritjof **The Tao of Physics** Fontana/Collins 1976
Milsom, John **Field Geophysics** John Wiley and Sons 1996
Dames, Michael **The Silbury Treasure** Thames and Hudson Ltd 1992
Gilbert, Adrian G & Cotterell, Maurice M **The Mayan Prophecies** Element 1996
Maclaine, Shirley **Going Within** Bantam Press 1989
Rogo, D.Scott **Miracles – A Scientific exploration of Wondrous phenomena**
Aquarian Press 1991

INDEX

EVOLUTION DAY

If you feel that you would like to know more about the concept of *Evolution Day*, what it is about, what is happening and how you can join in, then the following information will be of interest to you.

Visit the *Evolution Day* web site at

www.evolutionday.com

You will discover how groups of people will be making a positive difference to life on this Earth by 'collapsing' new realities that will be of benefit to mankind. You will learn how you too can play a part even in your own home.

At the Web Site you will also find a list of the top fifty recommended books on mental and spiritual development. Find out what they are and how they can change with your votes from month to month.

This is not a club, nor an association, nor or a society. It requires no registration, nor any fee. It is just for people who feel the need to do something that they know, if done collectively, will bring about a change for the better.

Carol Everett has produced a new Booklet and C.D; program entitled 'Meditating with the Higher Energies'. It provides a unique form of training for those people wishing to improve their abilities, whether they are novices or experienced at meditation. It is widely acclaimed to be the best assistance of its kind in the world and that it helps people in their 'healing' and 'communicating' in ways that are far ahead of anything that has been done before. If you would like to know more about this C.D. or wish to purchase it, please contact M.10 Services or go direct to Carol's web site

www.everetthealthcare.com

Front Cover Prints

There are a limited number of prints available of the design on the front cover. If you would like to purchase one or receive more details on Alasdair Urquhart's work, then please contact M.10 Services for more details, or visit his web site

www.alasdair.urquhart.com

M.10 Services, Courses & Seminars

Personal Courses

Unleashing your **creativity**
Increasing your **intuitiveness**
Reducing stress to safe levels
Learning and thinking strategies
Planning your financial **freedom**
Success modelling & goal setting
Enhancing performances within **sports**
Increasing levels of **confidence** and self esteem
Control over fears, phobias & negative habits
Meditating with the higher energies
Improving your **healing** abilities
Realising your psychic talents
Finding your **vocation** in life
Tailored **exercise** programs
Astrological profiling

Corporate Courses

Improving all forms of **communication** within organisations
Influence & persuasion techniques for **sales**
Management skills workshops
Coaching & **mentoring** skills
Creative thinking service
Stress management
Supervisory skills
Customer **care**

If you would like to find out more about these courses, please write to M.10 Services, P.O. Box 7, Exmouth, Devon, EX8 5YT sending the details shown on the form on the next page. Or contact us via our Web site. www.evolutionday.com/m10

M 10 Services is a training network run by Rory Macquisten dedicated to the improvement in communication, mental & physical health, self motivation and the pursuit of personal excellence. Whether it is in the field of sport, business or at home, M.10 aims to assist you and your colleagues to reach your full potential. Our combination of personal development tools, based on the latest research done on the mind and the brain, together with many years of extensive experience, enables us to offer uniquely powerful courses.

An M 10 Coach is a person that continually strives for improvement in the area of human performance and it's development. All have wide practical experience and are required to have carried out and continue in-depth research into their subjects. Each has a good understanding of the others expertise and all share the same fundamental philosophy of assisting people to attain more freedom through the decisions and choices they make through life. M.10 training puts the emphasis on results, their constant measurement and your continued development. Each course is individually tailored to your requirements and draws on our specialist learning skills that empower individuals to grasp new ideas and habits.

M.10 can arrange individual sessions on some of its services if required. Personal seminars are organised depending on demand in particular geographical areas. Registering your interest in them will hasten one nearer to where you live.

Please send further information on the above services, courses and seminars to:

Name..

Company (if applicable) ....

....

Address..

....

Postcode..................Country...

Tel................................Fax...

Email...

Mobile...

Specific interests...

....